BLACK LIST

BLACK LIST

A THRILLER

Brad Thor

EMILY BESTLER BOOKS
—
ATRIA

New York   London   Toronto   Sydney   New Delhi

ATRIA BOOKS
A Division of Simon & Schuster, Inc.
1230 Avenue of the Americas
New York, NY 10020

This book is a work of fiction. Names, characters, places, and incidents either are products of the author's imagination or are used fictitiously. Any resemblance to actual events or locales or persons living or dead is entirely coincidental.

First Emily Bestler Books/Atria Books hardcover edition July 2012

EMILY BESTLER BOOKS / ATRIA BOOKS and colophon are trademarks of Simon & Schuster, Inc.

For information about special discounts for bulk purchases, please contact Simon & Schuster Special Sales at 1-866-506-1949 or business@simonandschuster.com.

The Simon & Schuster Speakers Bureau can bring authors to your live event. For more information or to book an event contact the Simon & Schuster Speakers Bureau at 1-866-248-3049 or visit our website at www.simonspeakers.com.

Manufactured in the United States of America

10 9 8 7 6 5 4 3 2 1

Library of Congress Cataloging-in-Publication Data

Thor, Brad.
   Black list : a thriller / Brad Thor.—1st Emily Bestler Books/Atria books hardcover ed.
      p.   cm.
   1. Terrorism—Prevention—Fiction.   2. Intelligence officers—Fiction.   I. Title.
   PS3620.H75B56 2012
   813'.6—dc23   2012014513

ISBN 978-1-4391-9298-6
ISBN 978-1-4391-9306-8 (ebook)

To Barrett Moore
An exceptional visionary, patriot, and friend

AUTHOR'S NOTE

All of the technology contained in this novel is based on systems currently deployed, or in the final stages of development, by the United States government and its partners.

PREFACE

On August 17, 1975, Senator Frank Church appeared on NBC's *Meet the Press* to discuss the results of his full-scale investigation into America's burgeoning intelligence capabilities.

Senator Church revealed startling information and closed with a dire warning to every citizen of the United States:

[America's intelligence gathering] capability at any time could be turned around on the American people and no American would have any privacy left. Such is the capability to monitor everything: telephone conversations, telegrams, it doesn't matter. There would be no place to hide.

If this government ever became a tyrant, if a dictator ever took charge in this country, the technological capacity that the intelligence community has given the government could enable it to impose total tyranny, and there would be no way to fight back because the most careful effort to combine together in resistance to the government, no matter how privately it was done, is within the reach of the government to know. Such is the capability of this technology.

I don't want to see this country ever go across the bridge. I know the capacity that is there to make tyranny total in America, and we must see to it that [the NSA] and all agencies that possess this technology operate within the law and under proper supervision so that we never cross over that abyss. *That is the abyss from which there is no return.*

PROLOGUE

There were a lot of places in which Caroline Romero could envision being murdered—a dark alley, a parking lot, even a nature preserve—but a shopping mall in broad daylight wasn't one of them. Especially not one just steps away from the Pentagon. Nevertheless, here she was.

The team following her appeared to be made up of three men, one of whom she recognized, a tall man with almost translucent white skin and a head of thick, white hair. The trio took turns rotating in and out of view. There was no misconstruing their intention. The speed with which they had uncovered what she was up to and had locked on to her was astounding. As good as she was, they were better.

It wasn't a matter of simply being careful or of properly covering her tracks either. She had done all of that. The organization was just too big, too omnipresent to escape. Now it was coming after *her.*

She needed to work fast. When the team moved in, there'd be nothing anyone could, or would, do to stop them. First they would interrogate her and then they would kill her. She couldn't let them take her or what she was carrying.

The mall was large, with lots of upscale shops and closed-circuit cameras. They would be tapped into that system, watching her. She knew it because she had done it herself countless times. Knowing how they worked was the only thing that gave her an advantage.

She walked with a moderate pace, purposeful, but not frightened. If they sensed any panic in her, they'd know she was on to them—they would close ranks immediately and snatch her. She couldn't allow that to happen, not until she finished one last thing.

All around her, shoppers ambled in and out of stores, woefully unaware of what was taking place in the world just outside. It was their world too, after all, and she wanted to shake them. She wanted to wake them up. She knew, though, that they'd only look at her like she was crazy. In fact, until very recently, she probably would have agreed with them. What she had discovered, though, was beyond crazy. It was insane; frighteningly insane.

Her job had been pretty simple, with one primary directive: to tie up loose ends by clipping the loose threads. But along the way, she had committed a cardinal sin. Instead of clipping threads, she had begun to pull on one, and now she was about to pay the ultimate price.

In the first store she entered, she paid cash and bought multiple items in order to hide what she was doing. She politely told the clerk that she didn't need a receipt.

Back out in the mall, she merged with the stream of people and tried to keep her anxiety under control. She took a deep breath through her nose and shoved the fear as far down as it would go. *Only one more step,* she told herself.

Before that step, though, she needed to lay a little more cover. Paying cash again at two additional stores, she emerged toting two bags filled with nonessentials that would hopefully further mislead her pursuers. Her plan was to fill the figurative theater with so much smoke that no one would know where the fire was until it was too late.

The last store was the most important. It was also the biggest roll of the dice. Everything depended on it, and if it didn't go perfectly, her entire operation and everything she had risked would be for naught.

Entering the lingerie store, Caroline scanned for cameras. There were three—two covered the store itself, a third was trained on the sales desk where the registers were.

She moved casually from rack to rack examining items. As she moved, she looked to see if any of the men had followed her inside. She doubted it. While male customers might come in to buy items for their wives or girlfriends, they wouldn't loiter. Nothing would grab unwanted attention faster than a man aimlessly hanging around a women's lingerie store.

The team following her seemed to have realized that and had stayed outside, exactly what she had prayed they would do. It was time to make her final move.

With several items in hand, Caroline asked for access to a dressing room. As a clerk showed her into the dressing area, Caroline was relieved to see there were no cameras overhead.

The clerk unlocked one of the rooms and Caroline entered. Setting her bags down as the door clicked shut behind her, she removed several items and quickly got to work. Time was of the essence. The organization following her didn't like it when people fell into "shadows" and couldn't be monitored.

Cracking the dressing room door, Caroline extended a camisole and asked the clerk if she could bring her a larger size. When the clerk had walked back out onto the floor, Caroline closed the door and, keeping her voice as quiet as possible, recorded her transmission.

Now came the difficult part—sending it. This was where she had decided to go as low-tech as possible. It was the only way it had any hope of sneaking by unnoticed. She prayed to God it would work.

Exiting the dressing room, Caroline strode purposefully toward the sales desk, fighting to appear relaxed as she conducted her transaction. It took everything she had to maintain her smile and laugh with the chatty clerk. Out of the corner of her eye, she saw the white-haired man pass the store entrance.

Once the purchase was complete, Caroline accepted the latest addition to her collection of shopping bags, squared her shoulders, and left the boutique. She had done it.

As she stepped outside, her heart began to pound. There was nothing else for her to do, nowhere else for her to go. She knew how this had to end. Threading her way through the crowd of people heading toward one of the mall's busiest exits, she spotted the row of glass doors and began to pick up her pace.

The urge to run was overwhelming. She couldn't fight it anymore. The team that was following her seemed to know exactly what she was thinking, because that's when they struck.

But they were already too late.

CHAPTER 1

K urt Schroeder glanced down at his iPhone while his Nissan subcompact crunched across the estate's pebbled motor court. *No signal.* It was the same with his navigation system. He didn't need to turn on his satellite radio, it wouldn't have a signal either. Everything had been blacked out about a mile before the gates—*just as it was supposed to be.*

None of the locals had ever made a connection between the signal loss and the fact that it only happened when the owners of the estate were in residence.

Some blamed atmospheric conditions, while a few local conspiracy theorists pointed to the government, as neighbors laughed them off. Little did those neighbors know how close to the truth the conspiracy theorists were.

A company called Adaptive Technology Solutions had developed the signal-blocking technology for the use of the U.S. military in Afghanistan and Iraq. ATS was one of the most successful American tech companies most people had never heard of.

Practically an arm of, and indistinguishable from, the National Security Agency, ATS also conducted highly sensitive work for the Office of the Director of National Intelligence, the Central Intelligence Agency, the Defense Department, the State Department, the Federal Bureau of Investigation, the Department of Homeland Security, the Treasury Department, the Department of Justice, and a host of other agencies, including the little-known United States Cyber Command—the group in charge of centralizing U.S. cyberspace operations.

Whether via software, hardware, personnel, or training, there wasn't a move the United States government made in relation to the Internet that didn't somehow involve ATS.

So intertwined was it with America's political, military, and intelligence DNA, that it was hard to discern where Uncle Sam stopped and ATS began. Very little was known about the organization, which was exactly what ATS wanted. Had its board of directors ever been published, it would have read like a who's who of D.C. power. In addition to two former intelligence chiefs, it included a former Vice President, three retired federal judges, a former Attorney General, a former Secretary of State, a former Federal Reserve Chairman, two former Secretaries of the Treasury, three former Senators, and a former Secretary of Defense.

Some believed that ATS was a front for the NSA, while others speculated that the CIA might have been involved in its creation. All, of course, pure speculation. Anyone who knew anything about ATS only really knew about that particular facet they were dealing with, and even then, they didn't know much. The highly secretive company had worked for decades concealing its true breadth and scope. What was visible above the waterline was only the tip of the iceberg.

The organization was also exceedingly careful about whom they brought inside. Nowhere was the selection process as rigorous as at ATS. Its members shared a very particular worldview, along with a deeply held belief that not only could they shape domestic and international events, it was their duty to do so. Their goals were not the kinds of things they wanted discussed in newspapers and on the Internet. They took great pride in their anonymity.

The corporation's retreat, with its sophisticated countersurveillance and anti-eavesdropping measures, sat on more than two hundred rural

Virginia acres of rolling green countryside. It featured a clutch of buildings, the centerpiece of which was a large, redbrick neoclassical home
fronted by thick white columns.

The estate had been named Walworth after the ruins of a small, walled
farm at the south end of the property predating the Revolutionary War.
Its ownership was hidden behind blind land trusts and offshore corpora-
tions. No records existed at the county recorder's office, and no overhead
imagery of the property could be accessed via satellite. For all intents and
purposes, the estate didn't even exist, which was exactly what the powerful forces behind Adaptive Technology Solutions wanted.

Kurt Schroeder had been to Walworth a handful of times, having
helped to oversee the installation of several of its computer and security
upgrades. But he'd never been to the property for a gathering of the firm's
board of directors. He had only seen the full board together on one occasion, when he had been invited to accompany his boss to a winter board
meeting at the ATS property on Grand Cayman.

With its vast wealth, the company hierarchy never failed to do things
first-class. The motor court of the Virginia estate looked like the parking lot of a luxury European car dealership, with multiple BMWs, Audis,
Mercedes, and Range Rovers. Off to the side, the security teams had
parked their armored, black Chevy Suburbans.

Schroeder located an empty spot and parked. He looked into the mirror and dried the perspiration on his forehead. Tightening the knot in his
tie, he took a deep breath. His boss, the man who ran ATS, was a lot like
his deceased mother. Both had considerably volatile tempers.

Schroeder climbed out of his unimpressive yet efficient Nissan and
detected the scent of woodsmoke from one of the house's many chim-
neys as he walked across the motor court. Martin Vignon, the head of
corporate security, met him at the door. Like the rest of the team, Vignon
wore a dark suit and had a Secret Service–style earpiece protruding from
one ear. He was a tall man with impossibly pale skin and neatly combed
white hair. Behind his back, the boss—who seemed to have a demeaning
nickname for everyone—referred to Vignon as "Powder." Whenever he
threw the slur around, most of the employees uncomfortably laughed it
off or pretended they hadn't heard it.

Schroeder didn't know much about where Vignon had come from nor how he'd secured his job with the organization. Some said he was former military, others said he was former intelligence. Nevertheless, it was widely agreed that the man was discourteous and off-putting. Schroeder had looked into his background once, but the man was a black hole. Everything had been erased. The sick joke that had sprung up around his cold demeanor was that he was possessed of unusual powers; instead of seeing dead people, he created them.

He was the only American on the security team; the rest were Israelis, all handpicked by the security chief himself.

Vignon gave Schroeder a curt nod and waved him toward two of his men, one of whom was holding a metal detector wand. Considering all he was entrusted with at ATS, being wanded was an indignity. These wannabe Secret Service morons were out of control.

Not wanting to cause a scene, Schroeder simply submitted to the search. Before the security team could fully sweep him, though, his boss appeared.

"Where have you been?" the man demanded.

It was a stupid question. He knew where he had been, and Schroeder didn't bother answering.

"You'd better not have bad news for me."

Schroeder was opening his mouth to respond when his boss cut him off.

"Not here." He gestured for him to follow and led him down a wide hallway to an opulent study. A myriad of exotic animal heads adorned the walls. A fire in the fireplace warded off the chill from outside.

Schroeder waited for his boss to offer him a seat, but the offer never came, so he just stood there.

"Well?" the boss asked, as he walked over to a wet bar and poured himself a drink.

Schroeder took a deep breath into his lungs and let it out. "I'm sorry. Nothing yet."

"What do you mean, *nothing yet*?"

"We haven't been able to locate anything."

"Don't give me that *we* bullshit," the older man turned and said. "I made myself perfectly clear. I tasked *you* with this, and failure is *not* an option."

Craig Middleton was in his early sixties, had a thin build and curly gray hair that resembled a scouring pad. Despite sporting a perpetual tan and laser-whitened teeth, the most distinct feature of his rather unremarkable appearance were his deep-set eyes, which were rimmed with dark circles. Contrary to Craig Middleton's opinion, he was not an attractive man.

Schroeder eyed the matching purple silk tie and handkerchief that his peacock of a boss was sporting and, masking his distaste, focused carefully on his words. "It's only a matter of time," he replied. "Don't worry."

Middleton eyed his subordinate as he took a long draught of scotch. "Do you like your job, Kurt?"

"Excuse me?"

"I said *do you like your job?*"

"Of course I—"

The older man shook his head and motioned for him to be quiet. "I could have taken anyone under my wing, but I took you."

"And I'm grateful for—"

"I don't think you are, Kurt. I think, like the rest of your spoiled, entitled generation, you take everything for granted. I don't think you know the meaning of hard work. What's worse, I don't think you know the meaning of loyalty. Do you have any idea what I put on the line to bring you in and raise you up through the ranks? Do you have any idea at all?"

Schroeder knew all too well. If it weren't for Craig Middleton, he'd be sitting in a federal prison, or worse. "I think you know where my loyalty lies."

The older man took another sip and then looked at his watch. "Do I? *I'm* the one who has to go sit down with the board in ten minutes and look like I have zero control over this organization, and it's all because *you* aren't doing your job."

"We're talking about a needle in a haystack."

"We own the *fucking* haystack," Middleton spat. "Every last fucking straw of it. We own every rock. We own every drainpipe. We own every hollowed-out fucking tree. You can't even change your fucking mind without us knowing about it. So don't tell me you've got nothing yet. You've got *everything* you could possibly need at your disposal. Which means you'd better get me something and get it to me soon. Do you understand me?"

Schroeder nodded.

"Don't you fucking nod at me," snapped Middleton. "Answer me."

"Yes, sir," he piped up. "I understand."

His boss then raised his hand and pointed at the door. The pep talk was over.

As Schroeder left the house and climbed back into his car, Middleton crossed over to the desk and picked up the handset of his encrypted telephone, known as an STE, short for Secure Terminal Equipment. Inserting a dummy NSA Crypto Card into the slot, he dialed.

After two rings, the call was answered. "What's the verdict?"

"I think he's lying," Middleton stated.

"What do you want me to do?"

"Follow him."

"And if he *is* lying?" replied the voice.

"Add him to the list."

CHAPTER 2

G un!" yelled Scot Harvath, launching himself into the apartment as a hail of bullets splintered the door frame around him.

Knocking Riley Turner to the floor, he flipped onto his back and kicked the door shut.

"Move! Move! Move!" he ordered as he struggled to get to his feet, but Riley didn't stir.

Looking down, Harvath saw blood and pieces of gray matter from where one of the bullets had torn through her head. He didn't need to feel for her pulse. It would have been useless. She was dead. For a split second, everything stopped.

But just as soon as it had stopped, his survival instinct kicked in, and right along with it, his training. The shock of seeing Riley dead was relegated to a far corner of his mind as he focused on the here and now. Running his hands along her body, he searched for a weapon but didn't find one.

Leaving his dead partner on the floor of the entry hall, he jumped up and ran for the living room. Everything now was about staying alive.

All of the Carlton Group safe houses were set up in the same way.

Rushing toward the two sleeper sofas, he yanked the cushions off the first one but immediately abandoned it when he saw the pullout mattress beneath. The next one was where the capabilities kit should be.

Capabilities kits were Espionage 101. Though they could be tailored to fit specific assignments, in general they contained all of the hard-to-acquire items an operative might need in a foreign country: cash, sterile SIM cards, cell phones, lockpicking tools, a small trauma kit, tracking bugs, Tuff-Ties, a Taser, OC foggers, folding knife, multitool, an infrared and laser designator strobe, a compact firearm, suppressor, loaded magazines and extra ammunition, and a handful of other items.

Removing the cushions of the other couch, Harvath tore out the faux panel beneath and exposed a long metal box. He punched in the code, a green light illuminated, and the box's electronic lock released.

As he threw open the lid, he didn't need to hear the boots of the shooters staging outside in the hallway to know he didn't have much time. Judging by the suppressors on their weapons, not to mention the fact that they had located the highly secretive safe house, they were professionals.

Also, this wasn't some Parisian ghetto where gunshots and violence might go ignored. Even suppressed weapons made a very distinct and audible sound. In all likelihood, neighbors had already called the police. The shooters would be under pressure to finish their job and get away from the building. Harvath had to work fast.

His heart pumping and adrenaline coursing through his bloodstream, he snatched a .45-caliber Glock 21 pistol and spun the suppressor onto the weapon's threaded barrel. After racking the slide, he shoved two additional magazines in his pocket and grabbed a couple of foggers.

The only lights that had been on were in the living room and he quickly extinguished them. He needed every advantage he could get.

Peering back into the darkened hallway, he could see Riley's body still on the floor exactly where she had fallen. He punched the top of the fogger against his thigh and then pitched it into the hall.

It rolled a few inches as it hit the floor and then began to hiss as an aerosolized cloud of pepper spray was released into the air. It wouldn't prevent professional hitters from entering the apartment, but it was unlikely they had come prepared for it. Anyone who had trained to do entry work expected furniture and other obstacles, as well as the target being armed when they entered, but a fog of OC was an outlier, and that's why Harvath had deployed it.

True professionals would have been subjected to pepper spray as part of their training and could move through it, but it still sucked when immediately your mucus membranes dumped, your eyes began to water, and saliva ran from your mouth. Your lungs felt like you had breathed in thousands of needles. On top of everything, your eyes burned like hell and your vision was impaired, which was what Harvath was counting on. Now he could focus on the back door.

No safe house had only one way in and one way out. There had to be at least two means of ingress and egress. The fact that the shooters had not only located the apartment but had waited until he had shown up to start shooting told him they had access to way too much information and had done their homework. They would have nailed down all means of entering and leaving the building and therefore had him at a distinct disadvantage.

He had never been to this safe house before, though he'd been inside similar apartments in Paris. Often in these older buildings, there was a servant's entrance via the kitchen.

If this apartment had such an entrance, it wouldn't have been left uncovered. In fact, there was likely another team assembling there right now, poised to burst in. Harvath wasted no time finding out.

Entering the kitchen, he stood stock-still and listened, his eyes scanning the room. A shaft of ambient light spilled through a pair of weather-beaten French windows. Just as he had assumed, a door at the other end served as an exit.

Slowing his breathing, Harvath readjusted his grip on his weapon. He couldn't hear anyone on the other side of the door, but he didn't need to. He could *sense* them. He was an apex predator—at the top of the food chain. People didn't hunt him. He was the hunter, and he hunted *them*. Whoever had decided to put an X on his back had made a very, very bad mistake.

Creeping to his left, he opened the cabinet beneath the sink and quickly rummaged through it until he came up with what he was looking for. He removed the top from the bottle of dishwashing liquid, crept to the door, and dumped it all over the floor. When it was empty, he laid it in the sink and backed out of the kitchen.

Though the OC fog hung like a thick cloud in the entry hall, Harvath could already smell it from where he stood. His eyes weren't watering yet, but they would be soon.

He took one final deep breath and readied his weapon as an icy calm overtook him. It would be any moment now.

Five seconds later, he heard the distinct *thock* from outside the apartment's front door as the automatic timer turned off the lights.

"One, one thousand. Two, one thousand," he said to himself.

Just before reaching *five,* the assault came as both the front and back doors of the apartment were kicked in at exactly the same time.

CHAPTER 3

The distractions Harvath had set up took both of the breaching teams by surprise.

The two men who charged through the kitchen hit the slick floor and fell down in a tangled knot. Stepping into the kitchen, Harvath shot the first man in the head and the second in the back.

He was on his way out, when the man he'd shot in the back raised his pistol and tried to fire. Harvath re-engaged with two rounds to the side of the head, and the man's body fell limp.

Quickly, Harvath approached, pulled aside the man's jacket, and placed his hand against his torso. *Body armor.*

From the direction of the entry hall, Harvath heard the cough of a muffled shot as someone must have put an additional round into Riley Turner to make sure she was dead.

He knew there was absolutely nothing he could have done for her. Even if she had still been alive, the only first aid you provide in a firefight is to put rounds on your attackers. If you stop to tend to someone else, you're both going to end up being killed. Riley had been trained the same way and would have done the same thing.

She also would have kept her cool and would have focused on getting out, even if her colleague had just been killed. It was the professional, responsible thing to do, and Harvath knew it was exactly what he should do, but anger had gotten the better of him. He was now committed to a more dangerous and violent strategy, and he wasn't leaving until every single one of the attackers was dead.

With the element of surprise still on his side, he swept through the living room toward the hallway. The shooters knew he was in the apartment but had no idea where. He knew where they were, though, and he began putting rounds through the wall.

On the fourth shot, he heard a man in the hallway grunt and fall to the floor. His partner had figured out what was going on and began returning fire through the wall. Harvath, though, had already inserted a fresh magazine into his Glock and moved to a new position.

As the man continued firing through the wall, Harvath appeared like a wraith at the end of the hallway. The OC gas began to burn his eyes and before it could take full effect, he lined up his sights and fired.

The shot caught the man in the head and he dropped instantly. Harvath then locked in on the other man, who had been shot through the wall and was lying in a heap on the floor but still alive. The man was bringing his pistol up to fire when Harvath depressed his trigger and fired a round into him just inches above his body armor, right into his throat.

The attacker's weapon clattered to the floor as blood gushed from his wound. Harvath closed in and finished him with a shot aimed right at the bridge of his nose. He fired another round into the man's accomplice just in case.

With his lungs burning and his eyes and nose watering, he retreated from the hall and rushed into the living room. He wanted to throw open one of the windows and suck in a deep breath of cold, clean air, but he knew he couldn't. The shooters might have had more men positioned outside, possibly even a sniper, so he stayed away from the windows and moved around the darkened apartment as quickly as possible. Outside in the distance, he could hear the wail of approaching Parisian police cars.

He located a black Camelbak backpack that contained Riley's wallet, passport, and multiple personal effects. He stuffed the remaining items from the capabilities kit inside and zipped it up.

One of the safe house closets contained an array of spare clothing in different sizes. He hurriedly switched into a larger jacket to help downplay his muscular, five-foot-ten frame and grabbed a dark baseball cap to cover his brown hair. It wasn't the best of disguises, but it was better than nothing.

Shouldering Riley's pack, he returned to the apartment's entry hall only long enough to snap photographs of her, as well as the two dead shooters, both of whom looked to be in their early twenties.

He turned their pockets inside out, but there wasn't a scrap of paper to be found on them. Besides their weapons and extra magazines, they were completely clean. For communications, they carried cheap walkie-talkies and headsets—all likely sourced at a local outdoors or electronics store.

With no time to say a proper good-bye to Turner, Harvath made for the kitchen where he conducted a similar quick search of the men lying on the floor. Both of the men looked to be in their mid-twenties and were clean of any pocket litter as well.

Normally hitters were older, more seasoned. Besides their youth, everything else suggested a thoroughly professional job.

After grabbing a kitchen towel and a container of milk from the fridge, Harvath photographed the men and tossed another fogger down the back stairs. He listened for sounds of movement down below and when he didn't hear any, he stepped into the service stairwell and cautiously made his descent.

When he reached the ground floor, he moved away from the fogger and soaked the kitchen towel in milk. After wiping his face and hair as well as he could to mitigate the effects of the OC, he tossed the towel and put the baseball cap on.

He then removed the battery, as well as the memory and SIM cards from his phone, and slid them into one of his coat pockets. He did the same with the suppressor, after unscrewing it from his weapon. He tucked the Glock into one of the jacket's larger pockets on his right side, where he could hold it in his hand and shoot through the fabric if necessary. That done, it was time to step outside.

The apartment building chosen for the group's safe house was part of a cluster of buildings that formed a rough oval and shared a communal courtyard. Exiting his building and walking across the courtyard, Harvath gained access to the service corridor of another building facing an entirely different street. There was only one way of knowing if the hit team had every exit covered.

Using his left hand, he turned up the collar of his coat and stepped out.

He quickly scanned up and down the street. The kind of men he was looking for wouldn't be hard to spot—they had a certain build, a certain bearing. There were a handful of people about, but none of them even noticed him. Turning north, he began walking.

He needed to get out of Paris fast. He needed to get someplace safe where he could let Reed Carlton, the head of the Carlton Group and his boss, know that Riley had been killed and that their safe house had been "burned."

The sounds of police cars were now practically right on top of him and seemed to be coming from every direction. Soon the neighborhood would be locked down and cordoned off. Harvath picked up his pace.

He knew they would eventually get around to checking security camera footage. Paris, like London and Chicago, was a very dangerous city to operate in. It contained innumerable security cameras, which the authorities had networked and which recorded everyone and everything that happened. Keeping his head down and his chin tucked in, he tried to avoid being photographed.

He ran options through his mind as he moved. He could steal a car, but that would only increase the odds of getting caught. His only course of action was to get out of Paris, and then France, as quickly as possible without being noticed. The best way for that to happen was by train.

There were seven major stations in Paris that served a combination of domestic and international destinations. All Harvath had to do was decide where he was going.

He knew he needed to remain inside the EU for the time being. Though he carried a fake Italian passport, crossing into a non-EU country would subject him to a potential customs inspection. Considering what he was carrying in Riley Turner's backpack, that wasn't something he wanted to risk.

He needed to pick a destination where he had someone who could help him. And until he knew what was going on, whomever he turned to for help should be as far removed from his professional life as possible. The greater the degree of separation, the more difficult it would be for someone to make any connection and track him down.

He raced through a list of people he believed he could trust as he skirted the Montparnasse cemetery. The Gare Montparnasse was the closest train station to him, and it served western and southwestern France. From there, he could make his way into Spain and the Basque country, where he knew someone who could help. *But would there be any trains running from Montparnasse this late at night?*

He decided that the Gare d'Austerlitz would be a better bet. Among its many destinations, it ran trains directly into Spain.

Near rue Boissonade, Harvath found a taxi and told the driver to take him to the Gare de Lyon, on the other side of the river from the Gare d'Austerlitz. There he purchased a first-class ticket on the high-speed TGV for Lyon in his name and presented his American passport to the cashier when she asked for ID. He had no intention of going to Lyon, but the more red herrings he dragged across his path, the better.

Slipping out of the Gare de Lyon, he executed a surveillance detection route, or SDR, to make sure he wasn't being followed. Finally, he crossed back over the Seine and entered the Gare d'Austerlitz.

On the schedule, there was an overnight train leaving for Hendaye, a town in the French Basque country along the Spanish border. It was the fastest and most direct route available, so he purchased a second-class ticket in cash. He was ready with his Italian passport just in case, but the cashier didn't ask to see it.

With his ticket in hand, all he could do was keep as low a profile as possible until it was time to leave.

At 11:06 p.m., five minutes before the train was scheduled to depart, he boarded.

It wasn't until the train had gotten beyond the outskirts of Paris that he closed his eyes. But even then he was only pretending to sleep. Too much had happened. Too much didn't make sense. His mind was struggling to put together the pieces and figure out what to do next.

He was anxious to contact his boss, but he knew he had to follow protocol. The rules were clear—in a situation like this, there couldn't be any communication until he had gotten away to someplace safe. Even then, he would have to be very careful about everything he did.

In the meantime, he kept replaying the scene from the Paris safe house. He couldn't believe that Riley, whom he had slowly been getting to know beyond their professional relationship, was dead. He was crushed.

How the hell had it happened? No one outside of their group should have known about that safe house. It was only the beginning of the many questions he had. Carlton had sent him to Paris on an errand. Once it was complete, he had been instructed to go to the safe house. He had no idea Riley was going to be there, but when she answered the door, he had been thrilled to see her. Then the shooting had started and she had been killed.

What was she doing there? What was Carlton planning for them? Had someone sold them out? Someone in the organization? He had made a vow as he had left the apartment building and he reaffirmed it to himself now. If it took the very last drop of blood in his body, he was going to find whoever was responsible for this attack and make them pay with their life.

CHAPTER 4

A swath of green at the southernmost tip of Texas, the Lower Rio Grande Valley rests upon the northern bank of the Rio Grande, which separates the United States from Mexico.

Referred to by locals simply as "the Valley," or "El Valle" depending on your choice of language, the area stretches over four counties and has a population of about 1.1 million people. Its two biggest cities are Brownsville and McAllen, its two biggest "legal" industries agriculture and tourism. Its two biggest illegal industries are also of the agriculture and tourism variety; drugs and human smugglers passing through daily on their way north.

The Valley was a popular destination for wealthy Mexican families looking to escape the violence on the other side of the border, and many had second homes there. It was also a magnet for wealthy Texans, who had established stunning private ranches complete with every luxury imaginable, even private airfields.

It was upon one such private airfield that a Citation X had just landed.

The jet taxied to the end of the runway, where a white Ford F-150 was waiting. Emblazoned on the side of the truck were the words *Three Peaks*

Ranch. Beneath the words appeared the ranch's brand, a row of three tri-angles that looked like jagged mountain peaks.

Coming to a stop near the truck, the plane's engines were shut down as the crew opened the forward door and lowered the air stairs.

The Valley's subtropical climate meant that May through September could be oppressively hot, with humid daytime highs in the hundreds and evening lows remaining in the seventies. In October and November, though, the Valley was a completely different place. At this time of year, upper seventies to mid-eighties were the usual highs, with evenings in the fifties or sixties.

It was exactly sixty-seven degrees when the private jet discharged its passengers—a dwarf followed by two enormous white dogs.

Known to Western intelligence agencies only as the Troll, the little man had made an extremely lucrative career for himself in the sale and purchase of classified and highly sensitive information. He was a hacker par excellence and had also distinguished himself by engineering highly sophisticated trading algorithms and secretly selling them to some of the world's largest banks.

Following him down the air stairs, his dogs, Argos and Draco, were equally unique.

Standing over forty-one inches tall at the shoulder and weighing more than two hundred pounds each, the giant animals, known as Russian Ovcharkas or Caucasian Sheepdogs, had been the canines of choice for the Russian military and the former East German border patrol. They were exceedingly fast, intensely loyal, and could be absolutely vicious when the situation called for it. They made the perfect guardians for a man suffering from primordial dwarfism, who stood just under three feet tall and had some of the most powerful enemies on the planet.

On the tarmac with their noses in the air and their ears forward, the dogs took in the scents and sounds of this new environment. So too did their master. He could just make out the scent of honey carried, no doubt, on the wind from the many honey mesquite trees this part of Texas was known for. It was a part of America he had never been to before, and it was quite different from where he had been raised.

As a boy, his Soviet parents had abandoned him, selling him to a brothel on the outskirts of the Black Sea resort of Sochi. There he had been starved, beaten, and made to participate in unutterable acts that no child should ever be witness to, much less engage in.

It was there, though, that he learned the real value of information. Pillow talk from the alcohol-loosened lips of the brothel's influential clients proved to be a gold mine, once he knew what to listen for and how to turn it to his advantage.

Much like him, many of the women who worked in the brothel were society's castoffs, and they took pity on him. They were the first human beings to ever treat him with respect. They became the only family he had ever known, and he repaid their kindness one day by securing their freedom. And for their inhuman cruelty and the years he had spent suffering at their hands, he also had the madam who ran the brothel and her husband appropriately dispatched.

Despite having put significant physical distance between himself and the horrors of his youth, doing the same thing mentally hadn't been as easy. He carried with him a tremendous burden of shame that had shaped his character and had been his excuse for the many unsavory things he had done after leaving the brothel in Sochi.

But even in the dark, black pit inside himself that he thought was devoid of any soul, there actually was some light. Not all of the things he had done were bad. With the vast amounts of money he had accrued over the years he had actually done some good things, things that even bordered on noble.

He was a study in contradiction, but it would be a fatal mistake to assume that any contradictions in his character hinted at a hidden weakness. Human beings are the most successful of animals because of their capacity to learn, and an abused animal learns very quickly how to defend itself. It also learns very quickly to trust very few people—if any.

The handful of people the little man had allowed himself to get close to knew him as Nicholas. It wasn't his given name, but seemed to him just as good a name as any. It was an odd choice, though, for someone who had been forsaken as a child to choose the patron saint of children as his namesake. Again, a study in contradiction.

The man was also a study in deception, one of the primary talents necessary for survival in his field of endeavor. While his coterie of friends might know him as Nicholas, to the rest of the world he was an ephemeral string of aliases and assumed identities. He wove lie after lie after lie and had an amazing ability to keep the entire Web straight. It also made him exceedingly adept at ferreting out other people's lies. At this moment, though, certainty eluded him. He couldn't tell if he was being lied to or not.

As he descended from the jet, he reflected on the woman he had come here to see.

For many reasons, most notably his size, Nicholas was a committed recluse. The Internet had been a boon not only to his business but also to his social life. In the digital world, he could be a king—a god among men. There he was judged not by his physical stature but by the power of his mind.

Many of the people he met in those early days of the Internet saw the world in much the same way as he did. They were misfits like him, people who felt more comfortable in front of a keyboard than at a cocktail party.

So enjoyable were the friendships he had struck up there and so strong were the bonds he had formed, that after years of saying no, one day he agreed to meet his digital comrades in person at one of the annual hacking conferences.

It was a long time ago now, and the event had been held at a large hotel in a major American city. It was the most excited Nicholas could remember having been in ages.

He had arrived two days early to help get over his jet lag and didn't leave his room. He didn't want anyone to see him, not yet.

Attendees started arriving late Friday afternoon, and his circle of cyberfriends had arranged to meet in the hotel bar before attending the welcome reception.

Nicholas was so concerned about what kind of impression he was going to make that he changed clothes five times before settling on what to wear. Once dressed, he sat on the edge of his bed and waited until it was time to go downstairs.

When the moment finally arrived, he straightened his clothes one last time in the mirror and then turned and left the room. He could feel his heart pounding in his chest as the elevator opened and he stepped inside and pressed the button for the lobby. Two floors later, the car stopped and a group of young men, who had already been drinking, got on. Judging from their matching attire, they were part of a large contingent staying in the hotel for a highly anticipated college football matchup.

As the elevator descended, there were a handful of snickers, but Nicholas ignored them and faced forward. It was just as the car arrived at the lobby that one of the drunks asked, "Hey buddy, where are you from?" but by then the elevator doors had begun to open and Nicholas could pretend he hadn't heard the question. Nodding politely once more, he stepped out of the elevator and headed toward the bar, where he found his online friends all waiting for him.

They were a collection of every "hacker" stereotype one could imagine. Some were younger, some were older, and some fell right in the middle. They ran the gamut from obese to dangerously underweight. There was a mix from post-punk-geek-chic with plenty of piercings and hair dye, all the way to a guy with a black cowboy hat and Buddy Holly–style glasses.

He had never shared his photo with the group, so no one knew what to expect until Nicholas showed up. When he arrived at the table, the conversations immediately stopped.

Nicholas's heart caught in his throat as he introduced himself. For a moment, he was frozen with the notion that he had made the mistake of his life coming to the conference. Then someone broke the ice. "You're actually a lot taller than I thought you'd be," said the man in the Buddy Holly glasses. The group laughed and made room for Nicholas to sit down.

They shared stories and bonded over drinks until it was time for the reception.

It was a crowded event in an adjacent ballroom. The group managed to find a table and Nicholas was put in charge while the others broke into teams to get more drinks and bring back food from the buffet.

Despite the impolite stares he inevitably received, Nicholas was having a wonderful evening. As much as he disliked going out in public, there was no substitute for real, human companionship.

When nature finally called, he asked if anyone else at the table needed to visit the facilities. For the moment, everyone else was content to remain at the reception, so he excused himself, slid off his chair, and stepped away.

Buoyed by alcohol and his overwhelmingly good mood, Nicholas paused at the ballroom door, and with an exaggerated bow, stood back to allow an attractive woman with short, dark hair and leather pants to exit before him.

Instead of staring at him, as most people did, the woman smiled genuinely and said, "Thank you."

How Nicholas could enjoy himself any more was beyond him. The evening was just about perfect. All he needed to do now was find the men's room.

At the first set of restrooms, there was a line out the ladies' room door, but he was able to walk right into the men's room. The only problem was that the urinals were too high, and the lone handicap-accessible stall was taken. He waited as long as he could, but the pressure on his bladder eventually became too great and he set off in search of another washroom.

Close to another cluster of ballrooms, he found one. It was completely empty. At least it was until he finished his business and was exiting the handicap stall.

"Well, look at this," said one of the drunks who had ridden with him on the elevator. One of his colleagues stood swaying next to him, trying to aim into the urinal.

Nicholas smiled and nodded politely, but as he passed, the man stepped back and blocked his way.

"Where are you going, little buddy?" the man asked.

Nicholas didn't answer. He had found that if he remained quiet, people often lost interest in him. Engaging them only seemed to act as encouragement.

"I said, *where are you going?*" the man repeated adamantly.

Nicholas attempted to step around him, but the man quickly moved to block his path.

"What's your problem?" the drunk demanded. "Do you have a bridge to get back under, or something, you rude little fuck?"

"He doesn't seem to like you much, Stu," said the other man.

"Why do you suppose that is?"

"Probably afraid you'll make him turn over his pot of gold."

"Is that what you are?" slurred the drunk. "A leprechaun?"

Nicholas remained silent and kept a neutral expression. He had no intention of giving these two assholes the satisfaction of knowing they were getting to him.

"Do you have any gold?"

"You can't fucking ask him, Stu," said the man at the urinal. "You gotta catch him first."

The drunk thought about it for a second and then lunged. With his short legs, Nicholas was unable to move out of the way in time.

The man grabbed hold of Nicholas by the shirt and picked him up off the floor. "Now I want my gold," he said, shaking him. "Give me my gold, you little fucker."

"Put him the fuck down, Stu," said the man at the urinal.

"Shut up," said the drunk, turning his attention back to Nicholas. "You'd better have some gold for me, you little shit. Cough it up."

Having been set upon before, Nicholas always traveled with an ace up his sleeve. This time the ace was a razor, but it wasn't up his sleeve, it was behind his belt, and the way the man was holding him, he could move neither of his arms far enough to grab it. There was only one thing he could think to do.

Moving his mouth, he began to mumble, and the ruse created exactly the right response.

"What the fuck are you trying to say?" the drunk spat.

As Nicholas continued, the man drew him closer in an attempt to better understand what he was saying. That's when Nicholas struck.

In one lightning-quick snap, he whipped his head forward and slammed the drunk right on the bridge of his nose. There was a crack of cartilage and a spray of blood.

The drunk dropped Nicholas, screamed in pain, and staggered backward.

"What the fuck?" demanded the other man, looking over his shoulder to see what had just happened.

Nicholas drew the razor from behind his belt and got to his feet just as the man at the urinal spun to face him. He didn't wait for the man to engage. As soon as he was in range, Nicholas swiped at him with the blade.

He caught the man just above the knee, slashing through his trousers. He failed to cut him, though, and the man became enraged.

"You sneaky little bastard! Now you're going to get it."

"Kill that little fucker!" the other drunk yelled from behind his hands, as blood gushed from his nose.

Nicholas kept his razor ready, and when the man he had tried to cut lunged, he slashed at him again. But the lunge was only a feint. As the razor sliced through the air, the man pivoted and kicked it out of his hand. He then followed up with a punch to the side of Nicholas's head, which sent him sailing across the tile floor.

His vision dimmed and his ear began to ring as blood rushed to the site of the blow. Since he was unarmed, there was no mystery as to what was going to happen to him next. The only question was how bad it was going to be.

He saw the man with the broken nose, blood covering the front of his shirt, stand and come over to join his colleague.

"Now you're going to pay, you little fucker," he hissed.

As the words came out of his mouth, there was a gentle whoosh of air as the bathroom door was opened and someone entered.

From his perspective, all Nicholas could see were a pair of leather pant legs. He heard a distinct *schlink* as a collapsible baton was flicked into place, and then the real attack was on.

The woman dropped the drunk with the broken nose first via a blow to the back of his right knee. When his friend spun to see who was behind them, she swung the baton and broke his right arm. As he howled in agony, she hit him in his left leg, sending him to the floor alongside his buddy.

Without a word, the woman tore out both their wallets, studied their IDs, and then pocketed their business cards. Tossing their wallets back to them she said, "You've got five minutes to get the hell out of this hotel. If I ever see either of you again, I'm going to tell the world you tried to rape me, only to get your asses kicked by a man less than half your size. Now get the fuck out of here."

The woman emphasized her point by putting the boot to each of them until they began crawling toward the door.

After they had regained their feet and limped away, she turned to Nicholas. "Punching a bit above your weight class there, weren't you?"

His head hurt like hell, but he smiled.

"Let me help you up."

"Thank you," he said as she led him over to the sink, wet a paper towel with cold water, and handed it to him. "My name's Nicholas."

"I'm Caroline," the woman replied. "Caroline Romero."

That had been more than twenty years ago, and since then, Caroline Romero had never asked anything more of Nicholas than friendship—at least not until now.

There were multiple ways she could have contacted him, yet the method she chose had been very unorthodox, as was her warning.

As the ranch vehicle approached and the crew started unloading his belongings from the plane, Nicholas was concerned about why Caroline would have ever drawn him out of seclusion and into the open.

CHAPTER 5

Awakening to his room filling with smoke, Reed Carlton leapt from his bed and ran for the door. When he couldn't get it open, he raced for the nearest window, only to find that the security shutters had been locked down.

He snatched up his iPad, and scanned the electronic blueprints of his house. Each man on his protective detail wore a special bracelet that pinpointed his location on the property. The men who watched over his house and him while he slept were the most professional and loyal operatives he had ever worked with. None of them was moving, which could mean only one thing. They were dead and he was under attack.

Whoever had set the fire had likely used accelerant in order to get it burning so hot and so fast. No matter how soon the firemen got there, they weren't going to be able to save his house.

He noticed as he rushed into the bathroom that the overhead sprinklers weren't working and neither were the smoke alarms. He turned on all the taps, but there was no water pressure. Someone had locked him in and was trying to burn him and his house to the ground.

How they had managed to pull it off was immaterial. Right now all that mattered was getting out.

Though the entire bedroom was a hardened safe room, Carlton had always known that even the best security measures could be circumvented, or worse, turned against their owners, which was why he had brought in a team from another state to construct a clandestine escape route from his bedroom and the house. It was a feature no one else knew about, not even his security detail. The sixty-five-year-old was old-school in that respect, but his habit of trying to anticipate the worst had kept him alive through decades in one of the world's most dangerous professions.

For thirty years, he had been one of the Central Intelligence Agency's most vaunted spies and had learned to compartmentalize everything. He took this characteristic with him when he left and implemented it across his own private intelligence organization, the Carlton Group. There were certain elements of tradecraft that never expired. And, like the flooding of a canal lock, many of them now came rushing back to mind.

Fire could create severe panic, and the first thing he had to focus on was staying calm. It wasn't easy. It was so hot that the hair on his arms was beginning to singe. All around the room was the roar of the fire like the breaking of an enormous wave. The thickening smoke was acrid and the fact that it had permeated the seals of his safe room meant that he didn't have much time left. Unable to save his people, he did the only thing he could do, he saved himself.

The passageway from his bedroom led to a tunnel beneath the house. When he had emerged into the cold night air some distance away, he turned to look back at the fire. He didn't want to think about all the things he had lost inside, all the things that could never be replaced. He couldn't afford to be preoccupied with what was gone. If he did, it would only make him angry. He needed to remain calm, detached.

His was a world of three-dimensional chess. In order to succeed at it, one needed to remain clearheaded and be able to think steps ahead of the opponent. The last thing Carlton needed was to go off half-cocked. That would be a mistake, and he couldn't afford any right now.

By surviving the attack, he held the upper hand, at least for now. A fire this bad was going to take time to get under control and even more time for the authorities to get inside and begin investigating. They were going to have their work cut out for them identifying the bodies. That meant that right now, he had time on his side—what he did with it would make all the difference.

The protocol for a situation like this was very clear. First, he needed to get someplace safe. Only then could he start trying to piece together what had happened and begin to plan his next move.

CHAPTER 6

With his brown hair and blue eyes, Scot Harvath didn't exactly look like a local. In fact, despite the call sign *Norseman,* which he had picked up while dating a string of Scandinavian flight attendants earlier in his life, he looked more German than anything else.

He was a handsome man in his early forties and carried himself with an unmistakable bearing that, to the uninitiated, simply appeared to reflect relaxed self-confidence. The initiated, on the other hand, noticed how he took in his surroundings, how he was aware of everything and everyone without appearing to be paying particular attention to anything. In the parlance of an operator, they could see he was "switched on," and this heightened awareness could be attributed only to high-end military or law enforcement training.

Indeed, Harvath had received the best training both the military and law enforcement had developed. Leaving a career as an amateur athlete to follow in his deceased father's footsteps, he had undergone the grueling training and selection process to become a United States Navy SEAL. Always searching for a bigger challenge, he had gone from SEAL Team Two to the Navy's storied SEAL Team Six, where, among his many exploits, he assisted on a maritime presidential detail and caught the eye of the Secret Service.

The Secret Service invited him to help bolster their counterterrorism expertise at the White House. While it was an incredible honor, playing defense after years of being on offense and taking the fight to the bad guys didn't sit well with Harvath. It didn't take long for the President to realize that the young man's talents weren't being fully utilized.

Having long desired to level the playing field with the terrorists who threatened America's citizens and interests, the President set up a top-secret program for Harvath called the Apex Project. In essence, Harvath had only one rule of engagement—don't get caught.

The program was incredibly successful, but when the President left office after his second term, his successor had a different view of the world. Instead of killing America's enemies, he wanted to sit down and talk with them. The Apex Project was shut down and its funding directed elsewhere. Harvath had been downsized and was out of work.

He had then taken a job with a company in the mountains of Colorado that specialized in intelligence gathering and highly advanced special operations training. Soon after, the company was purchased by the Carlton Group—an obscure, private organization funded completely from Department of Defense black budgets.

In the post-9/11 world, quality, timely intelligence, and the ability to act on that intelligence were paramount. Deeply concerned with the entrenched bureaucracy at the CIA and the hobbling of the nation's defense apparatus, the Carlton Group had been established to boldly do what the nation's politically correct, vote-chasing politicians and cowering cover-your-ass bureaucrats were too timid and too inept to attempt.

It was based on the Office of Strategic Services, or OSS, the wartime intelligence agency that had preceded the CIA, and the modus operandi of the Apex Project was quite similar. In addition to the group's intelligence-gathering mandate, Carlton, or the Old Man, as he was known, had assembled a small group of operatives with specialized military and intelligence experience to carry out "direct action" assignments.

Operating under the simple charter of "Find, fix, and finish," Carlton had offered Harvath a position identifying terrorist leadership, tracking or luring them to a specific location and then capturing or killing as many of them as possible. Harvath would then be expected to use any intelligence gleaned to plan and execute the next assignment. The goal was to apply constant pressure to the terrorist networks and pound them so hard that they were forever rocked back on their heels, unable to even take a step forward. Harvath had accepted the job on the spot.

Carlton spent the next year personally training him, putting Harvath through the most comprehensive intelligence training he had ever experienced. In essence, Carlton distilled what he had learned throughout his career in the espionage world and drilled it into Harvath.

On top of the intelligence training, Harvath was expected to keep his counterterrorism skills razor sharp. He took classes in Israeli and Russian hand-to-hand combat, and continually updated his training in firearms, driving, and foreign languages.

He made excellent progress and despite having leapt the fence from his thirties into his forties, was in the best shape of his life. All his training had been to prepare him for any eventuality, but what happened in Paris had stunned him to the core.

Riley Turner had been an incredible operative. She was one of the first recruits the U.S. Army had approached for its elite, all-female Delta Force unit, code-named the Athena Project. He had worked with her on a handful of occasions and respected her skill and expertise. He had also been attracted to her but tried to keep things professional between them.

Years ago, he had resigned himself to the fact that in order for the American dream to exist, someone had to protect it. He understood that he was one of those people and that by protecting the American dream for others, he had to forgo a certain portion of it for himself, namely his personal life. He had been okay with that. The world was made up of good people who needed sheepdogs to keep the wolves at bay. Harvath had been a sheepdog ever since he was in grade school and had defended the developmentally impaired boy next door from the neighborhood bullies. Being a sheepdog was what he was good at. It gave him a sense of purpose. But he still wanted purpose beyond simply being a sheepdog. He wanted a family.

Even though he dragged a string of unsuccessful relationships behind him like cans strung to a bumper, he hadn't given up looking for the right person; someone who understood who he was, why he did what he did, and who could live with all of it. He had wondered if Riley Turner might be that person and had decided that the next time he saw her, he was going to begin to find out. With a heavy heart, he realized that opportunity now would never come.

Disembarking from the train in the seaside resort town of Hendaye, Harvath tried to put those thoughts out of his mind and focus on his next step.

If it were evening, he might have stolen a car from one of the hotel parking lots, relatively secure that the theft wouldn't be reported until the next morning, if not days later, when the hotel guest finally asked for it. But it was 7:30 a.m., and he needed a better plan.

Walking to an adjacent station, he bought coffee and something to eat before boarding a Basque commuter train that carried him across the border into Spain.

In Irún, he caught the bus to Bilbao, a city he knew from having been there over the summer. He found a small hotel in the city's medieval Casco Viejo neighborhood and, after presenting his Italian passport for identification, paid in cash for two nights. He had no idea if he would need the room that long, but at least he had it.

After showering and changing into new clothes he had bought en route, he left to surveil his target.

It was warmer in Bilbao than it had been in Paris, too warm to be wearing a jacket. Harvath was grateful to have Riley's backpack. Not only could he carry all of his possessions with him at all times but he didn't have to worry about having to walk around with an untucked shirt, beneath which his weapon might print through.

Designed by Camelbak for the Special Operations community, the pack had a hidden handgun compartment at the small of the wearer's back. It was an ingenious design that allowed him quick access to his weapon while he looked like just another tourist and blended right in.

To round out his look, he picked up a guidebook in Italian and a map of the city, both of which he consulted repeatedly as he strolled the neighborhood's popular Siete Calles, or Seven Streets, conducting his SDR.

Behind the cathedral on the Calle de la Tendería he walked into a small Basque restaurant and chose the same table he had taken on his previous trip, two back from the window, and sat down.

Making himself comfortable, he glanced over the menu and ordered some food. There was no telling how long it was going to be before, or if, the tobacconist would make his move.

CHAPTER 7

Because of the tobacconist's age, Harvath had counted on his being a traditional Spaniard who still observed the siesta. The man didn't disappoint.

Harvath watched as he closed up his shop, tucked a newspaper under his arm, lit a cigarette, and began walking.

At this time of day, there were plenty of people about, and he didn't need to work hard to avoid being seen. He hung far enough behind that if the man should happen to glance back, he wouldn't notice him among the throngs of people up and down the narrow street.

Having dealt very briefly with the man before, Harvath had pegged him as a very low level operative, and even that might have been entirely too generous a characterization.

He watched as the tobacconist continued on his way, passing up opportunity after opportunity to ascertain whether he was being followed. He was definitely not a professional.

He hoped that the man lived within walking distance of his place of business. If he took public transportation or had a car parked somewhere that he intended to drive home for siesta, it was going to put Harvath in a difficult situation.

Two blocks later, the man turned left and a block after that, Harvath realized he had been given a gift. Leaning out a second-story window was a buxom woman with flaming red hair. She looked half the tobacconist's age. Seductively, she blew him a kiss as he approached. Harvath had a pretty good feeling she wasn't the man's wife.

Slowing his pace, he removed his city map and pretended to study it as the tobacconist entered the building and disappeared. Ten minutes later, Harvath went in after him.

The locks were easy enough for him to pick, and once inside the small apartment, he quietly made his way toward the sounds of lovemaking from the bedroom.

He stood in the doorway for a moment waiting to be noticed, and then finally cleared his throat.

Looking over and seeing Harvath, the woman shrieked and clutched the sheet to her chin as she rolled off her partner, leaving the tobacconist completely naked.

Before he could find something to cover himself with, he saw Harvath's pistol and his look of anger shifted to fear. He told the woman in Spanish to shut up. *"Callate. Cierra la boca!"*

The man gestured at the bedspread, asking if he could cover himself and the woman. Harvath nodded and said, "Go ahead. Slowly."

"Englishman? American?" the tobacconist asked in heavily accented English.

Harvath ignored his question. "You don't remember me?"

The tobacconist studied him for a moment. "No."

"I bought some cigarettes from you over the summer."

The man smiled. "Señor, I sell cigarettes to tourists all day long."

"These were ETA cigarettes," he said, referring to the Basque separatist organization. "I was told to ask for your Argos and Draco brand."

Whether the man recognized the pass phrase or not, he couldn't be quite sure, but there was an unmistakable microexpression that flashed across the man's face. It was a subtle "tell" that Harvath had been taught to look for in the Secret Service. It indicated when a person was under duress because they were not telling the truth or intended to do harm.

"I don't sell any ETA cigarettes and certainly none with that name. I think you have made a mistake."

Harvath saw the tell again. "I don't think so. I was told to see you and only you. When I asked for that brand, you sold me a pack of cigarettes. Inside was a car key and an address to a garage not far from here."

The woman, who had been staring at Harvath, must have understood enough English to figure out what was being said as she turned to him and asked, *"Eso cierto?"*

The tobacconist ignored her and motioned with his head toward his cigarettes on the nightstand. Harvath nodded that it was okay.

He removed a cigarette from the pack, lit it up, and adjusted the pillows behind him with his elbow before sitting up and taking a deep drag. "I do favors sometimes."

"I know you do. And now I need a favor."

The man shrugged. "How can I possibly do you a favor?"

"After you sold me the cigarettes and I left your shop, two men followed me."

"Two men? What two men?"

Harvath described the pair and their very distinct features.

The tobacconist's eyes went wide. *"It's you."*

"So you do remember me."

"Those men were very angry for what you did."

"That's not my problem," replied Harvath. "Right now, you're going to contact their boss for me."

The tobacconist grimaced and drew in a deep breath. "He was not happy with what you did to the men."

Harvath raised his weapon and pointed it at the man's forehead. "There's only one person's happiness you should be concerned with at this moment and that's the guy holding this gun."

The tobacconist raised his hands in self-defense. "I don't have contact with him. He calls me."

Harvath noticed the wedding ring on the man's hand. "Does your wife know where you are right now?"

"Ay, dios mio," said the woman as she launched into a tirade about not wanting his wife to find out.

"Cierra la boca!" he ordered once more before turning to Harvath and saying, "As I told you, I do not know how to make contact. But there is someone else I know who can get a message to him."

Harvath lowered his weapon. "Do either of you have a car?"

The man looked at his paramour, then back at Harvath, and nodded.

"Good," Harvath replied. "Both of you get dressed. We're going for a drive."

CHAPTER 8

Parked alongside a narrow country road outside Bilbao, Harvath allowed his two guests to get out of the car. Removing the keys from the ignition, Harvath slid them into his pocket.

The tobacconist lit up another cigarette while his mistress spread a blanket on the grass. Before leaving her apartment, Harvath had suggested she bring along something to eat. The people they were waiting for wouldn't be in any hurry to get here.

It was pretty basic fare as far as picnics were concerned, which was understandable considering the hasty circumstances in which it was thrown together. The woman had brought bread, cheese, a few apples, and some sausage. She had also brought a plastic bottle filled with homemade wine, which Harvath declined.

He had no idea what the tobacconist had said to her, but she had lost her apprehension and had even tried to smile at Harvath once or twice. He wasn't in the mood and didn't return the gesture.

His mind was on Riley and what had happened. The protocol he was following was correct, but it was maddeningly slow. He needed to make contact with Carlton. The Old Man would know immediately what their next move should be and he'd move heaven and earth to get to the bottom of the attack. Once he had all the puzzle pieces in place, he'd set Harvath loose to exact revenge.

A lot would have to happen between now and that moment, so he tried to think of something else. Unfortunately, he couldn't get the image of Riley Turner out of his mind.

While he was lost in thought, the tobacconist noticed a car in the distance. "Eh," the old man said, drawing Harvath's attention to the vehicle.

Harvath recognized it right away and wondered who would be behind the wheel. He didn't have to wonder long.

When the black Peugeot pulled up alongside them, Harvath saw the two Basque separatist operatives he had crossed paths with over the summer. They were both beefy men with thick necks. One had a sloping forehead and eyebrows as thick as Brillo pads. The other had a thin scar running down his right cheek.

Last summer, the men had been sent to make sure Harvath made it safely to a meeting deep in ETA territory. They weren't supposed to be seen, but Harvath had picked up on them fifteen kilometers after leaving Bilbao. At a rest stop along the Autopista, he ambushed them and forced them to drive to a remote country road. After hog-tying the men, he dropped them in the trunk of the Peugeot and drove on to his meeting.

When they were cut loose and let out of the trunk in a tiny village called Ezkutatu, that was the last Harvath saw of them. Judging by the looks on their faces, they weren't happy to see him again. He couldn't care less. They were his ticket to where he needed to go.

Fishing the car keys out of his pocket, he tossed them to the tobacconist and walked over to the Peugeot. "Do I sit in back," he asked Scarface, signaling with his hand, "or in the trunk?"

Neither of the men spoke English, but they understood when they were being insulted. They had little choice but to take it, since they had been told to go get Harvath and bring him back.

Eyebrows, who was driving, stared out the window and grunted in response. Harvath took that to mean that it was up to him and slid into the backseat, placing his pack next to him.

Closing the door, he leaned back and said, "Ready whenever you are, ladies."

The drive up and into the mountains was longer than he remembered. It was also quite beautiful. It reminded him of Switzerland. The only difference was stone buildings with red-tiled rooftops that took the place of chalets.

They passed oxen pulling wooden carts and meadows filled with sheep. Every once in a while, Harvath caught a glimpse of the stout, wild Pyrenean horses.

After winding their way through several towns and villages, they finally drove through Ezkutatu. Harvath remembered the squat buildings and the tall church steeple, all untouched by time. No sooner had they entered the village than they had already left it behind.

What followed next was a drive Harvath had only done once and in pitch-black night. He would have been hard pressed to do it again without some sort of guidance.

The road rose and fell, bent and switched back as it climbed higher into the mountains. Harvath could feel the pressure changing in his ears.

They drove farther still until they came upon a small gravel road bordered by high rock walls. Had Harvath been driving and blinked, he would have missed it.

They turned onto the road and about three hundred yards later came to a gate. Beyond it was a pasture filled with livestock being watched over by several Basque shepherd dogs. As the car came to a stop, two of the dogs ran toward the fence and began barking.

Two large men stepped from behind a formation of tall rocks and approached the car. Each was carrying what the Italians referred to as a *lupara*. Harvath was not familiar with the Basque word for the traditional, double-barreled shotgun that had been sawed off, with a rounded, pistol-style grip of checkered wood. The shortened barrels made it easier to conceal the weapon and also made it easier to handle in the woods and other close-quarters situations. Without any chokes in the cut-down barrels, the shotgun dispersed a wide pattern of shot that was particularly devastating at closer range.

One of the guards chatted with Eyebrows and Scarface, while the other silenced the dogs and swung the gate open wide enough for the vehicle to drive through. As the Peugeot rolled forward, Harvath saw the wooden guardhouse with its propane heater and additional manpower, all of them heavily armed and similarly attired in insulated down jackets and traditional black Basque berets.

Eyebrows and Scarface were the cousin and brother-in-law of the district ETA commander, and this was his ranch. But it wasn't the district commander Harvath had come to see. It was another man, equally revered in the area, if not more so.

Eyebrows rolled to a stop in front of the stables and, grunting again, gestured with his chin toward the stairs. Harvath knew the drill.

Getting out of the car, he nodded at the two men and then watched as they drove off back toward the gate.

He stood for a moment and took in the view. The sun was dipping low on the horizon and the temperature, already considerably lower at this altitude, was beginning to drop. It was going to be a very cold night.

He climbed the stairs and opened the door to the small apartment above the stables. On the stove was the same traditional dish that had been left for him last time, Basque beans flavored with ham and chorizo. In the center of the kitchen atop an old wooden dining table there was a chipped glass and half a bottle of wine.

Though he'd spent less than four hours in the apartment last summer, the familiarity of it all helped to take the edge off of his tension. For the moment, he was safe.

Setting Riley's backpack on the counter, he reached for the bottle and poured himself a glass of wine. The next step was going to be very dangerous. Before taking a sip, he offered up a silent prayer that the man he had come to see would be up to the task.

CHAPTER 9

There were very few people Nicholas would ever risk his life for, but Caroline Romero was one of them.

That didn't mean, though, that he had thrown caution to the wind and gone rushing blindly to her aid. There were still precautions that he needed to take. First and foremost among them was selecting his base of operations.

Three Peaks Ranch spanned more than twenty thousand acres and belonged to a wealthy Texas family headed by Peter Knight. From cattle and aerospace to mining and biotechnology, Knight's business interests spanned the globe, and Nicholas had facilitated multiple transactions for him over the years.

The ranch was the family's primary retreat, maintained by a full-time staff. In addition to taking care of the Knights when they were in residence, the staff was expected to see to the needs of other guests who visited throughout the year. Before Nicholas showed up, they had had no idea what to expect. Mr. Knight had simply called and stated that a VIP guest was coming, that he'd be staying for an indeterminate length of time, and that the staff should see to any needs he had.

The man's first request was waiting for him outside the guesthouse the next day: a black Yukon Denali that had been sourced from a leasing group in Brownsville catering to disabled drivers. It looked and functioned just like any other SUV, except that it also offered hand controls so that the driver could control the vehicle's acceleration and breaking without touching the pedals. Per Nicholas's instructions, the staff had tinted the windows and removed the rear seats in order to give the dogs as much room as possible.

Hopping into the front passenger seat with a Leatherman tool, he peeled back the headliner and snipped the wires that connected to the vehicle's cell phone and onboard GPS/OnStar navigation system. After replacing the headliner, he then scoured the entire vehicle inside and out, making sure there were no other fleet management or tracking devices that might have been installed. It was a time-consuming exercise that required he get under the vehicle and use a step stool to poke around the engine compartment, but he had no intention of letting anyone follow his movements.

Once satisfied, Nicholas loaded the dogs inside and with the assistance of a booster seat he had brought along, took the Denali for a test drive to familiarize himself with the ranch.

The Knights had populated it with all sorts of wild and exotic game. If Nicholas hadn't been awake for the entirety of his flight in, he could easily believe he'd been dropped onto a wildlife preserve in Africa. In the time it took him to drive across the game enclosure, he saw addax, oryx, kudu, impala, water buffalo, zebra, gazelle, and wildebeest. The dogs, their heads out the lowered windows, noticed them too.

Confident he could now handle the vehicle out on regularly trafficked roads, Nicholas eventually turned back to his guesthouse.

Sitting on the front steps was the Knights' ranch manager, an attractive woman in her late thirties named Maggie Rose, who gave a friendly wave as Nicholas drove up.

Putting the car in park and turning off the ignition, Nicholas hopped out and then used the remote on the SUV's key fob to open the rear tailgate and let his dogs jump down.

"How's the truck working out?" she asked.

"It's just fine, thank you," he replied. Maggie had an easygoing way about her that he liked. Upon first seeing him, people often did a double take, but when she had met him at the plane last night to escort him to the guesthouse, she treated him just like any other guest. She had been professional, with just the right amount of Texas charm thrown in.

"I hope you don't mind, but since you weren't here I let myself in and put away the groceries you asked for."

Nicholas did mind. He didn't like the idea of anyone being in the guesthouse while he wasn't there. Nevertheless, there wasn't anything he could say. He was a guest, and he was sure she had done it only as a courtesy.

"Thank you," he replied.

"You're welcome," said Maggie as she smiled at Argos and Draco. "I did a little research on your dogs last night. They're an amazing breed."

Nicholas smiled. "It's the only type of dog I'll ever own."

"I bet they get expensive pretty quick in the eating department."

"You can't put a price on animals like these," he said, patting each of them.

"May I?" asked Maggie as she approached.

Nicholas nodded and Maggie walked over to Argos and Draco. She held a hand out to each of them to smell and then scratched them behind the ears. "You could probably make up half your food bill renting them out for pony rides at birthday parties."

Nicholas smiled again.

Lowering her hands, Maggie took a step back. "If there's anything else you need, just give me a buzz. My number is posted next to the phone in the kitchen."

"I'll do that," he replied.

He watched her as she walked back to her truck and climbed inside. She honked the horn and gave him a wave and a warm smile as she drove off. Nicholas waved back.

Once she had gone, he mounted the stairs along with the dogs and let himself inside. The dogs needed to be fed, but he wanted to check his equipment first. While he didn't have any reason to distrust Maggie, he didn't have any reason to trust her either. She was a nice woman, but he'd had plenty of nice women try to slip knives between his ribs over the years.

He made his way to the master bedroom, where he looked the equipment over. All the cases were still locked and appeared to be just as he had left them.

Unpacking two of them, he set up his satellite uplink and connected his laptop. As everything was powering up and signals were being established, he fed and watered the dogs. By the time he was done, he was ready to go online.

Sitting at the dining room table, he navigated to the site Caroline Romero was using to communicate. He had left her a message alerting her that he had arrived in Texas. Now there was a message waiting for him in return. It read: *Tonight. 8 pm. Casa De Palmas. McAllen. Parking garage. Top floor. Thank you for helping me.*

Caroline's previous appeal for help had contained such intimate information, things only the two of them could know, that he had no doubt that she was the author and that she was in very deep trouble.

Being the man he was, he wanted to rescue her immediately, sweep her into safety, but he needed to be careful. Telling her about the ranch and where he was staying was out of the question, at least for the moment. A lot of time had passed since they had last seen each other. A million things could have changed. Plus, he still had that twinge that something about this entire thing might not be right. Meeting in public was a much better option.

He also liked the idea that they would meet someplace where he wouldn't have to get out of his car. It made him feel better about traveling into McAllen.

Conducting a quick search for Casa De Palmas, he learned that it was a three-star hotel in the heart of the city. Next he pulled up satellite imagery and got a good feel for the layout of the property. Once he was familiar with the location, he began planning his routes to and from the hotel—as well as likely locations for an ambush. He was taking nothing for granted.

CHAPTER 10

McAllen, Texas, sat only five miles from the U.S.-Mexico border, and just beyond that was the highly dangerous Mexican city of Reynosa. Nicholas had both stolen from and sold information to some of Mexico's worst organized crime figures. He could envision a million scenarios, none of them good, whereby the meeting at the Casa De Palmas was only a ruse to draw him across the border to an undesirable end, so he had made sure to take appropriate precautions.

Because of his size, even weapons designed for children were usually too large and unwieldy for him to handle. They also fired only lower-caliber ammunition that didn't have enough knockdown power for his taste. To remedy the situation, Nicholas had all of his equipment custom made by some of the finest gunsmiths and engineers in the world.

His favorite weapon was a three-shot, .45-caliber handgun with a tiny grip and a dramatically ported barrel that helped significantly reduce the pistol's recoil. Despite the clever design, it took everything Nicholas had to control the weapon and bring it back on target for follow-up shots. Nevertheless, it was an incredible equalizer—an elephant gun that put the mouse on equal footing.

There was an array of other gear that Nicholas never traveled without, and he took his time loading up the Denali. If he couldn't return to the ranch, if he had to run, or if any of a million other things happened, he always wanted to be prepared. He had learned at a very young age that no one else was going to look out for him. Only *he* was going to look out for him. And for him to survive, he needed to think of everything and be as prepared as possible. The problem, though, was that no one could be prepared for *everything*.

Be that as it may, Nicholas hadn't come all this way to allow himself to be paralyzed by his doubts. He had come to repay a favor.

Once all his gear was loaded, Nicholas gave the dogs a few minutes of exercise and then had them hop into the cargo area. He closed the tailgate, walked around to the front, and climbed into the driver's seat.

A white-tailed hawk spun circles in the sky above as the Denali made its way across the ranch and out onto the county road, south toward McAllen.

Had he wanted to, Nicholas could have enlisted the help of Knight's security team, but he had decided against it. This was personal. He refrained from involving others in his affairs whenever possible. The less people knew about him, the better—even Knight's security team.

And while Caroline hadn't specifically asked him to come alone, the message had been clear. She was in trouble and didn't want anyone else to know that she had reached out to him. Fair enough. He could understand that. He had his dogs and more than a few aces in the hole, just in case.

As he drove, he was gripped by a tumult of emotion. There was apprehension, of course. It was always that way when he traveled outside his comfort zone. There was also a twinge of excitement. It had been so long since he had last seen Caroline. She was not only brilliant, she was beautiful, and much like that evening at the hacker conference years ago, he had found himself changing clothes multiple times before settling on the right thing to wear for this meeting.

Even he knew the effort was ridiculous. Their relationship had never been anything more than friendship, but still, she mattered to him and he wanted to look his best. In a sudden bout of impulsiveness, he had even shaved off his neatly trimmed beard in the hope that along with it he might be able to shave off a few years. It was ironic that a soul dealt such a miserable hand and treated so cruelly by life could possess such hopefulness; his insecurities were both heartbreaking and incredibly endearing to those closest to him.

To his credit, Nicholas was no fool. He knew how the world saw him. He was well aware that romantic entanglements were not something he would ever have to worry about. And, as he grew older, he began to make peace with the idea of spending the rest of his life alone. This had caused him to place even greater value on the handful of friendships he did have. It also played a significant role in deciding to answer Caroline's call for help.

His mind was drawn back to the task at hand as the rugged, rural landscape of south Texas began to give way to the outlying residential communities of McAllen.

Just over one hundred years old, McAllen was one of the fastest-growing urban areas in the United States. It had benefited tremendously from the North American Free Trade Agreement, or NAFTA, as well as the *Maquiladora* economy that allowed Mexican factories to import raw materials tariff free and produce goods to sell back to the United States. McAllen was in essence a boomtown catering to Americans and Mexicans alike. International trade, cross-border commerce and health care, on top of drug running and human trafficking, were making a lot of people in the Lower Rio Grande Valley very wealthy.

And for every wealthy person the border towns of south Texas produced, there were a thousand more who would do anything just to become wealthy. It was just this category of person Nicholas was on the lookout for as he rolled into McAllen.

One of the most common get-rich-quick schemes in Mexico was kidnapping, and it had already spilled across the border into the southern United States. While holding victims for ransom meant big paydays, "express" kidnappings were starting to come into vogue. Express kidnappings were a step above a mugging. Kidnappers first cleaned out your wallet, then forced you to the nearest ATM, where they made you withdraw the maximum amount allowed by your bank. Victims were normally then released, although some were held until the next day in order to make a second run. Nicholas didn't plan on falling prey to either crime.

Every time traffic slowed or he was required to stop for an intersection, he made sure to keep enough space between vehicles so that he could always see the rear tires of the vehicle in front of him. That meant he would be able to drive around the vehicle and not be boxed in.

He was well aware of the minor "accidents" carjackers orchestrated in order to steal high-end vehicles right off the street, and he was on his guard, constantly monitoring not only what was happening in front of his SUV but also along the sides and behind.

South Main Street was lined with old-fashioned streetlights and mostly single-story retail shops that looked like they had been built in the 1950s, their signs written in English and Spanish. Parked at an angle to the narrow concrete sidewalks was a mixture of pickup trucks, minivans, and cheap American sedans, cheek-by-jowl with BMWs, Porsches, and Mercedes. The contrast couldn't have been more stark.

Crossing from South Main Street to North was to literally go from one side of the tracks to the other. Instead of single-story shops, majestic palms now bordered each side of the street. There was a small, green square called Archer Park and across from it, the Casa De Palmas hotel.

Nicholas drove past slowly, taking everything in, including the adjacent parking structure.

A device sitting on the armrest next to him chimed and he glanced down at the screen to see "Casa De Palmas WiFi acquired." Smiling, he continued on, familiarizing himself with the neighborhood and the different routes he might have to take on his departure.

Half an hour later, he pulled into the McAllen Convention Bureau and Visitors' Center parking lot and found a spot facing Archer Park and the Casa De Palmas beyond. It was now time to do what he did best.

CHAPTER 11

Casa De Palmas had been built in the Mission style, with archways, a mock bell tower, red Spanish roofing tiles, and a cream stucco façade offset with brilliant white trim. The original structure dated back to the early 1900s, and as far as Nicholas was concerned, so did its security.

Using the hotel's own WiFi service as his access point, he had the Casa De Palmas' firewalls defeated within minutes. And once he was in, he owned everything inside the hotel. Anything that touched the Casa De Palmas computer system now belonged to him.

Nicholas began the next stage of his reconnaissance by scrolling through the guest registry. He searched for Caroline Romero's name but came up empty. He searched credit card transactions at the hotel bar and restaurant and also came up empty. He remotely searched the concierge's computer and still found nothing. As far as he could tell, Caroline had left no electronic "fingerprints" at the Casa De Palmas. He wasn't surprised.

He next shifted his attention to the hotel's less than impressive CCTV feed. Pouring himself a small cup of espresso from the thermos he had brought, he took a sip as he clicked back and forth, studying the different images.

All of the closed-circuit cameras were placed exactly where he expected them to be. There were feeds from the lobby, the loading bay, the different levels of the garage, and so forth. All the footage was recorded on two inexpensive, motion-activated DVRs located in the security office. As far as Nicholas could tell, they kept the footage for a week and then purged it, possibly making a hard-copy backup on a DVD or a removable drive of some sort. It didn't make a difference. One week's worth of footage would be more than enough.

After studying the live camera feeds, he tapped into the DVRs and scrolled backward through the day's traffic. He had plenty of time until his meeting with Caroline, so there was no need to rush. He was looking for anything out of the ordinary; anything that suggested he might be walking into a trap.

When he finished scrolling through with the current day's footage, he scrolled back and reviewed the footage from yesterday, paying particular attention to who arrived and who departed. While there were some visitors that gave him pause, most notably security men accompanying wealthy women to lunch with their girlfriends, there really wasn't anything that set off any alarm bells. So far, so good.

Just to be sure, Nicholas scanned one more day's worth of footage. Content for the time being, he moved on to the next phase.

There wasn't anything a business did these days that wasn't done on computer, and Casa De Palmas was a perfect case in point. Locating the HR director's computer, Nicholas was able to figure out which security guard would be on desk duty for the evening and when he had last been off. With that knowledge, he was able to select the garage footage from which he would build his loop.

Once he had partitioned a portion of the DVR and copied the garage footage over from two nights ago, all he had to do was rebuild the time-stamp data and make sure that when the switch took place, everything synched up. It wouldn't do any good to have the true feed to the guard be nighttime while the bogus feed from the garage still showed daylight outside.

At best, the work was tedious, but that was all. Soon enough, Nicholas had built himself a virtual cloak of invisibility that would cover the garage. Even better was the fact that while the guard inside the security office of the hotel would be unknowingly watching footage from two nights ago, Nicholas would be able to monitor the live feeds from the garage cameras. Sitting in his SUV on the upper level, he'd be able to watch all the comings and goings from the garage and would still have access to all the footage from the remaining hotel cameras. It gave him the edge, and that edge could make all the difference between life and death.

Checking the time, Nicholas reviewed the recent spate of arrivals at the hotel. The Casa De Palmas shuttle had recently disgorged a group of guests, presumably from the airport, and several expensive sports cars had dropped off groups of attractive, well-dressed women, many of whom seemed to know one another and had proceeded to the hotel bar.

Watching the mostly dark-haired, Latina women arrive at the hotel, he realized that he had no idea what he was looking for. Caroline could look exactly like she had the last time he saw her or she could look completely different. It was amazing how women could so easily change their appearance. She could be a blonde for all he knew or she could look exactly like any of the women who had entered the hotel over the last half hour.

Exercising his talents by taking over the hotel's camera system had made him feel empowered, but realizing that he didn't know what he was looking for began to put him on edge again.

He thought about pouring himself more espresso but decided against it. He was amped up enough already. "Focus," he told himself as he continued to scan the faces throughout the Casa De Palmas. Nobody was like Caroline Romero. If she was here, he had to be able to pick her out.

He watched the video feeds for another forty-five minutes, until it was time for him to get in place. Removing the custom pistol from inside the armrest, he placed it in his lap and covered it with a jacket. It was showtime.

Placing the Denali in reverse, he backed out of the parking space and pointed it toward the street. At the edge of the lot, he sent the "bump" to the monitors of the hotel security office. There was a flash of snow and then everything was fine. If the guard had been watching and not distracted by paperwork or texting on his cell phone, it would have appeared as if the power had momentarily dipped before coming back full strength. Unless he was attentive enough to notice that the valets taking cars at the front of the hotel weren't driving those same cars into the garage, then everything would be fine.

Nicholas wasn't worried about the guard. He had enough camera feeds to keep him busy without making distinctions among the separate feeds. Besides, from what his personnel file said, the guard was a twenty-eight-year-old single male. With all the attractive women in short dresses climbing out of low-slung sports cars at the front door, it was easy to determine where his attention would be focused.

With a quick SDR to make sure he wasn't being followed, Nicholas rounded the corner, passed the entrance to the Casa De Palmas, and drove into the parking structure.

He kept his eyes open for any vehicles that didn't belong there or might portend trouble, such as a delivery truck or a large windowless van. As he wound his way to the third floor, he didn't see anything out of the ordinary.

After conducting a slow crawl of the upper deck to examine the other cars, he found a spot toward the center and pulled in. The sun had set over an hour ago. A smattering of lights on tall poles cast an incandescent pallor over the exposed roof of the parking garage.

In his rearview mirror, Nicholas could make out the pedestrian bridge that led back to the hotel. As he was studying it, a chime rang from his computer.

He looked down and clicked on one of the windows he had left open. Caroline had just posted a message for him: *Coming out.*

Nicholas looked around. *Was she in one of the cars? The hotel?* He couldn't be certain.

When none of the car doors opened, he assumed she meant she was coming out from the hotel itself. Bringing up the live camera feeds from inside the hotel, he began searching for her.

Near the bar area on the ground floor, a woman stood waiting for an elevator. *Was that her?* She wasn't facing the camera. Her head was down and she seemed to be looking at her phone. She was about the right size, but so was every other woman who had walked into the hotel that night. When the elevator doors opened, she stepped inside and disappeared.

Less than a minute later, the elevator arrived at the third floor and the woman walked out. Once again, he couldn't see her face. She seemed to know where all the cameras were. Nicholas's heart had begun beating faster but not because he was excited to see Caroline Romero. He had a bad feeling something wasn't right.

Even so, he tried to tell himself to calm down. Caroline was an exceedingly intelligent woman. If she was in enough trouble to call him for help, she was very likely in enough trouble that she didn't want her face captured on a security camera. Nicholas wanted to believe in her abilities, but he was having a hard time. Instinctively, he reached down and wrapped his hand around the butt of his pistol. The dogs could sense their owner's unease and leapt up in back, their eyes scanning out the cargo area windows as they tried to figure out what was going on.

Suddenly the woman appeared on the pedestrian walkway. She stopped when she got to the parking area and looked around, unsure of where to go.

Nicholas took a deep breath and tapped his brake lights. The woman began walking forward.

She was attired like the other women he had seen entering the hotel that night, in heels and a short dress that clung to her body. A small cocktail purse hung from her left shoulder. The phone now gone, both of her hands appeared empty. His eyes flicked from her hands to her face, which he still couldn't see. She walked with her head tilted down. *Was she trying to throw off the cameras? Or was this all about throwing me off?*

The woman was closing in on the Denali, and Nicholas's trepidation was going through the roof. As she neared, alarm bells started going off inside his head. Everything inside him was yelling that danger was approaching. *Put the truck in gear and go—drive and don't look back,* the voices told him. Yet he ignored them. Argos and Draco had started growling.

Any time he may have had to react was now gone. The woman was so close she could touch the vehicle. And as quickly as that, he lost sight of her.

The dogs were now barking as they lunged at the back window. Nicholas craned his tiny neck from side to side as he tried to figure out where she had gone. *A trap.* He should have known.

Revving the Denali, he prepared to slam it into gear, when a face suddenly appeared at the passenger-side window. Without even thinking, Nicholas raised his pistol to fire.

He centered it on the woman's forehead and began to depress the trigger. But before he could fully engage, he jerked the weapon to the left.

The barking of the dogs was so loud that Nicholas couldn't hear himself think. They had raced forward and were straining to leap into the passenger seat to get at the figure outside. He yelled for them to be quiet.

He had never seen this woman before in his life. It wasn't Caroline, but there was something familiar about her.

She reached down and tried to open the passenger door. It was locked. She looked back at Nicholas.

"She was wearing leather pants," the woman said through the glass. "She had short, spiky black hair back then."

Before he knew what was going on, the woman was reaching into her purse. Nicholas reflexively swung his weapon back toward her, ready to fire.

But she wasn't reaching for a gun. From her purse she produced an old photograph and pressed it up against the window. He now realized why the woman standing there was so familiar to him.

Lowering his pistol, he reached behind him with his left hand and hit the unlock button.

As soon as she saw the lock pop up, the woman opened her door and climbed in. "I can explain everything," she said, before Nicholas even had a chance to speak, "but we need to go. *Now.*"

CHAPTER 12

The sun had just begun to rise when the knock fell upon the door. "It's open," Harvath said from the stove. He didn't bother to turn around. He knew who it was.

A Basque man in his early forties stepped quietly inside and shut the door behind him.

"There's coffee on the table."

The man walked over and pulled out a chair. Sitting down, he withdrew a pack of cigarettes from his pocket, shook one out, and lit it up. "It looks like I'm right on time."

He had dark hair and a clean-shaven face. His serene countenance was juxtaposed by his impeccable, military-style posture and a pair of brown eyes that seemed a little too alert for a man of his profession.

"I heard the dogs as your horse got near," Harvath said as he approached the table with a pan and spatula. "I hope you like eggs, Father."

The priest took a deep drag on his cigarette and held the smoke in his lungs for a moment before releasing it into the air and nodding.

After serving the food, Harvath walked over, put the pan in the sink, and joined his visitor at the table. He was just about to begin eating when the priest fixed him with his gaze. Harvath set his fork down and waited.

Setting his cigarette on the edge of the table, Padre Peio bowed his head and gave the traditional blessing. When he was finished, he made the sign of the cross and looked up. "I probably should say that I'm surprised to see you, but I assume that was your intention."

"I needed someplace safe."

The priest picked up his cigarette and gestured with it. "I suppose you could do worse than the ranch of an ETA commander. But someone with your resources could also do much better."

Harvath scooped up a forkful of eggs and nodded. "I needed a location that I couldn't easily be connected to."

The priest thought about this for a moment before responding. "What happened?"

"I don't want to discuss specifics."

"Fine, let's discuss generalities."

Harvath was silent for a moment as he reflected on what he knew about Peio.

The man had not always been a priest. In fact, his background was quite unusual among those who end up devoting their lives to God.

Peio and his family had left the Basque country for Madrid when he was in his first year of high school. With so many members of the family involved in the separatist movement, they had been worried about him and also his older brother becoming involved with ETA. They were right to have been concerned.

Within a year of graduating high school, Peio's older brother had returned to the Basque country and joined up. Three months later, he died in a shootout with police. Peio, though, took another path.

He undertook his compulsory military service and proved quite adept in military intelligence. He stayed in the military while he completed his college degree and eventually transferred into Spain's National Intelligence Service. It was there that Peio met his wife.

They deeply loved their jobs and each other. They had a plan to work five more years in the intelligence field and then transition into something less dangerous so that they could begin a family. They were six months away from that goal when, on a cold March morning in 2004, Alicia boarded a rush-hour commuter train for Madrid.

At 7:38 a.m., just as the train was pulling out of the station, an improvised explosive device planted by Muslim terrorists detonated, killing her instantly.

It was part of a series of coordinated bombings and became Spain's 9/11. The entire nation was in shock. Peio was shattered. As an intelligence operative who specialized in Muslim extremism, he felt that he had failed his wife and his country by not having prevented the attack. This unhealthy sense of responsibility drove him over the cliff into a dark emotional abyss.

When he requested to be part of the investigation, his superiors said no, and placed him on forced medical leave in order to recover from his loss. Three days later, he disappeared.

Colleagues who had stopped by his home to check on him assumed that he had returned to the Basque country to get away from Madrid and the scene of his wife's murder. They had no idea how wrong that assumption was.

Over the next thirty-six hours, Peio hunted down and brutally interrogated several Muslim extremists, severely hampering Spain's investigation into the bombings. No matter which leads the authorities chose to follow or how fresh those leads were, they arrived to find that someone had already been there. That someone was Peio.

He finally captured two key members of the terror cell who had planned and facilitated the attacks. After torturing them for three days in an abandoned building, he executed them both. It was but a mile marker on his personal descent into hell.

After drawing all the money out of his bank account, he left Madrid for the tiny Spanish island of Cabrera. There, he drank. And when the drinking no longer assuaged his pain, he turned to heroin, and a whole new circle of hell was opened to him. He became addicted. When his money ran out, he attempted suicide.

He was already dead emotionally, and had it not been for a local priest who found him, he would have died physically as well.

The tiny island priest was tough but compassionate and dragged Peio back from the dead. "God has other plans for you," he said, and when it came time for Peio to decide whether or not to return to Madrid and put the pieces of his life back together, God spoke to him directly and Peio learned what those plans were.

He confided in Harvath quite candidly not long after they had met that his biggest regret wasn't over anything he had done. It wasn't the brutal interrogations, the tortures, or even the executions of the terrorists he had captured. He had repented for those things and would ultimately answer to God. He had even forgiven himself for not having been able to prevent the attack that had taken his wife's life. What he regretted the most was never having had children with her. If they had had children, even just one, he couldn't help but wonder how different his life would have been in those days and months after Alicia's death.

Harvath found that hard to believe. Any real man, especially a man with Peio's background, would have done exactly what he had done. He would have hunted down and killed his wife's killers. But Harvath had learned that, man of the cloth or not, what Peio said and what Peio did were often at odds with each other. And, as good as Harvath was at reading people, he also found it difficult to discern whether Peio had taken to him because of their similar operational backgrounds or because the priest saw in him a soul in need of saving.

Peio's contradictions were most fully on display when it came to the man who had introduced them—Nicholas, or simply the Troll, as the intelligence world referred to him.

Peio and Nicholas had met at an orphanage, in Belarus. Nicholas was one of its patrons and the priest had been doing missionary work there, ministering to the *podkidysh,* or "abandoned children," many of whom were part of the continuing legacy of Chernobyl. Through their work at the orphanage, the two men had developed an unlikely, yet deep bond.

So strong was that bond that when Nicholas needed someplace safe, a place to disappear, he had turned to Peio, just as Harvath had done.

Peio lived two and a half hours farther up into the mountains at a remote monastery dedicated to Saint Francis Xavier. The ETA commander was a friend from his childhood and his fortified ranch served as a base camp and a gateway to the monastery beyond.

It was hard for Harvath to believe that it was less than a year ago that he and Peio had met. They had been drawn together by Nicholas, a man who had grown on both of them and whom each called his friend.

This same man had drawn Peio back into the field and his old way of life, though Harvath suspected the priest hadn't put up much resistance.

Harvath had been thrown into an operation with Peio and had watched him work. He was good; his instincts on the money. So adept was he and so suited to the field that Harvath secretly wondered if the man would be able to remain a priest or if God might have yet another plan in store for him.

Whether He did or didn't wasn't Harvath's concern. Right now he needed Peio. That meant he was going to have to trust him.

Reaching for his coffee cup, he settled on the words he was going to say and then began to fill the priest in.

CHAPTER 13

P adre Peio had only left the table once, to get an ashtray, and had motioned for Harvath to keep talking, which he did. When he finished, the priest exhaled a cloud of smoke and leaned back in his chair.

"I am deeply sorry for the loss of your colleague," said Peio. "I will pray for her, as well as the other men you were forced to kill."

The idea of Peio praying for Riley's killers didn't sit well with him at all, but Harvath kept that to himself.

"Now then," continued the priest, "what else can I do for you besides provide sanctuary? I assume you want to make contact with your superiors?"

"I do."

"Considering your circumstances, using a telephone, at least from here, is out of the question."

"Agreed," replied Harvath. "It would be too easy to trace. If I had access to a computer, though, I could route it so that it looks like I'm someplace else entirely. Is there one here that I can use?"

"There is. I'll speak to your host and see what I can do."

Twenty minutes later, Harvath was sitting in the main house in front of a small laptop. After laying a long digital trail through servers in multiple countries, he accessed his Skype account. Clicking on Reed Carlton's icon in his contact list, he typed a message the Old Man would recognize, letting him know that he had gone to ground and that Riley had been killed. *Am on the road. My companion couldn't make the trip.*

It was all he needed to say. Carlton was pretty much glued to his Skype account. If he wasn't communicating with his people in the field via computer, he was doing it on his smartphone. Harvath sent the message and then sat back and waited. Forty-five minutes later, he was still waiting.

The Old Man's icon showed that he was online, yet he still hadn't responded. The only thing he could think of was that he had to be in a meeting of some sort. But with the time change, it didn't make any sense. He didn't like it, but he had no choice but to continue waiting.

An hour later, Peio knocked on the open door and asked, "Everything okay?"

Harvath shook his head. "No word yet."

"It *is* the middle of the night back in the U.S."

"I can't reach Nicholas either and he's always online."

"I haven't been able to contact him either," said the priest.

"Since when?"

"Since yesterday. I reached out to him when I heard you were looking for me."

"Via cell phone or the Web?" asked Harvath.

"The Web," replied Peio.

Harvath went back into his contact list to check Nicholas's Skype status. It showed him as being off-line. Nicholas was never off-line. Something was wrong.

Scrolling through his contact list he pinged one of the other operators he worked with at the Carlton Group, a man named Coyne. His icon showed him as being online, but he wasn't responding. Harvath decided to call him on Skype. Clicking on the number, he activated the call and listened to it ring until it went to voice mail.

He then tried another operator, a man named Moss, and had the same results. Working his way down the list, he reached out to the two dozen or so other operators. Not a single one of them answered. Something definitely wasn't right. In fact, something was very wrong.

Peio could see the look on Harvath's face. "What is it?"

"I can't reach anyone. Not on their Skype accounts. Not on their mobile phones. *Nothing.*"

"Could there be a reason?"

Harvath was sure there was a reason, but the only one that came to mind was so unfathomable that he didn't want to even think about it. But he had to. There was no such thing as coincidence, not in his line of work. He had to assume that something very bad had happened. "I need to get back."

"To the States?"

"Yes. Now. As soon as possible."

"Do you think that's wise?" asked Peio. "You have no idea what you might be rushing back to."

The man had a point. He could be rushing right into a trap. That said, he couldn't just sit still. He had to do something.

He was running options through his mind when a chime rang from the computer and a message from the Old Man suddenly appeared on his screen. *Received your message. Are you okay?*

Peio had heard the chime and saw the expression on Harvath's face change. "What is it?"

"The Old Man just responded," stated Harvath as he keyed in his response to Carlton. *Am okay. No damage.*

There were a million things he wanted to tell his superior, but he knew better than to do that, even on Skype. Instead he waited.

Moments later, the Old Man typed, *Are you somewhere safe?*

Yes.

Good. Stay there. Wait for further communication.

It was just like the Old Man to tell him to sit and wait, without giving him any further information. The fact that he didn't ask where Harvath was or try to move him to one of the other Carlton safe houses was a bad sign. The organization must have been very deeply penetrated.

Roger that, Harvath replied.

Do not communicate with anyone else, the Old Man added. *Not until I figure out what is going on. No one.*

That was a prohibition Harvath should have expected. Technically, he had already "communicated" by reaching out to the other team members, but there was nothing he could do about that and decided to keep it to himself.

He wanted to ask what, if anything, the Old Man knew about the Paris attack, but he knew better. Carlton had contacts everywhere and had probably already been in touch with French intelligence. The fact that he wasn't asking for any details at this point spoke volumes. When he wanted Harvath's report, he'd ask for it. In the meantime, Harvath would do as he had been instructed.

Understood, he typed and then watched as the Old Man's icon changed from green to gray, indicating that he had logged off.

CHAPTER 14

That was actually worth getting out of bed for," Craig Middleton said as he patted his protégé on the shoulder. "Well done."

Kurt Schroeder tried to not grit his teeth. It was like working for Sybil. The man had to have been manic-depressive or bipolar or something. He ran so hot and cold, you never knew what the hell was going to come out of the faucet next. More often than not, though, the safe bet was that it would be pure liquid asshole. He was a screamer too, and prone to throwing things. Employees at ATS derisively referred to him as "Chuckles, the laughing boss" and called his twisted style of debasing encouragement "blamestorming." Schroeder, though, seemed to be keenly adept at handling him or, more appropriately, ignoring his less than professional, the-floggings-will-continue-until-morale-improves management style.

Middleton had never been able to hold an assistant for more than a year until he brought Schroeder in. Whether either of the men would ever admit it, they were made for each other.

Colleagues had marveled at Schroeder's ability to ignore Middleton's never-ending torrent of slights and petty insults. "Like water off a duck's back," they remarked, but they were incorrect. The insults didn't just "roll" off. Each abusive strike found its target, which Schroeder quietly cataloged and buried. When he did exorcise his demons, he attempted to do so as far from the prying eyes of ATS and Craig Middleton as possible. He knew all too well the lengths his boss was prepared to go to in order to leverage information.

It was by understanding Middleton so intimately that he was able to work with him so closely. And understanding Middleton wasn't difficult at all. He had to look no further than his own youth to find a nearly identical personality.

Schroeder had been born and mostly raised in a world of exceptional privilege, but in one afternoon, it had all been taken away. The fancy prep school, the magnificent house, the cars, the security afforded by bottomless bank accounts, all of it. Yet the worst part for Schroeder had been the loss of his father.

At the time, Schroeder was fourteen and a freshman in high school. The scandal was of epic proportions and its fallout horrible. It rained incessantly that autumn and the weather seemed to mirror the overwhelming sorrow welling up from the very pit of Schroeder's young soul. As the media trampled their Greenwich, Connecticut, lawn, they pounded down on the boy's sodden family and turned everything into mud.

Until that day, the family had been regarded with respect and admiration, even awe. Their wealth and prominence defined who they were. But it was all a lie, all of it. The media had a term for what Schroeder's father had been doing, a term he had never heard before. They called it a "Ponzi scheme."

In an instant, his father, the man he had idolized, the man he was named after, went from being a "wizard," a "magician," and a "genius," to a "liar," a "thief," and a "con man." As those words rained down, a vise clamped down on his heart, forbidding it to beat.

He loved his father, and even though he was no more than a boy, he desperately wanted to defend him. He refused to believe what everyone was saying. This was his *father* they were talking about. His father was a good man. He was being bullied, and Schroeder hated bullies.

As he reached out to him, looking for an explanation, looking for reassurance that everything was going to be okay, his father withdrew. Then a nightmare more horrible than anything he could ever imagine took place.

While home on bail, awaiting trial, Schroeder's father committed suicide. The vise that had been clamped around his heart now ripped it fully from his chest. From that moment, it was a cold, dark spiral downward.

Everything the family had was taken from them. Every bank account was seized. Every asset, every car, all of it, gone. And with it, so too went their prominence and their identity. In their place was insupportable, unbearable shame.

His mother, an already unhappy woman battling depression and a host of her own problems, slipped into a vodka-induced haze and carpet-bombed what was left of her psyche with pills as their world fell apart around them.

She was already a strict authoritarian, but now she became downright abusive and mean. She and her son moved from their once exceedingly comfortable life in Greenwich to a threadbare, one-room apartment in Hartford, where she proceeded to drink through what little of her own savings she had managed to hide from the courts.

Soon after, they went on welfare. Schroeder's few friends who hadn't abandoned him in the midst of the scandal did so now. None of them came to visit. It was as if upon leaving the tony ZIP code, he suddenly ceased to exist.

The public school his mother shoved him into was beyond rough. With the continuing accounts in the papers of the suicide and all the lives his father had ruined, the students soon put two and two together and figured out who he was. They mercilessly bullied him.

They called him "poor little rich boy" and hurled insults at his deceased father. A stammer Schroeder had worked hard as a child to overcome returned with a vengeance and served only to further embolden the bullies. Soon psychological torment gave way to physical, and he was beaten up repeatedly after school. When he had his jaw broken in three places and his left ear cauliflowered, Schroeder dropped out.

He found a job delivering Thai food. His mother either didn't notice or didn't care that he was no longer going to school. When the social services people made inquiries, she told them in no uncertain terms to "fuck off," and that it was her "right" to home-school her child. She reveled in being vile to anyone who crossed her path.

It also gave her a perverse pleasure to exercise her rights as she saw them and lord even an illusion of power over the same sector of the government that was subsidizing her rent, groceries, and utility bills. She didn't give a damn what they thought of her.

She also didn't give a damn if her son was getting any sort of education at all. She certainly wasn't going to waste any of her time on him.

That was fine with Schroeder. He had lost his taste for dealing with people and when he wasn't working, he preferred to be alone.

He immersed himself in a world of books. He read title after title whenever he could steal away from his mother, or while she lay passed out on the sofa bed after an all-night bender.

As his shattered life failed to improve, he went from missing his father to blaming him, and he blamed his lousy excuse for a mother as well. When the day came that he had saved up enough of his hidden money, he left.

Her abuse had become insufferable. The alcohol had eaten away at her brain and had completely destroyed any vestiges of a nurturing, mothering instinct. He taped a two-word note to a half-empty vodka bottle, which read, "Fuck you." At least he knew she'd find it.

For the next two years, he read the Hartford papers daily until he came across her obituary. After that, he never read another newspaper again.

He moved from his private world of books to the world of computers and the Internet. There he could carry on conversations without worrying that his stammer, which he fought daily to bring back under control, would draw any attention.

On the Internet, he found companionship and common purpose. He also found an exceptional outlet for his anger. With a soaring IQ, no adult supervision, and a moral compass that had been crushed beneath the tank treads of life, he quickly became one of the Net's leading "hacktivists."

He worked his way through a couple of years of easy hacks and then started getting into the harder stuff. For a long time, he took a perverse joy in targeting the media, but even that grew tiresome after a while. Finally, he arrived at a challenge worthy of his intellect and his skill set: hacking government and military networks around the globe.

While Schroeder focused on symbols of power, he wasn't above hacking NGOs and charitable organizations that offended his unbalanced sense of right and wrong. Organizations he thought were "phonies" or were failing to live up to their own mission statements particularly drew his ire. He was a perpetually angry loner who had a bone to pick with almost everyone, from the Red Cross to Amnesty International. When they finally identified and located him, he was the perfect hire for ATS.

Schroeder didn't just feel he was smarter than everyone else, he knew it. Nothing pissed him off more than stupid people, and as far as he was concerned, almost everyone he came across was stupid. He had an elitist streak running through his core that Craig Middleton loved and exploited to the fullest.

The more authority he was given, the more Schroeder wanted. Middleton had doled it out to him slowly, always watching to see what he would do with it.

Though he tried to hide it, he craved it like a drug and would do anything to get more. He was incredibly intelligent, but as far as Middleton could tell, he possessed zero courage. At his most base level, Schroeder was a coward. He wanted power so he could use it to punish others in order to feel better about himself. The man was a sadist. He took pleasure from giving other people pain. He was a weakling, and behind his back, Middleton referred to him as Renfield, the quisling mortal who served Dracula in Bram Stoker's novel.

Middleton had had high hopes that Schroeder would one day rise to a position of prominence within the organization, but after trying to develop his management talents, he had given up hope. Schroeder had very poor people skills and, like many of his kind, he related much better to computers. He lacked empathy, and worse, didn't appear capable even of faking it.

Middleton had resigned himself to the fact that Schroeder was exceptionally gifted, but that those gifts were limited. That was where the other nickname he used for him, Rain Man, came from. On occasion, if Middleton was pissed off enough, he mocked Schroeder by rocking back and forth in his chair as he shouted lines at him from the movie. Because Schroeder's stammer reared its ugly head from time to time, Middleton took particular pleasure in drawing out the line, "I'm d-d-d-definitely a good driver."

Schroeder buried that insult along with the rest and added another entry to the long and ever-growing list.

Now, backing out of Carlton's Skype account, Schroeder looked up at his boss and asked, "Do you think he suspects anything?"

"Of course not. Why the hell should he?"

"Because guys like him are paid to be suspicious."

"We're all paid to be suspicious. Get used to it. That's how we make our money."

"Yeah, but—" began Schroeder.

"Stop worrying about it," Middleton interrupted. "You've isolated his account so no one can contact him on it, right?"

"Yes, I did."

"Good, then. Now, what have you got on his midget data wizard? The Gnome or whatever the fuck he's called."

What an imbecile, Schroeder thought. *He can't even keep a simple code name straight.* "He's called the *Troll,*" Schroeder clarified, "and I don't have anything on him. He's gone completely dark."

"This is the twenty-first century and you work smack dab in the middle of its power center. There's no such thing as *completely dark.*"

"I know. I'm working on it."

"Well, work harder. People run, but they can't hide. What about that coroner's report we've been waiting for?"

"It hasn't been filed yet," said the young man. "IDs after a fire, especially a bad one like that, take longer. It'll hit their server soon enough, and when it does, we'll have it."

"I want it *before* it hits their server. Understood?"

Schroeder wanted to call his boss an *asshole,* or grab a pencil and plunge it into his eyesocket, but his rational self delivered a more appropriate response. "I'll get it to you as soon as it's available."

"Good," said Middleton as he rose. "How much longer until we'll have a lock on Harvath's location?"

Schroeder glanced back at his computer. "It's populating now," he said, studying a map that was unwinding all the servers the Skype connection had been routed through. "It looks like he's in Bulgaria. No, wait. I take that back. It's not Bulgaria."

Middleton was getting impatient. "Where the hell is he?"

"I've almost got him. One more second. It looks like . . . *Got him.* Spain."

"Spain? You're sure?"

"Yes," said Schroeder. "Near a village called Ezkutatu."

"Never heard of it."

"It's in Basque country. The Pyrenees."

"Send it all to my screen," Middleton ordered as he opened the door and started to step out into the hallway. Halfway there, he stopped and turned. "I almost forgot," he said. "About that data Caroline Romero stole."

"What about it?"

"Were you aware that she had a sister?"

Schroeder looked up from his computer. "A *sister*?"

"Am I not speaking English, jackass? *Yes*, a *sister*," he said, drawing the word out like Schroeder was an idiot. "Actually, she's her half sister. Same mother, different father."

"She never mentioned her."

"Really?" replied Middleton. "It never came up any of those times you two were out shopping for shoes or having your nails done?"

Weathering the insult, Schroeder made another hash mark in his emotional catalog and came back with a response a bit more caustic than usual. "You're aware that if I hadn't been friendly with Caroline, we never would have caught on to what she was doing?"

Middleton laughed in his face. "Bullshit. Like every other guy in this place, you just wanted to get in her pants. You didn't find out about her by being her friend. You found out because you were stalking everything she did."

"I wasn't stalking her. She was nice to me."

"You're a fucking sap, you know that? She was nice to you, moron, because you work for *me*. It's what a woman like that calls job security. Look it up. And while you're at it, check out *strategic alliance*. You're a flipping eunuch. God didn't give you balls, he gave you a pair of fucking raisins. You never would have said word one to her unless I'd ordered you to do so. And even then, she probably already suspected we were on to her. God only knows how much information you unwittingly passed to her during your *friendship*."

Schroeder was indignant and fought to keep himself under control. "I-I-I . . . ," he stammered.

"*You-you-you* what?" Middleton mocked. "Spit it out."

The young man could feel his cheeks flush and he balled his fists, digging his nails into his palms. He took a deep breath and let it out. "I d-d-d-d-didn't pass *anything* to her. And f-f-for the record, I never wanted to *get in her p-p-p-pants*. She-she-she wasn't my type."

Middleton laughed even louder. "You're either an idiot or a liar. She was *everybody's* type. In fact, I think that sexy piece of ass made you forget who butters your bread."

"I haven't f-f-forgotten."

"If that idiot Powder knew a flash drive from a fucking coffee cup, I would have given *him* the assignment. But he doesn't know shit about what we do around here, so I asked you. What a mistake that turned out to be."

"It w-w-wasn't a m-m-m—"

"Stop stuttering," Middleton snapped.

"Then stop m-m-mimicking m-m-me," Schroeder replied. "It m-m-makes it w-w-worse."

Middleton locked eyes with him and gave him an icy glare. "What makes it worse is that I can't trust you."

"That's not true. I've always been l-l-l-loyal to you."

"You'd better be."

"I've been g-g-giving this everything I've got."

"Yet you still didn't know about her sister."

Schroeder broke his gaze and looked toward his monitor. "I would have found her eventually."

"Of course you would have," the older man said, his tone thick with condescension. "You know what, Kurt? You have no idea what it's like to count on someone, only to have them consistently disappoint you."

Schroeder knew all too well and wished his boss would just leave him alone and let him go back to his job. "D-d-do you want me to look into the sister?" he offered, eager for the conversation to be over.

"Half sister," Middleton retorted. "No. *I'm* already working on her. I just wanted you to know that she's out there and that I have to be the one wasting my time trying to find her. Maybe that'll incentivize you to work harder."

There was only one thing that could incentivize Kurt Schroeder to work harder than he already was, but there was no way in hell he was ever going to reveal it to Craig Middleton. Before he could summon a response, his boss had left the room.

CHAPTER 15

Returning to his office, Craig Middleton closed his door and sat down at his desk. Waiting for him on his screen was the file with Harvath's coordinates and a smattering of other pieces of peripheral information. Making sense of data, massaging it and making it speak to him, was Middleton's gift. He wasn't simply good at it, he was practically a savant. There were only a handful of people in the world who understood the capture, synthesis, and manipulation of data as well as he did. In the world of data and information, he was more than a king, he was something akin to a god.

Middleton had been with ATS for as long as anyone could remember. IBM had spotted his brilliance in high school and gave him a blank check for his college and postgraduate studies. When his schooling was complete, he went to work in IBM's classified Fathom division, working on top-secret, cutting-edge projects for the United States government.

With Fathom, it was said that IBM had amassed the greatest assemblage of brainpower since the Manhattan Project. As might be expected with such an incredible collection of intellect, there were more than a few personality quirks within the division. Eccentricity and brilliance were often two sides of the same coin.

Craig Middleton though, possessed a genius that even his exceptional peers found unsettling. There wasn't a single project any of them were working on that Middleton couldn't immediately identify a way to improve. He wasn't shy, either, about telling his colleagues what they had overlooked or how even the smallest details of what they were working on could be made better. While his suggestions were always correct, his delivery was arrogant, and he grated on everyone who worked with him, even his superiors.

While never missing a chance to defame him for his rude and boorish behavior, no one could deny his brilliance, which was off the charts, and even his most vehement detractors at Fathom used names like Einstein and da Vinci when describing him. They also used names like Hitler and Mao.

Middleton's scorched-earth personality eventually succeeded in burning every bridge with his coworkers, and IBM was forced to seal him off from Fathom or, more accurately, seal Fathom off from him. Placed in an entirely new building on campus, Middleton was given an unlimited budget and his choice of what he wanted to work on, alone. His choice shook IBM to its core.

In the 1930s, International Business Machines began working with Adolf Hitler and the Nazis to help organize and utilize population data on a scale never before seen. It was a taboo period in the company's history, and one that IBM desperately wanted to forget. Middleton, though, was fascinated by it, in particular how the Nazis used data to surveil and control people.

Through a proprietary system of punch cards and punch card sorting machines, IBM assisted the Nazis in every stage of their persecution and eventual genocide of the Jewish people. It began with sorting census data to identify Jews in order to keep them out of particular fields of endeavor and eventually led to identifying where every Jew lived and how many family members they had so that they could be evicted from their homes and forced into the ghettos.

An American in Washington, D.C., named Herman Hollerith had developed the punch card system. At the height of the Third Reich, IBM was leasing, servicing, and upgrading two thousand sorting machines across Germany and thousands more across Nazi-occupied Europe, and manufacturing 1.5 billion custom punch cards each year in Germany alone.

There were "Hollerith Departments" at nearly every single concentration camp to compile and sort prisoner data, which ran the gamut from when a prisoner arrived to what slave labor he or she should perform and, of course, when each died.

The IBM partnership helped make the Nazis an incredibly efficient killing machine, far more efficient than they ever would have been on their own, and there was nary a facet of their operations that IBM didn't have a hand in. As Hitler sought to expand his Third Reich, IBM had salivated at the opportunity to gain even greater market share.

Knowing the culture at IBM and that nothing, especially data and information, was ever purged—no matter how damning or dangerous—Middleton demanded access to everything they had on the Nazi program. IBM declined his request. In fact, they went further, they told him it didn't exist. He knew they were lying, and he demanded the information again.

When he was turned down the second time, it was explained in no uncertain terms that if he made the request again, or even spoke of the project, his employment with IBM would be terminated, end of story.

Realizing that they weren't willingly going to grant him access to the material, he devised a plan to steal it.

After sufficient time had passed, he cobbled together a series of projects he knew IBM would be pleased to see him working on and began in earnest in his private lab, which was tucked away on the far side of the campus. What the higher-ups at IBM didn't know was that he had chosen each of the projects as cover and was slowly gaining access to the genocide program and siphoning copies of everything away.

By the time his superiors discovered, quite by accident, what he was up to, Middleton had made abhorrent progress. Using only simple mathematics and the rudimentary computing equipment available to IBM and the Nazis at the time, he had completely reworked and improved their program for genocide.

The detail into which his obsession plunged was beyond sickening. Improved train schedules and boxcar capacity studies, the construction and location of concentration camps, the means for prisoner selection, their murder, and the disposal of their corpses . . . Middleton's vision, not to mention his deplorable admiration of the process, which bordered on reverence, was repellent.

According to his calculations, IBM had dropped the ball. Hitler and the Nazis could have been at least 80 percent more "productive" in their killing of Jews and anyone else they saw as an enemy of the state.

When Middleton's research was uncovered, not only was he fired, but for the first time in the company's history they actually burned an employee's papers. They didn't stop there. Upon terminating him, they confiscated his identification, his keys, and escorted him off the campus. They then collected his folders and notepads and every single book and physical object in his office and burned those as well. Middleton's disgruntled colleagues, who were never informed of the research, weren't surprised to hear that he had eventually been let go. What they would never know is how accurate they were in comparing him to monsters like Hitler and Mao.

Unwittingly, IBM had helped Middleton unlock a box that should never have been opened. The genie, if it could be described in such benign terms, was now out of the bottle. Middleton had discovered his calling.

He worked for multiple competitors of IBM before ending up at Equifax, the nation's oldest consumer credit reporting agency. There, he was in his element, swimming in data and learning how he could use it.

He pioneered a division that gathered, analyzed, and provided consumer information to government and law enforcement agencies. It made him an extremely wealthy and powerful executive. The division would eventually be spun off as a company called ChoicePoint, a data-aggregating firm described as a "private intelligence service," which peddled its information to government and private industries. But as good as he had it, it wasn't enough. Even Equifax and ChoicePoint were not a large enough launching pad for him and what he wanted to do.

Soon enough, his talents came to the attention of the powers that be at ATS. They could have offered him a token salary of a dollar a year and he would have jumped at it. He could see the organization's potential. He could also see that their approach hadn't been an accident.

Toward the end of the vetting process, one of the board members asked him about his work on the Nazi program that had gotten him fired from IBM. However they got their information, they were incredibly well informed.

As Middleton answered their questions, he hedged his information; at least, until he realized that they were not unsympathetic to what he'd been doing. At that moment he realized how well suited they were for each other.

ATS needed a man like him to run their operations, and he was bright enough to recognize a once-in-a-lifetime opportunity when it was offered. Up to that point, he had had no idea ATS even existed, but once he grasped the breadth and scope of what they had created, he realized that it was the very platform he had dreamed of.

The education IBM had put him through was nothing compared to what he received the moment he began working with ATS. It was like having the doors of the Vatican's secret archives thrown open wide. There wasn't a single prominent American that ATS didn't have a dossier on. The amount of information the organization had access to was stunning.

When he asked why they had files only on prominent Americans and not on everyone, his initiation into the deepest, darkest circle of ATS began.

In fact, ATS had every intention of building files on every single American. That was a large part of why he had been brought on board. They liked the work he had done, including the research that had gotten him fired from IBM.

They believed the concept of the nation-state was destined for collapse, and they had every intention of helping it along. They believed that data was power. The more they collected, the more powerful they would become. Eventually, their goal was to assemble files not only for every American but for every single human being on the planet.

At the moment, their focus was on the United States, and there wasn't a single sphere of influence within it that ATS didn't control. Who got elected, what laws were passed, what judgments came out of the courts, stock market performance, the price of commodities, who the U.S. went to war with and why, the rise and fall of outspoken voices across the political spectrum, reshaping what was taught in schools to American children . . . ATS had even successfully inserted themselves into theology and was influencing what was being preached in many churches. They had a honed, singular vision of the world upon which they were focused with absolute precision, and the greater their advancements in technology, the more able they were to reshape the country, and soon thereafter the world, exactly as they wanted it to be.

It was like walking through your house in pitch darkness, confident you knew where all the furniture was, only to have someone flip on the lights and show you that everything, every single thing, was not at all where you had thought. Middleton had been sleepwalking his entire adult life. Only now had his eyes been opened. The depth of the deception was so amazing, so total, so complete that it was beyond even a man like Craig Middleton's ability to describe. Everything he wanted, everything he had ever envisioned, was within his grasp. He was home.

Though he was already out front on the power curve of leveraging data, his ATS mentors helped refine his skills and taught him many things he had never even considered possible, particularly when it came to influence operations. They demonstrated how to bring powerful figures to heel and keep them there.

One of Middleton's earliest and most ingenious contributions to ATS was the development of a software program to help screen for individuals ripe for leveraging. Similar to the program they would sell to tax assessors, which constantly monitored satellite imagery for unpermitted home improvements, Middleton had built a similar overlay program for government, intelligence, and military data. It searched for inconsistencies, contradictions, or holes in personnel files, briefings, and reporting. When it found any, a digital flag was raised as the system then attempted to decipher and address the problem.

It was this very system that had helped Middleton identify the man he was about to call.

Picking up the handset of his STE, Middleton inserted a Crypto Card into the slot and dialed.

"Do you have any idea what time it is?" said the man who answered on the other end.

"We've located your lost dog," Middleton replied. Taking one more look at the Harvath information on his screen, he then e-mailed the file. He didn't care how secure the telephone system was. He always spoke in code unless he was in a completely secure situation and the person was sitting right in front of him. "I just sent you the file."

"I'll look at it in the morning."

"It's morning now. Look at it."

"I'm putting you on hold," the other man said as he got up and walked downstairs to his study. There he turned on his computer and waited for it to boot up. When it did, he opened the e-mail, read the pertinent details, then picked up the phone again. "All this information has been confirmed?"

"I wouldn't have called if it hadn't. Let's get coffee." It was their code for a face-to-face.

"It'll have to wait," the voice replied. "I've got a lot on my plate today."

"Let me guess. Double-booked the wife and the mistress for lunch?"

"Fuck you."

"I'll see you in an hour," Middleton said, hanging up.

Though he would later claim he was in shock from the accident, it had been nothing more than cowardice. Somehow, though, Bremmer's reptilian brain was overruled by another part—his ego. He realized what a fool he was being. This was the perfect opportunity to prove himself a hero.

Rushing back to the café, he struggled to pull his driver from the vehicle. Sadly, the man had already expired. It was at this point that Bremmer took a bad situation and made it worse.

Unaccustomed to the capacity of Middle Eastern men for histrionics and lacking any Arabic skills whatsoever, Bremmer completely misread the screeching and wailing of the Kuwaitis struggling to extricate the two café patrons trapped beneath the SUV. Because of his military uniform and air of authority, they were beseeching him to help them. That wasn't how Bremmer saw it. To his inept mind, they were blaming him; and the men off the street who were now flooding into the café to help weren't good Samaritans, they were the beginning of a mob that very well might have torn him apart had he not acted. And act he did.

As the crowd swelled and the men tugged on his sleeves, trying to get him to do something, anything, Bremmer drew his sidearm and fired not one but four "warning shots" through the ceiling of the café and into the dwelling above.

Terrified, all of the locals, including those trying to lift the vehicle and pull the seriously injured men from underneath, backed off. But it was only temporary.

Like a nuclear reaction, white-hot rage instantly infused the crowd. While Bremmer had misread the group as a burgeoning mob, there was no mistaking it now. They were out for blood—his—and they were bound and determined to get it.

When one of the men turned on him with a broken chair leg, the lieutenant, who was not the best of shooters, punched two 9mm rounds directly through the man's heart, killing him instantly.

Bremmer didn't bother waiting for the man's lifeless body to hit the floor; he turned and took off running.

Within a block, his chest was heaving and his lungs felt like they were

CHAPTE

W hen Middleton arrived at the Pentagon, Colc
"Chuck" Bremmer was waiting for him.

Bremmer was in his late fifties, with close-c
and-pepper hair. He stood a foot taller than Middleton and ʝ
aura of prowess and integrity. That aura, though, much like t
surrounded his career, was false.

Jowly and out of shape, Chuck Bremmer had been a medi
of above average intellect who had risen to the rank of coloi
ever having served in actual combat. He was what was known
parlance as a Chairborne Ranger. He was a man who had su
the Army by kissing ass, not necessarily kicking it. The most
assignment the man had ever seen was more than twenty yɛ
Kuwait City; a full month after the U.S. had driven Iraqi forces
country.

While chauffeuring then-Lieutenant Bremmer to a mɛ
driver had suffered a heart attack. He had lost control of their
it barreled into a Kuwaiti shisha café and pinned two men uɪ
It was a terrible accident, made worse by Bremmer's reaction.
fuel tank ruptured and fearing it would detonate, he had baile
retreated across the street, leaving his driver behind to die.

on fire. After another block, he felt like he was going to vomit. Three blocks later, he did.

As the first wave of nausea subsided, Bremmer looked at his surroundings and something else took hold of him—panic. He had no idea at all where he was. He hadn't paid any attention while he was being driven to his meeting and had taken limited interest in the layout of the city. Now he was completely lost.

He needed to get off the streets. He needed to get someplace safe where he could think. He chose the first apartment building he saw and, after multiple attempts, succeeded in kicking in the lobby door.

It was a small building with two apartments per floor, and Bremmer trudged up the stairs toward the roof. He had to figure out where the hell he was.

The top floor consisted of a single unit, a modest penthouse with a small rooftop garden. Using his shoulder, Bremmer charged the door and knocked it wide open, startling a woman and two small children inside.

Before the woman could scream, Bremmer pointed his weapon at her face and placed his index finger against his lips. His message couldn't have been any clearer. Pulling her children to her, tears rolled from her eyes, but she never made a sound.

Pointing at the food the children had been eating, Bremmer gestured for the woman to pick it all up and then he confined the three of them in the bathroom.

A cabinet in the living room hid a small bar filled with cheap knock-offs of American brands. At this point, Lieutenant Bremmer wasn't picky. To steady his nerves he helped himself to what vaguely resembled a bottle of Jack Daniel's.

Unscrewing the cap, he tossed it on the floor and stepped out onto the roof. Immediately, his heart dropped through his boots. He couldn't make out a single landmark. Placing the bottle against his lips, he turned it upside-down and took a long swallow.

The substandard booze tasted like shit, but instantly its heat began to radiate throughout his body. He followed his first swig with two more and then tossed the bottle into a planter. He could get bombed later. At the moment, he needed to get his story straight.

Bremmer ran everything that had happened through his mind multiple times. With his driver dead, there wasn't another American to contradict his story. The locals could say anything they wanted, and he expected them to, but he knew whose side the military would want to come down on. The key to making everything work was to tell as much of the truth as possible. If he did that, the locals would actually end up unwittingly supporting the tale he would weave. And what a tale it was.

By the time the extraction team arrived to pull him out, Bremmer's story was airtight. It was so simple, so ingenious, that he surprised even himself.

The military not only bought it, their investigation actually supported it. Bremmer even received a commendation. Everything would have worked out perfectly, except for one thing. One of the men crushed by the SUV was the brother of a local CIA asset, who raised so much hell with his handler that the CIA's Kuwait City station chief launched his own, quiet investigation of what had happened. If ever the word *clusterfuck* deserved to be applied to an event, this was it.

When the station chief tried to share his findings with U.S. military command, he was told in no uncertain terms where to file his report. They had conducted their own investigation and stood by the findings. The station chief had stepped outside his authority and was threatened with all sorts of recriminations.

Bremmer was damned if he was going to have his career dragged through the mud and possibly even destroyed over a few dead Kuwaitis. The station chief filed his report back to Langley, along with a recommendation that no further action be taken. As a result, no further action *was* taken. Chuck Bremmer had slipped the noose and in the process had crafted an action-guy history for himself, which invariably grew a little bit larger each time it was told.

Basking in the glow of a lie that had helped boost him up the ladder of success, he had never harbored any concern that one day all of his accomplishments might be undone. All of that changed the day Craig Middleton had stepped into his life, armed with much more than just the truth of what had happened in Kuwait City. Middleton had come loaded for bear.

Colonel Bremmer had allowed himself to become the biggest believer of his own bullshit and enabler of the misplaced confidence his superiors had in his abilities. As his ego exploded, he had engaged in all sorts of indulgences he felt he was entitled to, including extramarital affairs and influence peddling in the realm of military contracts in order to line his own pockets.

When Middleton showed up and dropped it all on him like an atomic bomb, Bremmer knew he only had two choices—cooperate or lose everything. He might have been sorely lacking in character, but he certainly wasn't lacking in self-preservation skills. He knuckled under, and Middleton had owned him from that point forward.

When Middleton stepped into Bremmer's office, the Colonel, who never knew when he might be summoned to the White House, was wearing his blue service uniform.

Pointing at the door for Bremmer's SCIF, or Sensitive Compartmentalized Information Facility, Middleton said, "Shall we?"

No good morning, no nothing, the Colonel thought to himself as he picked up his mug and stood. *What an asshole.*

Walking over to the SCIF, he punched his code into a small keypad. When the locks released, he pulled the door open and waved Middleton into the secure conference room.

Once the door was closed, they picked their conversation up where they had left off. "So you're sure this information on his location is good?"

Middleton pulled out one of the leather chairs and sat down as if he owned the place. "I already told you it was good."

"Fine. The team will need access to some sort of surveillance."

"You'll have everything I can give you. How quickly can you get them there?"

"I've already got a team in Lyon. Harvath bought a ticket on the high-speed train from Paris the night before last."

"Why wasn't I told?" asked Middleton.

"I'm telling you now."

"Well, that's pretty stupid considering the resources I have."

"They're professionals," said Bremmer, ignoring the man's condescension. "They know what they're doing."

"That's why they're in France looking for a guy who's in Spain?"

"They'll be retasked. Is there anything else?"

"Yeah, there is. Why haven't I heard anything back from you on Kurt
Schroeder?"

"*Schroeder?* You mean the kid in your office?"

"No, the kid from the *Peanuts* cartoon. Of course the kid from my
office."

A twitch rippled across Bremmer's jowls. Middleton was an insufferable prick. "I assume you haven't heard anything because the men following him haven't found anything."

"Bullshit. There's something there. I know it."

"If you're so sure," said Bremmer, "then you should yank his access
before we have another Caroline Romero on our hands."

Middleton thought about Caroline Romero for a moment before his
thoughts shifted back to Schroeder. "He knows too much to simply yank
his access."

"Then we'll add his name to the list. Just make up your mind."

Middleton didn't like the man's tone. "Is that an order, Colonel?"

"Take it however you want. I've got enough of my own problems
without dealing with yours."

"Listen to me, Chuck. My problems *are* your problems and don't you
forget it. This is a national security issue. The names on that list represent
the most pressing threat to this nation. If this is not handled properly,
people will burn, including you."

"Is that a threat?"

"Me? Threaten a full-bird colonel? A special adviser to the National
Security Council? Of course not. Let's just call it a friendly piece of career
advice."

"I'll take it under advisement. Anything else?"

"We don't have closure on the concierge yet." *Concierge* was their code
name for Reed Carlton.

"You're paranoid," Bremmer replied. "You saw the pictures from that fire. He got burned to a crisp. No one could have survived that. He's dead. Trust me."

"Oh, I trust you," said Middleton. "It's your men I'm having trouble with. We should have used real operators."

"For all intents and purposes, these guys *are* real operators."

"Like hell they are. They're fucking criminals, and on paper it might have seemed like a great idea to secretly arrange commutations and spring them from the stockade to join your wet work team, but they're a disaster."

Bremmer didn't care for having his judgment called into question. "I told you, the Spec Ops community is too small. We couldn't send true operators after operators. There was too much of a risk they'd know one of the targets and not do the job. I don't care what we told them they were accused of. . . .

"It doesn't matter anyway. The men I'm using have had *exceptional* training and the proof is in the pudding. They've taken care of Carlton and every one of his people on the list."

"Everyone but Harvath," Middleton corrected.

The Colonel wasn't interested in rehashing the failed Paris operation. They had already had that pissing contest. "They'll get Harvath."

"They'd better."

Bremmer changed the subject. "In the meantime, I'm still waiting on you to give me the whereabouts of that dwarf."

"You'll get it soon enough."

The Colonel kept his eyes locked on Middleton as he raised his coffee mug and took a sip. The dislike between the two men was palpable. Lowering the mug, he walked over and deactivated the lock mechanism on the door.

"I guess that's it then," said Middleton as he rose from his seat. "Keep me up to speed on Spain."

Bremmer stood back and allowed the man to pass. Pausing before leaving the office, Middleton allowed a smile to crease his mouth. "I hear your daughter's field hockey team is doing pretty well this year. She's at Fredericksburg Academy, isn't she?"

The Colonel's frosty glare intensified. "You stay the fuck away from my family," he said, slamming the SCIF door and securing himself inside.

The smile on Middleton's face broadened. He loved pushing Bremmer's buttons. The man would do exactly as he was told. He had entirely too much to lose and Middleton had every shred of it buttoned down. Blackmail was an art form and Middleton a master at its execution.

What was about to happen next, though, was where the real art would unfold. Taking out the Carlton Group was only the first step. America was about to see an attack like it had never seen before. And once the dust had settled, things would never be the same again.

CHAPTER 17

Reed Carlton had escaped his burning home with nothing more than a green Barbour jacket, a change of clothes, and a bugout bag he kept behind the panel in his bedroom closet. Ready to go at a moment's notice, it contained cash, false ID and a credit card, a clean laptop, an encrypted IronKey thumb drive, three clean cell phones, maps, a suppressor, and a Les Baer 1911 pistol.

Staying off the main roads, it took Carlton over three hours to hike to the storage unit where he kept a green 1980s Jeep Cherokee loaded with additional supplies. Its license plates traced back to a dummy LLC and dead-ended with an aging attorney in a small Richmond law firm.

Avoiding the major thoroughfares, the Old Man drove northwest toward Winchester. As a county seat and home of Shenandoah University, there were plenty of affordable accommodations to be found. He picked a hotel with a business center, checked in under an alias, and got to work.

The Internet was like a vast pool of water and the best way not to be noticed on it was to avoid breaking the surface. Carlton knew that it was better to skim. If he had to take a plunge, he was well aware that the deeper he dove, the more attention he was going to draw to himself.

He started by surfing the websites of local newspapers. He didn't enter any search terms, he merely clicked on links that led him from story to story, website to website. Eventually, he found mention of the fire. It was a short, "breaking news"–style article that reported only the name of the town and how many fire companies had been called in to respond to the blaze. He needed more information.

The easiest thing would have been to call his office, but only an amateur would have risked such exposure. Whoever had managed to kill his security team, lock him in his own safe room, and disable the alarm and sprinkler systems would surely be monitoring everything that was tied to him until they had confirmation of his death. And when they learned that he hadn't died in the fire, then the noose was going to get a lot tighter. For the moment, he had the benefit of no one knowing that he was still alive, and he needed to leverage that advantage for all it was worth.

Logging off the business center's computer, he poured himself another cup of coffee in the lobby and headed back out to his Jeep. He drove south on I-81 until he found a busy enough truck stop and pulled in.

After gassing up, he parked and walked inside the restaurant, where he took a small table and ordered breakfast. As he waited for his food to arrive, he fired up his laptop and plugged in the encrypted IronKey drive. The rapidity with which technology was advancing never ceased to astound him. The IronKey was an off-the-shelf device, available to anyone, built to military grade specs with 256-bit encryption and a self-destruct feature that kicked in if the correct password wasn't entered within ten tries. *Simply amazing.*

Bringing up a list of cell phone numbers labeled "Car Club," Carlton tried to decide which of his people to reach out to first. He settled on Frank Coyne, a former Delta Force sergeant major. Coyne was exceptional at gathering intel and had worked under him at the CIA before he was hired on at the Carlton Group. Removing one of the clean cell phones from his bugout bag, he turned it on and dialed the man at home.

The phone rang, but Coyne didn't pick up and Carlton was dropped into voice mail. It was possible that Coyne was screening calls and, not recognizing the number, didn't answer. The Old Man didn't bother leaving a message.

Choosing the phone's SMS feature, he typed a short text message—*Blue#*—to let Coyne know he was about to call him and that he should pick up. He waited two minutes and then dialed. It rang several times before ending up in voice mail. Carlton disconnected the call and looked back at his list.

He tried another operator named Douglas with the same results—no answer at home and no answer on his cell. He was 0 for 2 and a bad feeling was beginning to grow in the pit of his stomach. Not only had he been targeted but now he couldn't reach two of his top people. He decided to pull out all the stops.

POL, or proof of life, was a term used in kidnappings as a prerequisite to a ransom being paid. Carlton had trained his people to utilize the term but had disguised it in order to protect its true meaning. He now went through his list and group texted his operators the message *Earnings Report: Blue Petroleum, Oil, & Lubricant.* It was both a warning that an imminent threat existed, as well as a call for them to report back to him via the cell phone he was using.

The phone should have begun vibrating instantly with responses. Not a single one came; not even from Scot Harvath, who, though overseas, had his phone with him 24/7.

Jumping on the truck stop's free WiFi, he enabled the flash drive's secure browsing feature. Using the Tor anonymity network, or the Onion Router as it was known, to help hide his location, he was routed through multiple servers worldwide before winding up at his final destination, Skype.

Carlton entered his name and password and then hit the sign-in button. He was greeted with the message, *Can't sign in. Wrong password.* He tried two more times before coming to the conclusion that it wasn't an accident. Somehow, someone had frozen him out and was denying him access. No one but his top people knew about his Skype account, or that it was his primary means of communicating with his operatives. That meant that his organization had been penetrated to its core.

There was only one reason to freeze him out of Skype. Someone wanted to cut off the team's primary means of communication with one another. The fact that none of his people were responding to his calls and texts told him someone had wanted to make sure they were all isolated in order to take them out. It was a "night of the long knives," and Carlton could only assume the worst.

But the worst was something he always planned for. PACE was an acronym for Primary, Alternate, Contingency, Emergency. Carlton surfed to an assortment of predetermined Internet dating sites and left messages for his people just in case.

After shutting down his computer, he paid his bill and followed two truckers into the men's room. At the urinal, he played the chatty retiree and was able to ascertain which direction they were headed, which rigs they were driving, and what their final destinations were. With that information in hand, the rest was just a matter of course.

Whoever he was up against was extremely adept at what they did. At some point, they were going to place him in that truck stop. Whether they back-traced him through his attempt to access his Skype account or the use of the cell phone didn't matter. He wasn't going to fool himself into believing he was safe. He needed to buy himself more time, or at least throw them off track.

He located the rig of the man driving to Bakersfield, sealed the cell phone in a Ziplock bag, and duct-taped it underneath good and tight. Until the battery ran out or it was discovered, the phone would leave a digital trail of bread crumbs, which would hopefully take his pursuers in a completely different direction.

Back at his hotel in Winchester, Carlton spent the rest of the day and into the evening on the computer in the business center, once again link-walking. But instead of searching for details on his attack, he looked for any stories that might be about attacks or "accidents" involving his operators. He was devastated to find multiple references, including one about a deadly firefight in Paris, which, while not mentioning names, had to have been about Harvath and the Delta Force operative he'd been sent to meet, Riley Turner.

Everything Carlton had built was destroyed; the center of his operation, the very backbone, had been ripped out. He should have felt lucky to be alive, but he didn't. He was beside himself at having lost so many good operators, many of whom were like family. He was also angry, and that anger was turning into rage. He was all too familiar with the feeling and knew that if he didn't control it, it would not only control him, it would consume him. He was too old and too experienced to allow his emotions to run roughshod and dictate his course of action. He needed to be cold and calculating; as cold as he had ever been, if not more so.

Returning to his room, he took a shower, shaved, and then drew the blackout drapes and stretched out on his bed. He hadn't slept since escaping the fire. He needed to rest.

He was exhausted, and it didn't take him long to fall asleep. But even as he slept, his subconscious was still working, trying to find answers, trying to find a way forward.

It was just after four in the morning when he awoke. He felt more tired than when he had gone to sleep, but he had something he didn't have when he lay down. He had a plan.

Looking over at the clock on the nightstand, he realized he'd have to move fast. There was a very narrow window for what he was about to do.

CHAPTER 18

Nicholas probably shouldn't have brought her back to the ranch. In fact, he shouldn't even have let her into his SUV, but the picture she had removed from her purse and pressed up against the window had changed everything.

It showed her hugging her older sister, Caroline, and the two of them laughing. But it wasn't just the picture that had changed his mind, it was the look on her face. She was absolutely terrified. It wasn't a show, it was genuine, and so he had unlocked the Denali's door and let her in.

Nina had the same high cheekbones and deep green eyes as her sister, but her hair was jet black, *probably dyed,* Nicholas figured, and she wore a tiny stud through her left nostril.

Exiting the garage, he began a long SDR to make sure they weren't being followed. Right away, Nina began talking, but Nicholas stopped her. It wasn't safe. Not yet.

He asked if she had any electronics with her. All she had was a cell phone; she took it out and showed it to him. As they passed the Donna Reservoir, he had her pull the battery and throw all the pieces out the window into the water. She did exactly as he asked while he continued to drive.

Just before the Rio Grande, he changed direction and headed west, and shortly afterward changed direction again and headed north up through Las Milpas and back toward the Three Peaks Ranch.

As they drove, they talked, or more specifically Nina talked, and Nicholas interrupted from time to time to ask questions.

She explained how a package from a D.C.-area lingerie shop had arrived and that in it were a couple of bra and panty sets, a tiny flash drive, and a recordable greeting card with a message from her sister.

The message warned Nina not to plug the drive into any computer but to wait until she found Nicholas, and then Caroline quickly explained how to contact him. There wasn't a lot of recording space, so she had to be fast. She told Nina that she was in trouble and that she loved her. That was it.

Nina tried repeatedly to contact her sister after receiving the message, but to no avail. Very soon thereafter, she had a bad feeling that she was being watched, both at her apartment and at work, and so decided to go to ground.

After calling in sick, she had holed up at the home of a wealthy Mexican family for whom she pet-sat from time to time. They were back in Reynosa until at least Christmas and had left their Hide-A-Key in the usual spot. She knew from past experience that they never bothered to set the alarm.

She was a sharp woman with good instincts, and Nicholas was impressed. He was equally impressed when she glanced back again at the dogs and said, "Ovcharkas, right?"

"How did you know?"

"I'm a vet tech."

"Do you see a lot of Caucasian Sheepdogs in south Texas?" he had asked.

Nina's mood seem to brighten, if just for a moment, as her thoughts were distracted from her concern over her sister, and she smiled. "Not really," she replied. "I just like dogs. Especially big ones."

After ascertaining that she had burned the greeting card, per Caroline's instructions, and watching as she pulled the flash drive from the left cup of her bra to show to him, he decided to keep their conversation light for the rest of the drive.

He asked personal questions in an effort to help keep her mind off her sister. It worked for a while, until he ran out of things to ask. He wasn't as socially skilled as he would have liked and felt awkward not being able to come up with anything else to talk about.

They fell into an uncomfortable silence that lasted the rest of the way back to the ranch. He was relieved when they finally arrived at the property and suspected that she was too.

At the guesthouse, he gave Nina her pick of the remaining bedrooms and placed a call to Maggie Rose asking if she could bring over some additional women's size 6 clothing.

Fifteen minutes later, Maggie dropped off a small bag, smiled, and left Nicholas alone. She didn't ask who the clothes were for or who was in the far bathroom taking a shower. He appreciated her professionalism.

Nicholas placed the items in Nina's room and then retreated to the kitchen. They tried to open the flash drive right away, but it was encrypted. Despite working with Nina for several hours trying to come up with the password, they had no luck. He needed a break.

Cooking was one of his greatest passions, providing a Zen-like experience in which he could lose himself. In fact, when Nina emerged from the guest room and entered the kitchen, he didn't even notice she was there.

Standing on a stepstool with his eyes closed and his nose in a glass of recently opened chardonnay, he was like nothing she had ever seen. For several moments, she just watched him. Finally, she asked, "Blackberries, apricots, or green apple?"

"Excuse me?" Nicholas replied, surprised to find her standing there.

"Somebody once told me that if you wanted to sound like you knew about wine, all you had to do was say you found a *hint* of blackberries, apricots, or green apples when you breathe one in like that."

Nicholas smiled and set his glass down. "I hadn't heard that."

"Oh, yeah. Then you roll out the gardening terms."

"Gardening terms?"

Nina thought for a moment and then gave him her list. "Grassy, oaky, mossy, or peaty."

"I think those last two are for scotch."

"Really?"

"Really," Nicholas affirmed.

"I'm obviously not an expert."

"Do you like wine?"

"Yes."

Picking up the bottle in his tiny hands, he poured a glass for her. "That's all that matters," he said as he placed the bottle back on the counter, slid the glass toward her and then picked his back up. "To Caroline."

Nina stood where she was. "They killed her, didn't they? She had the lingerie store mail me the package and then she ran out of the mall and got hit by a car. It wasn't an accident, was it?"

Nicholas had no idea. They had talked about Caroline's death multiple times since he had picked her up in McAllen, but he just didn't have enough information.

"They aren't going to stop until they kill me too," Nina continued.

"No," said Nicholas. "I'm not going to let anything happen to you. I promise. We're going to get to the bottom of this. Okay? I know it's hard, but you need to stay positive."

She didn't respond, so the little man repeated his toast.

Slowly, she reached for her glass and said, "To Caroline."

They each took a sip.

Nicholas waited a beat and then asked, "So?"

"So what?"

"Blackberries, apricots, or green apples?"

A reluctant smile spread across her lips. "I don't know, green apples?"

"Definitely green apples," he agreed.

Whether it was the wine or the fact that he was in his element in the kitchen, Nicholas was much more successful at keeping their conversation upbeat this time. He talked about two of his favorite things, food and wine, and Nina seemed genuinely interested. Before she knew it, dinner was ready.

Nina helped serve and they sat down to a meal of roast chicken with thyme and garlic mashed potatoes. Comfort food, something she was sorely in need of.

After dinner, they returned to the flash drive and Nicholas opened another bottle of wine to "help him think." He was throwing every tool in his toolbox at it, but the damn drive wouldn't open.

Convinced the answer was staring him in the face and he just wasn't seeing it, it was well after midnight when he staggered into the kitchen for a third bottle of wine and it hit him.

Rushing back into the master bedroom, he climbed up into the chair at his desk and began clicking away at the keys. Nina, who had lain down on his bed and fallen asleep, was awakened by the flurry of activity.

"What's going on?" she asked.

"How much do you know about what your sister did for a living?"

"She was a programmer for a company in Maryland called ATS. They do a lot of government work. Why?"

"And before that?" asked Nicholas as he continued working.

"She worked at some big Wall Street bank writing trading software or something."

"How close were you?"

"Caroline's fifteen years older than me. She was a sophomore in high school when I was born. Same mom, different dads."

"So you weren't that close," stated Nicholas.

"By the time I was two, she'd already left for college. I saw her over the summers a little bit and most of the holidays, but that was it."

"Did she ever tell you why she left the bank?"

Nina could tell this was headed somewhere, she just didn't know where. Propping herself up on one elbow she replied, "She said she got sick of all the pressure. She also said she hated living in Manhattan."

"She told me that too. Then I learned the real story."

"What do you mean the *real* story?"

Nicholas turned so he could look at her and replied, "Your sister was fantastic with computers and wrote some amazing software. Like every other programmer in the world, she crafted an insurance policy, a way she could slip back inside the bank's software if she ever had to. Call it a back door. The only problem was that her back door conflicted with someone else's on the system. And that someone else used it to screw your sister."

"How?"

"Another IT person was stealing the bank's client data and selling it on the black market. He rigged it to make it look like your sister had done it."

"She never mentioned any of this," said Nina.

"It gets more interesting. As I said, this other IT person, some guy named Sanjay, framed your sister in a very clever way. That said, Caroline was able to point out several inconsistencies that argued for her innocence. Nevertheless the bank fired her anyway. Two days later, she launched an attack on their system and knocked all of their ATMs off-line for a week."

Nina shook her head and smiled. "Ever since we were kids, she's always had a serious temper."

"Well, her *serious* temper got her into serious trouble. It didn't take long for the authorities to show up on her doorstep. Within two days of the ATMs going down, they picked her up."

"Wait a second. You said she had knocked the ATMs out for a week."

Nicholas now smiled. "She did, but no one could figure out how to break the program she had written and get them back online. They threatened to lock her up and throw away the key, but she refused to give in. It was a Mexican standoff. Finally, the bank blinked. They apologized for firing her and offered her a severance package. The authorities, though, were another matter.

"A crime had been committed and they had no intention of letting your sister walk. They wanted to throw the book at her, or so they said."

"What did they want?" Nina asked.

"They wanted her. And seeing as how no bank was ever going to hire her after what she had done, she took them up on their offer, in exchange for immunity from prosecution, of course. That's how she wound up at ATS. They're basically the IT people for the entire U.S. government."

"She never told me any of this."

"It took me a while to get it out of her, believe me," said Nicholas.

"So what does this have to do with Caroline's flash drive?"

Turning back around, he made several more keystrokes. "I think your sister built one of her back doors into this flash drive."

"You do?" replied Nina as she got off the bed and walked over to the desk.

"I do. And if I can find it, I think I can get us in."

Nina watched over the next ten minutes as Nicholas continued to type in strings of code into his computer.

Suddenly he hung his head and then shook it slowly from side to side.

"What's wrong?" she asked.

Nicholas smiled.

"You found it?"

"I did. There's a back door, but you'll never believe what the password is."

Nina put her hand on his shoulder and gave it an excited squeeze. "Tell me."

Nicholas pointed at a small box on the screen and then typed the six-letter code that opened up the drive: S_A_N_J_A_Y.

CHAPTER 19

It was unlike any drive he had ever seen before. The amount of data it contained was staggering. There were literally thousands of files stored on it and room for multiple terabytes more. Nicholas had heard about theoretical jumps in microstorage capability using discs coated in protein from salt marsh microbes, but he had never interacted with one until now.

"What's all this?" Nina asked.

Nicholas scrolled through the directory. "I'm not sure."

"Caroline said you'd know what to do. Whatever's on that drive, she said they were going to kill her over it. You have to figure it out."

"I'm trying, but it's like being given a puzzle without the top of the box."

"So start lining up the edges," replied Nina. "Do what you have to do to work your way in. I need to know what happened to my sister."

"I want to understand all of this as well, but deciphering what we're looking at is not that easy."

"Neither was figuring out how to unlock the drive, but you did it," she said, placing her hand again on his shoulder. "You can do this too."

Nicholas liked the confidence she had in him.

"What can I do to help you?" she asked. "I'm not a computer person, but there must be something. Just name it."

"How about some coffee? I think our long night is about to get much longer."

When Nina returned with a pot and two mugs, she asked, "What have you found?"

He had been chewing on the top of a pen, an exercise that sometimes helped him focus. "Are you familiar with filter bubbles?"

"No."

"It's a term used to describe how search engines, Google in particular, are studying every online move you make and then tailoring what results get returned in response to your search queries. You and I could both conduct the exact same search and Google would kick back completely different results. If we each typed in 'Egypt,' you might get sightseeing and travel information, while I get information about politics and the Arab Spring. Everyone is being placed in their own bubble online."

"But they're not getting the same information," Nina stated.

"Exactly. By controlling what you see, they can reinforce, or even shape, how you think. It's like going to the library only to have the librarian hide half the card catalog when she sees you coming. Information is being filtered based on what computer algorithms think you want to read. The problem is you have no idea what's being left out. However you see the world, whatever your politics or belief system is, you have to work to uncover any contradictory information."

"So much for the Internet existing to bring people together," she replied.

"Actually," said Nicholas, "the Internet was created to be a military communications network that could withstand a nuclear first strike. It was developed in the 1950s, but didn't transmit its first message until October 29, 1969. It was supposed to be the word *login,* but only the *l* and the *o* were transmitted and the system abruptly crashed."

"How ironic."

"Indeed," he replied as he exited out of an article and scrolled through the other files. "Filter bubbles are only one kind of issue Caroline saved articles on. There's a bunch of material on Internet legislation as well, Net neutrality, the Protecting Cyberspace as a National Asset Act—"

"Why would she have saved all of those?" Nina wondered aloud.

"I can't tell."

"It must mean something. What's Net neutrality?"

"Basically, it's a move by elements within the government who want to have authority to censor the Internet," replied Nicholas.

"That's not good."

"No, it's not, and the PCNA Act is even worse."

"I haven't heard of that one either."

"The PCNAA is also called the Internet 'kill switch.'"

"That, I have heard of," replied Nina. "That's the law that would place a giant off button in the President's office, right?"

Nicholas nodded. "And if there's ever some sort of mega cyber attack, the President would have the ability and sole discretion to shut the Internet down."

"Until the attack was gone?"

"For as long as the President saw fit. All he or she would have to do is keep renewing the state of cyber emergency."

"You act like it's that simple," Nina said as she raised her hand and snapped her fingers. "Once the threat's gone, the President would have to turn the Net back on. You can't just continue to say there's a state of emergency when there isn't one."

Nicholas raised an eyebrow. "You don't think so?"

"Lobbying for the ability to censor the Web isn't good in my opinion. I don't like censorship of any kind, anywhere. I want the Net to be free and open. But I find it hard to believe that a U.S. President would claim there was an ongoing emergency and use it to keep people off the Internet when there really was no emergency at all."

"Three days after the 9/11 attacks," said Nicholas, "the President of the United States declared a national state of emergency. Over a decade later, it's still in effect."

"What?"

"The United States has been under a continuous state of emergency since 9/11."

"And Congress just allows that?" asked Nina.

"It's not something Congress votes on. Under the National Emergencies Act, the President is required only to inform them of his decision. The act was created so the President couldn't establish a never-ending situation. A state of national emergency is only supposed to last for two years. The 9/11 state of emergency has been renewed repeatedly since it was established."

"On what justification?"

Nicholas looked at her. "Terrorism."

"But terrorism was around before 9/11," said Nina, "and it's going to continue to be around."

"And so will America's continuing state of national emergency."

"I don't understand that, though. Why? What's the point? What power does it give them?"

"You hit the nail on the head. It's about power. Supposedly, there are about five hundred legal provisions that can be bent or absolutely thrown out the window under a national state of emergency."

"Such as?" she asked.

"The most famous are the ability to suspend two major Constitutional rights—the right to habeas corpus, which deals with unlawful detention, and the right of National Guard troops to appear before a grand jury."

"Why would a National Guard soldier ever need to appear before a grand jury?"

"I'm not an attorney, but I would assume that because they're citizen soldiers that they have some right to civilian courts and aren't bound specifically by the military tribunal system," Nicholas said with a shrug.

"But that doesn't answer my question."

"Well, when do charges normally get brought against a member of the military?"

"When they break the law," Nina replied.

"Or," Nicholas pointed out after thinking a moment, "when they refuse to obey."

The look on the young woman's face immediately changed. "If National Guard troops refuse to carry out actions against their fellow countrymen, the last thing the government would want is for those issues to be adjudicated in a civilian court."

"Agreed," he said. "There's a school of thought that believes that buried within the Patriot Act are certain additional provisions the government can call upon only in a state of emergency and that is why it has been kept going. Again, I'm not a lawyer, but power is a heady drug. Only the very strong can resist its pull. Those with power tend most often to search out more in order to solidify their positions and prevent themselves from being dislodged. It's how a republic slips from freedom into soft tyranny and eventually despotism."

"But I still don't understand why Caroline would be interested in all of this."

Nicholas shrugged. "Maybe it had to do with what she was working on at ATS."

"But all that is policy stuff. I thought she was on the tech end of things, working with Homeland Security and things like that."

"That's in here too," he said as he opened another file, "and it makes a bit more sense, since DHS is responsible for cyber security across the civilian, military, and intelligence communities. Caroline copied truckloads of DHS Web pages and wiki articles. The acronyms for their programs and divisions go on and on—NCCIC, NCSC, NCRCG, NCSD, NPPD, CNCI, CS&C."

"Still nothing, though, that points specifically to what she was on to."

"There was an interesting article about the National Operations Center at DHS and something called their Media Monitoring Initiative," said Nicholas. "Apparently, since 2010, Homeland Security has been gathering personal information on journalists, news anchors, and reporters. Interestingly enough, they consider anyone who uses social media like Twitter, Facebook, or any of those platforms as being in the *media.*"

"So they spy on everyone, all the time. It *is* just like China. How come no one knows about this?" she asked.

"Some do, but I don't think anyone appreciates the extent to which this goes. Your sister seemed to and that may be what she was warning us about. There's lots more here, but like any puzzle, we have to take it one piece at a time."

Nicholas tried to sound confident, but the task was overwhelming. There was no key to why Caroline had archived all of this material. It all dealt with computers or cyber issues in one form or another, but why shouldn't it? Caroline was an IT specialist. None of this was anything unusual, much less something worth killing over. There had to be a bigger picture. *What was it she wanted me to see?* Nicholas went back to chewing on his pen, pausing only for an occasional sip of coffee.

For hours he scrolled through article after article; cached Web page after cached Web page. The whole drive was like some enormous digital scrapbook.

Scrapbook! What if that's exactly what it was? The articles obviously only told part of the story, like pictures. What if there was something written on the back of them—something that explained why the articles were significant?

Reopening one of the articles he had been reading, he looked at it from a new perspective. Most of the hackers he knew were incredibly bright, and Caroline Romero had been no exception. Many enjoyed the digital art of steganography, disguising messages or information but hiding them right in plain sight. They could be hidden among the millions of pixels in an image or even inside a digital sound file. The possibilities were endless. It was known as security through obscurity.

Caroline, though, was practical. Considering the hoops Nicholas had jumped through to gain access to the drive, he couldn't believe she would have set up another huge leap of security challenges.

Studying the document in front of him, he realized something. The Web article, like all the others, was the printable version. That meant it didn't contain pictures, but it did still contain links.

Even though he knew none of his equipment was currently connected to the Internet, he still checked one more time, just to be sure.

Convinced that he was safe, he floated his cursor over the article he was reading and clicked on one of its links.

Instantly he was transported into a whole new area of the drive he hadn't known existed.

CHAPTER 20

Whatever new technology was being used for the drive, it was impressive. Not only was the storage capacity unlike anything that had come before, so was its ability to partition off and disguise enormous chunks of data as simply unused space. It was like a movie lot—the building façades look perfectly real, but open up one of the windows, or walk through one of the doors, and there's an entirely different reality behind it.

Nicholas was tempted to wake Nina, who had once again fallen asleep on his bed, but decided to keep reading.

Clicking back and forth between the surface articles and what Caroline had attached beneath, he began to understand what she had attempted to do. It was a complete, painstakingly thorough documentation of every single venture and initiative that Adaptive Technology Solutions had ever been involved in. From the articles and wiki pages on DHS to investigative reports on the NSA, every piece of hardware, every software program, every patch, every string of code ever written, updated, or sold was documented. The depth to which ATS was entangled with the United States government astounded even him. The deeper he delved into the information, the further down the rabbit hole he was taken.

Considering his history in the sale and purchase of classified information on the black market, Nicholas was particularly interested in the dossier Caroline had assembled on the National Security Agency. Much of what he had always suspected was suddenly confirmed.

Within weeks of the 9/11 attacks, the unparalleled listening ability of the National Security Agency—which had always been aimed outside the United States—was turned inward. No longer was the NSA restricted to tracking foreign spies and terrorists, whose surveillance had to be signed off on by a judge of the U.S. Foreign Intelligence Surveillance Court. Now, in the name of national security, all American citizens were suspects, and due process had been completely abandoned.

Under contract from the NSA, Adaptive Technology Solutions' personnel entered telecommunications buildings across the country and secretly installed devices called beam splitters onto their switches so that duplicate copies of all landline, cell phone, e-mail, text message, and Internet traffic would be sent to highly secure, top-secret NSA server farms located across the country.

There, every citizen's electronic traffic was sorted and sifted by NSA analysts, using ATS software and equipment to search for and flag particular words and phrases. Anyone and everyone could and was being targeted. Privacy had been obliterated.

No matter how fast the technology moved or how secure devices were touted as being, ATS, and thereby the NSA, always got hold of new technology before the general public, thanks to secret national security directives, as well as an active campaign of industrial espionage spearheaded by ATS itself. Though he had long suspected it, Nicholas was stunned by the extent to which the United States had become a burgeoning surveillance state. In the name of "security," the liberty of citizens was being eroded, not on a yearly basis, not even on a daily basis, but continuously, around the clock, 24/7.

In addition to the warrantless wiretapping and the all-encompassing dragnet the NSA had spread across the Internet, Caroline had chronicled in her files a host of other operations geared toward what she termed Total Surveillance, much of it either unknown to the population at large or being deployed in such a fashion as to appear harmless, or better yet, useful.

Radio Frequency Identification—RFID tags—were a perfect example. They could be used to track everything from casino chips, livestock, and bottles of shampoo at Walmart to people. In fact, multiple high-end nightclubs in Europe were encouraging VIPs to be "tagged," whereby an RFID tag the size of a grain of rice—similar to what's implanted in many pets in order to ID them if they get lost—was placed under the recipient's skin to facilitate faster access to the club and an easier way to run a tab and pay for drinks. In return, the nightclub was able to cut down on employee theft and harvest a wealth of useful data about its best customers.

National governments were even getting into the game. The Mexican Attorney General's office had tagged eighteen key staff members in order to control access to their secure data rooms, and the United States, which was already inserting RFID tags in all of its passports, was actively considering tagging sex offenders. The potential abuses of this technology were beyond calculation, and Nicholas was reminded of the identification numbers tattooed on Nazi concentration camp victims.

Smartphones and onboard vehicle navigation systems regularly spied on customers, with the data being sold left, right, and center, as well as being handed over to the government on demand with little or no recourse. Many Americans were either unaware or unconcerned that GPS had been developed and was maintained by the Department of Defense, the organization under which the National Security Agency fell. There wasn't a single GPS device the NSA couldn't locate at a moment's notice if it wanted to. And when the NSA did go searching for particular GPS devices, it didn't have to report to anyone why it was doing so, what information it was gathering, or for what reason.

The same was true, Caroline noted, of the FBI. Not only did the Bureau maintain a database in a secure vault on the fourth floor of its headquarters building in D.C., code-named Guardian, which held files on tens of thousands of Americans never accused or suspected of any crimes, but who had simply acted "suspiciously" at some point in their lives in the eyes of a local law enforcement officer, but the FBI was regularly placing GPS tracking devices under suspects' vehicles without ever appearing in front of a judge and obtaining a warrant. They had also fielded "Stingrays" without warrants—new devices that could track suspects' cell phones even when they were not being used to make a call. Even DHS had jumped on the surveillance bandwagon.

In fact, DHS had gone so far as to outfit unmarked vans with large X-ray machines and was driving them around every major American city X-raying whatever and whomever they wanted—families in minivans, bakery trucks, school buses—all of it was fair game and none of it was being done with a warrant.

Inspired by "intelligent" streetlights in the Netherlands and the UK, DHS had also gotten behind another ATS surveillance project and was already testing it in a small U.S. city. The streetlights not only provided light but also included tiny, remotely controlled functions like audio recording, video recording, and the ability to X-ray anyone who passed by.

Even though Nicholas considered himself a political agnostic and had admittedly made his living as a thief, he was stunned that there was no outrage, no hue and cry from the day-to-day citizens who were being spied upon. The only people screaming bloody murder were the usual handful of privacy advocates. The majority of people seemed to have bought into the fallacy of believing that if they hadn't done anything wrong, there was nothing for them to worry about.

They had no idea of the likelihood that these technologies would one day be used against them. Like the tax code, the body of laws that governed national security would eventually make everyone a criminal, no matter how honest they were or how hard they tried to abide by the letter of those laws. It was only a matter of having attention turned on you. Those same measures that kept "you and your family safe" today could be used to track down and imprison anyone tomorrow.

Were Americans more concerned with having the latest and greatest app than in fighting how those apps kept track of their every move, their every communication, and even, via their search queries, their every *thought*?

People's thoughts, and the invasion of them, was another disturbing development that Nicholas had heard whispered about only to find confirmation of in Caroline's notes. In addition to algorithm developers trying to use data to anticipate customer behavior, the NSA and Google were using the millions upon millions of Tweets, Facebook entries, E-Z

CHAPTER 22

Reaching for his weapon, Harvath rolled out of bed and hit the floor. *What the hell was happening?* he wondered. Seconds passed.

As he lay there, his ears strained for any sound that would explain what was going on. There were no additional shots.

But he knew what he had heard. *The dogs had barked. A round had been fired.* But how much time had passed between the two? He had no idea. It seemed like maybe a minute, but it could have been ten minutes, or more.

The barking and the gunshot had to be connected. There must be a predator nearby. And if there was, it raised a very important question—was it the four-legged variety, or the much more dangerous kind that came in on two?

Harvath waited, but no other sounds came. For all he knew, it was nothing—the Basque equivalent of a coyote or a mountain lion had wandered onto the property and had been shot. But what if that wasn't what had happened?

Without a telephone or even a walkie-talkie with which to call down to the guard shack or reach out to Tello in the main house, Harvath had no choice but to investigate for himself.

He quickly got dressed and slipped soundlessly from the apartment. The night air was colder than when he had gone to bed, the fog thicker.

He could barely see his hand in front of his face. He chose to leave the flashlight in his pocket. If someone was out there, somewhere in the fog, a flashlight would only draw them to him.

Stepping outside, the fog parted and almost seemed to pull him in. As the sheets enveloped his body, he strained for sounds, any sounds. There were none; not even sounds from the livestock.

They have a very large pasture, he reminded himself. Maybe the animals moved closer to the mountain and away from the ranch buildings when the fog was so dense. Maybe, or maybe there was another reason.

Any moment now, he would draw the attention of the dogs. They were used to Tello and his men, but Harvath was a stranger and they still reacted warily to him.

None of them were coming to investigate his presence outside the stables. Unless they were all huddled with the livestock on the far side of the pasture, something was wrong.

As he walked toward the main house, he kept his pistol in his coat pocket, his hand wrapped around its grip and his finger on the trigger. He wanted to be ready for any surprises, but he didn't want to be one himself. Too often, the first and only thing people keyed in on was a gun. He didn't want to get shot by one of Tello's men.

Halfway to the house, he almost tripped over a pair of leather boots. He bent down through the fog and saw they belonged to one of the men he had nodded to before mounting the stairs to the apartment earlier.

Next to him was a lupara, and Harvath could smell that the weapon had recently been fired. He reached out to check the man's pulse. He was still warm, but he didn't have a heartbeat. When Harvath drew his fingers back, they were slick with blood. The man's throat had been sliced from ear to ear. The front of his jacket was damp from exsanguination.

There was nothing he could do for him. The man was dead, and the ranch was under attack. He needed to focus on the threat.

Three questions spun through his mind as he moved away from the body and crept toward the main house. *Who's on the property? How many? And why had they come?*

As soon as the last question popped into his mind, he had a bad feeling that he was going to get all his answers in short order.

Moving toward the main house, he wondered if the dead Basque had fired his shotgun at an intruder, or to warn his colleagues. Either way, it should have been like kicking a hornet's nest. The fact that the ranch hadn't immediately become a maelstrom of activity was a bad sign. From what he knew of Tello's men, they were serious customers, not the type to run away from a fight.

When Harvath got to the side door he had been using to come and go, he found it ajar and all *too* inviting. He decided to move along the outside of the house and conduct a quick reconnaissance before going in.

Moving through the fog, he felt his way along the outer wall so as not to lose his way. The windows were dark and didn't reveal anything inside.

Coming up to the corner of the house, he heard something and pulled up short. It sounded like someone choking back a cough, but he couldn't be sure.

His Glock already out, Harvath reached into his other pocket and withdrew the flashlight. He heard the cough again, followed by groaning.

He held the flashlight in his left hand, up high and away from his body. Then, taking a deep breath, he exhaled and spun around the corner.

He pressed and released the tailcap switch on the flashlight. It was a drill he had done thousands of times in the SEALs and the Secret Service. The pulse of light lasted only for a second or less, but it was amazing how much information the brain could process in such a short amount of time.

Because of the fog, it was like peering through Vaseline, but he was able to see enough.

There were two men. They wore jeans, hiking boots, and windbreaker-style jackets that seemed ill-suited to the altitude and temperature. They were fit and had short, military-style haircuts. One man was sitting, while the other crouched next to him, pressing a bandage of some sort at the top of his leg near the groin. The wounded man held a silenced pistol, and even though Harvath couldn't see it, he assumed the other man was armed as well.

That assumption was affirmed almost instantly when a hail of suppressed gunfire sent pieces of chipped stone from the wall near Harvath flying all around him.

Rapidly, Harvath retreated back around the corner. These weren't Tello's people. In fact, they reminded him a lot of the men from Paris.

Crouching down, he aimed his pistol around the corner and fired multiple times in rapid succession. The men had no cover and he intended to press his advantage.

He hadn't affixed the suppressor to his own weapon, but even as the fog gobbled up much of the sound, the shots from the big .45 still boomed like claps of thunder.

Standing up, he pressed his back against the wall and changed magazines. When he was ready, he reached around the corner and let another vicious volley fly.

He drew the pistol back, changed magazines, and waited, his ear as near to the edge of the wall as possible, but there was no sound from the other side.

Cautious not to make any sound himself, he took a quick peek around the corner. Nothing happened. Either they hadn't been able to see him through the fog, or they were no longer capable of returning fire. Harvath needed to find out.

After readying his weapon, he prepared to peek around the corner once more, but then thought better of it and stepped back. If they were waiting for him, that was the direction they'd expect him to come from. He reminded himself that the only first aid you give under fire is putting rounds on target. If the situation had been reversed, Harvath would have returned fire as he dragged his comrade to safety. Then he would have tried to flank his attacker.

As Harvath moved, his only thought was to neutralize the threat. Fifteen yards or so on, one of the men who had come to flank him stepped out of the fog and Harvath got his chance to take him out.

The man wasn't expecting to see him and while his reaction was quick, Harvath was quicker.

Remembering the body armor the men in Paris wore, Harvath depressed his trigger and double-tapped the man's forehead, dropping him to the ground dead.

He kicked the man's weapon away and quickly patted him down. Just as he had suspected, the man was wearing body armor. He was young, maybe mid- to late twenties, just like the men in Paris. And just like the men in Paris, there wasn't a scrap of paper anywhere on him that might identify who he was, where he had come from, or who had sent him. All he had was a small walkie-talkie clipped to his belt, along with a headset, which Harvath removed.

Standing up, he strained his ears through the fog for the sound of anyone who might be approaching. It was all quiet. *Too* quiet.

After putting on the headset and clipping the walkie-talkie inside his coat, he went looking for the other shooter.

He found the man almost exactly where he had last seen him, though now he was slumped over dead. He was also somewhere in his twenties. His upper left leg, as well as a portion of his stomach below his body armor, had been blown away with what looked like a close-range shotgun blast. Harvath gave him a quick pat-down, but like his partner, it didn't turn up anything at all.

Stepping away from the body, he crept back around the house to the side door, which was still ajar. He stepped inside and stood still for several seconds listening. There was barely enough light to see by.

Finally, he started moving, slowly. From the small mudroom where he had entered, he slipped through the pantry area and into the kitchen. All of his senses were on high alert. The only noise he heard was from an old wooden clock ticking in the living room farther ahead.

He moved from the kitchen into the dining area and stopped. The hair on the back of his neck suddenly stood up. In the living room, he could see an overturned side table and what looked like a pool of blood on the floor. It was too dark to tell any more from this distance and Harvath wasn't about to use his flashlight.

Walking over, he saw Tello's enormous frame sprawled facedown on the floor near the couch. After scanning the room, he made his way to him and carefully rolled the body over.

The man had taken a round to the forehead and one just beneath the nose. His eyes were open but lifeless and unfocused. The ETA commander was dead.

Was that what this was? A hit? Carried out by some rival faction? Maybe an organized crime element? Was the Spanish government involved?

The thought only just materialized in Harvath's mind when he had his answer. "Don't fucking move," said a man's voice from somewhere behind him. It spoke in English and sounded American. There was a cocky, urban edge to it. "Drop your weapon right there, asshole."

The room was so dark that even if Harvath had spun and tried to shoot, the man behind him would probably have ended up shooting him first. He had no choice but to comply and placed his weapon on the floor alongside Tello's body.

"On your knees," the man ordered. "Do it now."

Harvath followed the instructions.

"Hands behind your head. Interlock your fingers."

"Who are you?" Harvath demanded. "What are you doing here?"

"Shut up," said the man. "Hands behind your head. Now!"

"Not until you tell me who you are and what's going on."

The man pumped two suppressed rounds into the couch right next to where Harvath was kneeling.

Harvath raised his arms and locked his fingers behind his head. "You're fucking with the wrong guy, my friend."

"Shut up," the man repeated as he got on his radio. "Red Two to Red One. Target in custody. Building B. Over."

Harvath still had the headset on and could hear the radio traffic. "Roger that, Red Two," a voice replied. "Building B. Over." *Were there only four of them?* So far he hadn't heard traffic from anyone else.

"Red Two to Red Three. Give me a SITREP. Over," the man behind Harvath said. SITREP was shorthand for situation report.

There was no reply.

"Red Two to Red Three. Do you copy? Over."

Several seconds passed. There was still no reply. If there were only two other guys, they were both dead and Harvath had killed them. "You should have brought more men," he said.

The man ignored him. "Red Two to Red Four. Over." He waited and then tried hailing Red Four again. Finally he gave up and hailed Red One.

"Go ahead, Red Two. Over."

"Is the property secure? Over."

"Roger that. Over."

"I want you to begin looking for Red Three and Red Four. Start near Building B and work your way out. Over."

"Roger that. Red One out."

The man then turned his attention and his full anger on his prisoner. "My orders only say you have to die. They don't say how fast."

"Orders from who?" Harvath replied.

"None of your fucking business, traitor."

Traitor? The term stunned him. For a moment, he didn't know how to respond. Finally, he said, "You've definitely got the wrong guy."

"No, I've got the right guy, you treasonous motherfucker."

It was like getting punched in the face. *Traitor? Treason?* "What the hell are you talking about? You think I'm a traitor?"

"I don't make the judgment. I simply carry out my orders," said the man.

"Who gives you those orders?"

"None of your business."

"I'm a traitor and you're here to kill me, but who sent you is none of my business?"

"You talk too much," the man snapped.

"And you don't talk enough. You're making a big, big mistake. I'm telling you, you've got the wrong guy."

"Shut up."

Harvath could sense he was running out of time. "You're military, right? Or at least you were military at some point. What branch?"

The man ignored him.

"I was a SEAL before joining the Secret Service."

"I've seen your file," the man replied.

"Then you know what I've done for my country. You owe me an explanation."

"I don't owe you shit," he stated, as he turned his attention back to his radio. "Red Two to Red One. What's your status? Over."

"Haven't found anything yet, Red Two. Over."

"Hurry up. Red Two out."

There was something about this guy that didn't make sense, something Harvath couldn't put his finger on. He acted military, but at the same time there was a street thug vibe about him. "Listen," Harvath stated. "You can't kill an American citizen without benefit of a trial."

"I can if you're on the list, traitor."

"*List?* What list? What the hell are you talking about?"

The man was distracted by something and didn't reply. When Harvath tried to get him to answer his question, he dropped his voice and whispered sternly, "Shut the fuck up."

There was the barely perceptible creak of a floorboard as the man began to shift his weight, turning to his right.

It was followed by a thunderous blast that set Harvath's ears ringing. Reaching for his pistol, he spun and brought it up just in time to see the man fall forward and land flat on his face, dead. A shotgun blast had ripped through his neck all the way up and through the base of his skull.

Standing in the dining room, a smoking lupara in his hands, was Padre Peio.

Before Harvath could say a word, he saw a shadow of movement behind the priest from the kitchen. "Peio! Gun! Get down!" he yelled. He was too late. Instead of dropping, Peio spun.

It was hard to tell who fired first, Harvath or the man who must have been the voice from the radio, Red One.

As Peio dropped to the floor, Harvath depressed the trigger again and again, walking his shots up from the top of the attacker's chest into his throat and finally into the cleft beneath his nose.

The attacker's weapon clattered to the kitchen floor as he collapsed and Harvath rushed to the aid of his friend.

CHAPTER 23

Thankfully, Padre Peio's wounds weren't life threatening. He had taken two rounds to the shoulder. One passed clean through, the other was still inside, and judging from the reaction when Harvath applied a pressure bandage, it was near the bone and more than a little painful.

He kept trying to stand up. "I need to minister to the deceased."

Praying for the dead was the last thing Harvath wanted to do right now. He wanted answers—foremost among them, who had labeled him a traitor and put a hit out on him? And for what? What had he supposedly done? How had they tracked him down?

That last question was the easiest to answer. It had to have been through the Old Man. Their exchanges over Skype were the only connection to his location. He'd tried to hide himself by routing and rerouting through servers around the planet, but someone had untangled his Web.

Peio struggled to get up again, and Harvath's mind was drawn back to stopping the priest's bleeding. As soon as he had stemmed the bleeding the best he could, he helped the priest to his feet.

Peio walked over to Tello and prayed for the dead Basque, while Harvath searched the corpses of the two attackers. Like the others, they were young and not carrying any identification at all. The kid who had been about to kill Harvath had a handful of tattoos, a couple of which were crude and obviously not inked by a professional.

After praying over the two attackers inside, Peio let Harvath help him out the door and showed him where the other two were. The priest said a few words and they moved on.

Approaching the dead Basque halfway between the main house and the stables, Harvath figured out where Peio had picked up the lupara. What he didn't understand was why he had come back.

He put the question to the priest, but he declined to answer. He wanted to save his strength. Harvath understood and offered Peio his shoulder. They could speak afterward.

He knew the ranch well enough to navigate them through the slowly lifting fog and locate the bodies. Whoever the team was, they had been good. Tello's men were all dead, including Eyebrows and Scarface. Not a single one of them had been left alive. *What the hell was going on? Why were these killers so young, and what was this "list" the kid had said Harvath was on? More importantly, why had he called him a traitor?* None of it made any sense.

They soon came across the dogs. Harvath hated for animals to be killed. He understood why it was done in a raid, but he still hated it. Even when animals had been a factor in his assaults, he always tried to find another way to handle the situation without killing them.

When Peio was satisfied that he'd accounted for all of the dead, Harvath tried to lead him back to the main house to rest, but he refused. "The sun will be coming up soon," Peio said. "You need to go."

"What about you?" Harvath replied. "You need to see a doctor."

The man shook his head. "A priest with a bullet wound would fuel enough gossip to last a century around here. I cannot be connected to what happened here. Father Lucas will take care of my wounds."

"Do you have any idea how highly contaminated bullet wounds are?" Before the words were even out of his mouth, Harvath regretted uttering them. Of course Peio knew. He'd had plenty of experience with bullets before becoming a priest. "You're going to need antibiotics."

"We have all that at the abbey. Don't worry."

Peio was one tough guy. "You still haven't told me why you came back."

"I heard from Nicholas."

Harvath stopped and turned to look at the priest. "When? How?"

"We use the website of the orphanage where we met in Belarus to leave messages for each other. Nicholas set it up in such a way that our communications couldn't be seen."

Harvath had trusted his Skype communication with the Old Man, but after what had just happened, nothing was safe. "How do you know you were actually communicating with Nicholas? How can you be sure?"

"There's an authentication process," Peio answered. "It's similar to a dead drop. There is another site where I leave a nonspecific indicator. I believe Nicholas uses it for a lot of his contacts; sort of a messaging radar screen. I leave an indicator there to signal that there is a message waiting for him on the orphanage site. He then comes to the orphanage site, but cannot unlock my message and reply without using my indicator and how it was placed as a password."

"How many other people know about your chat system?"

Peio looked at Harvath to see if he was serious. "Have you ever met anyone more concerned with the security of his communications than Nicholas?"

The priest had a good point, and while no system was ever one hundred percent secure, Nicholas had developed some of the toughest to crack, often by hiding them right in plain sight like the orphanage. "What did he say?"

Peio grimaced suddenly as he took in a breath.

"You've got to let me get you to a hospital, Father. You can't make the ride back to the abbey."

The man forced a smile. "I can and I will."

"Peio, it's three hours on horseback."

"And I will need every minute of it to make peace with God and atone for what I did."

"You saved my life. Thank you."

The priest held up his hand. "We don't have much time. Let me tell you what Nicholas said."

Harvath nodded.

"When you reached out to me through the tobacconist, I knew something was wrong. As I said, I left a message for Nicholas. I wanted to
know why you were coming. Several hours ago, I finally heard back. He
said that he's uncovered something and he needs you to get back as soon
as possible."

"Did he tell you what it was?"

"No. When we communicate, we do so in generalities. Despite Nicholas's belief that he's created a secure system, he's still careful. Everything
is disguised to sound like orphanage business. He did, though, want me
to pass along a specific message to you."

"What was it?"

"'Make sure you do not promise or tip anyone anything.' Does that
make sense to you?"

Indeed it did. The message referred to two software programs used by
intelligence agencies around the world. PROMIS was the acronym for
the first program—the Prosecutors Management Information System. It
was the precursor of TIP—the Total Information Paradigm.

PROMIS worked 24/7, looking for correlations between people,
places, and organizations. It was brilliantly adept at accessing proprietary
databases like those of banks, credit card companies, e-mail providers,
phone companies, and other utilities. Running complex algorithms, it
built detailed relationship trees outlining a subject's every move, whom
they knew, and with whom they interacted.

Because it could develop a baseline from utility records, if the subject of an investigation started using more water or power, it would realize that people had likely joined the suspect at the suspect's residence. It
would then search through the suspect's phone records and e-mails and
look for contacts whose utility consumption had gone down. It would go
through credit card receipts to see if the contacts with diminished utility
usage had purchased airline or train tickets, and if so, where. It would find
all the towers that the contacts' cell phones were pinging off of, as well as
where they were paying for tolls and gasoline, all in an effort to try to figure out who was inside the subject's home contributing to the increased
use of power and water.

It worked around the clock, never sleeping, never stopping, and so had earned itself the nickname the Terminator. It was an appropriate moniker for its day, but the real terminator is what followed—TIP.

The Total Information Paradigm took PROMIS and wedded it with artificial intelligence. At that moment, the intelligence-gathering capabilities of the world's intel agencies went supernova. It was like going from a Prius to a Lamborghini. Not only could TIP think like a person, it was alleged that it could actually anticipate human behavior.

Nicholas didn't need to warn him about staying "off the grid." He was the one, after all, who had schooled Harvath so deeply on both the PROMIS and TIP programs. Aside from observing good tradecraft, those programs were why Harvath had chosen to reach out to Peio and to do so in the manner he had. The priest was outside of practically any relationship tree anyone or any data-mining program could assemble around him.

For Nicholas to reinforce the need to avoid getting flagged by either program had to mean those programs were actively seeking him out.

"Did he say anything else?" Harvath asked the priest.

"He told me I needed to do everything I could to help you get back. Unfortunately, my contacts aren't what they used to be. Getting you a new passport under a different name is going to take some time."

"I already have one, so don't worry."

Peio nodded. "I should have expected that."

"What I need, though, is a means to buy my airline ticket. All I have is cash, and that sends up red flags immediately."

"I know someone with Iberia Airlines. Employees often book tickets for friends through their intranet system. The employee pays with a personal credit card and the friend reimburses the employee."

Peio had obviously used this "friend" for similar travel arrangements before. No doubt, "reimbursement" meant the price of the ticket plus a premium for Peio's contact who did the booking.

Traveling on an Italian passport, Harvath wanted to select a U.S. point of entry popular with Italians. "How often does Iberia have flights to New York City?" he asked.

"That's just it," replied Peio. "I think Nicholas has a different plan for you."

"Why do you say that?"

"Before coming home, he suggested you stop at an orphanage he has a relationship with."

"The one in Belarus?" asked Harvath.

"No, this one's in Mexico."

CHAPTER 24

There were over 1,300 historical structures within the 184.5 mile long Chesapeake & Ohio Canal National Historic Park. Many of them were open to the public, including six "lockhouses," or "canal quarters," as they were known, which visitors could rent for overnight stays in order to experience what life was like along the once thriving canal that ran parallel to the Potomac. They came complete with all the modern conveniences of full kitchens, bedrooms, and bathrooms with showers. They were known as Lockhouses 6, 10, 22, 25, 28, and 49. The "blue" lockhouse, so named for the color of its shutters and front door, was also very historic and equipped for overnight stays, but it had never been opened to the public—and with good reason.

The blue lockhouse was the property of the Central Intelligence Agency. Inside, some of the most valuable defectors from the Soviet Union had been debriefed over the course of the Cold War. The term "Behind the blue door" had become synonymous with interrogations at the highest level. The majority of the agents who used the term had no idea where the blue door was, much less that it was attached to a diminutive C&O canal house. Many simply assumed the door existed somewhere deep within the bowels of headquarters, where only the Director and a handful of privileged others were ever allowed to go.

Reed Carlton saw the signal—a bird feeder propped against the porch—and knew the front door would be open. He didn't bother knocking; he didn't need to.

In a chair near a small, wood-burning fireplace a man sat reading. He didn't look up when Carlton walked in. He seemed content to read his book and listen to the crackle of the fire.

The man's name was Thomas Banks. Those who knew him called him Tom. Those who knew him from the war called him Tommy. Carlton hadn't served with him, but he had served under him and eventually took over for him at the CIA and had earned the right to call him Tommy.

One of the youngest OSS operatives in World War II, the exploits of Tommy Banks had been the stuff of legends. With no other marketable skills other than "Indian fighting," as Banks liked to call it, he had agreed to help establish the Central Intelligence Agency. He found his niche in the Directorate of Plans, which would eventually be called the National Clandestine Service—the branch of the CIA that recruited foreign assets and ran clandestine operations around the world.

For decades, Banks worked in the field before settling down to "raise his chicks," as he called the younger operatives, and teach them how to conduct ops even better than he had. Eventually, Banks would head the division as its deputy director, back when it was known as the Directorate of Operations.

Much of what Reed Carlton had learned about espionage and clandestine activity, he had learned from this incredible man, a quiet rock star in America's intelligence and political arenas. Though most citizens would never know his name, there wasn't a single powerful person in D.C. he couldn't get on the phone in minutes.

"I could hear you crunching up the path from a mile away," the man said as Carlton closed the door. "Looks like we're going to have to train you all over again."

He shook his head. "I think I'm getting too old for any more training, Tommy."

"You're never too old, Peaches. Just too lazy."

Peaches. Carlton hadn't heard that nickname in a long time. He had trouble remembering exactly who'd given it to him, but it had been in reaction to his style of interrogation. Though in every other way he maintained the appearance and persona of a gentleman, he could be absolutely ruthless when interrogating a prisoner. If Americans or American interests were on the line, he would do anything it took to get the information he wanted. He could be the antithesis of sweetness, which is why so many of his colleagues and even a supervisor or two so enjoyed his ironic nickname.

"Speaking of lazy," Banks continued, the slight Tennessee drawl still evident in his voice despite having spent the bulk of his life living within a half a tank of gas of the nation's capitol, "You didn't bring a cell phone to this meeting, did you?"

"I was taught better than that."

Banks grunted his approval. "All this damn technology is dangerous. You didn't use a GPS to get here, did you?"

Carlton shook his head. "I drove my old Jeep. It doesn't have GPS."

"And none of that damn OnStar either?"

"No. No OnStar."

"Good," replied Banks. "People have grown so soft they'd rather allow a company to catalog their every move and listen in to their private conversations than learn to read a map."

Carlton hung his coat on a peg near the door. "It's not all useless. They helped unlock my assistant's car once when she had locked her keys inside."

"That's why God gave us rocks," Banks stated. "No offense, but if you're dim enough to lock your keys in your car, maybe you need an hour or two to sit and wait for the man with the slim jim to arrive while you reflect on your IQ."

The man was as irascible as ever. He didn't have much time for stupid or lazy people. He came from an age, as did Carlton, where people were expected to make their own way. They didn't sit and wait for people to do things for them. "Thank you for meeting me like this, Tommy."

"You made it irresistible," the older man responded as he closed his book and waved his guest over.

Carlton joined him, taking the chair opposite his in front of the fire. "It shouldn't have been so easy to get to you. You're a creature of habit. That's dangerous."

Banks nodded. "I like my morning walk."

He lived on his own in a small town house in Georgetown, and his morning walk took him past many of the dead drops he'd used during the Cold War. They were the same drops the old spy had used to train Carlton and his young CIA colleagues years ago. "Lucky for me I know your route."

The older man was momentarily transported. "Seeing that chalk mark really took me back. At first I thought it might have been a mistake, or maybe a new bunch was using my route for training, but then I checked the drop and found your message. I figured you were either jerking my chain or this was serious."

"I'm not jerking your chain, Tommy. This is serious. You're the only one I could come to with this."

"If I'm the only one you could come to, then you really *are* in trouble. What's going on?"

"The long knives are out. Somebody has killed all my operators, and they tried to kill me too."

Banks' eyes widened. "Who? How?"

Carlton relayed everything he knew. He told the old spy about the fire at his house, his inability to access his Skype account and his inability to reach any of his operators via any of the established protocols set up for just such an emergency, as well as the multiple articles he found online about several of their deaths.

When he was done, he leaned back and held the gaze of his former boss. The wheels were already turning in the old man's mind. He could see it.

"I'm going to ask a stupid question," said Banks. "Any chance a Muslim terrorist organization could have penetrated your group this deeply?"

Carlton shook his head. "No way. They not only don't have the sophistication necessary to pierce our network, they don't have the talent to take out all my men the way they did. This isn't some terror organization."

"What about someone inside your group?"

"A mole?"

"Or someone who wanted to make some money and didn't care about the damages."

Carlton thought about it for several moments. "All of my people are solid, except . . ." His voice trailed off.

"Except for what?"

"Nicholas."

"Who's Nicholas?"

"The Troll."

Banks couldn't believe his ears. "I've heard about him. He's really on your payroll?"

"It's worse than that," said Carlton. "We physically have him in-house, in the center of our operations. We even built a special SCIF for him."

"You do need to be retrained—completely. Why the hell would you bring a person like that into the heart of your operations?"

"I didn't bring him in. Harvath did."

Banks had met Harvath before and he liked him, but still. "What the hell does Harvath know about running an intelligence organization?"

"Harvath knows plenty," Carlton said. "Initially, I was against bringing Nicholas in—"

"That's his real name?" Banks interrupted. "Nicholas?"

"What difference does it make?"

"It makes a hell of a lot of difference. Did you even vet the little thief?"

"Yes, we vetted him, for all the good it did. There's not a lot out there on him that can actually be verified."

"So you just threw the castle gates wide open and let him in. I'm surprised at you."

"We firewalled a lot of stuff off," Carlton said in his defense. "We made sure he only had access to certain things."

"You should have assumed he'd find a way to get access to everything."

"He was primarily Harvath's asset, but you should've seen the amount of stuff he did for us, for the country. If he's a con man, he's the best there ever was."

"Could he have accessed your operators' files?" Banks asked.

"According to you, we should assume he was able to access everything."

"And would have been able to find a buyer for whatever he wanted to sell. A leopard doesn't change its spots. Once a thief, always a thief."

Carlton shook his head. "I'm not saying I don't agree."

"Where is he now? Have you reached out to him since all this went down?"

"No, I haven't."

"Then that's our first step," Banks replied. "The next step, though, is going to take some doing. Your guys were all Tier One operators. They weren't killed easily. It took a pretty high level of proficiency to go after them."

"Which is why I came to you. Whoever is behind this has access to some serious military or intelligence personnel."

"You think this is domestic? The Agency settling up its score with you?"

"In all honesty, I don't know what to think," said Carlton. "Have we been an embarrassment for the CIA? Of course we have, but killing American operators just to get us out of the picture? No way. I think this is something else."

"Like what?"

"I don't know."

"I can't help you, Reed, if you don't give me *some* idea. Who else's toes have you stepped on?" Banks demanded. "Who else would have a score this big to settle with you?"

"That's the problem. I've had on-and-off disagreements with a couple of investors, and the company board has stood up a couple of good pissing matches, but that's corporate stuff, and I deal with it when it pops up. That's not what this is. This is something else; something more. And frankly, I can't think of anybody at this level who'd have a score to settle with us."

"*Cui bono* is the question then."

"Exactly," said Carlton. "Who benefits from having me killed, my operators killed, and my organization zeroed out? That's what I've been racking my brain over and why I need your help. I have to be very careful about what doors I knock on."

"Knock on the wrong one and you could get shot in the head."

"True. You, though, don't have that problem."

Banks understood what his former protégé was asking. "It doesn't take much work to connect the two of us you know."

"I'm aware of that, but I think there's a way we can use it to our advantage."

CHAPTER 25

Schroeder double-checked the information on his screen and then ran it again before picking up the phone and calling his boss at home.

"What?" Craig Middleton snapped as he answered on the fourth ring, having been roused from a deep sleep.

"It's Kurt."

"What time is it?"

"Four thirty."

"A.m.?"

"Yes, sir."

"Why can't you work during the day like everyone else?"

"I've been working around the clock. You told me to keep at it until I found something," said Schroeder.

"Did you track down the data that Caroline Romero stole?"

"Not yet."

"Well, whatever you have, it better be worth waking me up again for. What is it?"

"I think I found something."

"You *think* you found something?" replied Middleton. "I *think* I'm going to get in my car, drive to the office, and throw you out a window. How about that for *thinking*? Get to the point, idiot. Why'd you call me?"

"A Google search."

Middleton waited for the man to elaborate and when he didn't, said, "I'm starting to look for my car keys, Kurt."

"Somebody did a search for Caucasian Ovcharka."

"What the hell is *Caucasian Ovcharka*?"

"It's a breed of dog," replied Schroeder. "A breed of very big dog. The type of dog we believe the Troll owns."

"So what? There's probably a lot of people in the world who Google that dog breed."

"Maybe. But how many people go from Googling Caucasian Ovcharka to a search on primordial dwarfism."

Middleton was wide awake now, and his tone of voice changed instantly. "Where?"

"Texas. The search is a couple of days old."

"Where in Texas?"

"South Texas. Closest point on the map is an unincorporated community called Agua Nueva."

"Shit," stated Middleton. "How close is that to a city called McAllen?"

Schroeder zoomed out on his map and made the calculation. "It looks to be about eighty miles. Why?"

"That's where the half sister is."

"Caroline's?"

"No, Wayne Newton's, moron. Of course Caroline's."

Schroeder absolutely hated his boss. "If I knew more about what was going on, maybe I could help figure out what data Caroline had stolen and where she's hidden it."

"You know all you need to know."

"Which is next to nothing except that we're hunting down some private group of treasonous mercenaries and a pile of data of indeterminate size, allegedly stolen by Caroline."

Middleton was pissed off and it was obvious in his voice. "You don't like being in the dark, Kurt?"

"No. It hampers my ability to do my job."

"Well, join the club. This isn't about what we like or don't like. This is about national security. All you need to know is that we're looking at the biggest domestic terrorist plot ever mounted against the United States, and the Carlton Group is behind it. Caroline Romero was a traitor about to divulge critical data that would have assisted in that attack."

"And she just happened to get hit by a car as she was leaving Pentagon City Mall."

"You've seen the footage," Middleton replied. "She rushed into traffic all by herself. No one pushed her. She had committed treason, she knew we were on to her, but instead of facing the music, she committed suicide. If there was ever an admission of guilt, that was it."

"God works in mysterious ways."

"God had nothing to do with it. If God were even remotely involved in all of this, he'd help us find what Caroline stole in order to protect this country. You keep your mind focused on that and maybe we'll be able to help save this nation."

Schroeder relented, "What do you want me to do?"

"I want an address and full workup on anyone and everyone associated with where that Google search took place."

"Okay. And then what?"

"Then get some sleep. You've earned it," said Middleton.

"I'm not tired. What else do you want me to do?"

"You've done enough, Kurt. After you're done, go home."

There was something about the way his boss told him that he'd "done enough," that made him uncomfortable. "I'll open a file and pull everything I can. You'll have it within the hour."

"Good boy," said Middleton, and then the line went dead.

Middleton swapped one of his dummy NSA Crypto Cards into the slot of his STE and dialed.

Several seconds later Chuck Bremmer answered, "Don't you ever sleep?" he asked.

"I think we've got the midget."

"Call me back when you *know* you have him."

"We've got him," Middleton repeated. "Coffee in forty-five minutes. Don't bother brushing your teeth. I'm not in the mood for heavy petting."

They met at the Pentagon and neither man spoke a word until they were inside the SCIF.

Middleton handed him a file. "You need to launch a team right away."

"Don't tell me what I *need* to do. Where is he?"

"Texas. About eighty miles northwest of McAllen."

"You want me to send a team back to Texas? We've already been on one wild-goose chase looking for that vet tech woman who dropped off the grid. Which, by the way, you claimed was impossible. *No one drops all the way off the grid*, you said. *Don't worry. We'll find her.*"

Middleton didn't like having his words turned back on him. That said, he didn't have time for a dick-measuring contest. He tried not to let the man get to him. "We believe the Troll has been helping her."

"What kind of confirmation do you have?"

"It's complicated."

"It's *bullshit*. That's what it is," Bremmer replied. "Has anyone actually had eyes on the target?"

"No, not yet, but trust me, he's there. And when we find him, I think we're going to find her too. Now, how soon can you get a team back down there to pinpoint them and take them out?"

The Colonel shook his head.

Middleton looked at him. "Don't you shake your fucking head at me, Chuck. How long?"

"These resources don't exactly grow on trees."

"No, they don't. They grow on military bases and get packaged into nice little off-the-books kill teams that are overseen and *tasked* by you."

"*After* the President's black panel reviews and makes a determination."

"Are you suddenly having second thoughts?" Middleton asked.

"You're damn right I am. We lost four operators in Paris. *Four.* How the hell do I explain that?"

"You don't. You're Colonel Chuck fucking Bremmer. You head one of the most sensitive covert programs the U.S. has ever stood up. I don't care if the Secretary of Defense himself walks into your office and demands answers. He doesn't need to know. No one does. That's why we influenced getting it set up. It's why administrations come and go, and yet *you* remain at the White House. This thing is a fucking stovepipe on purpose."

Bremmer was well aware of how the program was constructed. DOJ lawyers consulted with the President and key members of the black panel to review each case before a kill order was issued. It was the process by which American citizens Anwar al-Awlaki and Samir "Sammy" Khan, one a senior al-Qaeda figure and the other coeditor of al-Qaeda's terrorism magazine, were placed on the kill list and taken out in Yemen. No one in the administration had any idea that Bremmer had been padding the list. Need-to-know, especially when colored with the patina of ongoing counterterrorism operations, was an amazing tool for shutting down any questions in a city like D.C.

"So how soon?" Middleton repeated.

The Colonel looked at his watch. "Probably by this time tomorrow. They're going to need imagery, though. Either drone or satellite."

"No problem. I should have a preliminary file in about an hour. I'll make sure you get a copy."

"I'll watch for it. Anything else?"

"What about the job in Spain? Do we have any confirmation yet?"

"Negative. Nothing yet."

"Why the hell not? It's already daytime there," said Middleton. "The operation should be complete by now."

"They're professionals and they'll follow the protocol. They're not going to make contact until they're safely out of the country."

Middleton wanted to inquire as to whether they were more professional than the first team the Colonel had dispatched to Paris, but he let it go. The word *protocol* made him wonder what the protocol at the White House would be when Blue Sand kicked off. He knew they had enough supplies on hand to weather things for a bit if they wanted to, but they wouldn't. It would take them about ten minutes to really figure out what had happened, and once they did, there'd be a rush for the doors. The Se-

CHAPTER 26

P adre Peio's airline contact made all Harvath's travel arrangements and booked the tickets under the name on his Italian passport.

Using the car Eyebrows and Scarface had been driving, Harvath navigated his way back to Bilbao and abandoned it near the train station. He caught public transportation to the airport, where a ticket was waiting for him at the counter for the first leg of his journey.

He flew from Bilbao to Madrid, where Peio's contact, an older man named Gomez, met him at the gate. He escorted Harvath to the "Sala VIP" lounge, checked him in and then led him to a quiet corner to finish transacting their business.

Gomez provided Harvath with forms and two padded FedEx shipping envelopes, then left him alone while he fetched them each a coffee. When he returned, Harvath had the packages ready to go.

The first envelope contained Gomez's fee. Harvath had sealed the cash inside and scribbled down an imaginary address in Barcelona. The second envelope contained his real passport, as well as Riley Turner's, along with the handful of other personal items that had been in her backpack. Harvath addressed it to one of his aliases in care of a fly-fishing cret Service would want to enact the continuity of government plan and move the President right away.

The President would fight it at first, of course, but as soon as the reports started feeding into the situation room about the panic and the chaos, his resolve would begin to leach away. The death counts were what would really unnerve him. That's when he'd realize that he needed to gather up the first family and go.

For a moment, Middleton thought about filling Bremmer in the rest of the way, of giving him a warning and thereby a chance to make preparations for his own family, but as quickly as this spark of altruism was ignited inside him, it was extinguished. He didn't care if Bremmer and his family survived what was coming.

Taking out Carlton and his people was a sensitive assignment that required highly specialized labor. There were very few people who could handle the job. Until the list was closed out, Middleton had no choice but to put up with Bremmer. But as soon as Blue Sand launched, everything would be different.

Smiling as he rose from the table, Middleton looked at him and gave him a final word of caution. "Just make sure your people haven't screwed the pooch in Spain."

"Don't worry about my people," the Colonel replied as he stepped over and unlocked the SCIF door. "One way or another, they'll get him."

resort in Alaska owned by a buddy of his. The man had received packages for Harvath before. When he saw the name on the label he would simply take it and put it in his safe until Harvath contacted him for it.

After accepting the two mailers, Gomez handed over a small wheelie bag that had been packed with clothing in Harvath's size and a small toiletries kit. Traveling from Bilbao to Madrid with a small backpack was one thing, but traveling all the way to Mexico City without any real luggage would definitely arouse suspicion and added scrutiny. Gomez had agreed to supply the bag, probably liberated from the airline's lost luggage department, as well as to handle Harvath's FedEx drop-off for an additional fee.

Peio had vouched that Harvath could trust Gomez completely, which was good, since Gomez was the only man who could provide what Harvath needed.

When their business was concluded, the Spaniard wished Harvath a pleasant flight and left the VIP lounge. Harvath finished his coffee and then took his newly acquired luggage into one of the private shower rooms, where he unpacked the entire thing and stripped it all the way down. He wasn't about to board an international flight and then attempt to clear customs in Mexico, of all places, carrying a bag someone else had given him.

Satisfied that there was nothing in it that could get Harvath in any trouble, he turned on the shower and cleaned himself up.

When his flight to Mexico City was ready to board, he shuffled out of the lounge with a Spanish daily newspaper tucked under his arm and attached himself to a group of businessmen as they made their way to the gate.

Onboard, Harvath studied the passengers around him in the business class section as he stowed his bag. No one appeared the least bit interested in him, which was just the way he liked it. Informing the flight attendants that he didn't want to be awakened for the meal, he donned the headset from the seat pocket.

He had no idea what awaited him in Mexico, but he knew he needed to be rested for whatever came. It was much easier said than done. As the plane sped down the runway, his mind was overrun by the same questions that had been plaguing him since Paris and which had only been compounded in Spain, foremost among them—who had accused him of treason and why?

And while he didn't want to believe he might have been betrayed, he had to ask himself how the Old Man was involved. Had he set him up? It seemed almost impossible. There were so many other ways he could have gotten to him if he had wanted. But Carlton was like a father to him. The idea that the Old Man would ever want to "get to" him at all was insane. No matter what charge anyone could ever trump up against him, the Old Man wouldn't blindly issue a kill order. He knew Harvath too well. They had history together, a bond.

The more he thought about it, the more it pissed him off. None of it made any sense. He couldn't get a handle on any of it, and each time he tried to fit the pieces together he only got angrier and more confused.

He knew alcohol normally wasn't the answer, but sometimes it could be. Feigning a fear of flying, he talked a flight attendant into leaving him with several mini bottles and a glass of ice. As the liquid warmth spread through his body, it soon worked its way into his thoughts, disconnecting him from his mind in a dull haze, which allowed him finally to drift off to sleep.

It wasn't one of the best chunks of sleep Harvath had ever had, but it was better than nothing. He awoke quite a few times, uncomfortable even in the business class seat, but was able to fall back asleep.

An hour before the plane touched down in Mexico City, he awoke again when the lights were brought up and the crew came through to serve a final meal. Harvath was hungry and downed two cups of coffee along with his food.

Despite the fitful sleep, he felt more exhausted when he stepped off the plane than when he had gotten on.

As he moved through the airport, he kept his hat on, his collar up, and his eyes looking down, trying to avoid the cameras as best he could. At least three people knew that he was on his way to Mexico, and that was already three too many.

The customs and immigration agents seemed more interested in one another than in Harvath and his Italian passport. They simply stamped it and waved him on through. He would make his flight to Monterrey, Mexico, with time to spare.

Walking through the terminal, there were countless opportunities to relieve any number of oblivious travelers of a cell phone or a laptop computer, but he resisted the urge. It wasn't worth the risk while in transit. Staying off the radar meant staying *completely* off. Hopefully he'd have answers to his questions soon enough.

After getting more coffee, he killed time in an adjacent gate area until the final call came for the flight to Monterrey. He had surveilled all of the passengers on his flight and none of them gave him any pause. Boarding, he found his seat, stowed his bag, and sat down next to an attractive young woman who seemed more interested in her stack of Mexican fashion magazines than in striking up any sort of conversation with the man sitting next to her. They were perfectly suited for each other. An hour and twenty minutes after takeoff, when the plane touched down in Monterrey, the woman was still engrossed in her reading.

Harvath made his way through the drab airport to the transportation counter and purchased a ticket into the city, then exited the terminal and walked over to a cab stand. He counted the number of vehicles in the queue and watched them as he moved forward. At the last minute, he allowed two families to step in front of him and take the awaiting taxis. They thanked him for being such a gentleman, and he smiled. None of them realized that they had done him more of a favor than he had done for them.

After showing his ticket, the driver unlocked the doors and Harvath climbed inside with his bag. Leaning over the seat, he handed the driver the address Peio had given him. The man looked at the slip of paper and then turned and looked at his passenger. *"Con permiso, señor,"* he said. *"Estás seguro de saber lo que haces?"*

Even if Harvath didn't possess a minor grasp of Spanish, he would have understood the question just by the look on the man's face. Was Harvath sure he really wanted to be taken to that part of town? *"Sí,"* Harvath replied. *"Vámonos."*

The man shrugged, put his cab in gear, and pulled out into evening traffic.

It was a twenty-minute drive from the airport into the city, one of the largest in Mexico. It was hard to believe that in 2005 it was ranked the safest city in all of Latin America. Now it was wracked with cartel violence and incredibly dangerous, each year bloodier than the one before.

Harvath had no idea where the address was that the taxi driver was taking him to, but he had a feeling it wasn't one of the city's garden spots. By the same token, Harvath hadn't expected it to be anything spectacular. Orphanages didn't usually occupy prime real estate.

He had to hand it to Nicholas, though. Being plugged into a worldwide network of orphanages was very much akin to how intelligence agencies used NGOs. They provided a certain amount of cover at ground level and allowed you to tap into what was happening "on the street" better than at almost any other level save for narcotics or law enforcement organizations. Orphanages often had a religious affiliation that put them above reproach and scrutiny. On top of that, if they had been treated well, former charges who were now adults could be incredibly loyal and prove extremely helpful in certain situations.

Harvath didn't doubt Nicholas's sincerity, but he also didn't doubt that Nicholas structured many of his relationships with a secondary benefit in mind.

Nearing the city, the driver—who had wisely stayed off the highways because they were controlled by the drug cartels—began taking narrower side streets. Many of the buildings were dilapidated and covered with graffiti. At the next stoplight, a street vendor appeared and the driver double-clicked the cab's door locks. It was the man's subtle way of giving his passenger a heads-up. It happened again two blocks later as a motorcycle came up from behind and slowed down next to them, its rider taking a particularly long look at Harvath before moving on.

Five minutes later, the cab came to a stop not outside an orphanage, but a dimly lit tavern. Sensing his passenger's confusion, the driver read the address aloud from the slip of paper as if to say, "This is where you asked to be taken," and handed it back to him. Harvath turned over the fare ticket along with a U.S. twenty dollar bill as a tip, grabbed his suitcase, and got out.

He looked up at the battered colonial façade and checked the address himself. Sure enough, it was the one Peio had given him. The cab idled as Harvath stood on the sidewalk studying the tavern. The sound of Mexican pop music could be heard from inside. A bad feeling began to overtake him. He couldn't help but wonder if he was walking into an ambush.

The longer he stood waiting outside, the more attention he was going to draw to himself, so he decided to walk in. As he moved toward the door, he heard the cabdriver put the taxi in gear and drive away.

Harvath was now totally on his own.

CHAPTER 27

Calling the tavern a hole in the wall would have been a compliment. The place was an absolute dump. Faded 1960s reprints of Mexican artwork adorned the worn plaster walls, which had been stained brown over the decades, like the ceiling, by a patina of cigarette smoke. A string of red, Italian-style Christmas lights looked like it was left up year-round, adorning the dirty mirror behind the bar.

Tables of men conversed as waitresses carried drinks from the bar and plates of food from the kitchen. A bouncer at the door looked up as Harvath walked in but went back to the paperback he was reading, as if tourists with wheelie bags were their bread-and-butter customers. Judging from the neighborhood and the cabdriver's reaction, Harvath was pretty sure no gringos had seen the inside of this joint in a long time, if ever.

He picked a table off to the side, away from the majority of customers, where he could watch the door.

A couple of minutes later, a waitress came over to take his order. Just like the bouncer, she didn't seem to be the least bit surprised to see him there. *"Cerveza, señor?"*

What he wanted was a coffee, but having a beer bottle in front of him at the moment was appealing on several different levels. He saw that they served Bohemia in the bottle and asked for one.

As the waitress left to get his beer, he could see beyond the bar and into the kitchen, where some sort of meat was being roasted on a spit over hot coals, probably *cabrito,* young goat. It was a popular dish in this area of northern Mexico, as was something called *discada,* a combination of meats cooked in beer inside a plow disc that's been welded shut.

Harvath must have been paying a little too much attention to the kitchen. After dropping off his bottle of beer, the waitress returned with a plate of meat, accompanied by onions and fresh salsa, and a container with hot tortillas. Though he tried to explain to her that he hadn't ordered it, she simply told him to eat and walked away to see to another table of customers.

Not knowing when he'd be able to eat again, Harvath spooned some meat into one of the tortillas, added some onion and salsa, and dug in.

It was *cabrito,* and having eaten as much goat as he had in his day, most of it lousy, he knew good goat when he tasted it. This was very good goat.

When he was done, the waitress returned with some sort of custard for dessert, which Harvath politely declined. She asked if he wanted any coffee and though he was still slowly sipping at his beer, he said yes. She returned with *café de olla,* a rustic style of coffee brewed with cinnamon, and cleared his dinner dishes. Missing, though, was the steak knife Harvath had tucked carefully beneath his leg.

An hour later, there were only two other tables of customers left in the place. Harvath declined a third cup of coffee and watched as the bartender waved the bouncer over and handed him two pieces of paper.

The bouncer delivered one to each table and stood there as the groups of disgruntled patrons were forced to pay up. Harvath waited for his bill to come, but it didn't. Instead the bouncer saw the last of the customers out and then bolted the door.

"Stand up, please," the bartender said in English as he joined the bouncer at Harvath's table. "You can leave the knife on your chair."

The bartender was a barrel-chested man in his late fifties. He wasn't as big as the doorman, but he looked like he could hold his own and had done so on many occasions. Harvath didn't want to take on either of them, much less both, but he could if he had to. *Have a smile for everyone you meet, along with a plan to kill them,* had long been one of the mantras that had kept him alive.

Harvath removed the knife from beneath his leg, set it on the table, and stood up. If he needed it, he wanted it close.

The bartender took two steps back and beckoned Harvath forward. "Over here, please."

Harvath stepped around the table and walked toward the man.

"That's far enough. Hands on your head, please."

"What's this all about?" asked Harvath.

"It's just a formality. Hands up, please."

Harvath did as he was told and was given a thorough pat-down by the bouncer.

When he was finished the bartender told Harvath he could lower his arms and added, "Norberto is going to look through your luggage now. Okay?"

It sounded like a question, but Harvath knew better and simply nodded.

As the doorman did his due diligence, the bartender continued talking. "As best we can tell, no one followed you from the airport."

"Who's *we*?"

"My name is Guillermo," said the bartender. "But beyond that, I don't think we want to know much more about each other. Correct?"

"Probably not," replied Harvath as he watched the bouncer going through his bag. "Are things this dangerous now in Monterrey?"

"Things are this dangerous everywhere now, *señor.*"

True, thought Harvath. "Interesting orphanage you're running here."

The bartender smiled and gave a slight bow of his head. "Consider this a portal. You can't get there without going through here."

Harvath wondered what Nicholas had gotten him into. "Your devotion to protecting children is admirable."

"Let's just say that I have a personal interest in making sure nothing happens."

He wasn't surprised. If there really was an orphanage and Nicholas was somehow using it for his own ends, why shouldn't other shady characters be doing so as well?

He was about to ask the bartender a question when the bouncer zipped up his wheelie bag and nodded.

"It looks like you're ready to go," Guillermo stated.

"What do I owe you for the food?"

"It's on the house."

Harvath pulled out another twenty-dollar bill, left it on the table for the waitress, and followed the bartender out the back of the tavern.

CHAPTER 28

A block over, they came to a three-story building surrounded by a high concrete wall with a heavy wooden door that looked like it could be a couple of hundred years old. Guillermo produced a ring of keys from his pocket while the bouncer, Norberto, watched the street.

The bartender located the proper key, inserted it into the old iron lock, and turned. There was a loud click and then the door swung open. Harvath followed the man inside, and Norberto brought up the rear.

They had entered a wide rectangular courtyard. A jungle gym a stone's throw from a statue of the Virgin Mary was all he needed to see to tell them where they were.

The walls were covered with murals of children playing interspersed with stories from the lives of the saints. Above the entryway was an inscription in Latin: *ALERE FLAMMAM VERITATIS—Let the flame of truth shine.* It was an interesting motto for an orphanage, but it resonated with Harvath. If anyone needed the flame of truth right now, it was he.

Beneath the inscription, Guillermo produced another key, opened the door, and shuttled his party through. "Wait here," he said, once they were inside. "I will find Sister Marta."

The interior reminded Harvath a lot of his grade school—the linoleum floors, the wooden lockers, the black-and-white photographs along the walls, even the faint scent of disinfectant—were almost identical. With all the similarities, and remembering how so many of the nuns had looked alike to him back then, he wouldn't have been surprised if Sister Marta had been a dead ringer for the principal of his school, Sister McKenna. Sister Marta, though, turned out to be nothing like Sister McKenna.

When she appeared, she was wearing blue jeans and a Rutgers sweatshirt. She was in her late thirties with dark chin-length hair and, despite not wearing any makeup, was quite pretty.

The bartender said something in rapid Spanish to her that Harvath didn't catch. All he was able to understand was how he addressed her. It wasn't as "Sister Marta" but rather Martita, adding -*ita* to her name as a form of endearment. The young nun, in kind, referred to Guillermo as Momo and gave him a kiss on the cheek before he and the bouncer turned to leave.

As the door closed behind them, Sister Marta welcomed Harvath and extended her hand. "I'm Sister Marta."

"It's nice to meet you, Sister," said Harvath, trying to figure out what her relationship with the bartender was.

"You may call me Marta if you like. We're not very formal around here."

"Is that why Guillermo called you Martita?"

The nun laughed. "We may be informal, but we're not *that* informal. Only family call me Martita. Guillermo—Momo, as I call him—is my uncle."

"Your English is very good. Did you go to school there?" Harvath asked, indicating the university on her sweatshirt.

"No. We get lots of clothing donations here. The items that are too big for the children, we pass on to the poor. Occasionally, the staff will find something that they think will fit me and they set it aside. That's where this came from."

"What about your English?" Harvath asked, intrigued. There was an aura of instant likability about her. She was strong and, like most nuns he'd known, could probably be quite strict when she had to be, but she was also very personable.

"My family takes education very seriously. I learned English in school and French too. I teach both to the children here."

"They're all somewhere sleeping right now?"

"Yes," said Sister Marta with a smile. "Upstairs. It's the only time I can honestly say that most of them remind me of little angels. During the daytime, it can be a different story."

Harvath smiled in return. "I'm sure you have your work cut out for you."

She waved her hand as if to sweep the topic aside. "It's late and you're not here to learn about the running of an orphanage."

"To be honest, Sister, I don't exactly know why I'm here."

"You're here because it's where God wants you to be."

"I'm sure that's true," said Harvath, "but in this case, God used an intermediary."

"You're referring to Nicholas."

"Yes, and I'm assuming I'm here because you can help me get to him."

Sister Marta nodded. "I have arranged to get you aboard a special flight tomorrow that will take you across the border."

Harvath looked at her.

"It's not that kind of flight," she replied, sensing that he suspected it might be drug related. "It's all completely legal. I have contact with someone who runs a shuttle service that flies wealthy Regios back and forth to Texas for daily shopping trips."

"*Regios?*"

"*Regiomontanos*—*Regios* for short—is what we call people from Monterrey."

"Where do they fly into?" Harvath asked.

"A city called McAllen."

"What about customs and immigration?"

"It's a small airport," she responded, "and the pilot is American. He brings people in and out all the time and they all know him there."

"But his passengers still need to clear customs and immigration, even if they're just visiting for the day to go shopping and then turning around and flying back to Monterrey."

"That is correct, but it is much less formal than at a major port of entry. As long as you have a valid passport, they swipe it and you get waved through. You do have a valid passport?"

Harvath nodded. "I do."

"Then you shouldn't have any problem. You should be able to walk right through."

"I don't understand why you're doing this."

"You don't need to understand."

"Why would you risk yourself for Nicholas?" he asked.

"What am I risking? I helped arrange a seat for you on a popular charter flight."

"You know what I mean."

"Do I?" she replied. "Nicholas has been very generous to our orphanage. When he found out that Momo was having trouble with the cartels, when they wanted to use his bar to move money and weapons and drugs, he made it all go away, all of it. He didn't want any of that near us. He's a good man. I have no idea about his past and I don't want to know. That is between him and God. All I know is that he has made a significant difference in the lives of the children here."

"Do you do many favors for him?"

"In all these years, he has never asked me for one until now. I can only imagine you are very important to him."

Harvath wasn't quite sure how to respond to that.

"He told me that you're a good man," she continued. "He said that you have spent most of your life in the service of others. That was all I needed to know. That's why you're here and that's why I'm taking you to the plane in a few hours."

"And when I land in McAllen?"

Sister Marta removed a piece of paper from her pocket and showed it to him. "He said you're supposed to look for this."

CHAPTER 29

R eed Carlton wanted to avoid the D.C. area at all costs, and that included Georgetown. There were just too many cameras. He had
risked it once to load Tommy's dead drop and set up their first
meeting, but that was enough. Banks agreed with him.

Banks suggested that they communicate via the classified section
of the *Washington Post* until they could develop drops outside the city.
It was an old espionage tactic that would allow them to fly beneath
the radar. All they would need was a debit card purchased with cash
at any drugstore, grocery, or Walmart. The only drawback was the
lag time from when the ad was placed to when it actually showed up
online.

Carlton explained to Banks how classifieds worked on the Internet.
Thankfully, the older man was well versed enough in the Web that they
were able to set up a system quickly.

The best way to hide their communications was to go to Craigslist
where they selected two crowded but not obvious source cities. Outgoing
messages were disguised as ads on the Oakland list and responses were
posted on Tampa's. This way, there was no billing trail. And while their
communication wasn't exactly instantaneous, it was about as close to

real time as they could get in exchange for such a low-level risk of being intercepted.

Twenty-four hours after setting everything up, Banks placed a coded ad on the Oakland Craigslist, requesting a meeting as soon as possible. Carlton responded through an ad of his own on the Tampa list, and a few hours later, they were seated at a late-night restaurant outside Fredericksburg.

"You've got big troubles, my boy," Tommy said after the waitress had poured their coffees and walked away. "Your office has been locked up tighter than a bank vault."

"What are you talking about?"

"It's been sealed and they have guards on it."

"Who does?" said Carlton.

Banks raised his coffee cup and took a sip. "FBI, but it feels like CIA."

"So this *is* payback from them."

"It's suspicious, I'll give you that. I reached out to a whole bunch of my Agency contacts and not a single one of them would talk to me. Not one."

"So what does that tell you?"

"It tells me," replied Banks, "that something pretty serious is afoot."

"Yup."

"But just because nobody wanted to talk to me didn't mean I rolled over and gave up. Somebody, somewhere in the chain, scared the hell out of everyone and ordered them to play dumb. That's some pretty serious pressure, so I decided to apply a little pressure of my own."

Carlton studied the man sitting across from him. "I love you, Tommy. You Hoover'd somebody, didn't you?" Much like storied FBI Director, J. Edgar Hoover, Thomas Banks had been rumored to have developed dossiers over the years on Agency higher-ups he didn't care for. He wasn't a blackmailer per se. The files in his mind were only for insurance, to be played like cards if and when he ever needed to accomplish an honest objective while a dishonest obstacle sat in his path.

"It's probably better you don't know the details, but yeah, I pulled a file I have on somebody there and I played it. It's some pretty bad stuff from the 1970s. I don't know what the statute of limitations is, but it's enough to cause him a whole mess of problems and hold up his pension, not to mention the PR nightmare it'd be for the seventh floor."

"I appreciate your doing this for me."

"Don't thank me," Banks replied. "The guy's a weasel. He deserves it. The problem is that he didn't give me very much."

"One step at a time. I'm all ears. What'd you get?"

"The Agency can't go after American citizens on American soil. That's why the domestic legwork has fallen to the FBI. The real momentum behind this thing, though, seems to be coming from somewhere else. Someplace pretty clandestine with a lot of power."

"More clandestine than the Agency? What are we talking about? The Director of National Intelligence?"

"Whoever it is, they're the ones who appear to have built the case against you."

"Me?" replied Carlton. "What are you talking about?"

"Actually, it's not *just* you. It's multiple players in your organization."

"My ops division, you mean?"

"My guy wouldn't say."

"What's their case? What do they think they have?"

Banks again raised his coffee cup for a sip, but this time stopped partway. "Treason," he replied, half whispering the word.

Carlton was stunned. "*Treason?* You've got to be kidding me. That's insane."

"I agree, and I could tell just by the look on my guy's face that he didn't believe it either."

"Is he someone I know?"

Banks set his coffee cup on the Formica table. "Like I said, it's better if you don't know the details."

Carlton understood and, leaning back in the booth, pulled his cup and saucer toward him. "So, what specifically is the charge? What is it we've allegedly done?"

"That's what I'm still trying to find out. The minute anyone hears the word *treason,* it's like a toxic chemical spill just happened. Everyone takes a giant step back. Nobody wants to go anywhere near it. Get too close and it could affect you too."

"There's more to this. Somebody can't just accuse us of treason and put a hit on all of us. There has to be due process."

"You and I both know we've been carrying out extrajudicial activities since the birth of this nation."

"Against foreign enemies of the state," said Carlton, "not American citizens."

Banks shrugged. "A few Americans have also been helped on to their just rewards over the years."

"True, but very, very few, and there's always been a review process."

"How do we know there wasn't one this time?"

Carlton looked at him. "Is there something you're not telling me?"

"Not at all. I'm just playing devil's advocate."

"But there's no way any panel could come to the conclusion that I, or any of the people that work for me, could even be capable of treason."

Banks shook his head. "You really do need to be retrained. Take your emotion out of this."

"Do you know how many of my people, exceptional people, exceptional *patriots,* were murdered?"

"Yes, I do, and I'd be angry as hell too, but I'd lock it away somewhere and save it until I figured out what the hell was going on. Because if I didn't, it'd probably get me killed."

The older man let his words hang in the air for a moment as he took another sip of coffee. "You're smart, Peaches," he finally said. "Smarter than I ever was, but you're going to need every last ounce of cunning you can muster to get yourself out of this.

"You've been labeled a traitor by your own government, and based on whatever evidence they have, they found the threat so compelling that it called for your immediate termination. I don't see how anything could ever get more serious than that. So you can be pissed off all you want *after* this thing has been laid to rest and we've found a way out to the other side of it."

Slowly, Reed Carlton nodded.

"Now that we seem to know who is out to get you, we need to winnow down the how and the why," said Banks. "If we can reverse-engineer this thing, we may be able to get you your life back."

"It won't bring my operators back," Carlton replied. Though he kept checking the Net for messages on the dating sites they used for emergency messages, there hadn't been one. He knew they were dead.

"No, it won't bring your men back. But once we have this thing figured out, that's when I'm going to stand back and let you take your anger out of that box. That's when you make sure that every last person involved in this pays. I don't care who it is, even if this goes all the way to the Oval Office itself."

CHAPTER 30

Harvath grabbed a couple hours of sleep on the couch in the staff room. At 7 a.m., Sister Marta, wearing her full habit, knocked and invited him to the cafeteria for breakfast.

"I thought you said you were informal around here?" he said as they walked.

"We are. Normally I wear a skirt and jacket of some sort. What you saw last night was Sister Marta off-duty, casual. I'm still a human being, especially after the children have gone to bed and I have things to do."

"And now, the habit?"

"I'm driving you to the airport and then I have some other errands to run outside the city. There'll be cartels. They're filled with bad men, but they're not all irreligious. Being easily recognized as a nun can be a plus, especially when on the road."

She was indeed a smart lady.

The cafeteria, which looked like it also doubled as a classroom, was painted in bright colors. Along the walls were the letters of the alphabet with corresponding pictures—*A* for *ardilla* (squirrel), *R* for *ratón* (mouse), *J* for *jirafa* (giraffe).

"You're lucky," said Sister Marta as she picked up a tray and handed it to Harvath. "Today we have eggs."

He accepted the tray and got in line behind her. The sounds of the children filled the room. Most smiled and laughed. Occasionally one or two of the younger children argued or pushed. Harvath expected a stern reprimand from Sister Marta, but none was ever needed, as invariably an older child would step in and patiently handle the situation.

"What I have found," the nun said, "is that all children, no matter what their situation, look for love, they look for family, and they look for understanding. When they act out, they do so because they want to know that there are rules that apply to them. They understand that the rules exist because we love them."

Their breakfast consisted of small portions of rice and beans, along with a little bit of scrambled eggs. One of the staff members offered him coffee and Harvath gladly accepted.

He and Sister Marta sat at a table of boisterous children ranging from five to eleven years old. Several were siblings, and the nun explained that it was their policy never to split children up unless they absolutely had to. When everyone was seated, they said the blessing and then began to eat. Harvath watched as one little boy monitored his younger sister, making sure she got enough to eat and even giving her some of the food from his own plate.

The children were thrilled to have an American visiting, and those who had been studying with Sister Marta tried out their English on him. Their innocent mistakes and Harvath's attempts to reply to them in Spanish created much laughter around the table.

"You were a hit," said Marta as they slid into her aging Volkswagen for the drive to the airport. "I guarantee you it's all they'll be talking about for the rest of the weekend."

Harvath smiled thinking about the kids. It had been a long time since he'd enjoyed himself like that.

"Do you have children?" she asked.

"No."

"You're good with them. You should think about it."

He did think about it, or at least he used to.

"Are you married?" she continued.

"No. I'm not married."

"Why not?"

Harvath looked at her. She reminded him of Peio. He had taken an interest in his personal life right after meeting him as well. Harvath didn't like talking about himself. It made him uncomfortable. When the subject came up, he either ignored it, changed it, or made fun of it. All three forms of diversion had failed with Peio, and he suspected they'd have just about as much chance of succeeding with Sister Marta. "I'm not very good when it comes to relationships, Sister."

"I find that hard to believe. You are a nice man. You're handsome, you like children. What's the problem?" she said, pausing. "Do you not like women?"

He laughed. "No, Sister. That's not the problem. I like women, believe me."

"So what is it?"

"If you don't mind, I'd rather not talk about it."

"Well, I do mind," said the nun. "And if you had seen yourself with those children the way I did, you'd mind too. Is it that you have trouble establishing relationships? Is that it?"

He was convinced that somewhere in the Vatican someone was running a sales contest to get single people married. He didn't disagree with the concept, he was just getting tired of having to defend himself. "Starting relationships isn't my problem."

"But *finishing* them is."

Harvath nodded. "It takes a special type of woman to put up with my career."

"What is it exactly that you do?"

"Let's just say I travel a lot."

"And the woman in your life couldn't accompany you on these trips?"

An image of Riley Turner flashed into his mind, and he kept it there as he spoke. "That would take a *very* special woman."

"Have you ever met such a woman?" Sister Marta asked.

"Yes, I have."

"What happened?"

"She was killed," he replied as the image of Riley disappeared from the forefront of his mind.

"I'm very sorry."

"So am I," he replied.

"At least she knew that you cared for her."

"Actually, Sister, I'm not sure she had any idea."

The nun turned onto a busier street, and there was a sign for the airport up ahead. "She knew, trust me."

"How do you know?"

"It is very difficult to hide when something or someone makes us happy. Even if you had wanted to, you couldn't have hidden how the children made you feel at breakfast."

She was wrong, but simply by virtue of the fact that she had no idea who the man sitting in her passenger seat was. He had been trained to hide everything and to lie as if he was telling the most honest truth held in the deepest part of his soul. Had he wanted to, he could have convinced everyone, even Sister Marta herself, that he didn't care the least bit for children.

That of course wasn't the truth. She had caught him in a rare, unguarded moment—something he didn't normally allow strangers to see.

"I'm not only a nun," she continued. "I'm also a woman. Women can see many things in men that they themselves may not see or choose not to see."

A faint smile creased his face. She was relentless. "What do you see in me then, Sister? What is it that I don't see or don't want to see?"

"I think you are quite complicated, but as for most men, what you want, what you truly desire, is quite simple."

"Which is?"

"I think that—like the children God has entrusted to our orphanage—you want what all of us want. You want to be understood. You want someone to care for you and you want to have your own family."

"I'd also like to win the lottery," he remarked.

"Is humor something you use to avoid problems?" she asked.

It was a reflex. He didn't even realize that he'd made the joke until the words were already out of his mouth.

"You may think it takes those kinds of odds, but it doesn't," Sister

Marta continued. "All it takes is faith. And the best part is that when God does bring the right person into your life, it really will feel like you've won the lottery."

Harvath didn't want to argue with her. She was a wonderful, well-intentioned woman. "I'll tell you what, Sister. If you promise to keep praying for me, I'll keep looking. Deal?"

"I will pray for you either way," she stated as they arrived at the private aviation section of the airport.

The nun parked her Volkswagen and led Harvath to the terminal, where she introduced him without giving his name. The pilot didn't seem to mind and only asked if Harvath had a passport, upon which Harvath patted his backpack and nodded. He had left the wheelie bag at the orphanage and told Sister Marta to do whatever she wanted with it. He was supposed to look like a tourist who had flown up to Texas for a day of shopping, not someone who was staying overnight.

As the pilot did his preflight check and the other passengers, most of whom seemed to be acquainted, mingled, Harvath thanked Sister Marta and told her to be careful. When he asked where he should pay for his ticket, she told him not to worry, that it had already been taken care of. He wasn't sure if Nicholas was behind it or if the nun had paid directly out of her pocket, but either way, it was money that she could have used at the orphanage.

He tried to argue with her, but she wouldn't have it. "Keep your heart open," she said with a smile, changing the subject on him. "When God brings someone special into your life again, grab on with both hands and don't let go."

Harvath laughed. He didn't mean to, he just did. "Thank you, Sister," he said. "Your faith in my capabilities in that area may be a bit misplaced, but I appreciate it all the same."

"I'm in the business of faith," she replied as the pilot signaled that the passengers could begin boarding. "I'm blessed with a never-ending supply."

The flight was a bit choppy on the climb out of Monterrey, but once the plane had leveled off, it was smooth sailing all the way to Texas.

The Cessna Caravan aircraft landed at McAllen-Miller International in McAllen, Texas, and taxied to the immigration terminal. The pilot chatted amiably with the personnel in the small processing area as his passengers' passports were scanned and stamped. Once his own passport had been scanned and stamped, he led his customers back outside to the plane for the short taxi over to the general aviation area.

In front of a blue-roofed building labeled *McCreery Aviation,* he shut the plane down and the gaggle of cheerful passengers disembarked. As he had done for customs and for immigration, Harvath mixed himself into the middle of the crowd. It was amazing how many *Regios* had blond hair and either green or blue eyes. They were also a very international set, which played well for him at immigration, because two women had girlfriends visiting from Germany and another had a male friend in from Spain. Harvath's Italian passport didn't even draw a second look.

Waiting just beyond the McCreery building was a fleet of stretch limousines. Their drivers were holding up pieces of paper with the names *Melendez, Casas, Calleja,* and *Esquivel* written in heavy black marker.

Harvath wasn't looking for a name, though. He was looking for a symbol: three triangles that looked like jagged mountain peaks or a row of shark's teeth.

Once a handful of passengers had piled into one of the limos and it pulled away, he spotted a white Ford F-150 pickup with the three triangles painted on the side, along with the words *Three Peaks Ranch.*

As he moved toward it, his eyes swept the parking lot for any sign of danger. Fifteen feet from the vehicle, the driver's side door opened and an attractive woman with long blond hair, blue jeans, and cowboy boots climbed out.

CHAPTER 31

Maggie Rose introduced herself to Harvath, and the pair shook hands. She looked to be about his age, or maybe a couple of years younger, and spoke with a Texas drawl.

"We've got about an hour's drive," she said. "Is there anything you need before we get going?"

"Where exactly are we headed?" he asked.

Maggie was wearing an embroidered polo shirt with the Three Peaks Ranch logo, and tilted it toward him. "Your room's already made up and everything."

Harvath was apprehensive and hadn't gotten into the truck yet. "If you don't mind, Maggie, who sent you to pick me up?"

The ranch manager smiled. "A little fella with two of the biggest dogs you've ever seen."

"Did he give you his name?"

"No, sir, he didn't."

"How about my name?" asked Harvath. "Did he give you that?"

"No, sir, he didn't give me that either. He simply told me when your flight was coming in and that you'd find me."

"That's all?"

"He also told me I was supposed to play this for you," she said as she jumped back in the truck and turned up the stereo.

Harvath recognized the song immediately—"Rubber Duckie" by Bootsy Collins. There was no longer any question that Nicholas had sent Maggie to pick him up.

One of their first moments of détente had been over beers in Brazil. In the background as he cooked lunch, Nicholas was playing music. The song was "Rubber Duckie." Harvath had the original *Ahh . . . The Name Is Bootsy, Baby!* album in both vinyl and digital. The fact that the two shared a love of American funk was only the first of many things he would go on to learn about the little man.

Harvath walked around to the passenger seat of the truck and climbed in. Maggie got in on the driver's side and closed her door.

"Is all of that for you?" he asked looking at the grocery bags on the backseat.

"No, sir. That's for the other gentleman at the ranch. I came down early to do some shopping for him. A lot of the ingredients he likes I can't find up by us. A bit too exotic."

"And you were able to find them here in McAllen?"

"I found a couple, but most of the time people just looked at me like I was speaking Chinese."

She was definitely shopping for Nicholas. "How long has he been staying at the ranch?"

"Not long," Maggie replied as she navigated the truck out of the lot and onto the street. "Since the beginning of the week."

"He's a charming man, isn't he?"

The woman nodded. "Yes, sir. He's very polite."

"You can call me Scot, Maggie. You don't have to call me sir."

"Okay, Scot."

"So, tell me a bit about this ranch we're headed to."

As they drove, Maggie gave him a history of south Texas and its major ranches, focusing a lot on the world-famous King Ranch, which was over 825,000 acres and comprised portions of six Texas counties.

From the major Texas ranches she gave the history of the Three Peaks Ranch—who had owned it before the Knight family and what types of cattle had been bred there. It was a fascinating history, and Harvath was looking forward to catching a glimpse of some of the exotic animals the Knights had imported.

As the conversation continued, Harvath slowly pulled subtle details from Maggie about the ranch's security measures and its staff. Aside from a simple ADT home security system and a handful of security cameras, there really weren't any other active measures when the family wasn't in residence.

When the Knights were in residence, they brought with them their own security team that manned a twenty-four-hour checkpoint at the gate, as well as roving patrols and agents who watched the security camera feeds. Pushing a bit harder, he learned that there was a license plate camera at the front gate, as well as pressure plates that alerted the gatehouse and the main house when someone was coming up the driveway. The 3,000-acre exotic animal enclosure was surrounded by ten-foot-high "game" fences.

By the time they finally arrived at Three Peaks Ranch, Harvath had built a good rapport with Maggie and had assembled a much better picture of how the ranch operated, what its security was like, and who the staff were.

Off in the distance, he noticed buzzards flying over a windmill of some sort. "Somebody lost some livestock out there."

Maggie followed his gaze. "That's not our property. It belongs to the ranch next door, but they're not grazing cattle over there right now. The windmill pumps water into a trough, so it still attracts a lot of animals. A coyote or something probably took down a deer that had stopped to take a drink."

"Must have been a really big deer to get that many buzzards circling."

She smiled as she pulled up to a keypad and punched in her code. "As they say, *everything's* bigger in Texas."

The wrought-iron gates, emblazoned with the ranch's three-triangle brand, slid open and they pulled through.

As they drove, she pointed out the buildings. They had been built from Texas limestone, known as Ol Yella, quarried near San Antonio and brought down on flatbed trucks. There was also a hefty complement of Austin stone. The roofing tiles were clay. The wood beams, columns, rafters, and decking were cypress, while the hand-carved doors, cabinets, and accents were Texas mesquite. Saltillo tiles covered the interior floors, and the walkways outside were Oklahoma Sugarloaf flagstones.

In addition to the main house were a large guesthouse, the ranch manager's home, six small staff casitas, a vehicle storage building along with a walk-in freezer and game-processing area, stables, and a recreational building that included kitchen, dining hall, bar, arcade, and exercise facility. As they passed it, Maggie commented on the "liar's pit," a stone firepit that the Knights and their guests liked to gather around in the evenings with drinks.

From the moment she picked Harvath up, she hadn't asked him any personal questions or made any inquiries about Nicholas. They were the Knights' guests; that was all she needed to know.

Pulling up in front of the guesthouse, she smiled, put the truck in park, and said, "Here we are. I'll just get these groceries inside and—"

"Don't worry about the groceries," Harvath replied as he reached into the back and picked up the bags. "I've got them."

"Well, if you find there's anything you need, just let me know. My numbers are on the fridge inside and all the phones have me on the speed-dial list, home and cell."

"There is one thing. I'm going to need some clothes."

"The Knights keep a whole closet full of casual clothes for guests, in the rec building. If you don't find anything to your liking there, I can recommend a couple of places nearby, or if you give me a list, I'd be happy to go out and pick up whatever you want. Just let me know."

"I will," he said as he stepped down from the truck. "Thank you."

"You're welcome," she replied and then, remembering the CD Nicholas had given her, she pressed the eject button on the player. "Don't forget your 'Rubber Duckie.'"

"You keep it," Harvath answered. "I've got a bunch."

Maggie smiled and pushed the CD back into the player. As she put the truck in reverse and began to back up, he could hear the song beginning again.

Mounting the guesthouse stairs, he was just reaching for the door when it opened from within and Nicholas greeted him with Argos and Draco at his side. "You made it. Thank God."

"Where do you want these?" Harvath asked, holding up the grocery bags.

"You can put them inside. We've got a lot to discuss."

CHAPTER 32

Nicholas introduced Nina to Harvath and briefly outlined his friendship with Caroline. He then asked Nina if she could give them some time alone. They had a lot to catch up on, much of which was too sensitive to be discussed in front of her. He did his best to frame it so that she wouldn't be offended.

"I understand, Nick," she replied, setting aside the paperback she had been reading. "I think I'll take a walk."

Nina rose from the couch and as she walked past, she smiled and gave his arm a little squeeze. "See you later."

Harvath was fascinated. He'd never seen Nicholas interact with a woman before. Once the front door had closed, he turned and said, "She calls you *Nick*?"

"It's *complicated*."

"Yeah, I can see that."

"She's an incredible woman. She reminds me a lot of her sister."

"And you two . . ." Harvath let his voice trail off.

The little man didn't answer. His silence spoke for him.

"I wouldn't have figured you for the goth type."

"This isn't about her looks. We have a connection like you wouldn't believe."

guard tower with highly polished windows. The guards could monitor any of the prisoners at any time without their knowing exactly when they were being actively watched."

"And Caroline Romero believed ATS was doing the same thing, only digitally?" asked Harvath.

"Yes, and not to prisoners but American citizens. She cataloged how ATS was steering like-minded members of the U.S. government in order to create a fully encompassing, fully functioning digital panopticon. Hence the term *Total Surveillance*."

"But what does it have to do with me being accused of treason, or our organization being penetrated and Riley getting killed?" Harvath asked. "It doesn't make sense."

"It doesn't, you're right. That's why having a better understanding of what Caroline discovered might help us figure this all out. She made a big deal about a study from the Brookings Institute. Entitled 'Recording Everything: Digital Storage as an Enabler of Authoritarian Governments,' its premise was that as the costs for data storage fall, it becomes 'more cost effective for governments to record every scrap of digital information' its citizens produce.

"The easier and more cost effective that is, the more incentive there is to do it. The technology not only enables authoritarianism, it encourages it. Governments simply cannot say 'no' when offered more power. And as we know, information, and thereby knowledge, is power.

"Caroline saved a blog entry that summed it up best. Every e-mail, all your Internet activity, the entirety of every single phone conversation, every piece of GPS data, all your social media interactions, every credit card transaction, every single electronic detail about your life, like it or not, is being placed into a safety deposit box that you have no control over. The government can come in at any point, open that box, and conduct retroactive surveillance on you. They will be able to create a perfect profile of your behavior, and they'll be exceptionally well armed if they deem your behavior to be in opposition to the best interests of the state.

"While Brookings estimated that the conversations of every citizen could be recorded for seventeen cents a year, Caroline showed that ATS

He was right—Harvath didn't believe it. The only female com
ionship Nicholas had ever known had come with a price tag attached
suddenly, in the middle of an absolute shit storm, he had stumbled
a budding romance with an attractive woman likely half his age. It
the contrast with his own personal situation that much more stark.

"Riley's dead," Harvath said. It was an abrupt and perhaps cold cl
of subject, but in all fairness, there were much more serious things
pening than Nicholas's relationship with Caroline Romero's sister.

To the credit of the large heart that beat within his little body, N
las took no umbrage. "I'm sorry, Scot," he said. "What happened?"

From the way Harvath had spoken about Riley in the past, h
suspected there might have been something more than just profes:
respect between the two, and as Harvath recounted what took pl.
Paris, Nicholas realized that his friend had indeed developed feelin
her.

Once Harvath had filled him in on everything that had happ
it was Nicholas's turn. Before he started, he walked into the kit
grabbed a beer for each of them, and returned to the living room
handed one to Harvath and began to speak.

Layer by layer, Nicholas brought Harvath up to speed on what h
uncovered. He detailed his friendship with Caroline Romero, along
her background at Adaptive Technology Solutions. Harvath was un:
iar with ATS, so Nicholas read him in.

From there, the little man explained how Caroline had mailed a l
her sister in Texas, with a recordable greeting card containing instru
and an advanced flash drive. He then described how he had unlock
drive and what he had learned from it so far.

When he was done, Harvath stood up and fetched them ar
round. Returning from the kitchen, he remarked, "You said Ca
characterized what ATS was doing as a sort of 'digital panopticon.'
is that?"

"It's based on a concept developed in the late eighteenth centu
a British social theorist named Jeremy Bentham. The panopticon
vision for the perfect prison. The building was like a wheel, with :
cells facing the hub. In the center of the hub was an enclosed ci

and the NSA were not only already doing it, they had gotten the cost down to only five cents a year. They're storing all of your e-mails, GPS data, text messages, and Web activity too, for even less."

"Is there any data on private citizens they're not collecting?" Harvath asked.

Nicholas shook his head and filled him in on the testing of streetlights in Michigan that could record audio and video and then explained how ATS via the NSA had been behind the explosion in surveillance cameras in Manhattan and Chicago. Caroline had downloaded a PowerPoint presentation that outlined how ATS could have one surveillance camera for every five citizens up and running within three years.

There were new Japanese cameras ATS liked that recorded every single person who passed by and stored the information in perpetuity in a digital library. Using breakthrough facial recognition software, the camera could go back into its database and scan 36 million faces per second until it found the one it was told to look for.

Anticipating resistance because of the cost of all this surveillance technology, ATS had its in-house governmental lobbying firm craft a step-by-step case showing how Congress could orchestrate a "public safety" tax, whereby the citizens being surveilled would bear the cost themselves.

"Evil doesn't even seem to begin to describe these people," said Harvath.

"No it doesn't," said Nicholas. "And all the surveillance right now is being done without a warrant. Americans have no idea. But that's not even the worst of it."

CHAPTER 33

C aroline believed that while ATS had built this amazing, all-encompassing surveillance apparatus under the premise of national security, their goal actually had nothing to do with national security at all," Nicholas explained. "Their goal was control—complete and total control of every man, woman, and child in the United States."

"How the hell is that even possible?" asked Harvath.

"ATS is like an organism that survives only by feeding off a host. In this case, the host is the U.S. and its citizens. But ATS needs politicians, judges, bureaucrats, and innumerable other cogs in the Big Government wheel to help legitimize and push their agenda. Those whom they can't buy, they blackmail."

And *he* was being accused of treason. Harvath shook his head.

"Sometimes, though," Nicholas continued, "there are those who won't toe the line. That's when pressure is brought to bear. The targets can be individuals, or entire swaths of the citizenry, and they can be guilty of nothing more than holding an idea that the state finds threatening to its existence."

"I thought we were talking about ATS."

"We are. For all intents and purposes, ATS *is* the state. Caroline described that when people refer to a 'shadow government,' they're actually talking about ATS, whether they realize it or not."

"And they're planning to target Americans simply because of ideas they hold?" Harvath asked.

"They're not *planning*. It's already happened. The Department of Homeland Security recently issued a report identifying 'disgruntled' military veterans from Iraq and Afghanistan as potential 'right-wing' terrorists. Supporters of politicians and political causes that called for smaller government with greater accountability to American citizens were also labeled as potential terrorists. Owning guns, ammunition, or more than a week's worth of food now classifies you as a potential terrorist. Even certain political bumper stickers or flying the bright yellow Don't Tread On Me Gadsden flag can now qualify you as a terrorist.

"No matter what you do, your government sees you as the greatest threat to its existence—greater than al-Qaeda or any foreign invader—and it will do whatever it needs to do to protect itself."

"That's crazy."

"Is it?" Nicholas asked. "Under the rubric of 'homeland security,' Americans are being subjected to more invasive screening and intensive surveillance every day. TSA is now not only at airports but also train and bus stations. They're even appearing at highway rest stops. You're being told it's for your own good, for your safety, while this framework, this cage is being built around you. Very soon, construction is going to be complete and the cage door is going to swing shut. When that happens, there will be no way out."

"There's got to be a way to stop this."

"They've stacked the deck completely in their favor, right down to the federal court's guaranteeing immunity from criminal and civil prosecution to any private companies that assist the government, i.e., the NSA and thereby ATS, in spying on American citizens."

"I still don't understand what this has to do with why the Carlton Group has been targeted."

"From what Caroline uncovered, ATS is moving into some final phase of an overall plan to solidify its control."

"What kind of plan?" Harvath asked.

"That's where it gets interesting. According to her notes, the powers that be at ATS are obsessed with the Internet. They love social media because it does such a good job of mapping relationships for them. Online purchases, online searches, e-mails, all of it is invaluable. In that sense, the Internet has been a positive in their eyes. The 'negative' as they see it, comes from the free flow of ideas and information.

"In the days when there were only TV, newspaper, and radio, information could be controlled. That's no longer the case. In essence, information is no longer bottled up. It's no longer controlled. It has been unleashed, and that poses a danger to ATS.

"In Caroline's notes, she cited multiple political movements from different parts of the spectrum. These, ATS believes, would never have been possible without the Internet as a means for organizers and participants to communicate. ATS sees something coming in the very near future, and they don't want American citizens to be able to communicate about it. They want to deny Americans the primary vehicle by which they would likely organize and mount any sort of resistance."

"Whoa," interrupted Harvath. "*Resistance?* Resistance to what?"

"I haven't been able to figure that out," Nicholas replied. "I don't even know if Caroline fully knew. All I can say for certain is that ATS views the Internet in its current form as very dangerous."

"What does that mean, 'in its current form'?"

"I've been looking through quite a few articles that Caroline saved covering the idea of some sort of a digital Pearl Harbor. From what I've discerned, ATS was heavily invested in promoting this concept."

"Some sort of cataclysmic cyber attack?" said Harvath.

"Precisely. Whether ATS used it to spook clients into purchasing more hardware or software upgrades or consulting, I can't tell. What the evidence does seem to show is that they worked very hard behind the scenes to push the idea of America's vulnerability to such an attack. In order to bolster the gravity of the vulnerability, they enlisted the cooperation of former high-ranking government officials, now in the private sector, who would be in the know on the subject."

"You don't think America is vulnerable to that kind of attack?"

"Very much so," Nicholas replied. "The FBI Director, the Director of National Intelligence, even the head of the NSA, have said so publicly. But what's interesting is how badly ATS wants the American people to know. This goes beyond convincing the government. I think they already had them in the bag. The American people, though, needed more convincing, more of a campaign, in order for the narrative to take hold. That's where the former high-ranking government officials came in.

"These officials were used to write attention-grabbing books about America's cyber vulnerability. Others were booked on television programs and interviewed for newspaper articles. ATS went so far as to pitch a major cable news channel on a slick, two-hour televised war game entitled *We Were Warned: Cyber-Shockwave.*"

"I remember that," said Harvath. "It was like a who's who of former high-ranking government officials. National Intelligence, CIA, Homeland Security, the White House, even some military personnel and some folks from the Attorney General's office, right?"

Nicholas nodded. "They were all assembled in a mock situation room to respond to a major cyber attack. According to Caroline, the program's purpose was very straightforward, to precondition the American people."

"Precondition them for what?"

"Number one for the attack, and number two for expanding government power in order to deal with it. Federalizing the National Guard, nationalizing power companies and other utilities in order to keep the NSA up and running; they thought of everything, even a host of new and expansive presidential powers, which they put forth as not only necessary but also 'justified' by the Constitution."

"You're saying the entire thing was a propaganda piece?" Harvath asked.

"An exceptionally well executed propaganda piece. It just happened to coincide with a widely reported, real-life computer virus that infected more than seventy-five thousand computers worldwide and ten U.S. government agencies. How about that for timing? People tuned into the program in droves."

Harvath didn't believe in coincidences. "So ATS has been prepping the battlefield for an actual real-life attack?"

"Yes. And based on Caroline's notes, it's going to be much worse than the mock scenario they dreamed up for TV. The real attack won't focus just on the eastern seaboard, it will consume and cripple the entire nation."

"Why? What could they possibly get out of that?"

"Remember all of the changes made in the aftermath of 9/11? Those will pale in comparison to how radically different the country will be after this digital Pearl Harbor. ATS wants to usher in a brand-new version of the Internet. They call it Internet 2.0 and it will be completely controlled by the government."

"The government?" Harvath asked. "Or ATS?"

Nicholas smiled ruefully. "If Washington, D.C., is Oz, then ATS is the man behind the curtain."

Harvath nodded and Nicholas continued, "To use Internet 2.0 for any purpose, no matter how small, you'll be required to log on with a user-specific, government-issued identification number. Anonymity will be a thing of the past. Everything will be monitored: what you say, what you look at, all of it. The government, under the guise of 'safety' and 'national security,' will have sole discretion as to who should be allowed on the Net, and for what purpose. They'll have a massive off switch that they can throw whenever they deem it necessary, and they could keep the older version of the Internet turned off indefinitely. It would be the ultimate curb on people's ability to communicate and would strangle the free flow of ideas and information."

It took a moment for all of it to sink in. Finally, Harvath said, "So if they control the Internet—"

"They'll control everything," said Nicholas, finishing his sentence for him.

"What is it that's coming down the pike, though, that they need all this control?"

"Like I said, I don't know. I don't think Caroline even knew. All I can do is speculate."

"So go ahead and speculate."

"An attack of this magnitude, to take down the entire Internet in order to replace it, is pretty spectacular. But what follows has got to be even more spectacular."

"And it has to be something that the American people are going to strenuously resist," added Harvath.

Nicholas nodded. "What Caroline was able to assemble hints that the people at ATS forecasted multiple scenarios, up to and including a full-fledged revolution. What would cause Americans to revolt?"

Harvath didn't need to think about his response. "Loss of their freedom, America's sovereignty being dismantled, the nation subverted to some foreign or international body like the UN."

"Whatever they have planned, replacing the Internet with Net 2.0 was the last piece of their puzzle."

"Why now? Why wait for the Internet to become this ingrained in people's lives? Why didn't they do this ten or even twenty years ago?"

"I can't even begin to understand the way these people think. Caroline's notes indicate that the Internet grew much faster than any of them had anticipated; that it took on a life of its own. It boomed so quickly, they couldn't get a fence around it. The haphazard attempts at levying taxes on it and establishing various control measures like a presidential kill switch are prime examples. It simply took them this long to develop and perfect Internet 2.0."

"And part of getting everything online was the preconditioning of the American people for the attack, the PR campaign so to speak," said Harvath. *"We've been warned."*

"Exactly. It's a clever form of the Hegelian dialectic—a psychological tool used to manipulate the masses. In this case, you create a problem, wait for the reaction, and then offer the solution. What people historically fail to realize, though, is that those offering the solution are the same people who caused the problem in the first place. They also fail to realize that no matter what the solution is, it always ends up providing its creators with more power."

"Do we have any idea what this digital Pearl Harbor will look like or how it will happen?"

Nicholas shook his head. "No. But to justify completely remaking the

Internet, its impact would have to be enormous; something that would surpass any attack America has ever known."

"When you sent word through Peio, you warned me to avoid tripping the PROMISE or TIP systems," Harvath said. "Do you think there's a connection between what Caroline uncovered at ATS and the hit on me and Riley in Paris and then what happened in Spain?"

This time Nicholas nodded. "Let me show you."

CHAPTER 34

Come in!" Craig Middleton yelled after slamming down the handset of his STE. He had been on and off with Bremmer for the last three hours. The operation in Spain had been an utter failure.

Kurt Schroeder stepped into the office and closed the door behind him. He carried a file folder in his hand.

Middleton looked at him. "What the hell do you want?"

"It's about Reed Carlton."

"Is that the coroner's report?"

Schroeder nodded. He removed the report from the file, walked over to his boss' desk, and handed it to him.

The older man snatched it away and flipped to the end. "What the fuck is this? *Inconclusive?*"

"The bodies were very badly burned."

"Ya think?"

Schroeder ignored the sarcasm. "We're talking charcoal. They had to go by dental records. The only problem is that Carlton was CIA, so his records are classified."

"Bullshit. Nothing's classified to us. We practically run that place. Get the records."

"I did, but they're so old they were still on paper. I had to request a copy from the Agency's dead-file storage."

"So why are you wasting my time?" Middleton asked. "What's the bottom line?"

"Carlton's body was not among those recovered at the scene of the fire."

As a new wave of anger overtook him, the older man's face reddened like a rapidly rising thermometer.

Schroeder could tell that his boss was going to blow and tried to circumvent it. "I've already set up a dragnet. If Carlton uses his phone, a credit card, or reaches out to anyone on his relationship tree, we'll know."

"We'll *know*?" Middleton bellowed. "The fuck we will. He's not going to do anything under his real name."

"I've plugged in all known aliases for him too."

"And he's got a hundred or two others we're not aware of."

Schroeder felt his boss was overestimating, but he wasn't sure. "That many?"

"I'm exaggerating, you idiot. It doesn't matter how many aliases he has. Carlton has decades of field experience. If someone like that doesn't want to be found, it's almost impossible to find him."

The younger man bristled at being called an idiot but kept his temper in check. "You're the one who always says we own every haystack."

"Are you being a smartass?"

"No, sir."

"It doesn't matter if we own every haystack," Middleton asserted, "if we can't find the needle in time. Whatever they're planning, we know it's supposed to happen soon."

"Then let's call in some help with the haystack," said Schroeder, who still didn't have a complete picture of what his boss thought was coming.

Middleton looked at him. "What do you mean?"

"Let's get local law enforcement to put out a Be-On-The-Lookout for Carlton. Suspected arson and homicide."

The older man liked the sound of that. "Good idea. The more people searching the haystack the better. Just make sure it doesn't trace back to us."

"Don't worry. I can do it so it looks like it came through the FBI."

"Then do it. What else do you have for me?"

Schroeder pulled a sheaf of pictures from his file folder and handed them over.

"What the hell are these?" Middleton demanded.

"Surveillance photos."

"I can see that. What I want to know is *what* I'm looking at."

"They were taken this morning at the airport in McAllen, Texas. The woman in the truck outside the civil aviation terminal is Margaret Rose. She manages the Three Peaks Ranch near Agua Nueva. She's the one who conducted the Google searches for Caucasian Ovcharkas and primordial dwarfism," Schroeder replied.

Middleton was suddenly interested. "And who's the guy she's picking up? None of the cameras seem to have captured his face very well."

"I noticed that too. He flew in on a private charter from Monterrey, Mexico, but cleared customs and immigration with an Italian passport."

Middleton took an even closer look at the photos. "Do we know if he was anywhere before Monterrey?"

"We do," Schroeder replied. "I ran him through the Mexican databases and it turns out he just arrived in Mexico last night."

"From where?"

"Bilbao. He flew into Mexico City via Madrid."

"And how close is Bilbao to Harvath's last-known location?"

"As far as commercial airports go, it would have been one of the closest."

Middleton was suddenly very animated. "I want you to download all the CCTV footage from every airport he passed through. I want to know every step he made, every person he talked to."

"I'm already on it," Schroeder said as he headed for the door.

Staring at the final photograph that showed Harvath climbing into the truck branded with the Three Peaks Ranch logo, Middleton smiled and said, "Gotcha," as he reached for his STE.

CHAPTER 35

It was late. They sat with untouched plates of food in front of them at a desk in Nicholas's room while Nina slept down the hall. Storm cases and various pieces of computer equipment were stacked about. Harvath watched across three linked monitors as the little man walked him through Caroline's data. As Nicholas spoke, his tiny hand worked a wireless mouse, opening folder after folder, bringing up articles and notes for Harvath to read.

"This was one of the most interesting things I've found on the drive," said Nicholas as he clicked on a file labeled *Roundup*. "Have you ever heard of something called Main Core?"

"Only in passing," Harvath replied. "What is it?"

"Since the 1980s, there's been an allegation that the United States government actively maintains a database of U.S. citizens it considers a potential national security risk. Some say there are more than eight million names on the list. Supposedly, it's part of the government's highly secretive continuity of government plan. The idea behind Main Core is that if there should ever be a major national emergency, the government would have a list of people it saw as potential threats and could zero in on for additional surveillance, questioning, or even detention. For each name on the list, there was a full dossier, and the database could ID and locate any perceived enemies of the state almost immediately."

"So that's what it is, an enemies list?"

"Precisely," replied Nicholas as he pointed to the screen. "But there's something beyond Main Core, something that predates it by decades and doesn't need a national emergency to be activated. It's called the Black List. This list is much more than just citizens the government feels need tracking, questioning, or detention. This is a kill list, and once you're on it, your name doesn't come off until you're dead."

"Now I know what the operative in Spain meant when he said that I was *on the list.*"

"According to the data Caroline gathered, treason is one of the reasons you can be placed on the list."

"There's no review? It's completely extrajudicial? That's insane," said Harvath. "The American government doesn't just accuse a citizen of treason or terrorism and then go out and kill them."

"That's not what these files say."

"Then the files are wrong. Even Americans who have left the country to support al-Qaeda against the U.S. have gone through a vetting process before being targeted."

"That's true," replied Nicholas. "But this is something different. You yourself have been sent on multiple assignments to kill persons hostile to the U.S. Was every one of those sanctioned at the top?"

"No comment."

"See. You know how compartmentalization works. It's like a dresser divided into multiple drawers and subcompartments. Controlled access programs and special access programs exist not only to keep things secret but to keep politicians and agency heads in the dark. Not even the handful of 'superusers' in D.C., who supposedly have access to everything, have a full grasp of everything that's going on, particularly in the clandestine world."

Harvath shook his head. "Even so, the majority of people I've been assigned have not been American citizens. Those that were, had their cases reviewed and sanctioned."

"I'm simply telling you what Caroline discovered. According to her data, the Black List is real. It exists."

"Who's behind it? Who makes the targeting decisions and has the final judgment?"

"From what's on the drive," replied Nicholas, "it dwells in one of those divided-off subcompartments. They meet in secret and no one knows who makes up the panel."

"Are they intelligence people, or are they from DOJ? The White House?"

"It appears to be a mix."

"Do you have any idea how many of them there are?" Harvath asked.

"No. Caroline doesn't say."

"When someone has been found guilty and is targeted, who carries out the sanction?"

"A kill team of some sort," Nicholas replied. "They all have military training at the Special Operations level."

"Who runs them? Are they active military? Do we have any idea where they're based?"

Nicholas shrugged. "I have no idea."

"Why the interest in me?" said Harvath.

"From what I can gather, it wasn't specifically you, it was the Carlton Group in general and the fact that it employs former military and intelligence personnel."

"There are plenty of private groups out there who do that. Why would ATS come after us?"

"None of those groups match your size or proficiency. You're a threat. You operate outside the system and they can't control you."

Harvath was incredulous. "And they *can* control the CIA or the FBI?"

"Those are organizations inside the system, and yes, they can control them. They have enough influence to steer anything in D.C. in any direction they want it to go. It's all done covertly, quietly behind the scenes, but it's done."

"But we're small-time."

"No you're not. Not anymore," said Nicholas. "You've disrupted several international terrorist attacks, you conduct your own, unilateral clandestine operations, and what's probably most dangerous of all to them, you don't answer to anyone in the United States government. They know who you are and they know the trouble you can cause for them. The Carlton Group is the only organization they mention by name in the file. That's why I wanted you to get back here as soon as possible and make sure you stayed off the grid. I didn't know anything about Paris and Spain until you told me."

"I'm surprised they didn't try to just gobble us up."

"They did. On two separate occasions, ATS tried to purchase the Carlton Group. And both times, Reed Carlton said no," replied Nicholas as he pulled up a memo Caroline had downloaded. "They were not at all happy about it—you can see here some of the thoughts they had about your group afterward."

Harvath leaned toward the screen and read several of the remarks aloud. ". . . A danger to the intelligence community if left unchecked, zero accountability to any authority or governing body, a collection of renegade cowboys imbued with an excessive sense of nationalism, significant diplomatic and national security risk, if this group cannot be brought under control other steps must be taken . . ." He stopped reading at that point. "So those steps mean splashing all of us?"

"I'm not sure," Nicholas replied. "Caroline developed the impression that at some point ATS and the Carlton Group crossed swords, but that Carlton didn't realize it. Somehow, your group tripped up one or more things ATS had been working on."

"Like what?"

"Ops of some sort. She was trying to figure it out as part of what ATS was up to, but she was killed before she could get to the bottom of all of it."

"Did Caroline know that you were working with us?" Harvath asked.

"I never told her. I kept it a secret. In fact, I kept it a secret from everyone. I didn't even let Caroline know that I was in the country. ATS knew, though, and my name appears in their files, so at some point she found out."

Harvath studied the man's face. "Could she have been setting you up?"

"It crossed my mind, but I don't think so."

"Why would she want Nina to bring that drive to you?"

"Because," he replied, "Caroline and I were friends. Because she *knew* I'd do the right thing with it. She knew I'd warn the right people and that I'd help stop whatever it was that ATS has planned."

It was a reasonable answer. In fact, it was better than reasonable. It made sense. He could see he had offended Nicholas, so Harvath let it lie. Rubbing the back of his neck, he squinted at the clock. "It's almost midnight."

"What do you want to do?"

"Have you tried to contact the Old Man?"

"No," Nicholas replied, "and after hearing how quickly you were targeted, I'm glad I didn't."

"So we don't know for sure if he's alive or dead."

"We don't. We also don't know how many other people from the group were killed. But, seeing as how you couldn't reach a number of them, I think we have to assume the worst."

Nicholas was right, but Harvath didn't want to think about it.

"There's a message forum that the Old Man designated for emergencies. If you can set up a safe way for me to get online, I'd like to check it. After that, I don't know if there are any more bombshells in these files, but I'd like to split them up between us and go through as many as possible before we turn in."

"I'll put some coffee on," said Nicholas as he slid out of his chair. Nodding at Harvath's plate, he asked, "You want that heated up?"

Immediately, as the words came out of his mouth, the lights dimmed and went out. The alarms on his backup APU batteries sounded as they kicked in and supplemented power to the computer equipment. What didn't kick in was the generator Harvath had seen outside, and that should have happened almost instantaneously.

"Blackout?" Nicholas remarked.

Harvath signaled for him to be silent as he reached out and turned off all the monitors. The dogs had been sleeping nearby but sensed something was wrong, rose, and began growling. Nicholas commanded them to be quiet.

Unable to travel with his pistol internationally, Harvath had left it back in Spain. His voice just above a whisper, he asked Nicholas, "Did you bring any weapons with you?"

The little man nodded.

"Get them. Right now."

CHAPTER 36

Nicholas hurried over to a case next to the bed, but as he bent down to open the lid, the lights came back on. "Must have been a surge of some sort."

"Maybe," Harvath said. "Let's see what you brought with you."

Nicholas turned his attention back to the case and retrieved two weapons. One was a small handgun, and the other looked like an old, scaled-down M3 submachine gun or grease gun, as it was called back in the 1940s. Both had obviously been custom made for Nicholas.

Pulling two extended, stick-style magazines from the case, he closed the lid and laid everything out on the bed. "This is all I've got."

Harvath looked at both weapons. "What caliber?"

"The pistol is in .45 and the sub is .22LR."

A .22 was only a step above a BB gun as far as Harvath was concerned. It didn't have nearly enough power. That said, he understood that the larger the rounds, the heavier the weapon would be. A weapon of this caliber made sense for a man of Nicholas's size, especially if he wanted to be able to fire many shots without reloading. With a lot of skill and a lot of luck, a .22 could kill a man. It could also be one hell of a nuisance in trying to keep your enemy pinned down while you made your escape. "Do you have extra rounds for the .45?" he asked.

Nicholas reached back into the case, withdrew a small box of ammunition and handed it to him. Harvath picked up the tiny pistol and could only wrap a couple of fingers around the grip. He was able to get some of his index finger through the trigger guard, but it was going to be a nightmare to shoot if he had to.

"Stay here," he said, checking to make sure the weapon was loaded and then dumping the additional .45 rounds into his pocket. "Wake Nina and keep her and the dogs with you."

"Where are you going?" Nicholas asked.

"Outside to take a look around."

"You think somebody shut the power down and then brought it back up on purpose?"

"It's probably nothing. I just want to make sure."

Nicholas had a feeling he wasn't being told the truth, but he didn't press it.

"I'll be back in a bit," said Harvath. "Keep the doors locked and stay away from the windows."

The little man nodded as Harvath exited the master bedroom. Inserting one of the slim magazines into the mini M3, he charged the weapon and tucked the extra mag into his waistband before heading down the hall to get Nina.

Harvath slipped outside into the darkness. The night was cool and a thick cover of clouds hung overhead, blocking the stars from view.

There were no active exterior lights on the guesthouse, and it took a few seconds for his eyes to adjust. He tuned his ears to the sounds around him, trying to pick up anything unusual. There was the steady rhythm of cicadas and beneath it a slight breeze that shook the narrow leaves of a row of Texas olive trees close by. Other than that, there was nothing out of the ordinary.

He moved around to the side of the guesthouse where the generator was. Considering that it was on fenced, private property, he wasn't surprised to find it unlocked. He could make out boot prints in the dust around it. They weren't from cowboy boots like the ranch hands wore. They looked like hiking or tactical boots. Big, too.

Examining the generator, Harvath tried to run through his mind how he would rig it, if he wanted to cut power to the guesthouse in advance of an attack. Before the actual attack, he would always do what he called a "flicker," a quick cut-off of power, to make sure that everything was set and ready to go. Was that what they had just experienced? Were the boot prints some sinister, pre-attack indicator, or did they belong to a repairman who had recently been out to service the generator?

There wasn't much ambient light and he wished he had a flashlight.

Kneeling down behind the generator on the other side, he examined all the wiring. It looked fine at first glance, but he had learned that first glances could often be deceiving. If you could take out the generator without anyone knowing, when you were ready to cut power to the guesthouse, you could do that from a distance. It was the best way.

He was halfway through his inspection when he sensed someone approaching, moving carefully just beyond the olive trees, taking pains not to be heard.

Harvath stopped what he was doing and adjusted his grip on Nicholas's tiny .45. He had no idea whether he had been spotted or if the generator had shielded him from view. But, it appeared his suspicions about the power outage had been confirmed.

He took a deep breath and exhaled as he shifted to his right. He needed to keep his heart rate under control. He had only three shots before he would need to reload, and there was no telling how accurate or wildly inaccurate the weapon he was holding was going to be. The one thing he had going for him was that at least he had halfway decent cover. And, if he hadn't been spotted, he might even have the element of surprise.

That changed, though, when the figure stopped its approach just behind the row of trees and stood, waiting. *But for what? For me to make a move and give myself away?* Harvath could wait all night if he had to.

Seconds passed. He felt certain whoever was out there in the darkness knew exactly where he was.

The silence was broken by a weapon being cocked. It had been done very slowly in order not to make any noise, but Harvath had heard it and now he knew exactly where in the trees the shooter was hiding. In response he readied his own weapon and prepared to take action, but then something happened.

From behind the trees, the figure shouted out a command in Spanish. *"Levantese!" Stand up. "Suelte el arma!" Drop the weapon!*

Harvath had no idea if she could see it or not, but he stuck one hand over the top of the generator and waved. "It's okay, Maggie," he replied. "It's me, Scot. Lower your weapon."

There was the sound of her weapon being decocked and then Maggie Rose stepped out from behind the olive trees carrying a Mossberg lever-action rifle. "What are you doing out here?" she asked, walking over to him as he stood up and emerged from behind the generator.

"We had a problem with the power a few minutes ago. What are you doing out here?"

"I saw something on the CCTV cameras and wanted to come check it out."

"What did you see?" he asked.

"A group of illegals crossing the property. If the Knights were here, their security people would go out and question them. The problem is, we don't have a procedure for this. If it was just staff here, we're told not to engage, just let them pass. You're here, though, and that makes me responsible for you. Though maybe I don't need to worry," she added, looking at the weapon in Harvath's hand.

"When was the last time this was serviced?" he said, walking around the generator.

"About a month or two ago. Why?"

Harvath motioned her closer and pointed at the boot prints. "These are fresh. Does anyone on the ranch wear boots like these?"

She studied them for a moment and replied, "No. None of us do."

"I didn't think so," he said as his eyes tried to penetrate the darkness around them. "I want to know exactly what you saw on the cameras. Where are they now?"

"A group of what looked like four males, but by the time I noticed them, they were already leaving the property. I didn't see any others in their wake, but I wanted to make sure."

"Were they carrying anything? Any weapons?"

"If I'd seen weapons, I would have called the sheriff."

"How tall were they? What were they wearing—"

"Come up and see the footage for yourself," Maggie said, interrupting him and pointing in the direction of the main house. He was uneasy, and though she didn't know why, it was catching. Looking over her shoulder she added, "Suddenly I don't feel so comfortable standing out here like this."

CHAPTER 37

"There they are. Right there," the ranch manager said as she backed up the closed-circuit footage.

They were sitting in the security office on the first floor of the main house, built and decorated in the same Tex-Mex Mission style as the other buildings. "I have a monitor with a live feed at my place," she continued, "but I have to come here if I want to rewind anything."

Harvath used a trackball to slowly roll the footage backward and forward. "Do you get a lot of people who cross through the ranch?"

"The illegals, you mean?"

"Anyone. Illegals, poachers, whatever."

"Most of them tend to be illegals moving their way up from Mexico. They hide and camp during the day, then move across the ranches down here at night. With the cloud cover and no moon, they've got a perfect night for it."

It wasn't the only thing a night like this was perfect for. "Does this happen every night?"

Maggie shook her head. "A couple of times a month, maybe."

"When was the last time?"

She shrugged. "We'd have to go through all the footage. No one watches the cameras unless the Knights are here."

"But you were watching."

"I happened to be awake and something caught my eye. I wouldn't characterize that as watching. Like I said, I only came out to make sure you-all were okay."

Harvath froze a frame of video. Despite hunching over when they moved, they couldn't hide their size. "These guys look pretty big to me," he said, "or am I wrong?"

She leaned in next to him and looked at the monitor. "No, you're right. They do look big."

"Are the groups normally made up of four people?"

Maggie shook her head. "There isn't a standard. For every one you see, there can be five or ten more."

"What about clothing? Is this the kind of stuff you normally see?"

"The clothing is perfect."

"Even with all four men wearing baseball caps?"

"It's all perfect, but there's something missing."

Harvath looked at her. "What?"

"Anything these people own, they're usually carrying it with them. But these four aren't carrying anything. No food, no water, no plastic grocery bags. *Nothing.*"

It was a very good observation. "How do I zoom in?" he asked.

She showed him and Harvath tightened up as close as he could. "What do those look like to you?"

"Whatever they are," Maggie replied as she studied the pixilated, infrared image, "they definitely aren't cowboy boots."

She was right. In fact, even with the rough quality of the extreme close-up, the boots they were wearing looked exactly like what Harvath envisioned had left the prints near the generator.

Zooming out, he scrolled through the rest of the night's footage, trying to ascertain when and how the men had crossed onto the property, what they had done while there, and when and how they had left. The problem was that there were large gaps. The men had been captured on only a couple of the cameras, and they never showed their faces. They'd either been extremely lucky or had known exactly what they were doing, purposely avoiding the cameras.

As he played some of the footage again, Maggie said, "Freeze that."

Harvath stopped the feed and peered at the image. "What do you see?"

"Now that I look at it again, there's something not right about the clothes."

"How?"

"It can be pretty cold at night this time of the year. You normally see these people wearing multiple layers that they can take on and off as they need to. It's warm tonight, but none of these guys has any extra clothes tied around their waists. Now zoom in on the last one in that frame there."

"What am I looking for?"

"The shirtsleeves. See how high up the cuffs ride on his arms? Now pull out just a bit and look at all four of them. Their pants and boots fit, but nothing else does."

"Because those aren't their clothes," stated Harvath.

"Then where'd they get them from?"

Harvath remembered the buzzards from earlier that were circling the watering hole and wondered if maybe it wasn't deer that had stopped to drink there. "I think I may have an idea," he said.

Before leaving the house, Harvath talked Maggie into opening up the gun room for him. It looked like something out of a British castle: rows of mahogany cabinets filled with expensive hunting rifles, watched over by exotic animal heads adorning the walls. Down the center was a long glass table with drawers containing a range of handguns.

Some of their barrels were threaded, which meant there probably were suppressors somewhere. Maggie confirmed this, but explained to him that they were kept in a separate safe that only the Knights had the combination to.

It would have been a helpful thing to have, but he'd have to live without it.

Harvath selected a Heckler & Koch Mark 23 pistol, took a handful of spare magazines, and helped himself to one of Mr. Knight's Benchmade knives. All told, he was in and out of the room in under two minutes.

He had thought of using Maggie's cell phone to call Nicholas, but the man was already on alert. Besides, for all he knew, Maggie's phone was being monitored, and reaching out to Nicholas might set something in motion before he could get back, so he had decided against it.

Not knowing how many eyes were on the ranch, Harvath lay on the floor of Maggie's truck as she drove out one of the service gates.

A mile down the county road, she pulled onto a rutted access path and brought the truck to a stop. Harvath climbed out of the back and into the passenger seat. "How far away are we?" he asked.

"Less than a mile."

He nodded, and Maggie put the truck in gear and resumed driving. He needed to check out that watering trough. Seeing the ill-fitting clothing of the "illegals" on the CCTV footage had set alarm bells ringing in his head.

As they were nearing the trough, Harvath signaled for Maggie to stop.

"What is it?" she asked.

"I think there's a vehicle up ahead."

"Where? I don't see anything."

"Kill the lights. Shut off the engine."

Maggie did as she was told.

"Do you have a flashlight?" he asked.

The ranch manager nodded, opened the armrest, and handed him one.

"When I come back," he said, "I'll let you know it's me by flashing the light three times; two longs and a short. If you see anyone else, shoot them."

Maggie looked at him like he was crazy. "What are you talking about?"

"Trust me," he replied. Then, after disabling the dome light, he climbed out of the truck and disappeared.

Creeping toward the vehicle he had seen in the bounce of Maggie's headlights, he reflected on what he would do if tasked with assaulting Three Peaks Ranch. Surveillance would be the first order of the day, but before that, he'd need a place to hide whatever he was driving. You couldn't just leave a car parked along a county road out here. It would attract too much attention. You needed someplace to hide it, close enough that you could cover the rest of the distance by foot.

Using an adjacent ranch that abutted your target made sense, especially if the area you picked wasn't currently in use. The windmill was also a good landmark, easy to navigate back to.

It was the presence of water, though, that had bothered Harvath. Water didn't attract only animals, it also attracted human beings.

Moving through the darkness, he arrived at a dark Dodge Durango that had been pulled off the road and partially hidden behind a tall clump of scrub. The doors were locked and there was nothing inside. Reaching his hand out, the hood was cool to the touch. How long the SUV had been sitting there was anyone's guess. Twenty yards on, he could make out the silhouette of the windmill. Beneath it would be the trough that it pumped water into.

Harvath stood for several moments and listened for any sound indicating there were people up ahead. He didn't hear any and quietly continued on toward the trough. He came across the first body ten yards on.

It looked to be a young Hispanic man who had been shot in the back of the head, execution-style. He had been dead for at least a day, probably more, and his flesh had been picked apart.

Moving onto the trough, he found five more bodies, a mix of men and women. All had been shot at close range and dumped into a shallow grave. Whoever did the burying, though, hadn't realized how quickly the bodies would be dug up and feasted upon by scavengers.

Playing the light over the carnage, Harvath was able to re-create enough to figure out what had happened. Many illegals carried maps marked with "safe" places to camp and find water along their routes. Judging by what he saw, somebody else was already here when they arrived and it didn't end well.

Four of the victims had been stripped to the waist. Scattered around the trough were the illegals' few possessions, mostly in plastic grocery bags, just as Maggie had said.

Studying the ground, Harvath discovered perfect matches for the boot prints around the generator outside the guesthouse. He had seen enough.

After flattening the tires of the Durango with his knife, he rejoined

Maggie, making sure to signal her with the flashlight before he got too close.

"What did you find?" she asked.

"You need to get back to the ranch as fast as you can," he replied.

The look on his face must have said it all. Maggie didn't ask any more questions. Firing up the truck, she turned it around and stepped on the gas as Harvath began giving her instructions.

When they reached the main county road, Maggie headed toward Three Peaks Ranch. Half a mile out, she slowed down and Harvath opened his door and leapt out.

CHAPTER 38

Harvath used the wire cutters from Maggie's truck to cut through the game fence and slip inside. It was the one angle of attack he felt certain no one would expect.

Without knowing who or what he was up against, all he could do was envision how he would carry out a similar assault. Not only were the conditions favorable weather-wise, with heavy cloud cover and low ambient light, it was a Saturday night and most of the ranch staff was in town.

If Paris and Spain were any indication, this would be another four-man team. That seemed to be confirmed by the CCTV footage, as well as by the four dead males stripped to the waist back at the water trough.

He had no idea how long they had been surveilling the ranch, but they had accurately identified the guesthouse, and Harvath had no doubt that was the target. While Maggie had originally believed that the men had left the property, Harvath wasn't so sure. They had done their flicker test. Now they would dig in and wait to take their objective.

Other than the olive trees in back, there wasn't any vegetation obstructing the guesthouse. There were only two doors—the one in front and the one off the kitchen—and lots of windows. If Harvath were running this operation, he wouldn't risk sending all four men inside. He'd take his best long-range shooter and set him up in an overwatch position.

The best place was a clump of red maples about four hundred yards north of the guesthouse. From there, you could see almost the entire structure. If he had to set up a sniper, that's exactly where he would do it.

The breeze did little to keep Harvath's body temperature down as he raced across the exotic game enclosure. He had picked the most direct route, cutting off one of the corners and running at a diagonal. When he reached the fencing on the other side, he had to use the wire cutters again and pull back a small section in order to slip out.

He wasn't surprised that he hadn't come across any game. They knew he was there long before they could see him. The breeze had been at his back the entire time, pushing his scent out in front of him like an olfactory air horn.

As he swung around in a loop, a thousand yards out from the maple trees, the wind was coming at him, no longer at his back.

Using a row of tall grasses for concealment, he continued moving forward. He was in rattlesnake country and while he tried not to think about it, he wished he had some sort of night vision gear and should have asked Maggie. If the security cameras were IR equipped, they probably had other equipment, especially for hunting at night. At this point, though, it was too late. He'd have to rely on his own natural abilities.

The dry autumn grass crackled underfoot and rattled like dry cornstalks as he moved through it. He did the best he could to minimize the noise, but it resulted in little attenuation. Very soon, he was going to have to abandon the safety of concealment for a quieter path.

Halfway to the maples, he stepped out from the grass, steadied his breathing, and listened. All the sounds were as they had been when he had stepped outside the guesthouse almost two hours earlier. Had he not seen the CCTV footage and the bodies on the adjacent ranch, there would be no indication that an intense danger was lurking somewhere in the darkness.

He began moving forward again but stopped after thirty yards, when he thought he smelled something. It was only the faintest whiff, and the harder he tried to zero in on it, the more he smelled only earth and other odors.

Exhaling through his nose, he gave up and continued on. Ten yards further and the scent was delivered unmistakably on the breeze. *Cigarette smoke.*

Smoking was something you were never supposed to do on an op, but it was a rule that was broken all of the time. Harvath now knew there was definitely someone up in the clump of trees. Hidden away, at least four hundred yards from his target, whoever it was probably thought they could risk a quick cigarette without tipping anyone off. Most likely, he was using the soldier's trick of cupping both hands around the cigarette in order to prevent the glowing tip from being seen, but it didn't make any difference. Harvath knew exactly where he was.

If the man was in fact a sniper, he'd be equipped with some sort of night vision device. But with both hands cupped around his cigarette, he'd be incapable at the moment of anything more than peering through a fixed rifle scope. He wouldn't be actively looking to either side or, more to the point, behind him.

Quickening his pace, Harvath closed the distance to the copse of maples to thirty yards, then dropped to the ground and crawled in on his belly, inch by carefully silent inch.

He was less than ten yards away when he saw the sudden bright orange glow of the coal as the smoker uncupped his hands from the cigarette and crushed it out. There was a crackle of dry leaves while the sniper adjusted himself behind his rifle and peered into his scope. From his prone position, he slowly pivoted the rifle from side to side. Barely above a whisper, he spoke into his headset microphone and said, "Gold One, you're clear. Gold Two, also clear. Gold Three, you're good to go."

Harvath drew his knife. With his other hand, he felt around him for a rock just the right size. He needed only to distract the man for a second.

As his fingers closed around what he was looking for, he took a silent breath, let it out, and sprang.

CHAPTER 39

The distraction wasn't as effective as Harvath had planned, because when the sniper's attention was drawn in the direction of where the rock had been thrown, he immediately seemed to sense he was under attack.

Harvath had launched himself, expecting to land on the man's back. Gripping his forehead, he would pull his head back, expose his throat, and slice through his larynx, thus silencing him instantly. Then he'd push the head forward and plunge the knife into the base of his skull. With a twist of the blade, the brain stem would be severed and the man would no longer be a threat. That wasn't exactly how it unfolded.

The sniper rolled over, bringing his rifle with him. As Harvath landed on top of him, the young man swung the stock and connected with Harvath's left collarbone, creating a shock wave of pain.

His body wanted to roll away from the agony, but he fought to stay where he was. Rapidly his eyes swept the young sniper's face and neck; in a microsecond, he found what he was looking for.

Being on top, Harvath had the advantage of leverage. In the blink of an eye, he clamped down on the butt of the weapon and drove all his weight forward.

The sniper tilted his head to the side so as not to be hit in the face, and that was the opening Harvath had been hoping for. Reaching over the scope, he swept the knife. It entered behind the man's right ear and came down below his jawline, slicing through flesh and the wire of his headset.

Taking some of his weight off the rifle, Harvath added pressure to the blade, making sure to cut as deep as possible. As soon as he severed the larynx, he pulled the knife out and slid it between the man's ribs. He was wearing body armor, but it was soft and meant to stop bullets, not a knife. Adding more force, Harvath thrust the blade up and into the man's heart.

The sniper's body went rigid, spasmed, and then fell still. His hands dropped from the rifle. Harvath pulled it away and stood. The entire struggle had lasted only a matter of seconds.

Setting the rifle aside, he relieved the twenty-something sniper of his radio and then dragged him behind one of the maples and dumped the body. In a perfect scenario, he would have taken the man captive in order to interrogate him, but there had been no way to subdue him and he had nothing with which to tie him up. Even then, it would have been an impossible task to keep one eye on the sniper while figuring out where his colleagues were. If he could have done it another way, he would have. As far as he was concerned, he had exercised the only option available to him.

Though he had done it before, Harvath was not fond of using a knife. There was something barbaric about it. It was too close, too messy, too personal. He preferred using a firearm; it allowed him to keep a certain psychological distance.

He had lost track of the men he had killed by pulling a trigger. Those weren't the faces he struggled to keep banished to remote corners of his psyche.

It was the men he killed up close, inches away, whose faces sometimes loomed in his mind's eye. He had never figured out why. He was required to kill for a living, and he had little problem doing it. Why should one form of killing be any different from any other? The end result was the same.

The only conclusion he could come to was that civilized people were encoded with an aversion to murder. Throughout thousands of years of history, tales of morality and murder were handed down from one generation to the next. From childhood, human beings are steeped in stories about the unjustified taking of life, and the acts they find the most reprehensible are those committed with the most basic tools—stones or knives, clubs or bare hands—as if the tools most associated with murder are those that have been around as long as murder itself.

There was a dissociation Harvath felt when taking a life via the barrel of a gun. The bullet was his intercessor. He pulled the trigger; the bullet was released; the bullet killed the target. It was clean, simple, it all fit compactly inside an iron strongbox he kept buried away in his mind. And no matter how many times he killed, the box always had room for one more. It was only a handful of kills, no matter how justified, that were occasionally able to slip his mental jailer and prod the edges of his conscience.

Some of Harvath's strongest qualities, though, were his willpower and his ability to compartmentalize and focus on the mission at hand. He was not prone to doubts or second-guessing.

After clearing away the sniper's body, he set up the rifle and lay down behind it—a Remington Model 700 with a sound and flash suppressor, as well as a detachable box magazine. He had no idea what caliber it was but assumed it was powerful enough to get the job done from this distance.

Mounted to the top of the weapon was a powerful thermal scope with the ability to "see" in total darkness. Harvath set the radio down in front of him, made sure the volume was adjusted to low, and then peered through the scope.

From the sniper's last communication, it sounded as if there were three others, which meant he was dealing with a four-man team, just as in Paris and Spain.

As he began panning the area with the scope, the lights in the guesthouse suddenly went out.

"Come on. Where are you?" he whispered as he snugged the stock tighter into his shoulder.

For a fraction of a second, he was gripped by a fear that maybe the hitters were wearing gear that canceled their heat signature, but he soon saw the colored glow of a figure approaching the guesthouse from the northwest, carrying what looked like a suppressed tactical rifle.

To make a perfect shot at this range required a certain amount of data, most of which Harvath would have to guess at.

Bullets drop over distance, so he elevated his point of aim in order to correlate the point of impact. The breeze would blow the bullet slightly off trajectory, plus his target was moving, which meant he needed to aim not where the man was but where he was going to be when the bullet arrived.

He made the calculations instantaneously and adjusted the rifle. Exhaling, he pressed the trigger. The bullet spat from the weapon, raced toward the target, and *missed*.

He had no idea where it hit, but it was close enough to cause the man running toward the guesthouse to pull up short, turn his head, and look directly in his direction.

"Damn it," Harvath said aloud, as he cycled the bolt and chambered another round. Repeating the process, he recalculated and was preparing to fire when the target took off running. "Damn it," he muttered again.

Exhaling, Harvath anticipated where the man was going to be, readjusted his aim, and fired. This time the bullet was spot-on.

Before the man's body even hit the ground, Harvath had cycled the bolt and was scanning for the other two. He picked up his second target, also carrying a weapon and closing in on the guesthouse from the south. Taking aim, he exhaled once more and pressed the trigger.

The bullet connected with the man's torso, and he went down but only to one knee.

Harvath pulled back the bolt, ejected the spent casing, and drove it home, advancing the next round.

The target was trying to get to his feet when Harvath fired again, this time nailing him right in the head.

He looked back through the scope at his first target, who was lying facedown on the ground and hadn't moved, and then began searching for number four. Seconds ticked by.

The radio had been silent, which meant that unless the fourth man had seen his colleagues gunned down, he had no idea what was going on. Harvath kept searching for him, but he was nowhere to be seen. That could only mean that he was coming up on the guesthouse from behind. Harvath needed to warn Nicholas.

Identifying the windows of the master bedroom, Harvath aimed high and fired one round into the room, following it immediately with a second.

He then threw the levers of the scope mount, detached the device from the top of the weapon, and ran toward the guesthouse.

CHAPTER 40

Get behind the bed, lie down, and don't move," Nicholas said.

"Why won't you tell me what's going on?" Nina implored. "It's the people who killed Caroline, isn't it?"

"I don't know what's going on. The power fluctuated a little while ago. This may be nothing."

"Which is why you have me in here, along with the your dogs and a gun?"

"Shhhhh," he said. "You need to be quiet, Nina. Please."

The young woman did as he asked and the room fell silent. The dogs knew something was wrong and stood staring at the closed bedroom door, their ears alert, their noses sniffing the air for any foreign scent. Draco was the first to begin growling. Something had caught his attention.

As Argos joined him, two rounds pierced the bedroom's upper window. Nina shrieked but quickly muffled her scream by clapping her hand to her mouth.

Nicholas shuffled over to her. "I've changed my mind. Stay as low to the floor as you can and get to the bathroom. Crawl into the tub and stay there. Don't move until I come for you."

Nina nodded as he raised his weapon and took aim at the bedroom door. The dogs were growling louder, and he could tell someone was in the house now.

"*Stoy,*" he whispered to them sternly in Russian. *Stay!* "*Tzeeha.*" *Quiet!*

Harvath knew that Nicholas was armed. He wouldn't reenter the guesthouse without announcing himself. Somebody else had come in.

The little man glanced around quickly and came up with a plan. After positioning the dogs and ordering them to be quiet, he took his hiding place. The field of view was terrible, but at least he was concealed and would hopefully have the element of surprise on his side. If only he had his .45 as well.

Clutching the tiny M3, Nicholas felt his heart pounding in his chest and tried to slow it down. He took one deep breath after another. He was about to take in his fourth when a hail of bullets ripped through the door and the drywall beside it. There were sparks and the sounds of hisses and pops as the rounds chewed up the extensive computer setup. As soon as the shooting had begun, it stopped.

Nicholas knew he should breathe, but he couldn't bring himself to, for fear of giving away his location. Instead, he gripped his weapon tighter while he prayed that none of the rounds had found Nina or the dogs.

The seconds ticked by, and he half wondered if maybe the attacker had moved on to the other rooms, but he knew better; especially when the knob turned and the door slowly swung open.

He braced himself for some sort of distraction device. He had heard that the effects of a flashbang, or stun grenade, could be mitigated by closing your eyes, jamming your fingers into your ears, and opening your mouth slightly to equalize the pressure, which is what he did.

He counted to three, and when nothing happened, he opened his eyes and looked. The first thing he saw was a suppressor, quickly followed by a fraction of a barrel and then a short handguard. Soon the entire weapon appeared, as well as the person holding it.

The attacker crept cautiously into the room, sweeping his rifle from side to side.

Two more steps, Nicholas said to himself. *Two more steps.*

The attacker took one, and was about to take another, when something suddenly made him stop.

Don't stop. Just one more step.

But the man turned and started going in another direction. He was going toward the bathroom. Nicholas had to do something.

Cracking the lid of the empty equipment case he was hiding in, he raised his weapon. *Come back this way,* he silently pleaded, but the attacker had made up his mind.

In three more steps, Nicholas would lose sight of him. A shot from this angle wouldn't be lethal, but it was all he had. Steadying himself, he lined up his weapon.

The .22 rounds came flying out of the little gun, hitting the attacker in his rump and the back of his left leg. He screamed in pain and spun to face his assailant. As he did, Nicholas yelled in Russian for the dogs.

As soon as the attacker turned and began trying to get a fix on who had shot him, the dogs burst from the bathroom door.

Argos leapt into the air and onto the man's back as Draco attacked his wounded left leg. Together they brought him right to the floor and began tearing him apart.

In his fall, the man had lost his rifle, and Nicholas rushed from his hiding place just in time to see him draw a knife. Raising his weapon, he angled for a shot, but the dogs were all over him. He didn't want to shoot one of his own animals.

As the man's hand reached out and was just about to slice, Nicholas raced in front of the blade and used his weapon to parry the blow. There was the distinct clang of metal hitting metal, the force of which knocked Nicholas to the ground and made him fumble the little M3.

The man, still screaming while Argos and Draco mauled him, raised his knife again and prepared to bring it down. Nicholas found himself directly in its path. He tried to recover his weapon, at least to block the blade, if nothing else, but he knew he wasn't going to be fast enough.

With no other choice, he grasped the hot barrel of his gun just as a muffled pop made the attacker's knife fall to the floor, accompanied by a spray of blood and an even more powerful scream.

Scooting away from the man as he brought his weapon to bear, Nicholas looked up to see Nina, eyes wide with fear, grasping the attacker's rifle.

CHAPTER 41

Carlton squinted at the cheap motel alarm clock before picking up the vibrating cell phone beside his bed. He'd given the number to just one person, and it was to be used only in a life-or-death emergency. Flipping it open and raising it to his ear, he said, "Go ahead."

It was Banks, and he spoke in code. "It looks like someone has figured out you're up and around and has ordered you one of those fancy Western neckties."

A Be-On-The-Lookout, or *BOLO,* was out for him. Whoever these people were, they were now using law enforcement to help cast a wider net. "How long ago?"

"Around midnight." Banks replied. "I just learned about it."

"What's in it?"

Banks gave him the breakdown. They had a recent picture and his physical stats, but they didn't have a description of his vehicle or a plate number. Small consolation; they'd have them soon enough. Their focus would begin inside Virginia and spread out from there. As local law enforcement made the rounds of different hotels and motels, eventually they'd pinpoint where he'd been. Then it would be only a matter of time until they came up with his Jeep. He'd have to get rid of it.

"Anything else?" Carlton asked. He was already out of bed and shoving his few belongings into a small duffel. As soon as the call was over, he would disassemble the phone and scatter the pieces. It was no longer safe to use.

"I'm close on something. Just waiting for confirmation. When I have it, I'll drop it in the box."

"Understood."

"In the meantime, watch your ass," said Banks. "There's a whole bunch more eyeballs in the game now."

"You too," replied Carlton. "And as soon as we hang up, nuke whatever phone you used to call me on."

"I'm way ahead of you. Don't worry." With that, he disconnected the call.

Carlton removed the battery from the phone, pulled out the SIM card, and snapped the device in two at the hinges. After a careful sweep of his room, he turned out the lights and approached the window. Peering from behind the drapes, he looked out onto the parking lot. There was no sign of movement.

Tucking his 1911 into his waistband, he slipped on his coat, zipped up his bag, and gave the parking lot one last check before stepping outside.

The only way he was going to get a new vehicle that couldn't be traced to him was to steal one, and he ran the limited options through his mind as he unlocked the Jeep and climbed in. He powered up his laptop and set it on the passenger seat. McDonald's offered free WiFi, and there was one about two miles up the road. He backed out of the motel parking lot and headed in its direction.

Carlton had been taught early in his career that the most important factor in stealing a car was to steal one nobody was going to notice was gone, or at least not right away. For decades, spooks had been fond of haunting long-term parking lots. All you had to do was wait until someone showed up, parked, and got on the shuttle bus. As soon as the bus pulled away, you went to work. But that was then.

While some in the business still favored this method, Carlton disliked it for several reasons. With the surge in technology, most cars had sophisticated electrical systems that made them all but immune to hotwiring unless you had very specific tools, which Carlton didn't. That meant he needed an older vehicle. There was no telling how long he'd have to sit in a remote lot before the right car showed up. The longer he waited, the greater the temptation was to settle for a vehicle that had already been parked for an indeterminate amount of time. Giving in meant you could end up snatching a vehicle whose owner might be returning from their trip at any minute.

The biggest strike against stealing a car from a long-term lot, though, was the security. Spies weren't the only ones who liked the pickings in these lots; so did professional car thieves, so operators of long-term lots took great pains to deter thefts. In short, it just wasn't worth it; especially when there was a much better option available.

Pulling into a lot across the street from the McDonald's, Carlton logged onto their WiFi network, opened his browser, and plugged in his search terms. In less than a second, the results came back, along with a map studded with five digital pins. He browsed the website for each facility and then conducted cyber surveillance using the map's street view feature. Of the five, only one met all the criteria on his list. After computing his route, he turned off the computer and got back on the road.

Since his last meeting with Banks, he had all but resigned himself to the fact that he wouldn't be able to sort out the conspiracy he was embroiled in with brainpower alone. It was just too vast, and there were too many empty spaces, too many question marks. Whoever had set their sights on him and his people had incredible pull at an extremely high level. He still had no idea what the stakes were, or what they were planning, but he knew it had to be something big. That meant that the people involved would be excruciatingly careful.

It also meant that they likely had operational experience in this area. Banks had agreed with him on that. To create and execute a lie of this magnitude and to weave it with multiple murders, its architects had to be intimately familiar with Washington. They had to know its ins and outs. They had to know every card in the deck, how each was played, and how they could slip their own card in without anyone being the wiser. That meant one thing—these people were, or at one point had been, true insiders.

They would need firsthand knowledge of and connections within the intelligence community and the three branches of government. Then there was the military component.

Only highly trained, highly specialized personnel could have taken out his operators. These weren't simply contract killers. It wouldn't be impossible to put together a list, and Carlton had begun to do so. They could have come from only a handful of elite units around the world—the British, maybe Russians, possibly the Australians. To pull it all off with such precision meant that they were highly disciplined, which was yet another reason he leaned toward the killers having military experience.

He also had to consider that American Special Operations Forces had been used—that was harder to swallow, though. The SOF community was small and very tightly knit. Unless the kill teams were comprised of morally bankrupt men who had washed out of the Special Forces community, he couldn't envision American operators turning on their fellows. It just didn't make sense. Nevertheless, he couldn't rule anything out.

The questions kept spinning in his mind as he drove. The scope of the entire thing was so vast that he couldn't help but wonder if he was looking at a coup of some sort. It was the only framework upon which he could hang the few pieces he'd gathered and not have them fall apart. Why else take such an ultimate risk? Why lay everything on the line like this?

Carlton had seen enough to know that such plots existed. His own group had been instrumental in stopping one of the most sophisticated coups he'd ever encountered. Was this plot somehow connected? Was it simply another prong of an attack that they had failed to uncover?

He was suddenly consumed by the feeling that he might not be that far off base. A tuning fork had been struck somewhere inside his brain and the note was now resonating outward.

Here they had been striking at every snake that slithered out of the darkness, but what if those snakes weren't random? What if they were actually part of a many-headed Hydra?

Had Carlton and his team been so successful at chopping off the heads that the monster had no choice but to turn its attention on them and attack? The more he thought about it, the more the idea solidified in his mind. If he was right, then he was left with only two options. Either he forced the monster out into the daylight, or he tracked it into the darkness and fought it there. Whatever path he chose, he had little doubt that it would be one of the most dangerous assignments he had ever gone after.

He spent the rest of the drive obsessed with the Hydra image, trying to interlace all the snakes his people had killed and looking for a common denominator.

When he arrived at the retirement community on the outskirts of Richmond, his focus changed. It was a semirural area with a forest preserve about a mile away. Driving past his target, he pulled into the lot for the forest preserve and parked.

From the toolbox in the back of the Cherokee he removed a hammer, two screwdrivers, wire cutters, rubber gloves, a slim jim, and a thin roll of electrical tape. He placed the items in a small pack and then struck off through the woods for the retirement community.

It was a sprawling facility on several acres that incorporated a variety of buildings. This wasn't some shady nursing home where ungrateful children dumped their aging parents. With its manicured grounds and stylish architecture, it looked more like a high-end resort.

The community offered options from villas and condos all the way to assisted living and hospice care. All told, there were more than two hundred units. Carlton felt confident he'd find what he was looking for here. Less than ten minutes into his search, he did.

From the day people become old enough to drive, till the day they die, a car represented freedom and independence. Which was one of the reasons many aging drivers found it so difficult to give up their cars. Many, out of sentimentality or the refusal to admit they had grown too old, held on to their vehicles long after they stopped driving. As long as he chose correctly, it could be months, if ever, before the car's owner noticed it was missing and alerted authorities.

Making his way down the rows of vehicles in the open carport behind the facility, he spotted an aging Cadillac with slightly tinted windows. Based on the dust alone, he could tell it hadn't been driven in some time.

He gave it a quick once-over. Not only was the tire pressure passable, the license plates were still valid. The only concern that remained was whether the battery still carried a charge.

He slid the slim jim inside the rubber seal of the driver's door and popped up the lock. As he opened the door, he was greeted by the dome light coming on, which meant the battery did in fact have juice. Climbing inside, he turned the light off, closed the door, and removed a small penlight from his pocket. He looked through the car to see if its owner had left a spare key, but there was none to be found.

Placing the penlight in his mouth and slipping the flathead screwdriver into the ignition, Carlton gave it a strong tap with the hammer and attempted to turn it like a key. While it would ruin the ignition cylinder, it was often all that was necessary to get many older cars started. In this case, though, it didn't work, so he pulled the flathead out and went to plan B.

Using the Phillips head, he removed the screws that attached the plastic panels together around the steering column and pried them away to expose the ignition cylinder and the wires running into it.

Ducking down, he identified the set of wires running to the battery, as well as those going to the starter. Slipping on the rubber dishwashing gloves, he picked up the wire cutters and clipped the power wires running to the cylinder.

He stripped the ends and twisted them together to begin the flow of power. Next he cut the starter wires, stripped the ends, and made sure not to touch them with his hands, lest he get a healthy shock.

Holding an exposed starter wire in each hand, he took a breath and brought them together. The Cadillac groaned, but seconds later, its large engine roared to life.

Carlton separated the starter wires from each other, tore off two pieces of electrical tape, and wrapped each exposed end.

After quickly replacing the panels around the steering column, he stashed his tools in the glove compartment, put the car in drive, and quietly drove out of the retirement community.

Back at the forest preserve, he transferred his gear from the Cherokee into the trunk of the Cadillac and then drove the Jeep down a long fire road.

In the bouncing beam of his headlights, he spotted a narrow break in the trees and took it. He drove as far as he could and then turned off the ignition. In case anyone should stumble across it, he left a quickly scrawled note: *Hiking, be back soon.*

He walked back out through the trees and up the fire road to the Cadillac. As he pulled out of the forest, his mind returned to the image of the Hydra, and he began to plan what he needed to do next.

CHAPTER 42

After checking the two figures outside and seeing that they were both dead, Harvath slipped inside the guesthouse. From the direction of the master bedroom, he could hear a man's agonized cries. Thankfully, the voice was much too deep to belong to Nicholas.

Creeping forward and using the thermal scope, his weapon up and at the ready, Harvath made it about half the distance before Draco charged into the hallway and started barking. The dog's muzzle looked to be dripping with blood and its eyes were wild, as if it had gone feral. He gave no indication that he recognized Harvath. In fact, he looked primed to attack.

"Easy, boy," he said softly, but the dog continued barking and moving forward. He didn't want to hurt the animal, but he also didn't want to give himself away if he didn't have to by calling out.

The standoff was quickly broken by Nicholas's voice from inside the room. "Who's there?" he called out.

"Rubber Duckie," Harvath replied, knowing you never answered "me" to a who-goes-there question.

The little man shouted a command in Russian, and the dog ceased barking and returned to the bedroom. Harvath kept his pistol up and pulled it into his chest as he followed.

He stopped at the edge of the doorframe and lowered the scope. A faint glow spilled out the door into the hall, and again he heard a man's cries. "Are you okay?"

"Yes," Nicholas responded. "You can come in."

Harvath did a snap peek around the corner before stepping fully into the doorway. A man in his mid-twenties lay on the floor, covered in blood. Argos, whose snout was also covered in blood, stood nearby. Much of Nicholas's computer equipment had been shot to pieces. A badly damaged laptop still gave off enough light to see by.

Draco stood alongside Nicholas, who was covering the wounded attacker with his little M3. There was no sign of Nina. Harvath was about to ask what had happened to her when he heard the sound of vomiting from the bathroom.

He stepped into the room and trained his pistol on the young man bleeding all over the floor. The dogs had torn him to shreds. From where he stood, Harvath doubted he'd make it.

"Are you all okay?" he repeated to Nicholas.

"Nina's shook up, but we're okay."

Harvath removed the tiny .45-caliber pistol from his pocket and tossed it to him. "Here," he said. "Cover him with this."

Nicholas transitioned to the more powerful pistol and did as Harvath instructed.

As he approached the kid on the floor, he motioned for Nicholas to call off Argos.

"No," Nicholas argued. "He came to kill us. Let the dogs finish the bastard."

Harvath glared at him. "Keep those dogs back. That's an order."

Nicholas relented, issuing a command in Russian, and the dog retreated to his side.

Harvath looked down at the attacker and decided he wouldn't need his pistol. Tucking it into his jeans at the small of his back, he bent over and lifted the kid into a sitting position against the side of the bed.

It was a messy operation. When Harvath finally got him into place and drew back his hands, they were slick with blood.

The extent of the kid's injuries was very grave. His face had been savaged, and the dogs had done incredible damage to his limbs, as well as his groin area, and his throat looked like raw hamburger. Harvath was amazed he could make any sound at all. There was a wet whooshing noise that could be heard beneath the moaning as the man labored to take in oxygen. The fact that he hadn't slipped totally into shock was incredible.

"You're in bad shape," Harvath said gently. "I've got a trauma kit and will do what I can, but before I can help you, I need you to answer some questions. Who are you? Who sent you here?"

The kid's eyes were glassy and unfocused. His breathing was coming in gasps. There was a gurgle as he coughed up a mouthful of blood.

"He's not going to answer you," Nicholas replied. "Let me put the dogs on him."

Argos and Draco began growling again.

"I'm not telling you again," Harvath snapped. "Keep those dogs under control." Turning his attention back to their prisoner, he said, "It's up to you. I've got pain meds as well. We can stabilize you and get you to a hospital. It's your call. Just tell me who you are and who sent you."

The kid was dressed like his dead comrades outside. He wore 511 trousers, tactical boots, and an ill-fitting sweatshirt likely taken off one of the men he and his team had murdered at the water trough. On his wrist was a military-version Suunto watch, popular with SOF guys. He had short, dark hair and a fit build. Under different circumstances, he could have been some young SEAL or Green Beret Harvath had trained or operated alongside at some point in his career.

He waited for the kid to say something, but nothing came, so Harvath said, "All of the men I worked with were good, honorable men who had shed blood for their country. They're dead now, murdered by the same people who sent you here to kill us."

It caused the kid a lot of pain, but he tilted his head and rolled his eyes up to meet Harvath's. He was no longer moaning. His pupils were beginning to dilate.

"Whatever they told you, they lied," Harvath said. "You were used. This has to end here, now. If you help me, no one else has to die."

Moments passed. When the kid opened his mouth to speak, blood-soaked air rattled in and out of his lungs. The words that formed on his shredded lips were barely discernible, and Harvath had to lean down to make them out.

"Bremmer," the young man rasped. "Chuck Bremmer."

Harvath thought he recognized the name from when he was attached to the President's Secret Service detail. There had been a special Defense Department liaison to the White House named Bremmer. "Are you talking about Colonel Chuck Bremmer?"

There was no response. The kid had gone into agonal respiration, or "guppy breathing," and was gasping in very short, rapid breaths.

Harvath repeated his question, searching the young man's face for any sign of acknowledgment. All he got back was a cold, glassy-eyed stare. Seconds later, the guppy breathing stopped.

Harvath checked his pulse. He was dead.

CHAPTER 43

Coordinating with Nicholas as he cleaned up, Harvath rattled off a list of instructions before driving away in the Denali. It was the early hours of Sunday morning and the majority of the staff was still hitting the bars in town. He had posted Maggie Rose up the road to make sure none of them came back onto the property into the middle of a potential gunfight. Now that that danger had passed, there was something else he needed her to do.

Her truck was parked along the shoulder of the road and he pulled into the oncoming lane so they could talk driver's side to driver's side.

Her words tumbled out in a rapid cascade. "Are you okay? Is everybody else okay?"

Harvath reached his hand through his open window so he could place it on her arm. "Everyone's fine. Don't worry."

Maggie was expecting an explanation of what had happened, some sort of summary, but it didn't come. It took a moment for that to sink in.

Harvath could tell she was confused. "Maggie, listen," he said. "The less you know the better. Okay? The men who came onto the ranch aren't a problem anymore. Let's just leave it at that."

"What does that mean?"

He smiled, trying to reassure her. "It means there's nothing to worry about. Okay?"

Still confused, Maggie simply nodded.

"Good. Now, is there someone whose computer you could use right now? Someone not associated with the ranch?"

She looked at her watch before responding. "I think so."

Harvath searched the truck for a piece of paper and something to write with. When he found them, he scribbled down a Web address and several strings of numbers. Handing it to her, he explained what he wanted her to do.

Maggie listened, studying what looked like a list of serial numbers, and repeated back his instructions. "That's it?" she ended by saying.

"That's it," Harvath replied. "When you get the confirmation, write it down and then come back to the ranch."

Maggie checked her watch again. "What are you ordering anyway, in the middle of the night? I don't understand. How do you even know somebody will be there to get it?"

"They'll be there. Don't worry."

She shrugged her shoulders and nodded her head. "The bars will be closing soon. What do you want to do about the staff coming back?"

"As long as they steer clear of the guesthouse, we'll be okay."

"They will. They may continue drinking in one of their casitas, but you won't see any of them on the main property until morning."

"What about you? How long until you're back?"

She thought about it for a moment. "I have some friends who live about halfway into town. Figure it'll take me about twenty minutes to get there, twenty minutes back, plus however long it takes me to roust them out of bed and place your order. Are you sure I can't call to give them a heads-up?"

Harvath shook his head. "No. Don't use the phone. In fact, I want you to take the battery out of your cell phone right now."

He watched as Maggie shook her head and did as he asked. "Thank you," he said. "Don't stop for anything. I'll see you in about an hour."

Without waiting for a response, he then put the truck in gear, pulled a U-turn, and headed back to the ranch.

When he got there, he parked in back of the vehicle storage building. He would have to work fast.

A set of tall double doors led into a wide concrete bay with stainless steel tables, overhead cable hoists, gambrel systems, and a narrow channel that fed into multiple floor drains. Off to the side of the game-processing area was the walk-in freezer.

He spotted a game cart and in a cabinet behind it, a stack of large game bags. After tracking down an apron and a pair of heavy rubber gloves, he exited the building, loaded everything into the Denali, and headed back toward the guesthouse.

His first stop was the stand of maples. The sniper was right where he had left him. Dead weight was always a pain in the ass to move, and he hadn't been able to get the truck right up close. After slipping on the apron and the rubber gloves, he packed the corpse in a game bag and used the cart to wheel it over to the Denali.

Bending down, he slung the body over his right shoulder, stood up, and manhandled it in the cargo area. The two other corpses adjacent to the guesthouse were just as difficult. Pulling up next to each of the men, he mummy-wrapped them in game bags and hefted them into the SUV, then made sure he had gathered up all of their weapons. The last thing he had to take care of was the body inside the guesthouse.

Stepping inside, he found Nicholas and, surprisingly, Nina—who'd moved past her emetic horror—hard at work in the master bedroom.

The pair had already packed up Nicholas's salvageable gear and stacked it along the east wall. Next to the nightstand were a mop, a bucket, and various cleaning products from the kitchen pantry.

Neither Nicholas nor Nina had done anything with the corpse of the last attacker, not that Harvath had expected them to. Nicholas was too small, and Nina wasn't cut out for that kind of work. The man remained as he had died, propped up against the bed. One of them had draped a sheet over him. Where the blood had seeped through, it caused the sheet to cling and mold itself to those parts of the corpse.

"About that," Nicholas said, seeing Harvath looking at the shrouded body.

Harvath held up his gloved hand. "I'll take care of it. Just finish what you need to do."

"What should we do about my damaged equipment?"

"Leave it. We're only taking what we absolutely have to," he replied. "I'll ask Maggie to get rid of the rest. Is any of it traceable?"

"No," said Nicholas. "It's all clean and I've already pulled the drives."

"What about Caroline's flash drive?"

The little man tapped his right front pocket. "Good to go."

Harvath stepped over to the bathroom and held the door for Nina. "I'll try to be as quick as I can. You may want to wait in here."

He didn't need to tell her why he wanted her out of the room for a few moments. She knew what his role was the minute he appeared with the gloves and the butcher's apron.

Once she had stepped into the bathroom, he closed the door, retrieved the game cart he had left in the hallway, and wheeled it in.

"What are you going to do with the bodies?" Nicholas asked.

"If we had time, we'd drive them to a remote corner of the ranch, dig the biggest hole we could, and cap it with a thick layer of cement."

"And seeing as how we don't have time?"

"Plan B."

Nicholas didn't bother to ask what plan B was. Instead, he stood back and watched as Harvath tucked the corpse into a game bag and cinched it shut. Hefting the body onto the cart, he said, "Get Nina to help you pile whatever gear you're taking near the front door. As soon as that's done, scrub the hell out of the floor. Make sure there isn't a drop of blood left anywhere in here."

The little man put on a good show, but Harvath could tell that, like Maggie, he was a bit shaken. Nicholas flashed him a thumbs-up, and Harvath disappeared through the door, wheeling the last corpse.

Outside, he hoisted the body into the back of the SUV with the others and returned to the guesthouse. As fast as Nicholas and Nina could stack the Storm cases near the front door, Harvath snatched them up and piled them on the roof. He ran a length of cord through the handles and secured them all to the rack. After giving everything a quick tug to make sure it would remain in place, he took off for the recreation building.

CHAPTER 44

Daylight was still two hours off when the first strains of the Pilatus PC-12 turboprop aircraft began to be heard circling above the ranch.

Harvath flashed the lights of the Denali. Maggie threw the switch and illuminated the landing strip. The pair had already said their good-byes, and Harvath had coached her on how to report the bodies at the trough. She was savvy enough to understand why he didn't want her watching him loading the plane. It was for her own good.

After the white-and-blue aircraft touched down, it turned around at the end of the runway and taxied back to where the party was standing.

Pulling up alongside their stack of gear, the plane came to a stop and its single turbine engine spun down. After the main door was opened and the air stairs unfolded, a clean-shaven man in his early fifties stepped out.

He had thick brown hair and was wearing a denim shirt, khakis, and a pair of work boots. He studied the group amassed beside the runway, along with their gear and the two enormous white dogs, then gave Harvath a wave.

Harvath waved back and watched as the sinewy pilot descended the stairs.

The man crossed the tarmac and Harvath stuck his hand out. "Thanks for coming, Mike."

The pilot wrapped him in a bear hug and lifted him off the ground. "You're damn right I came. I always told you I would. I just didn't think it'd be in the middle of the night." Letting go, he stood back in order to take everyone in again. "Good Lord, if this isn't a great group of passengers." Looking down at Nicholas he added, "How the heck are you doing? You ready to go flying?"

Mike Strieber was a character. Quick to tell a joke, as well as to find the humor in any kind of situation, his happy-go-lucky personality was infectious.

Born and raised in San Antonio, he had joined the Marines after securing his engineering degree, because he wanted to kick ass *and* fly planes. He flew all sorts of aircraft before deciding that it wasn't planes he really wanted to fly but helicopters. In his indomitable fashion, Strieber went after his new goal with everything he had.

As it turned out, he made an excellent helo pilot and was eventually tasked to Marine Helicopter Squadron One, also known as HMX-1, the squadron responsible for flying the President, Vice President, cabinet members, and other VIPs. It was while Harvath was on the President's Secret Service detail that he and Strieber had met and become friends.

When Strieber retired from the Marines and HMX-1, he decided to return to his engineering roots. He had an idea for a tactical flashlight that he thought might be pretty good. Once again, he went after his goal with everything he had and created quite a name for himself.

Strieber flashlights, as well as a very creative line of knives he had begun producing, were in such demand with the military, police, and private citizens, that Mike ran his people and his fabricating shop around the clock. With U.S. troops deployed in so many different time zones, he always made sure he had someone checking their website and e-mails 24/7. He was fanatical about customer service. It was just the way he was and his success reaffirmed it. Harvath had had no doubt that the coded message he'd scribbled down for Maggie would get through to him. The words may not have made any sense to her, nor did the latitude and longitude coordinates that looked like serial numbers, but Mike had had no problem figuring it all out.

"So, where are we off to?" Strieber asked. He said it cheerfully, as if Harvath was his biggest client and he was eager to keep him happy.

Harvath waved him over to the Denali and showed him the game bags in the cargo area. "I'm going to need to get rid of these."

Strieber didn't need to have the bags unzipped to guess what was inside. "You know when I told you that joke about how a friend will help you move, but a *real* friend will help you move a body, I was only kidding, right?"

"I wouldn't ever want to put you in a bad spot, Mike, but these guys killed a bunch of people tonight and they tried to kill me. They got what was coming to them."

Strieber knew enough about Harvath's time with the SEALs, as well as what he had been doing since leaving the White House and the Secret Service, not to ask a lot of questions. "Should I assume this is official business, then?"

Harvath nodded.

"Okay," Strieber replied. "After we dispose of your dirty laundry, what else do you need from me?"

Harvath gestured to Nicholas, Nina, and the dogs and said, "I'm hoping you can put them up for a little bit. Someplace safe."

"I think we can do that. What about you?"

"I'll fill you in after we take off."

The answers were good enough for Mike. Sizing up the passengers, their gear, and everything Harvath had in the Denali, Strieber began making calculations about weight distribution and takeoff.

Harvath suggested that Nina and Nicholas climb aboard with the dogs, and then he and Mike got to work.

Twenty minutes later, the plane was loaded. Once Strieber had completed his preflight check, he gave him the thumbs-up. Harvath climbed into the plane behind him, retracted the air stairs, and secured the cabin door. He made sure Nicholas, Nina, and the dogs were all set before walking forward into the cockpit and taking the copilot's seat.

As he slipped on his headset, Strieber asked, "Are we all ready?"

"We're ready," Harvath replied.

Minutes later, they were at the far end of the runway and Mike was feeding power to the aircraft's enormous engine. It felt like sitting astride a thoroughbred in the starting gate. The muscular plane was vibrating and seemed to be itching to take off.

"Here we go," he said as he released the brakes, and the aircraft began racing down the runway.

Harvath watched the gauges as the speed rapidly increased. Finally, Strieber pulled back on the yoke and the sleek bird lifted off.

They headed south and then changed course and headed east toward the ocean.

The cloud cover was high enough that Strieber was flying VFR, or Visual Flight Rules, which meant that he didn't need to file a flight plan and there'd be no record of where he'd been.

Harvath pulled a map and balanced it on his lap. Using a red-filtered flashlight that Mike had handed him, so as not to ruin their night vision, he traced his finger along the coast and asked a series of questions.

"It's up to you," Strieber answered. "I guess it just depends on how soon you want the bodies found."

Harvath wanted it to take as long as possible, if they were ever found at all. That left them with two choices. They could either drop them in the marshy South Bay near the border or out over the Gulf of Mexico. Harvath didn't have enough information about the currents to know if dumping them in the ocean would result in them washing up in Texas or Mexico. Either way, the deaths would be chalked up to cartel violence. The only difference was that U.S. authorities would conduct at least a pro forma investigation, while the Mexicans very likely wouldn't bother. Harvath opted for the South Bay.

Mike explained how he'd make his approach and then gave instructions on where he wanted Nicholas, Nina, and the dogs while Harvath carried out his task. Harvath unbuckled himself from his seat, walked back in the plane, and got everything into position.

Using some of Mike's gear, he fashioned a rigger's belt and secured himself with a long enough tether to the inside of the aircraft. Back at the ranch, he had filleted each of the bodies from the pubic bone up to the sternum, slicing through their intestines. It was the only way for the gases inside the corpses to escape. If he hadn't, they would bloat and float to the surface. While working, he noticed that two of the men had crude tattoos similar to those he had noticed on the attacker in Spain.

After placing the bodies back in the game bags and reinforcing them with duct tape, he knotted heavy nylon cord around their ankles.

Stacked at the back of the plane were eight, forty-five-pound plates that he had taken from the ranch's exercise room. He tied ninety pounds' worth of weight to the ankles of each corpse, pierced the game bags in order to allow excess gases to escape, and relayed a message forward that he was ready.

Strieber decreased the plane's altitude and brought it around in a wide, sweeping arc. As they neared the bay, he signaled for Harvath to open the rear utility door.

The slipstream and the roar of the engine were deafening. Salty sea air swept into the fuselage as the aircraft descended even farther. Waiting for the last signal, Harvath kept his eyes forward. Twenty seconds later, Mike pointed his flashlight into the cabin, fired a series of rapid blinks, and Harvath shoved the first body out the door.

CHAPTER 45

Information was knowledge, and knowledge was power. By having access to every scrap of information, Craig Middleton was able to amass unlimited power. It gave him and his inner circle at ATS control over everything—money, politicians, and, whenever necessary, whether people lived or died. Middleton had always felt in control. Always, that was, until now.

Things had been going perfectly until Caroline Romero. He'd made a mistake sending his own security people after her. They'd botched the job, she had been killed, and they'd failed to recover the hard drive. He had no idea how much she had learned, but he had to assume that whatever she had uncovered, it would spell disaster for him and for ATS. That couldn't be allowed to happen. It was imperative to get the drive back at all costs.

Discovering that the lingerie shop had sent a package to Romero's sister had been a big break, but it hadn't come soon enough. By the time Bremmer had gotten his team down there, the sister had disappeared. Middleton had a pretty good feeling that it wasn't just underwear that had been mailed in that box. Caroline had sent her the flash drive as well.

She had also instructed her sister on how to remain hidden. Nina Jensen had abandoned her apartment, her job, her credit cards and cell phone. She hadn't contacted any friends or family. But based on the surveillance Bremmer's men had conducted at the ranch, she had managed to link up with Carlton's dwarf, as well as with Scot Harvath.

These were two streams Middleton would never have imagined intersecting. The nexus had to be Caroline. At some point she and the Troll must have become acquainted. She got the flash drive to her sister, and the little computer hacker followed not long after. He was likely the one who had reached out to Harvath and had drawn him to Texas. The fact that they had all managed to stay off the grid was significant. Had it not been for the ranch manager's Google search, they might have completely slipped through the net.

Two teams had been sent after Harvath, and both had failed. This time, Bremmer had instructed the Texas team to place one man in an overwatch position to act as a sniper. Middleton had pressed for details, but the Colonel didn't have much more to provide. The team would complete their surveillance and assemble their own assault plan. They understood that they were not to kill the girl until she gave up the flash drive. If they needed to torture her to get it, they were authorized to do so. Once they took physical possession of it, all three subjects were to be terminated.

After the hit, the team would put as much distance between themselves and the scene as possible. At some point, they would make contact. Bremmer would then detail how he wanted them to deliver the drive.

Middleton had not been able to sleep. He knew the assault would happen sometime in the early-morning hours. He had no way of knowing if the sister had secreted the drive somewhere, but he doubted it. In all likelihood she had it with her at the ranch. He hoped that the third attempt on Harvath would be the charm, but as the night wore on and Bremmer failed to report in, Middleton became more apprehensive.

As he poured himself another scotch, his mind turned to another of his problems, Reed Carlton. The aging spook was a slippery old fox. How he'd made it out of the inferno that had been set at his home was a complete mystery. Bremmer's men had been lying in wait, ready to take him out if he managed to escape his master bedroom, which had been locked down tighter than a drum. None of Bremmer's team had seen anyone leave the house. Everyone assumed Carlton had been consumed by the blaze. Yet when the smoke literally cleared, he was nowhere to be seen. He had completely vanished.

And while Middleton liked the idea of the BOLO being put out on him, he had his reservations about the efficacy of some law enforcement officer stumbling across a man who'd been trained by the best and had spent decades slipping in and out of hostile countries around the world.

Carlton and Harvath seemed to be cut from the same cloth. Both had been able to slip Bremmer's kill teams. Taking control of Carlton's Skype account had been a clever way to pinpoint Harvath, but in hindsight, Middleton wondered if they shouldn't have waited until the old spy had been confirmed dead. Maybe they could have used the account to lure both of them into a trap.

He was Monday-morning-quarterbacking himself and he knew it. They had every reason to believe that Carlton had died in that fire. When Harvath had popped up on Skype, they would have been foolish not to jump at the chance they had.

Leaning back in one of the leather club chairs in his study, Middleton swirled the scotch in his glass. Erasing everything and starting from scratch, he rebuilt the relationship chain in his mind. *Caroline had contacted her sister. The sister had contacted the dwarf. The dwarf had contacted Harvath who had attempted to contact Carlton. And who had Carlton contacted?*

Once the coroner's report had come in, he had posed the same question to Schroeder. It made sense that in an emergency, Carlton would have secluded himself someplace he felt was safe and then would have reached out to the people best able to help protect him, his hitters.

Schroeder got on it and came back a short time later. ATS had been monitoring the cell phones of Carlton's operators. Within twenty-four hours of the fire, each had been sent a text message reading *Stock Update: Blue Petroleum, Oil & Lubricant.* It wasn't a coincidence. It had to be some sort of code.

The phone that had sent the message was still emitting a signal, and Schroeder had tracked it to a truck stop in Arizona. He tipped the Arizona

State Police, who dispatched units to the location in search of Carlton. Middleton, though, felt something wasn't right.

When the signal started moving again, Schroeder, posing as a surveillance tech from the FBI, was able to help the authorities pinpoint its source. It turned out to be an eighteen-wheeler headed toward Bakersfield, California. While the driver was being questioned, other officers scoured the rig. They eventually came up with the cell phone, which had been placed in a Ziplock bag and taped underneath. Carlton was a clever son of a bitch.

Though they assumed the phone was clean and wouldn't offer any leads, Schroeder still arranged for it to be shipped back on the first commercial airline flight in the morning.

Middleton had to hand it to the old spook. It was a halfway decent red herring. But it was also a *tell*. Carlton obviously knew that eventually the phone was going to get tagged. He'd used it only once and then dumped it. This got Middleton to thinking. *What did he do next?*

Again, he reassembled the relationship chain in his mind—*Caroline to her sister, the sister to the Troll, the Troll to Harvath, Harvath to Carlton, and Carlton to his operators.* But when his operators didn't respond, who would be next on Carlton's list? Who would he have turned to for help?

Not only ditching the phone after one use by placing it under the westbound truck but having a clean phone to begin with showed that Carlton thought ahead; that he was a tactician. This didn't surprise Middleton. It was to be expected from a man with his training. He would have known that they'd be looking at all of his relationships, which in fact they were. Carlton would have had to turn to somebody. He would want answers, and he would need help in getting them. Either he reached out to a contact who wasn't in his relationship tree, or—like Caroline—the sister, the Troll, and Harvath had found a way to communicate that didn't trip any alarm bells at ATS.

Walking over to his desk, he set his drink down and brought his computer back from sleep mode. Pulling up Carlton's relationship tree, he studied the various branches and interlocking relationships for the hundredth time. He felt certain the answer was there; he just wasn't seeing it.

Whom did he trust? More importantly, assuming that he had figured out that all of his hitters had been killed, whom did he trust with his life? Without knowing what enemy had risen against him, to whom could he turn? If it was just one person, who could help him unravel a puzzle this complex, where the stakes were so incredibly high?

Staring at the chart, Middleton excluded candidate after candidate as he delved further back into Carlton's professional career. Very likely it would be someone local; someone with exceptional contacts in D.C., who could dig for him without arousing suspicion. That suddenly brought a completely different parameter to Middleton's mind—who might fit the bill perfectly, but at the same time be the least likely candidate of all?

Middleton searched for colleagues whom Carlton had been at odds with, people he had had professional or personal run-ins with. There were a few, but not many. Nevertheless, Middleton wrote their names down.

He was about to close out of the file when he decided to give it one last perusal and aim for the absolute least likely candidate of all. As he did, he came across a name and a bell went off somewhere in his head.

Highlighting the header, Middleton opened the subfolder for Reed Carlton's mentor, Thomas "Tommy" Carver Banks.

CHAPTER 46

Mike Strieber had always enjoyed getting his hands dirty and being connected to the earth. He liked watching things grow and wanted his children to understand that food didn't magically appear at the grocery store. In addition to all the other things he'd done in his life, he'd always wanted to give farming a try. So, after finding the right location, he had purchased his own farm.

Being a pilot with his own plane meant that he could fly from San Antonio to the farm whenever he wanted. It was his private refuge, and he chose not to talk about it much. It had great water and encompassed a couple hundred acres. There were horses for his wife, Angela, a pool for the kids, and of course a shooting range. Other than that, he hadn't done much to the property. It wasn't supposed to be a Four Seasons. It was supposed to represent a simpler time in his life.

The moment Harvath saw it he loved it. But it wasn't because it was so remote. It was because of whom Mike had hired to work and run the farm.

The three young Marines were all veterans and each had seen combat in Afghanistan and Iraq. They were standing with Mrs. Strieber alongside a white Suburban and a blue Ford Super Duty pickup as Mike touched the aircraft down on the dirt strip and taxied over to them. Each had been wounded, but there was no self-pity in them at all.

When Harvath stepped out of the plane, Angela gave him a big hug. They hadn't seen each other in almost two years. She was easily Mike's better half, and Harvath reminded him of it every chance he got. She was younger, funnier, and much better looking. More importantly, she had a heart as big as Mike's, if not bigger.

After finishing her hello, she turned and introduced Harvath to the three Marines—Matt, Jason, and Ryan; all from Texas. Matt had been shot behind his left ear by a sniper while on combat patrol near Ramadi, Iraq. Jason and Ryan had both been maimed in separate IED attacks in Helmand Province, Afghanistan. Jason lost his left arm and Ryan both legs beneath the knee. Even in civilian clothes, though, they still looked like Marines and stood proud and tall.

The men took turns shaking hands with Harvath, but their attention was immediately drawn to the other passengers coming out of the aircraft. One would have thought that three men working a farm in the middle of nowhere might have been captivated by an attractive young woman like Nina Jensen, but they appeared more preoccupied by Nicholas and his two enormous dogs.

Angela reached out, punched the nearest man in the shoulder as a lesson to the others, and with a smile asked, "Didn't anyone ever teach you that it's impolite to stare?"

"Sorry, ma'am," the men said almost in unison.

Ever the hospitable Texas lady, Angela walked up to Nina, introduced herself, and then met Nicholas before he reached the bottom of the air stairs and extended her hand. "Welcome to Five Star Farm," she said. "I'm Mike's wife. Angela."

He had no idea if she had done it intentionally or not, but he liked the fact that she had made her introduction before he had fully descended the stairway. In this fashion, she wasn't looking down at him, nor was he looking up at her. They met practically eye to eye. "I'm Nicholas," he replied, shaking her hand. "I'm pleased to meet you."

"Did y'all have a good flight?"

"It was very comfortable, thank you. You have a lovely plane. I've never flown in a Pilatus before. It's like a private jet inside."

Angela Strieber placed her index finger against her lips and quickly shushed him. "We don't use those two words around here."

"Private jet? Why not?"

"Because I'd like him to retire some day. I can't afford for him to catch the jet bug."

Nicholas nodded knowingly. "You're a smart woman. There are a lot of men out there who identify themselves by having the sleekest, most expensive thing on the tarmac. But from the little I've seen of your husband, I don't think he's that type."

Mrs. Strieber winked at him and said, "No man is immune. Trust me."

Nicholas smiled and stepped down. Joining Nina, he was introduced to the three vets, who then walked over and helped Harvath and Mike unload the plane and transfer everything into the Super Duty. Angela showed Nicholas and Nina to the Suburban, and once the dogs were inside, headed off to the ranch house, where they would all rally.

Mrs. Strieber already had a pot of coffee going and pointed people to the cabinet where the mugs were stashed as everyone filed into her kitchen. Nicholas and Nina saw to the dogs and then offered to help with breakfast, but Angela politely declined and encouraged them to sit down with the others at the kitchen table. With fresh biscuits in the oven, she set to work on bacon, sausage gravy, and fried eggs.

As the aromas of the country breakfast filled the room, Mike set his coffee cup down, took a seat, and called everyone to order. He and Harvath had held an in-depth discussion on the flight in, and the first order of business was operational security. Mike explained that there was to be no communication with the outside world until further notice. The vets were given a simple cover story to e-mail or text to friends and family explaining why they'd be off-line for the next few days. Once the messages had been sent, Mike respectfully asked the men to let him hang on to their phones. While he trusted them implicitly, they had no idea what they were up against. Harvath had explained it to him on the flight in, and frankly it scared the hell out of him. Better safe than sorry.

He also requested that they retrieve their laptops from the bunkhouse and drop them off after breakfast. None of the men argued. They understood operational security. For all intents and purposes, Mike was their commanding officer. They would do as he asked. Harvath could tell by looking at them that they found the possibility of impending danger more than a little exciting.

Once the operational security details had been hashed out, Mike assigned guard shifts. Angela was given one, as was his son, who was driving up from San Antonio. The younger daughter could pull a trigger, but she was too young to stand guard by herself. Mike and Angela's elder daughter could have held her own, but she was still away at school.

Though Nicholas admirably volunteered, Harvath told him he wanted him to continue to focus on Caroline's flash drive and anything else he could draw from it. As for Nina, she didn't have much experience with firearms and therefore didn't qualify. Angela Strieber told her not to worry. There'd be plenty for her to do.

Mike then explained that he would be flying Harvath to another location and would step into the shift rotation as soon as he got back.

Mrs. Strieber laid out breakfast and the group ate heartily. When it was over, she got Nina and Nicholas installed in the house, while the vets went to work on shoring up the perimeter and Mike led Harvath to one of his pole barns.

Bolted to the concrete pad inside was an Armag Arms Vault. It looked like a shipping container made of high-grade steel that had been painted desert tan. Mike removed a set of keys from his pocket, unlocked the door, and turned on the lights, revealing a mini armory.

Weapon racks held an array of long guns, pistols, sub guns, and Taser devices. There were suppressors, a host of weapons optics, knives, binoculars, radios, helmets, plate carriers, tactical vests, and of course Strieber flashlights. Stacked in ammo cans were hundreds of thousands of rounds in varying calibers.

Harvath took it all in and then looked at his friend. "What? No RPGs?"

Mike shook his head. "Just like a SEAL. All you ever want to do is blow shit up."

While that was true for some, Harvath was of the school that each specific job required a specific tool. The only problem was that you often didn't know what the perfect tool was until you were in the thick of it, and by then it was too late to go back and get what you needed. The key was choosing something that worked well in as many situations as possible.

"You haven't seen this yet," Mike said as he waved Harvath into the vault. "I just bought it."

He picked up a large briefcase and laid it on the armorer's table. "This is the new takedown rifle from LaRue Tactical," he said as he opened it up. Packed neatly inside were the component pieces of one of LaRue's high-end long guns. "Watch this."

Harvath watched as Mike rapidly assembled the rifle, spun on a high-end suppressor, and mounted a large scope in less than sixty seconds.

"It doesn't have to be rezeroed. You just put it together and it'll drive a tack at over seven hundred yards. Ain't that something?"

"What caliber is it? .308?" Harvath asked.

Strieber nodded. "And it breaks down just as quick. It allows you to get in, get it on, and get the hell out before anyone knows you've been there."

It was something indeed. "Can I borrow that?"

Strieber waved his arm and gestured at the entire vault. "You can take whatever you want."

Harvath wanted to take one of everything, but he couldn't. He'd have to choose carefully. He was going into very hostile territory alone. There'd be no resupply, support, no nothing. The last thing he needed was to look back and wish he had chosen one piece of equipment over another. But no matter how carefully he planned, he knew that Mr. Murphy, of Murphy's Law, was always destined to show up. The only thing you could count on when planning an op was to expect the unexpected.

Harvath let his operating environment be his guide. He chose equipment that was easily concealable and that he was the most familiar with. Laying everything he wanted on the armorer's table, he then returned half to the racks, packed the rest of it into his Camelbak, along with lots of extra ammunition.

"That's all you want?" said Strieber. "You're sure? I can probably scare up a bigger ruck for you."

He shook his head. "I'm good."

"Okay, then. I'll lock up here and get the plane fueled and ready. Angela or one of the guys can drive you out to the strip. How about we say forty-five minutes?"

"Thanks, Mike. I'll see you out there," replied Harvath as he picked up the briefcase with the takedown rifle in it and shouldered his pack.

Back at the farmhouse, he took a few minutes to strategize with Nicholas and debrief. He wanted to check the dating site for any word from the Old Man, but he didn't dare, not from the Strieber's farm. Nicholas agreed. They both suspected that Skype was how Harvath had been pinpointed in Spain. While Nicholas believed that ATS had gotten the Skype account through covert means, Harvath had a deeper fear.

His fear was that someone had grabbed Reed Carlton and had tortured all of the communication protocols out of him. That person or persons could be sitting on the dating site right now just waiting for him to show up. Which brought him to how a kill team had been able to find Three Peaks Ranch.

Nicholas had been very careful in his use of the Internet while there, but ATS was so sophisticated, there simply was no telling how they'd been discovered. They needed to assume that anything they did over the Net could and would expose them. They agreed that Nicholas would continue to study Caroline's flash drive and all its data off-line, but that anything beyond that was off-limits, including Strieber's landline phone. Nina and Nicholas had to completely cut themselves off from the outside world. Any contact, and even then only in an emergency, would be done through Mike.

"It's been a long time since I felt this powerless," Nicholas confided in his friend.

"You're not powerless," Harvath replied. "You're going to stay on Caroline's data. We need to know what these people are planning so we can stop it. The answer has got to be on that drive somewhere. Find it."

He pointed at Nicholas's tiny .45 and added, "Keep that loaded, keep it with you, and keep your head on a swivel. Got it?"

The little man smiled. "Got it."

They didn't say anything else to each other. Instead, Nicholas stepped forward and did something he had never done before. He motioned for Harvath to bend down, and then he gave him a hug. He had an awful feeling he was never going to see his friend again.

CHAPTER 47

Flying into North Carolina was going to end up being either a very good or a very bad idea.

When Mike came in to see customers at Fort Bragg, he always landed at the Moore County Airport. The people there were friendly, the staff didn't ask a lot of questions, and there was no tower. It was the perfect general aviation setup to have resting in the shadow of America's primary counterterrorist unit.

The First Special Forces Operational Detachment—Delta, also known as Delta Force, Combat Applications Group (CAG), or simply the Unit to its members, was headquartered in a remote section of Bragg behind high security fences and rows upon rows of razor wire. There, "behind the fence," as people referred to it, no expense was spared on training the world's most elite warriors.

These operators excelled in a wide array of clandestine operations including hostage rescue, counterterrorism, and counterinsurgency, as well as strikes inside hostile, off-limits, or politically sensitive areas. It was because of these operators that Harvath worried that coming to North Carolina could end up being a deadly idea. If Colonel Chuck Bremmer was tasking active military personnel for his kill teams, they might have something to do with the Unit.

But there was something else about the Unit, which was why Harvath had decided to risk the trip. Never content to rest upon its laurels, and always exploring new ways to make itself better, deadlier, and more efficient, several years ago Delta had asked one of its most aggressive and forward thinking questions—*Why not train and field female operatives?*

It was an exceedingly good idea. Women attracted less attention in the field than men, and when they did, it was often of a completely different kind. They were welcomed in places men were not and could get away with things men could never dream of. A female operative who was prepared to kick in your door and shoot you in the head, or cuff you and stuff you in a trunk, was the last thing most of the bad guys ever expected.

With the approval of the Army's Special Operations Command, under which Delta was chartered, a group of operatives agreed to become recruiters for the all-female team they were creating, the Athena Project.

The scouts were searching for intelligent, self-confident, polished women who could blend in and disappear into foreign cultures. They needed to be athletic and highly competitive. They needed to hate to lose, be mentally tough, and determined to win at all costs. Success needed to be part of their DNA. They also needed to be attractive.

People react to others differently based on how they look. If the female operatives were attractive, there was no end to what they could achieve. Men did things they shouldn't do just to be near them, extending opportunities and even information that would never be offered to their male counterparts. In essence, the majority of men could often be counted on to underestimate and act stupidly around attractive women.

The Delta recruiters haunted high-end female athletic events, searching for potential candidates at triathlons, winter and summer X Games, universities, and U.S. Olympic training facilities. They also utilized a myriad of front companies. It was one of those very fronts that Harvath was there to visit.

After arranging to have the plane refueled, Mike Strieber borrowed the FBO's courtesy car, a white Chevy Astro van, and he and Harvath drove into town.

"Pretty long way to fly for a manicure," said Mike as Harvath removed the SIG-Sauer from the concealment pocket in his Camelbak and tucked it into the back of his jeans. "Angela's never going to let me hear the end of this one."

Harvath had decided on the detour about a half hour into their flight, and Mike had rerouted. He had no way to know if Riley Turner had been a target in Paris or if she'd simply been collateral damage in a hit focused solely on him. While the operators in the Athena Project had worked on assignments with the Carlton Group, they weren't the Old Man's employees. They were simply tasked to him on an as-needed basis. Their group was so classified Harvath didn't have any contact information for any of them beyond e-mail addresses, which were locked away on his laptop in Virginia. This meant that he not only couldn't let them know what had happened to Riley, but he also couldn't warn them that they might be on the Black List as well.

The nail salon was in a strip mall not far from the center of Fayetteville. Owned by the wife of a retired Unit member, it was one of the first fronts Delta and the Athena Project started using when they began to broaden their search outside the ranks of the military. Not only did promising local candidates pass through the salon, it also gave the program a trusted location when it needed to quietly transact its affairs off-base. No one ever gave any of the women entering or leaving the salon a second thought. Even better, it was open seven days a week.

Harvath showed Strieber where to park and told him what to keep his eyes peeled for. Pulling one of Mike's baseball caps down over his forehead, he climbed out of the van, crossed the lot, and walked into the salon.

The place was packed. All of the stations were full, as were all the chairs in the waiting area. Dan McGreevy and his wife looked to be doing very well.

"Hi. Do you have an appointment?" the cashier asked.

"Actually, I'm here to see Dan. Is he in?"

The girl picked up the phone and pressed a button for an extension. "Whom should I say is here?"

"Tell him a mutual friend from overseas suggested I pop in and see him when I got to town."

The young lady seemed to know enough about what McGreevy did or had done in his past to be satisfied with that response. It wasn't unusual for operators to suggest to other operators to look up a friend if they ever made it to their town. Harvath probably wasn't the first person to have ever dropped in at the salon and to have floated a cryptic introduction to the receptionist.

Though he couldn't see them, he knew the shop would have security cameras, and he did his best to make sure none of them were picking up on his face. He turned his back to the young lady and leaning against the counter, pretended to be looking out the plate-glass window of the waiting area.

The cashier relayed his message and hung up the phone. "He'll be right up."

Harvath thanked her and moved over as a woman came up to pay her bill. A few moments later, Dan McGreevy appeared.

He was a compact man in his late forties, a couple inches shorter than Harvath. He had blond hair graying at the temples and a deep cleft chin. The minute he laid eyes on him, Harvath could tell the man was already suspicious of him.

"Can I help you?" he asked.

It wasn't exactly the way one normally greeted a friend of a friend who had stopped by to say hello. "Hey, Dan," Harvath replied, sticking his hand out. "Kevin Kirk."

The man shook his hand, but only briefly. "What can I do for you?"

"A mutual friend suggested I pop in and see you when I got to town."

"What friend?"

"Is there someplace a little less public where we can talk?"

It was quite apparent that McGreevy wasn't fond of people dropping in on him unannounced. "Why don't you give me this friend's name first?" he replied.

Harvath locked eyes with him and said, "Turner. Riley Turner."

A sudden microexpression gave him away. "Never heard of him."

"It's not a *him,* it's a her, but I can see you already know that. Listen, you're going to want to hear what I have to say. I'll be out of your hair in five minutes."

McGreevy jerked his thumb over his shoulder toward the rear of the salon. "We can talk in my office. And I'm not giving you five minutes. You've got three."

CHAPTER 48

McGreevy pointed at one of the chairs in front of his desk and told Harvath to take a seat. "Your three minutes start now."

Harvath decided to get right to the point. "Six days ago, Riley Turner was shot and killed in Paris."

"Let's assume for a moment that I even knew who this Riley Turner was and that I'd be interested in this information. Why would I believe you?"

"Because I was there," said Harvath, taking note once again of another tell when the man mentioned Riley by name.

"Were you the one who shot her?"

"No, but I killed the men who did."

"Men?" McGreevy repeated.

Harvath nodded. "Yes. There were four of them; a wet work team."

"And not only can you identify a *wet work* team, but you managed somehow to kill all four of them?"

"Yes."

"Your name isn't Kevin Kirk, is it?"

"No, it's not."

"You're not going to tell me who you are, are you?"

Harvath shook his head. "My call sign is Norseman. How about that?"

"I've never heard of you," McGreevy countered.

Harvath had anticipated the man's reaction and slid Mike Strieber's cell phone from his pocket. The SIM card had been removed and its memory card replaced with the card Harvath had been carrying in Paris. Clicking on the photo of Riley, he handed the phone over to McGreevy.

"Jesus," he said, all pretense of not knowing her now gone. "Who the hell did this?"

"That's what I was hoping you could tell me," Harvath replied as he placed his finger on the phone's screen and swiped to the next photo. "I've got pictures of each of the shooters."

He watched as McGreevy looked at each photo and then went back and looked at all of them again. If he recognized any of the men, he was very good at hiding it. Handing the phone back, he said, "Sorry. I can't help you."

"I think you can, and I need you to do me a favor."

"You've got pretty big balls to come in here, show me pictures like that, and ask me for a favor."

Harvath understood where the man was coming from. "I get it. You don't know me. You did know Riley Turner, though."

The man began to protest, but Harvath held up his hand to stop him. "For the record, you haven't admitted anything. I'm coming to my own conclusions, which is something I need you to do as well."

"Such as?"

"We've already passed the three-minute mark and I'm still here, so I'm guessing you've grasped that I'm the real deal. What you haven't made up your mind about is if I'm one of the good guys or one of the bad guys."

McGreevy smiled. "And I suppose you're going to tell me you're one of the good guys and that I should trust you."

"No," said Harvath, and then dropped the name of another Athena Team member: "Gretchen Casey will tell you."

Instantly, the smile fell from the man's face. "Who the *fuck* are you?" he demanded.

"You've already got my call sign. Call Casey. If you can't reach her, try Julie Ericsson, Megan Rhodes, or Alex Cooper."

McGreevy looked like someone had just walked up and hit him

with a pipe. The man sitting across from him had just rattled off the names of four operators from one of the most clandestine programs in the history of the United States military. "I don't know any of those people, and if I did, why would I tell you? You won't even give me your real name."

"For good reason," Harvath replied. "Whoever is responsible for Riley Turner's death is trying to kill me. And for all I know, Casey, Ericsson, Rhodes, and Cooper may also be on their list. That's why I need to talk to them."

The man leaned back in his chair and exhaled. Harvath could sense the wheels spinning in his mind. "I know what you're thinking," he said.

McGreevy cocked an eyebrow at him. "Oh, you do. What's that?"

"I think you're trying to make up your mind. I think professionally you're obligated to pick up that phone and place a call to someone back at the Unit. I understand that. For all intents and purposes, you need to assume I'm a threat and that I am here with bad intentions. You don't want to be the guy who sells anybody out. That's not how it works. We all cover each other's backs."

"We?"

Harvath nodded. "I've been on multiple assignments with those women. They know me. They'll vouch for me. You only need to contact one of them, describe me to her, give her my call sign, or put me on the phone, and everything will be good. To do that, though, means circumventing your chain of command and doing me, a complete stranger, a favor."

"You're right, it would be a *big* favor, and I don't even do *little* favors for people I don't know."

"I think in my case you're going to make an exception."

"Why is that?"

Harvath kept a close eye on the man's face as he prepared to drop a final name on him. Over the summer, six Athena Project members had been tasked to work with him in chasing down a deadly terror ring. As they narrowed in on a team of suicide bombers, one had detonated. Rubble was strewn everywhere and the building he'd been in front of began to collapse.

Harvath held up his hands and showed them to McGreevy. "I dug Nikki Rodriguez out of that building in Amsterdam with my own hands. And as I was pulling her out, she was pulling somebody else out, even though she had a piece of metal sticking through her chest that had collapsed her right lung."

McGreevy pinched the bridge of his nose. "Where'd you go after that?"

"We followed the terror cell back here to the States."

"Where specifically?"

"Chicago."

"Why wouldn't you want me to go to the top with this?" McGreevy asked. "If your story checks out, I'm sure they'll put you in touch with whomever you want. Hell, they might even be able to help you, but I *have* to call this in."

Harvath had him. He knew it. He just needed to pull him the rest of the way into his camp. All McGreevy needed was the right reason, which was what Harvath gave him, "What if making that call sets off a chain reaction that puts Casey, or all of them in even greater danger? Shouldn't they be allowed to decide what the next step should be?"

CHAPTER 49

Dan McGreevy had texted Casey and Rhodes simultaneously with a terse, three-word message. *Get over here.* Within twenty minutes, they were standing in the doorway of his office.

Megan Rhodes saw Harvath first. "Look who's here," she began excitedly but she fell silent when she saw the look on his face.

Gretchen Casey sensed something was wrong immediately. "What are you doing here?"

"It's about Riley."

It was identification enough. Dan McGreevy ushered the women in and offered up his office for them to talk in private. Anticipating Harvath's next words, he held up his hand and stopped him. "At some point, the powers that be need to know what happened. All I am going to say is that it should be sooner rather than later. Other than that, I'll leave it up to the three of you to decide."

"What the hell happened?" Casey asked. "Is Riley okay? Where is she?"

Gretchen Casey, or "Gretch," as she was known to her teammates, had grown up in East Texas and studied prelaw at Texas A&M. Her mother was a semisuccessful artist and her father a former Army Ranger who had her shooting from the first day she could hold a rifle. Her love of cross-country in high school and skill at shooting had led her to become a world-class summer biathlete. She dropped out of the sport when she fell in love with a hedge fund manager and moved to New York City. She received her law degree at NYU but moved back to Texas and resumed her career as a summer biathlete when the relationship ended. She was eight months back into the sport when a Delta Force recruiter spotted her and made her an offer that she found hard to resist.

She had brown, shoulder-length hair with highlights, and green eyes. At five-foot six, she was the smaller of the two women in the room, but that had no impact on her leadership abilities, which had seen her put in charge of her Athena brick.

Megan Rhodes was the quintessential "American" girl; blond-haired and blue-eyed. Her mother passed away when she was very young and her father, a cop, raised her in the Chicago suburbs.

Rhodes attended the University of Illinois, where she was a successful competitive swimmer. Thanks to her striking Nordic features and five-foot-eleven height, she'd been nicknamed the Viking Princess, and it had stuck with her all the way to Delta. Those who knew her loved the moniker. She was every bit the Viking, but there wasn't an ounce of princess in her. She was a stone cold killer when she had to be and endured the worst situations any assignment threw at her without ever complaining. Like her teammate Casey, Rhodes was in her early thirties, fit, and very attractive.

Harvath didn't feel comfortable speaking in Dan McGrecvy's office. There was no telling if he had it wired or not. Unless he knew for sure, he always assumed the worst.

Signaling his concern, he asked, "Is there someplace else we can talk?"

Outside the nail salon, Harvath swapped the memory cards and handed Mike Strieber's phone back to him. Strieber eyeballed the two attractive yet serious-looking women across the parking lot but didn't say anything. He knew this was business.

Strieber had plenty of customers he could see in and around Bragg and told Harvath to simply buzz his cell phone once he had figured out what he wanted to do. Harvath thanked him and as Strieber fired up the courtesy van and exited the lot, Harvath joined Casey and Rhodes at their car.

Fifteen minutes later, they were sitting in Casey's living room. Rhodes came back from the kitchen and handed him a beer. "You look like you can use one."

Harvath accepted it, twisted off the top, and proceeded to tell the two women everything that had happened. When Casey paused to ask him about the photographs, he pulled the microSD card from his pocket and handed it to her.

She slid it inside her phone as Rhodes leaned over to stare at the images. Both women, though tough as hell, were visibly upset by what they saw.

"We have no idea who did this?" Casey asked.

Harvath shook his head. "No. I only have the name of the person who supposedly tasked the kill teams, Colonel Chuck Bremmer."

"He's active U.S. military?" replied Rhodes.

"As far as I know. He was a special DoD liaison to the White House and the National Security council back when I was on the President's Secret Service detail."

"Was he running kill teams then?"

"He and I weren't exactly chatty."

"So we have no idea," Casey interjected, "whether or not Riley was specifically targeted or was just in the wrong place at the wrong time."

Harvath looked at her. "Have you spoken with Cooper and Ericsson?"

"I spoke with both of them last night. Julie is on leave visiting her family in Hawaii, and Cooper is doing a training rotation in New Mexico."

"What about Rodriguez?"

"She's fine; still recovering, but she's okay," Casey said.

"If nobody else was targeted on your team, then Riley had to have been killed because of me."

"What were the two of you doing in Paris anyway?" Rhodes asked.

"Carlton has an Israeli contact there. He sent me to pass off some information. After the meeting was over the Israeli handed me an envelope. Inside was the address for the Paris safe house written in Carlton's handwriting. When I got to the building, Carlton texted me the apartment number. I rang the bell, was buzzed in, and went upstairs. Riley opened the apartment door and that's when the shooting started from the stairwell."

"Do you know why she was there?"

"I never got the chance to ask."

Casey removed the SD card from her phone and handed it back. "Where's Reed Carlton now? Do you have a way to contact him?"

"Yeah, but there's no way to be certain it's secure. Based on everything else, I have to assume he's being watched."

"By ATS."

Harvath nodded.

Megan Rhodes balanced her beer on her thigh. "So in addition to not knowing if Carlton is alive or dead, we don't know who's pulling all the strings."

"Correct. We've got no idea."

Casey looked at her teammate and then at Harvath. "It seems like there's only one person at this point capable of giving us any answers. I think we need to pay Chuck Bremmer a visit."

"I agree," said Harvath. "But there are a few things we need to do first."

CHAPTER 50

R eed Carlton knew he wouldn't be able to stay long, maybe only a
day, two at most, and even that would be pushing it. He was a fugi-
tive and had to keep moving. If he stayed too long in one place, he
risked being discovered.

He passed through the sleepy towns of Lancaster County as he
wended his way north. The crowds of summer vacationers who thronged
to this area near the Chesapeake Bay had long since gone, and many of
the shops had closed for the season. He found a small ethnic grocery and
bought a bag of supplies. The man behind the counter took little interest
in his customer, transfixed by some foreign soap opera being beamed to
his TV from a dish on the roof. There were no cameras, and Carlton paid
in cash.

The turn-off to the rental home was exactly where he remembered
it. Three summers earlier, a lady friend of his had rented the home for a
month to entertain family and friends. Carlton had made the hour drive
from D.C. to visit with her on the weekends. He remembered it as if it
had been yesterday.

It had been July. All of the little towns up and down the Rappa-

hannock were decorated in red, white, and blue. It was straight out of a
Norman Rockwell painting, and American flags flew for as far as the eye
could see.

The weather had been hot and of course summer-in-Virginia humid.
Carlton had consumed more ice cream and Popsicles over that month
than in the previous ten years of his life combined. During those weekends, he had allowed himself to forget who and what he was. The only
paper he had picked up was the small local gazette, with its schedule of
parades, fireworks, and pancake breakfasts. The house didn't even have a
television. It was the most relaxed he had felt in ages.

The yellow house with its wraparound porch and white shutters
brought back a flood of memories, none of which he had time for.
He crept around the perimeter to make sure there was no one inside.
Window stickers from a nonexistent alarm company were the extent of
the property's security. Carlton ignored the management company's
key box hanging from the doorknob in the breezeway and removed
a set of picks from his jacket pocket. Unlocking the door, he walked
inside.

It smelled clean but empty, as if it had been buttoned up for the season. Walking into the kitchen, he checked the refrigerator. It had been
emptied out and unplugged. No one was planning on using this house
anytime soon.

Carlton checked the garage. All the summer toys were neatly arranged
along one wall. Against the other was a neat row of plastic garbage cans,
a lawn mower, rakes, brooms, and assorted tools. There was a kettle grill
and a half-empty bag of charcoal.

Opening the overhead door, he walked out to the Cadillac and pulled
into the garage. He retrieved his groceries from the passenger seat, along
with the few items he had in the trunk and then closed the garage door
and returned to the house.

He cooked himself a modest meal from his provisions and heated a
pot of coffee on the aging stove. Sitting down at the kitchen table, he took
out a pad of paper and began to make a list.

In it, he cataloged every operation he and his organization had been
involved with since its inception. He drew relationship and impact dia-

grams, detailing every single person and every single agency, whether foreign or domestic, that they had cooperated with or even brushed past in their assignments. It was an exhausting exercise, and when he had poured it all out, he had a pile of pages and a pounding headache. The Hydra in his mind's eye had sprouted so many heads, he couldn't focus on any of them.

Pushing himself away from the table, Carlton stood up and walked into the living room. On the mantel above the fireplace, just as he remembered, was a little armada of brightly colored wooden sailboats. He picked up the blue one, recalling how his hostess' grandson had dropped it and broken its mast.

The little boy had been panicked. Carlton could still remember how he had cried, certain that he had damaged some priceless antique and was in a mountain of trouble.

In fact, he hadn't stopped crying until Carlton had assured him that not only could the boat be repaired but that they would do it together and that it would be their secret—no one else needed to know. The two were inseparable for the rest of the boy's visit. Such was the power of a secret.

Secrets could isolate people from one another, but when shared, they could also draw people together. One had to choose very carefully, though, with whom to share and exactly *what* to share. Of Benjamin Franklin's many witticisms, few seemed as relevant to Carlton as the warning from *Poor Richard's Almanac* that three people may keep a secret only if two of them are dead.

That was the kind of world he lived in. Its very currency was secrets, and it was populated with lies, deceptions, and half-truths. For some in that world, trust was impossible, but those incapable of trust didn't last long. You needed to be on guard, but you also needed to be able to let your guard down. No one could be at code red twenty-four hours a day, seven days a week. At some point, you had to let people get close.

Carlton returned the sailboat to the mantel, its secret still intact, and his mind was drawn back to what Franklin had said.

Even though he didn't know what it was, Carlton was party to a secret, and someone was trying to make sure the secret remained kept, by having him and his people killed. The secret involved treason somehow, which made him think about the charge itself.

If accused of the right kind of treason, whereby there were pressing national security concerns, review of the case could be done in complete secrecy. The people who passed sentence could remain anonymous, and very few details, if any, would ever be made public.

Pressing national security concerns could also get a subject placed on a kill list. The speed with which the sentence was carried out would be pegged to how immediate the threat was believed to be. This was the point around which Carlton's thoughts began to crystallize. Whoever was after him had used the treason charge as a means of expediting his execution, as well as that of his operators.

But whoever had wanted him dead had to have known that he and his people wouldn't be easy to kill. To pull off the night of the long knives, someone would have needed personnel with exceptional training and access to very closely guarded intelligence.

That brought Carlton to the question of *why*? Why did someone want him and his people dead?

Murder, and the motivations for committing murder, had existed since Cain and Abel. The first answer that had come into his mind was that he and his people knew something they shouldn't and someone had ordained that they be silenced. But he had dismissed the thought as quickly as it had come to him. He purposefully kept all of his people compartmentalized. Try as he might, he couldn't come up with one specific piece of intelligence or operational detail that he and his men all shared in common and that could make them a threat.

Is there a different motivation? Was Tommy Banks right? Was this about revenge? Carlton turned the possibility over in his mind once more.

Yes, his group had been good at what they did, exceedingly so, but as bad as the blood had been between them and the CIA, this wasn't the Agency's style. If they had wanted to get rid of him, they would have done it through incessant and damaging leaks to the media and by pushing for congressional hearings. They would have trumpeted the Carlton Group as a rogue organization that answered to no one and made up their own rules as they went along. The powers that be at Langley would have targeted the group's contacts at the Defense Department and would have publically embarrassed them into severing the relationship.

That's how the CIA would have handled it. But what if it wasn't the Agency? *What if it's someone else?*

Returning to the kitchen and to his stack of notes, with a fresh cup of coffee, Carlton found his thoughts getting complicated again. If it wasn't an intelligence organization trying to take out his group for stepping on its turf, he wasn't left with many alternatives.

Carlton and his people had targeted only enemies of the United States. Most of those enemies had been Islamic terrorists. It was almost impossible to believe that somewhere a Muslim sphere of influence so powerful existed that it both knew about the Carlton Group and could also strong-arm the United States into wiping it out. *Was there a cog in the wheel missing?*

His group had recently dismembered two major terrorist rings—one in Europe and one in the United States—but not before the terrorists had succeeded in killing scores of Americans. It had been very bloody.

The attacks, though, were rumored to have only been a precursor to a much more sophisticated wave to follow. Someone had likened it to water draining from a bay before a tsunami came rushing in.

All of the attacks, Carlton's people had discovered, were part of a master plan, a blueprint entitled "Unrestricted Warfare." Suicide bombers and Mumbai-style shooters were meant to soften America up. The attacks that followed were to be even grander in scale and meant to cause such havoc that Americans would beg for any semblance of order, and would surrender much, if not all, of their freedom in exchange.

The man who had orchestrated the plot had been dealt with and his remaining coconspirators swept up and sentenced. For all intents and purposes, it had appeared that the cancer had been completely cut out. *But what if it wasn't? Could what was happening now be some sort of payback? With all of the people they had rolled up, could they have missed one?*

Carlton didn't think so. The number two man in the operation, the person who controlled all the moving parts, had been extensively interrogated. The man had broken and had given them every detail. Although Carlton knew better than to shut his mind off to any possibility, he needed to keep searching for the right answer.

This brought him to his most recent theory, admittedly his weakest: somewhere, another plot was under way, and the Carlton Group somehow stood in the plotter's way.

It was a concept he had trouble completely wrapping his mind around. With the extensive capabilities of America's intelligence and law enforcement agencies, it would seem that anyone intending to do the nation harm would have much more to worry about than Carlton's burgeoning organization. One thing bothered him about that, though. The ability to frame him and his people for treason, unleash kill teams, and highlight him in a nationwide law enforcement bulletin suggested that this was coming from somewhere within the government itself. If that was the case, it could only mean one thing—a coup of some type was brewing. It also explained why his organization would be perceived as a threat.

In a coup scenario, chaos reigned. Depending on what kind of influence the plotters had over agencies like the FBI and CIA, they could easily keep those groups tied up in bureaucratic knots, while the plot unfolded and they got the ball across the goal line. In that kind of situation, the Carlton Group would definitely be a wild card. It operated outside the law and could do things no other group could. One call from the DoD was all it would take, if even that. Carlton could task his own organization without a DoD request. The bottom line was that Carlton could move swiftly and effectively, but he would only move against an enemy of the United States.

The more he mulled that scenario, the more believable it became. He knew it was a possibility. Stripping the United States of its sovereignty was the ultimate goal of the last plot they had foiled. Simply put, there were many in the world who saw the U.S. not as a force for good but as a roadblock, an impediment that had to be crushed and bulldozed out of the way. Though he didn't have all of the pieces yet, the ones he did have were starting to click into place.

His operational hypothesis, until he developed any information to the contrary, had to be that there was a very serious threat against the nation, that it was being coordinated from within the government, and that team or no team, Carlton had to do everything he could to identify and stop it.

He'd had a growing feeling that it was going to come down to something like this. Now he was certain. It was time to develop and launch his own attack. Looking at his watch, he hoped Tommy Banks was up to the challenge.

CHAPTER 51

Ha, ha! See?" Middleton exclaimed as he reread the e-mail. "I told you Banks was the guy we needed to watch."

Schroeder was impressed. "How'd you know Carlton would reach out to him?"

"Because. If there's one thing I know from years of studying data, it's people."

"This is a pretty obscure e-mail account," the younger man said, tapping his screen. "Are we sure it belongs to Carlton?"

"It's his all right." Middleton elbowed him out of the way, took control of his mouse, and three clicks later brought up a diagram tracing the e-mails that had been sent to and from the account. "It's one of those Runbox.com e-mail addresses out of Norway that people think we can't crack. It hasn't been used that many times, but look at the interaction; all accounts tied to people on Carlton's relationship tree."

"But his message to Banks doesn't make any sense."

Middleton rolled his eyes. "You've got a lot to learn. He's requesting a meeting. He's got something for Banks."

Schroeder's eyes went wide. "You don't think he's talking about the flash drive, do you?"

"I don't have a fucking clue, but whatever he's got, we want it."

"What if what he's got is Harvath? Do we want that?"

Middleton drew his hand back as if he was going to strike him, but then got control of himself. Though Chuck Bremmer wasn't ready to concede the Texas operation, none of his operators had been heard from in more than twelve hours. It was obvious what had happened. It was a disaster. Three times, Bremmer had sent teams to kill Harvath, and three times his teams had failed. Middleton had torn the Colonel a new asshole and the two had almost come to blows inside the SCIF at the Pentagon.

Schroeder had a point, though. What if it was Harvath that Carlton had, or information as to his whereabouts? Even more important, what if Carlton had been passed Caroline Romero's flash drive? What if Carlton was using Banks to take everything public in order to help clear his name?

Any of those scenarios was more than plausible. Middleton's biggest challenge was deciding how they should handle the meeting between Banks and Carlton. The cloak-and-dagger stuff wasn't Middleton's forte. That said, it didn't appear to be Bremmer's either. Somehow Harvath had been able to smell those kill teams coming from a mile away. They'd have to take care of this in-house.

"If Harvath's a part of this," Middleton replied, "I'll take care of it. Do we know where Banks is right now?"

Schroeder nodded at his mouse and when his boss let go of it, he used it to pull up another screen. "It looks like he's at home."

"Good. I'll assign some of our security people for surveillance. Keep monitoring his communications. The minute Carlton sets a time or a place for their meeting, I want to know about it."

When Middleton returned to his office, Martin Vignon, his chief of security, was already waiting in one of the chairs. Even from across the room, Middleton could see the man's blue veins beneath his pale, nearly transparent skin.

Crossing the office and sitting down at his desk, Middleton summoned up a fake smile for Vignon. He didn't like the fact that the man had made himself right at home.

Vignon's pale lips curled into what should have been a smile but looked more like a sneer. It all but vanished when Middleton tilted his head toward the door he'd purposely left open and said, "Close it."

It was a petty power play. The security chief stared at Middleton for a moment before rising from his seat to carry out the command.

Middleton noticed that Vignon didn't use his hands to push himself up and out of the chair. Even in his fifties, the security man was quite fit.

When Vignon retook his seat, Middleton spoke, "If I ask you to follow an eighty-eight-year-old man and not fuck it up, do you think you can handle it?"

"Which part? Following an octogenarian, or being asked if I can do it without *fucking it up*?"

Middleton smiled. This time it was genuine. While he didn't care very much for Vignon, at least the pasty-faced man retained a modicum of self-respect. "Both."

"What is it specifically you want?"

Middleton removed two folders and handed them to him as he spoke. One was for Thomas Banks, the other for Reed Carlton. Vignon flipped through them as Middleton went into everything in detail.

When he was done speaking, he looked at his security chief and asked, "How do we keep this quiet?"

"Obviously, we involve as few people as possible."

"*Obviously.* How many men are we talking about?"

Vignon did the math in his head. "For right now, we keep it very low-key. Two men in a car ready to follow him if he drives and another two men a block away who can follow on foot if he goes that way."

"Why can't you use the men in the car to follow on foot?"

"If the subject walks a block away and then has another vehicle parked or he hails a cab, you'll want the team in the car immediately able to roll."

Middleton didn't like being reminded that he didn't have the kind of mind for this sort of thing. "Fine. Two teams. But no more than that. And I want to make sure the men you use can be *trusted*."

Vignon had been around long enough to understand Middleton's meaning by the way he pronounced the word *trusted*. "I'll see to it," he said, before changing the subject. "If we can get Banks and Carlton to-gether, what do you want—"

"*If?*" Middleton repeated, cutting him off.

"*When* we get Banks and Carlton, where do you want the interrogation to take place?"

The question didn't require a lot of thought. There was no sense reinventing the wheel. "Do you still have the location set up that you were going to use for Romero?"

"We cleaned the gear out, but we still have access to it, yes."

"Then use it," replied Middleton as he rose from his chair, indicating the meeting was over. "We'll keep gathering intelligence on this side and feed you anything relevant."

Vignon gathered the files from his lap and stood. "One last question."

"What is it?"

"If this Scot Harvath does show up, what do you want us to do?"

Middleton didn't waste a moment of thought. There was a perceptible tensing of his jaw as his teeth ground together and he said, "Don't wait. Kill him."

CHAPTER 52

Harry P. Davis Field in Manassas was a small, regional airport about thirty miles from D.C. It was easy to get into and out of and had a much smaller surveillance apparatus than Dulles or Reagan National. Mike Strieber used it whenever he had business in Washington. His aircraft's tail number, or N-number as it's called, appearing in their logs wouldn't be unusual.

He arranged to have his plane refueled and then went over to Hertz to select a rental car. He surveyed what was available, then filled out the paperwork in his name and drove off in a black Chevy Suburban.

After picking up Harvath, Casey, and Rhodes, Strieber parked out of sight of the rental car offices and the private aviation building known as the Fixed-Base Operator or FBO, so Harvath could remove the SUV's license plates. Five minutes later, he returned and attached the plates from another black Suburban on the small, unattended Hertz lot. It was a short-term fix, but if Mike's name was being put through PROMIS, TIP, or any of the other database screening systems, they'd have the plates tied to the rental contract, not the plates that were actually on the vehicle at the moment. If the police, for any reason, ran a check, it would come back as a black Suburban owned by Hertz. Harvath had yet to see a cop ever verify a vehicle identification number.

They dropped Strieber in downtown Manassas, where he planned to kill a few hours before returning to the airport by cab and flying his plane back to Texas.

Harvath, along with Casey and Rhodes, had spent the prior afternoon and well into the evening doing research on Colonel Charles Bremmer. Using DoD resources was out of the question. Harvath had no doubt that his name was flagged throughout their systems. That meant Casey or Rhodes would have to do the dirty work, and any search they did would trace right back to them. Harvath wasn't willing to risk it. They'd have to limit themselves to open source information.

As they began their search, it became apparent that Bremmer wasn't a total fool when it came to protecting his personal data. Neither his phone number nor his address was listed in any phone books, and it didn't appear that he had ever been mentioned in any news articles. Harvath thought about using ZabaSearch but decided against it, knowing that individuals could set up e-mail alerts on Zaba to notify them when someone ran their name.

They continued digging, hitting every popular military site and went as far as checking the business-networking site, LinkedIn. None of them turned up even a shred of information on Bremmer.

Harvath was beginning to get discouraged when Casey came up with a very promising lead. It was a list of benefactors who had donated to a small, private school in Virginia called Fredericksburg Academy. Among those thanked for their contributions in the $5,000 to $10,000 range, were "Mr. and Mrs. C. Bremmer."

Was it their "Charles" Bremmer? Possibly, but despite the somewhat uncommon name, it could have been any of the C. Bremmers in the world. Harvath hadn't known Bremmer very well. He had no idea if the man was an alumnus of Fredericksburg Academy or if he even had a child, or children, who attended the school. Their big break came when they began skimming the school's website.

Laid out in beautiful script atop images of the Fredericksburg Academy campus was a page dedicated to testimonials from parents. One of them was from "Patricia Bremmer, FA parent." It was followed by her child's class year, indicating that she, and ostensibly whoever Mr. Bremmer was, were parents to a current Fredericksburg Academy junior. Their search had just been narrowed.

It didn't take long to uncover a Ms. Molly Eileen Bremmer, who in addition to being a varsity field hockey player, also had an active Facebook account. The page included geo-tagged pictures of the Bremmer family home, their vehicles, and Molly Bremmer's parents.

As soon as Harvath saw the first one he said, "That's him. That's Chuck Bremmer."

Just as good as finding the family photographs was reading through the posts back and forth between Molly and her friends. It was in doing so that they discovered Ms. Bremmer had a major field hockey game the next afternoon and that her biggest wish, next to winning it, was that her dad would honor his promise and not be late to this one. Before Harvath could say anything to Casey, she was already pulling up satellite images on Bing and had begun planning all the potential routes Colonel Bremmer could possibly take to and from the match.

They spent the rest of the evening formulating their plan. He saved the last thing he needed to do on the Internet for the next morning before they took off. As Strieber readied his plane, Casey drove Harvath to a FedEx office in Fayetteville and waited in the parking lot while he went inside.

Paying with an untraceable $50 debit card that Rhodes had had a friend of a friend pick up the night before, Harvath got back on the Net and went to the dating site the Old Man had designated for use in absolute emergencies. Knowing that the majority of analysts would be male and loath to sift through ads of men seeking men, that was exactly where Carlton had explained their ads should be.

Harvath had resigned himself to the worst. Going from one ad to the next was like scrolling through the obituaries. The Old Man was more than a mentor. He was like a father, and Harvath had already lost one father in his life.

It was an agonizing process, and Harvath was tempted to skip right to the end, until one ad in particular caught his eye.

Seconds went by. He didn't blink, he didn't breathe; it felt like even his heart had stopped beating. Then everything started up again in a rush.

It was Carlton's ad. There was no question. It had been posted four days ago. That meant two days after the attack on him in Paris and a day before the attack in Spain. It had to be the Old Man. Even the burn code he used was right on the money. No matter how badly he was ever tortured, Harvath didn't want to believe that he'd give up their ultimate code, the code that existed just between the two of them.

Nevertheless, it troubled Harvath that a personal ad had been posted on the very same day that he had thought he'd been conversing with Carlton over Skype. *Damn it,* he thought to himself. This entire thing was so hard to make sense of. He was starting to second-guess everything. This was exactly the kind of doubt that he and the Old Man loved to sow in America's enemies. He didn't like that the shoe was on the other foot.

There were three status levels that Carlton could have conveyed in his transmission, coded X, Y, or Z. Z meant charcoal, the absolute worst; that he was completely burned and Harvath shouldn't try to find or contact him. But that wasn't what Carlton had transmitted. He had selected Y—situation severe, but he was okay and attempting to regroup. Harvath decided that for now he'd play along.

Making sure to mirror the language used in the other male-to-male ads he had read through, he crafted a careful, short response:

Really turned on by your ad. Am going to be in town on business. Would love to hook up.

Harvath then closed with the phrase he and Carlton had devised so that he would know it had come from him:

Let's do dinner, but not sushi. Am only into meat eaters.

With that, Harvath had logged out of the dating site and had signed off of the computer he was working on, and exited the FedEx office.

"So?" Gretchen Casey asked as Harvath slid back into her car. "Any news?"

Harvath took a moment to gather his thoughts before answering. Finally, he turned to her and with a reserved smile said, "I think, at least as of four days ago, he was still alive."

Casey turned her high-wattage smile right back at him. "That's fantastic. If he slipped the hit they put on him, he would have gone right to ground and there's no way they'd be able to track a man like him."

"I hope you're right," Harvath had replied.

That had been more than ten hours ago. Now they were in Virginia, Harvath was lying in the Suburban's cargo area, and Casey was unbuttoning her shirt. It was time for them to get it on.

CHAPTER 53

Because they didn't have the manpower to devote to a car that could follow Bremmer from the Pentagon to his daughter's field hockey game, there'd been discussion about the best place to lay their trap.

Rhodes had been in favor of waiting in the parking area and taking him there. Harvath disagreed. Even though this was an "away" game, there was still the potential of his being recognized by other parents. If they saw him pull into the lot, only to turn around and leave with a stranger, it could set off alarm bells. At the very least, someone might say something to Mrs. Bremmer, and Harvath needed her to stay put.

Rhodes did raise one point that Harvath agreed with. From what they'd been able to learn from reading Molly's Facebook posts, her father was chronically late to all of her matches. Rhodes used that as a selling point. There was probably a better than equal chance that Bremmer would be late. If so, the issue of other parents being in the parking area might not be a concern.

Having been a high school athlete himself, Harvath knew Bremmer wouldn't be the only father likely to be late to the game. They couldn't stage in the parking area and hope to take him down without notice. Too much could go wrong. The fact that Bremmer would probably be in a hurry to get to his daughter's game, though, worked to their advantage.

If Bremmer was in a hurry, he'd probably take the most direct route from his office and he'd be focused more on getting to his destination than on what was going on around him.

In almost any other situation, pulling up next to him as he got out of his car, throwing a hood over his head, and dragging him off in the Suburban would have been fastest, cleanest, and most effective. Today, they were going to have to be a little less fast and a whole lot less clean, but as long they were effective, the ends would justify the means.

After scouting the area where the match would take place, they left Rhodes behind to set up her part of the operation. Casey and Harvath then thoroughly scouted two additional locations they'd need, before driving back out to the highway and the exit they were confident Bremmer would be taking.

No sooner had Harvath shut off the engine than Casey restarted the argument they had been having since she had first heard Bremmer's name.

"It completely escapes me how you think we're going to go along with this."

"It's the only way it works, Gretch," Harvath replied.

"The hell it does."

He understood why she was angry. If the situation were reversed, he might feel the same way. "About Rhodes . . . ," he said, changing the subject.

Casey knew what he was referring to. "She'll do it," she replied. "She won't like it, but she'll do it."

"You've got to trust me on this."

"Trusting you and liking what you've asked us to do, though, are two different things."

"I know," said Harvath and he meant it. He respected Casey. She was a highly accomplished and highly skilled operator. Whether in spite of those facts or because of them, he knew he was going to have to keep an eye on her. If she changed course on him, it wouldn't be the first time an operator had decided their view of how to handle the situation was the best one. Harvath had done it more times than he could count.

He succeeded in changing the subject and they made small talk until one of the clean cell phones Casey had brought with her vibrated and several MMS messages came in with pictures attached. She scrolled through and then handed the phone to Harvath. Molly and her mother had arrived. Rhodes had taken pictures not only of them but also of their vehicle. Everything, so far, was on track. Checking his watch, he decided it was time to get ready.

Removing the wireless entry fob, Harvath left the key in the ignition, and he and Casey climbed out of the vehicle. After removing the license plate from the front bumper, they walked around to the back.

Triggering the hatch, he counted how long it took to open and then hopped up into the cargo area. Once he was in, Casey closed it and stood by as Harvath tested using the fob to open it from inside. Satisfied, he gave her the thumbs-up and she returned to the driver's seat.

Because of their position, they were stuck with an obstructed view of the highway. There wouldn't be much time between identifying Chuck Bremmer's vehicle and having to pull out after him. Checking her appearance in the rearview mirror, Casey adjusted her shirt.

"I'm not going to have to remind you to smile and turn on the charm, am I?" he asked, from the back, where he was lying out of sight.

"If he's like any other man I've ever met, it's not my smile he's going to be looking at."

"Good point," Harvath replied. "Don't forget your speed, okay?"

"How did I ever survive without you?" she snarked. "I know how fast I have to be going to get the airbags to deploy. Don't worry about it."

"Sorry. Just give me a heads-up so I can brace for impact."

"I'll try to remember."

Harvath shook his head and smiled. She didn't like being told what to do and what to remember. He couldn't blame her. He was the same way. He began to say something else, but she cut him off. "I can't hear you," she said, "I'm watching the road."

Harvath smiled again and contented himself with waiting. Ten minutes later, Casey said, "Contact," as she tossed her binoculars into the passenger seat, and started the engine.

He didn't like being positioned in the cargo area. He would much rather have been behind the wheel, but it had been his idea, and it was the right way to carry out their plan. Nevertheless, he didn't like the feeling that he wasn't 100 percent in control. "Remember," he cautioned, "watch your speed and let me know when to brace."

"Want to take a stab at what's worse than a backseat driver?"

"I get it. Just remember your precious cargo back here."

"I know you can't see," she replied, "but I'm rolling my eyes up here." Before Harvath could respond, she added, "He's exiting now."

"We're sure it's him?"

"Stand by."

The seconds ticked past. When Bremmer's vehicle hit the top of the exit ramp and turned right, Casey said, "We've got him. That's him," and pulled out onto the road.

It was a rural thoroughfare in suburban Virginia. Thick-trunked trees and grassy fields were interspersed with cookie-cutter housing developments. Based on how fast they were traveling, Harvath tried to picture where they were and how soon they'd arrive at their assault point. He was tempted to ask Casey, but she needed to focus on driving, so he kept the question to himself. The problem, though, was that she was continuing to accelerate, and even from where he lay, he could tell they were going well above the speed limit.

"What the hell is going on?" he finally asked.

"I guess Daddy doesn't want to disappoint his little girl."

"How fast are we going?"

"You don't want to know," Casey replied and then added, "The way he's driving, I don't know if he's going to stop when he gets to the stop sign. Should I pit him?"

Pitting, slang for the Pittman Maneuver, referred to turning the front quarter of your vehicle into the rear quarter of the target vehicle in order to cause them to spin out. It was an effective move, but it could also be deadly if the target vehicle hit a tree, crossed into oncoming traffic, or went into a ditch and flipped. Harvath didn't want to risk it. "No," he said from the cargo area, "don't pit him."

"Then what do you want me to do? It doesn't look like he's slowing down."

"He'll stop."

"I don't think so. I can already make out the stop sign, and if I can see it, so can he."

"How much distance do we have between us and him?"

"Maybe six car lengths," said Casey.

"He's not going to overtly risk a ticket. He'll do a California stop. He'll slow down and look left and right and then step on the gas again. You need to hit him before he accelerates."

"I'll try."

Harvath pressed himself up against the third row of seats and got ready for impact. Casey gunned the heavy SUV, only to step on the brakes almost immediately as she tried to time her arrival at the intersection for just the right moment. With the speed at which Bremmer was moving, Harvath sensed the calculation was extremely difficult.

He felt the shudder of the antilock brakes kicking in as Casey made another massive correction in the vehicle's speed. Five seconds later, she depressed the accelerator, ramped up speed, and shouted, "Brace!"

CHAPTER 54

Colonel Chuck Bremmer had done exactly what Harvath had said. He'd rolled the stop sign. Gretchen Casey had also done what Harvath had said and had timed her impact perfectly.

The SUV struck the rear of Bremmer's car just as it entered the intersection. The impact was hard enough to pop open the lid of Bremmer's trunk and give him a good jolt but, to Casey's credit, not so hard that it deployed her airbags.

Slamming on his brakes, Bremmer came to a complete stop in the middle of the road.

"The lid of his trunk released," said Casey, as she put the SUV in park. "He's getting out. I don't see any other vehicles headed toward us."

"Roger that," said Harvath.

As he heard her open her door, he counted to five and then activated the rear hatch. Even before he had slipped from the cargo area, he could already hear Bremmer yelling.

"You idiot! What the hell is the matter with you? I could have been killed!" he screamed as he leapt from his car. When he saw what he was yelling at, another part of his anatomy kicked in and his tone instantly changed.

"Are you okay? Oh, my God. I'm so sorry," Casey said. "Please tell me you're okay. I don't know what I was thinking. I'm trying to get to my daughter's field hockey game. The phone rang and I know I should have let it ring, but . . ."

Bremmer raised both his hands palms out. "I'm fine. I'm sorry for my language. I think we're going to the same field hockey game and it looks like we're both late."

Casey, who had met him at the rear of his vehicle, bent over, ostensibly to survey the damage, and didn't need to look up. She could feel his eyes on her chest. "I really did a number on your bumper."

"Are you sure?" he replied.

"It looks pretty bad. I guess we should probably trade information," she said as she straightened up.

Bremmer readjusted his focus from her chest to her face. "I guess we should. Let me get a pen out of my car."

Upon turning, he froze.

"I don't think you're going to need it," said Harvath, who had crept up on him from behind and was now pointing his weapon directly at the man's face. "Put your hands behind your back."

"It's you," Bremmer said, barely above a whisper.

"If you ever want to see your wife and daughter again, put your hands behind your back right now. Do it."

The Colonel complied and Casey removed a set of plastic Flex-Cuffs from her pocket and trussed him up tight.

"Jesus, those hurt," he said.

"Shut up," Harvath admonished as he slammed the lid of the man's trunk, only to have it pop back up.

"I'll take care of it," replied Casey. "Don't worry. Let's get moving."

Harvath led Bremmer to the rear of the Suburban, placed a hood over his head, and had him lie down in the cargo area on his stomach. After cuffing his ankles, he hog-tied him and rolled him over on his side. He then nodded at Casey, who returned to his car and used an extra set of cuffs to help hold the trunk lid down before they began moving again.

They rallied at the final location they had scouted, parking far enough off the road that they wouldn't be noticed. Opening the hatch, Harvath removed his knife and sliced through the restraints that had secured Bremmer's ankles to his wrists. He had him swing his legs out, but before he let him stand, he gave him a warning. "You know who I am, so you know what I am capable of. Do exactly as I tell you and don't piss me off. Now stand up."

Bremmer did as he was told. "What's going on?" he said through the hood. "Where are you taking me?"

"You'll see soon enough," said Harvath, jerking him forward. "Move."

He led the Colonel through a wooded area to the top of a small hill. When his hood was snatched off, Bremmer's eyes took a moment to adjust. "Oh, my God," he said when he noticed the field hockey match in the distance. "What are you going to do?"

"That's up to you. Do you see that over there?" asked Harvath pointing in the near distance. "Ten o'clock? About a hundred yards out, on top of that large rock?"

Bremmer strained to see what his captor was talking about. "I think so. Why?"

Harvath raised one of the Garmin walkie-talkies Rhodes had packed and said into it, "A-One."

Seconds later, the gallon of milk they had set up as a target exploded in an enormous spray of white. There'd been no discernible report from Mike Strieber's suppressed, takedown rifle.

A chill went down the Colonel's spine as he realized Harvath had a sniper with a suppressed weapon somewhere nearby.

Tucking the radio in his back pocket, Harvath pulled out Casey's cell phone and showed Bremmer three photos—Patricia Bremmer, Molly Bremmer in her field hockey uniform, and the car they had driven to the game. "Here's how this is going to work. If you lie to me, if I even think you are lying to me, I take my radio back out, I give the command, and two shots will be fired."

"No," the man said. "Please, no."

Harvath ignored him and continued. "The first shot will go into the stands. It'll be a head shot, killing your wife. The second shot will hit your daughter and she'll end up paralyzed. I'll make sure she knows that her mother died and she was paralyzed because her father put himself before his own family."

"Don't. Please."

"I'll then make sure that you're exposed and prosecuted for what you've done. It'll be a public relations firestorm. The story will break so big that there'll be no way the White House or DoD can cover their asses. They'll have no choice but to roast you alive in order to save themselves. You'll go down in flames.

"And when your prosecution is complete and they send you to Leavenworth or wherever they decide to cage you for the rest of your miserable life—and that's if you escape the death penalty—your torment will have only just begun. I'll make sure that every day inside that cage is a living hell for you. The prison shower scenes you've seen in movies are nothing compared to what's going to happen to you. You're going to have so many admirers that they'll have to put a revolving door on your cell and you'll need a social secretary to keep all your gentlemen callers straight."

"You can't—"

"I can't *what*?" Harvath said, getting in the man's face. "I can't make sure you pay for what you did? You just fucking try me, asshole. You killed friends of mine and it is taking every last thing I have right now not to kill you myself. And I don't mean just put a bullet in you. I *mean,* drag you to a farm in the middle of nowhere to torture you for months on end. It would be a hell you can't even begin to imagine. I have nothing left to lose at this point.

"You, on the other hand, have everything to lose. I am offering you the opportunity of your miserable lifetime. Don't throw it away."

He could tell by looking at Bremmer that the most dangerous thing the man had ever wrestled with was a stapler. He was a bureaucrat, a paper pusher.

Harvath hated using someone's children and family, but sometimes it was the most efficient and expeditious method. The key was to knock the man off-balance right away and scramble him emotionally, so he couldn't think and became psychologically unhinged.

"You've already sent everyone you could after me and you couldn't stop me. So how's this going to end? Are you going to kill your wife and cripple your daughter, or are you going to cooperate with me?"

Bremmer looked toward the field hockey game and kept his eyes there for several moments. When he turned back to Harvath, he slowly nodded.

"Have you sent men to kill me?"

"Yes," Bremmer replied.

Harvath studied the man's face as he asked questions he already knew the answers to. He wanted to have a baseline in case the man started lying to him. "Where did they try to kill me?

The Colonel swallowed. "Paris. Spain. Texas."

"In Paris, was I the only target?"

Bremmer shrugged. "You were the primary target."

"What does that mean?"

"We knew the woman would be with you and that our best chance would be to take you at the apartment."

"So you ordered her killed as well."

"She was a threat. Yes."

"You also targeted other people I work with," Harvath stated.

"Yes."

"Why?"

"Because," Bremmer replied, "you were on the list."

Harvath detected a slight change in the pitch of the man's voice. It was paired with a microexpression that lasted less than the duration of a camera flash, but there was no mistaking it. The Colonel was either lying or holding something back. "What list are you talking about?"

"It's called the Black List. I don't compile it. I just handle the names once they've been added."

Harvath conducted his interrogations much like a shark, swimming in wide concentric circles around his subject as he gathered information. The more information he gathered, the closer to the truth he came and the tighter the circles began to get.

There was blood in the water, though, and it was Bremmer's. His last answer had been a lie; the tell had reappeared once more. When a subject began to bleed lies, Harvath had to restrain his desire to strike. Sometimes, seeing a fin slice through the waterline was even more psychologically terrifying than having a bite taken out of you.

"Who's responsible for the list? Who compiles it?" he asked.

"I can't tell you that," Bremmer replied. "It's classified."

Harvath smiled. "You and I are way beyond classified, Colonel. What's more, I think you're trying to dance with me now, and I already explained what would happen if you did that." Taking the walkie-talkie back out, he lifted it to his lips and said, "He's not playing ball. Take out both targets."

Bremmer stepped forward. "No, no, no. I'll tell you."

Harvath raised his pistol and pointed it at the man's head. When Bremmer stepped back, Harvath lifted the radio again and said, "Cease fire. Do not engage targets. Stand by."

"It's a panel of national security people who are close to the President, and it also includes the Attorney General."

"Who put my name on it?"

"You were accused of treason."

"That's not what I asked you," Harvath said, noting the man's tell yet again. "Who put my name on the list?"

"I don't know. The meetings are way above my pay grade. They're beyond top secret. I don't attend. I just handle the list. I'm telling you the truth. You have to believe me."

"You're lying to me and I told you what would happen if you did. Never forget that you could have stopped this," replied Harvath. He raised the radio once more and said, "You are cleared hot. Fire when ready."

"Jesus, no. Please dear God. No," Bremmer begged.

"You've got a lot of nerve calling on God to help spare your family. You could have saved them, but you chose not to. For as long as you live, don't you ever forget that because you lied, they died."

Tears began to roll down Bremmer's cheeks as he blurted out "I did it. I added your name to the kill list. Tell your sniper to stand down."

"Why?"

The Colonel's eyes were wide with fear. "Call off your sniper, for God's sake, and I'll tell you everything."

"Tell me now."

Bremmer couldn't believe his ears. He darted his eyes from Harvath to the field hockey match and back again. "Craig Middleton," he implored. "He's the person who wanted your name added to the list."

"I've never heard of him."

"Please. You have to radio your sniper. Tell him not to engage. I'm begging you. He runs a company called Adaptive Technology Solutions. He's the one behind all of this. I had no choice. Please don't hurt my daughter. None of this is her fault. Please."

CHAPTER 55

Adaptive Technology Solutions had been the magic phrase. Based on everything Nicholas had shown him on Caroline Romero's flash drive, by naming the company, Harvath knew that Colonel Chuck Bremmer was telling the truth.

He spent the next forty-five minutes questioning him in the Suburban. Rhodes had been left in place just in case Bremmer needed a reminder not to stray from his newfound commitment to cooperation. As it turned out, no such reminder had been necessary. It was like opening a faucet wide and letting it run.

Though the man was loath to do it, he admitted how Middleton had co-opted him and revealed the extent to which he had organized wet work assignments on Middleton's behalf. He detailed to Harvath how the kill teams had been made up of convicted military personnel, selected because of their extremely aggressive personalities. The list of things they had been convicted of was disgusting. Many were former and even current gang members. That explained some of the tattoos Harvath had seen on the attacker in Spain, as well as tattoos he had seen when prepping two of the corpses in Texas.

It had made Harvath sick to his stomach to think that he had killed

American military personnel, but that was all changed now that he knew the backgrounds of the men who had been sent to kill him.

As Harvath continued questioning, Bremmer offered up one particularly good piece of news. He explained that the initial attack on Reed Carlton had failed and that as far as he knew, the man had gone to ground and disappeared.

He confirmed that the attack on the Three Peaks Ranch in Texas had come about after the ranch manager had conducted a Google search that led them to believe the Troll was hiding there. Via their surveillance of Maggie Rose, they had discovered Harvath's arrival, and that had cemented the decision to launch their attack.

Bremmer knew that his team had been killed and that Harvath had done the killing. Surprisingly, he made no inquiry as to the location of their bodies. They weren't people to him, they were pieces on a game board like Monopoly hotels. If you lost a few, you could always buy more. He was a heartless son of a bitch, and it hadn't slipped Harvath's notice that the man had been much more vociferous in pleading for his daughter than his wife.

The Colonel admitted that he had padded the kill list based on orders from Middleton. When pressed for an accounting of all the assignments he had carried out for the ATS Director, five times Bremmer tried to horse-trade for immunity from prosecution. It got so bad that Harvath had to reach back out to Megan Rhodes and threaten not only to shoot Bremmer's wife and daughter but to take out several of Molly's teammates as well.

He was astounded by how quickly the Colonel could go from concern for his daughter to thinking only of himself and of saving his own skin. Had the daughter not been an exploitable, psychological pressure point, they would have had to physically torture him to get him to cooperate. He was that terrified of Middleton and what he had the power to do.

To that end, Bremmer demanded to know how Harvath was going to insulate him from Middleton's wrath. Just because Harvath had promised no harm would come to his family didn't mean that Middleton wouldn't come after them. When he asked Harvath if he was going to kill

Middleton, Harvath changed the subject. It was none of the man's business. He was lucky to be breathing.

Once Harvath knew who was behind the kill orders, he wanted to know why.

"According to Middleton," Bremmer replied, "your group had been turned. He said you were conspiring with a foreign entity that was planning an imminent terrorist attack on the United States."

"And he brought this to you, rather than to the FBI?"

"He said your people had every agency penetrated; that it had to be handled this way."

"And you believed him?" asked Harvath, though he could tell from the look on the man's face that he didn't.

"I didn't have much choice."

Harvath wanted to rip the man's throat out. "You are the worst excuse I have ever seen for a human being. You have no code at all. There are barrels of innocent blood on your hands. You know that? There is nothing I want more at this moment than to snap your flabby neck with my bare hands.

"The people you are responsible for having killed were patriots who repeatedly went into the darkest corners of the globe to battle the most hideous evil you have ever seen. Middleton lied to you, and you knew he was lying, yet rather than do the right thing, you went along with him to save your own fat ass. You're disgusting."

Bremmer tried to hang his head, but Harvath wouldn't let him. "Don't you dare, you son of a bitch. Look at me when I'm talking to you."

When the man looked back up, Harvath railed for several more moments before resuming his interrogation. The more questions he asked, the more useless Bremmer proved himself. He had no idea what Middleton was attempting to frame the Carlton Group for, and he was completely unfamiliar with the term "digital Pearl Harbor" or what it might entail.

The only other thing he could offer was an interesting suggestion about how to get to Middleton. For a paper pusher, it was rather ingenious. Harvath asked a couple of follow-up questions but beyond that, showed no interest in pursuing the man's suggestion.

Before letting him go, he gave the corpulent colonel a final warning. "You sent the best you had after me and none of them returned alive. There is nothing you can do to me. I am beyond anyone's grasp. I also have a lot of friends, several of whom will be keeping an eye on you and your family. If you vary your routine even the slightest bit or try to take a sudden vacation, they have explicit instructions on what to do to you.

"If you tell anybody about our little talk, if you attempt to contact Craig Middleton, I will do worse than kill your wife and cripple your daughter. I know a very sadistic Bedouin who would love to add a young girl like Molly to his harem, and I'll make sure you get complete video documentation of it."

"No. I promise. I won't say anything," Bremmer pleaded.

"And if I even *think* one of your kill teams is on my trail, every single bet will be off and I'll personally come for you and your family. Is that clear?"

The Colonel nodded. Harvath cut him loose and motioned for him to get out of the truck. Casey watched from the front seat as Bremmer walked back to his car.

"Do you think we can trust him?" she asked.

Harvath, who was also watching, shook his head. "No. But we really don't have any choice."

"Listening to him speak, I wanted to put a bullet in him. I still do, for what he did to Riley."

"I probably couldn't have stopped you. Why didn't you do it?"

"Because you told me this was the right way to handle this and I trust you."

It was a frank and honest admission, one that he respected her for.

"When this is all over, though," she added, "I'm not the one who promised to let him live."

"I understand."

"Does that also mean you'll understand if Megan and I decide to do something about it?"

Harvath held her gaze for a moment. "I can't tell you what to do, one way or the other. Do I think the guy deserves to be croaked? Absolutely. But he also has a wife and daughter."

"How about the operators from your group who were killed?" Casey asked. "How many of them had spouses and children?"

"Most of them."

"So?"

"So, I think Bremmer should be made to pay, without killing him."

"Are you moralizing now?"

"Maybe," Harvath replied. "In fact, yeah. I am. At some point, there has to be a process. Putting a gun against his head and pulling the trigger is no better than what he had done to Riley and the others."

"At least justice would be served."

"Do you believe that?"

Casey looked away. "I'm done talking about this."

It was a convenient way to dump out of the argument, but Harvath let it go. She was going to do whatever she wanted to in the end.

What mattered now was getting to Craig Middleton and preventing whatever he had planned. Though it was fraught with more than a few pitfalls, Bremmer had given them a halfway decent suggestion as to the first part. Harvath just had to figure out how to make sure they weren't walking straight into a trap.

CHAPTER 56

The trick for Reed Carlton wasn't finding the men he needed, it was keeping them sober, or relatively sober, long enough to do their job. The operation was an exact duplicate of one he and Tommy Banks had run more than thirty years ago.

"Look for the Barbour jackets" was a piece of advice given to many Western intelligence operatives, especially in the early 1980s. The famous green, British all-weather jackets had many pockets to hide equipment, were stylish without being too flashy and quite popular with people in the intel game. If you ever found yourself in trouble, recruits were taught, look for the Barbour jackets. Chances were, you'd find a friendly.

The Soviets, it was rumored, had heard of this advice, and all their agents, from Bangkok to Berlin, had been taught to keep their eyes peeled for the low-key yet distinct outerwear. Whether this was true or simply Cold War–era paranoia, Banks wasn't certain, but he had decided to play it up. It could only help his plan, and certainly couldn't hurt.

He and Carlton had been working on a very sensitive operation behind the Iron Curtain. They had a highly placed Hungarian intelligence agent who wanted to defect and had been dispatched to Budapest to make contact with him. Their job was to ascertain if he was the real deal and, if so, to gauge his value and then mount an operation to get him out of Hungary and into Austria, where he'd be fully debriefed in Vienna before being flown back to the United States.

The two CIA operatives arrived in Budapest separately, and each was set upon by teams of Hungarian secret service surveillance teams augmented by Russian KGB. It was almost as if they knew they were coming. Both of the Americans sensed a trap, but they had little choice except to move forward.

They tried a series of different gambits to shake the surveillance teams, none of which worked. Someone, somewhere, was very invested in their not succeeding in their assignment. It was Banks who finally came up with the ruse that allowed them to give their pursuers the slip. Decades later, it was the same ruse that Carlton planned to employ, though not to give their pursuers the slip but rather to draw them into the open.

Washington, D.C.'s Union Station was a busy commuter hub. It was crowded during both the morning and evening rush hours, but the evening's rush was different. Instead of people pouring out of the station, anxious to get to their jobs, people were pouring into it, and their end-of-the-day, exhausted-from-work pace was less intense. While some moved with energy and purpose, many moved slowly and en masse, as if on some sort of collective autopilot.

Assuming his former mentor had been surrounded with digital trip-wires, Carlton had chosen to e-mail Banks. He'd been careful, though. He wanted to pique the other side's interest, but he had to do so without appearing obvious. He was, after all, setting a trap of his own. The last thing he wanted to do was to scare them off. He needed them to believe that they had the upper hand and were outsmarting him.

He also needed to make sure that Banks understood the message. As it turned out, he had nothing to worry about. Banks remembered the Budapest operation like it was yesterday.

Carlton found the two men near a homeless shelter in Baltimore. Both men were interested in making a couple hundred bucks, especially such easy money. After getting them cleaned up, Carlton bought them a meal, a new set of clothes, and drove them into D.C. to run them through what they were expected to do.

He then used them to load a dead drop for Banks with final instructions. After that, Carlton took them for coffee, controlling the amount of "flavoring" each would be allowed from a bottle of whiskey they had picked up on the way in from Baltimore. He wanted them to eat once more before the operation, but neither man was interested. Carlton figured he was lucky enough to have made it this far and worked on keeping the men sober enough to function.

At the appointed hour, wearing a false beard, a hat, glasses, and clothing that made him appear much heavier than he was, Reed Carlton entered Union Station, took up his perch, and waited.

The two homeless men proved to be more reliable than he had hoped and followed shortly after. No doubt, the men were eager for the rest of their money, and the only way they'd get it was to finish the job properly.

From where he sat, Carlton had a commanding view of what was about to go down. The thing he worried about the most was the cameras. If the two homeless men didn't walk exactly as he had shown them, and someone panned in and got a good enough look at one of their faces, it would be over before any of it got started. So far, though, the men seemed to be doing everything exactly as they'd rehearsed. All they were waiting for now was for their star to arrive.

Banks would have spent most of the afternoon conducting elaborate SDRs. If he hadn't lost his touch, which Carlton had every reason to believe he hadn't, he might have even lost his surveillance team once or twice. If he did, the plan was to allow them to reacquire his trail, but to do so in a manner that appeared as if it was entirely of their doing. When Banks did make for Union Station, it was to be at the very last minute. They couldn't afford to give the other side any time to set up a trap. The only way the con worked was to keep it moving and never give the other guys a chance to catch their breath. It would be a physically and mentally grueling day for everyone involved but especially for a man Banks' age.

The station was teaming with commuters when the old spymaster entered wearing a wide-brimmed Orvis hat, his old Barbour Beaufort jacket, and carrying a battered leather satchel. According to plan, he purchased a ticket on the high-speed Acela line to New York City and then milled with the crowds and made his way toward the restrooms.

Carlton was able to pick up two men tailing him. They wore dark suits and tan raincoats. Their hair was cut short, military-style. They were broad-chested and fit. They wore shoes that laced up and had comfortable soles. These were men who spent a majority of each day standing. Each was right-handed and he could tell they carried a concealed weapon somewhere at or behind their right hip. They moved deliberately; their heads on a swivel, alternately taking turns focusing on their prey as well as their surroundings. These were dangerous men, and Carlton had no illusions as to what they were capable of. All this he was able to discern in a matter of seconds. He'd been at the game long enough to assimilate and analyze data in an instant. It was the only way he had lived as long as he had.

Satisfied with his assessment, Carlton scanned the crowds for additional operatives. If there were two, there had to be more. What he didn't know was how many. Was there another team waiting in a car outside? Were there more men combing the station? Were they using women? Had they enlisted local law enforcement? The list of unknowns was a mile long. It was time to start getting some answers.

Checking his watch, Carlton stood and began moving toward the exit. Twenty seconds later, he spotted Banks' hat and green Barbour coat coming out of the men's room. Another man, also in a Barbour jacket and now carrying Banks' leather satchel, joined him. The two broad-chested men in trench coats were right on their tail. Carlton had yet to see anyone else following.

Outside, the men made a beeline for the cab stand while Carlton hung back. They were the third party in line. When the trench coated men emerged from the station, they didn't seem to know what to do. Carlton noted one of them raising his shirt cuff to his mouth and speaking into a concealed microphone. He hadn't thought they were working alone, but now he had confirmation. What he needed to know was who was on the other end of their radio.

He watched as the trench coats stood together on the sidewalk and pretended to make small talk, keeping their eyes glued to the two men working their way forward in the cab stand. Finally, a blue-and-white D.C. cab drove forward and the two men in Barbour jackets climbed in.

As the cab pulled away, the trench coats ran for the street and a black Chevy Suburban screeched to a stop. It stopped only long enough for them to hop in, but as the dome light came on, he saw there were two additional men inside, one with very gray, nearly white hair and very pale skin. No sooner had the men jumped in than the Suburban took off after the cab.

Carlton, who now had a much better grasp of how many players were on the other side of the net, stepped out into the street and watched as the Suburban rocketed into traffic. There didn't appear to be any other cars along with it. This was a four-man team driving a single vehicle. Carlton liked those odds and set off walking.

Two blocks away, at F and 2nd Streets, he entered Ebenezers Coffeehouse. There was an old man in a gray windbreaker and a USS *Ronald Reagan* ball cap who had just paid for his coffee. "Did they buy it?" he asked as Carlton walked up to him.

"So far, so good."

"Good," Tommy Banks replied as he placed a heat band around his cup and patted the weapon hidden beneath his own jacket. "Now we get to the fun part."

CHAPTER 57

Finding parking anywhere near Washington's major parks or monuments could be an absolute nightmare. For that reason, it was decided that Banks would stay with the car and Carlton would go on foot into West Potomac Park, near the Reflecting Pool and the National World War II Memorial.

The two homeless men had been given a sheet with specific instructions to hand to their driver. It was a circuitous route that made it appear the vehicle's occupants were running SDRs before arriving at their ultimate destination. If Carlton and Banks had really been in the cab, they would have gotten out and changed cabs and/or modes of transport several more times, but Carlton wanted the assignment to be as idiot-proof as possible for their stand-ins. Besides, Banks had spent all afternoon running them around. They knew something big was in the works and that's all they'd be focused on at this point.

By the time the two men arrived in the park, Carlton had already taped the last half of their money in an envelope beneath one of the many benches and around the arm of which he had tied a white plastic convenience store bag. All he had to do now was wait.

The homeless men climbed out of the taxi and talked quietly to each other as they walked along the footpath. Night was quickly falling, and

Carlton, who had lost the beard and changed his hat and jacket, watched from a safe distance. His challenge at this point was deciding who and what to handle first. As fate would have it, the surveillance team helped make up his mind for him.

This time, instead of sending two men, they had sent three. All were middle-aged men in trench coats. The white-haired man was nowhere to be seen and Carlton assumed he was somewhere nearby, double-parked with their vehicle. He would have to move fast.

Removing one of his clean cell phones, he flipped it open, called Tommy Banks, and rattled off a list of instructions before hanging up and returning the phone to his pocket. For this to work, it was going to have to be executed perfectly. His only concern was whether or not Tommy could handle his end.

Carlton had already written off the three men in trench coats. They were going to die. There was no other way. He hadn't asked for this war, but someone had chosen to bring it right to his doorstep. They had killed his people. They had tried to kill him. Tonight he would begin to take his revenge.

As the darkness thickened, the air was cold and damp. The smattering of tourists who were out seemed intent on taking their photos and getting back to the warmth of their hotels. They moved quickly and didn't linger. As the last set hurried past, Carlton removed his 1911, screwed the suppressor onto its threaded barrel, and secreted the weapon beneath a folded copy of the *Washington Post*. It was old school, indeed, but it was effective and that's what mattered.

He would have to withdraw the weapon from its hiding place in order to prevent the spent shell casings from failing to eject properly, but by the time his weapon was out, that would be the end of the three men in trench coats up ahead. Action beat reaction every time.

Carlton watched as the trench coats cautiously approached the two men sitting on the bench in their Barbour jackets. It didn't take long for them to realize they had been duped.

While two of the trench coats jerked the homeless men to their feet, the third removed what appeared to be photographs from inside his jacket and compared them to the faces of each of the men. The jig was up.

Raising his shirt cuff to his mouth, he relayed into his microphone what had happened as his eyes scanned the area. Carlton had positioned himself so that he couldn't be seen and began watching as they roughed up the two homeless men. Both received vicious blows to the stomach, doubling them over, and then they were kicked and struck repeatedly about the head and face. Carlton wanted to step in and help them, but he couldn't, not yet.

Finally, the homeless men were jerked to their feet once more and the trench coats began dragging them off toward 17th Street. Carlton was going to have to move very quickly if he was going to make this work.

As he sprinted away, he removed his cell phone and called Banks, letting him know the direction the men were headed. He had no idea if he'd even disconnected the call when he jammed the phone back in his pocket and picked up the pace.

Rounding the World War II Memorial, he slowed himself to a brisk walk as he headed north up the sidewalk. He stared into the glaring headlights of oncoming traffic, trying to make out the Chevy Suburban. It would be here any second.

A large group of tourists, having visited their last site of the day, was exiting the memorial and making their way toward two motor coaches that were double-parked along 17th Street. Carlton mixed himself into their group and kept his eyes peeled toward where the trench coats and the two homeless men would emerge from the park.

There was a sidewalk ahead that emptied out of the park, and unless the trench coats were cutting across the grass, this was where they would exit. It also meant that the fourth man, the one with white hair, would bring the Suburban up somewhere behind the buses, and that was exactly what happened.

As the crowd of tourists neared their coaches and began to board, Carlton spotted the trench coats. The bloodied homeless men were being spirited toward the street. He had no idea where the Suburban was. Any moment, he was going to lose his cover, as he'd already passed the first bus and the remaining tourists he was with had begun to slow down in order to queue up to board the second coach.

Suddenly the Suburban came racing up behind the second bus and stopped. Seeing the vehicle, the trench coats hurried their prisoners. That was when Carlton kicked into gear.

Stepping from behind the group of tourists, he bent forward and pulled his head down toward his shoulders. The newspaper and 1911 were tucked under his left arm. As far as he wanted them to know, he was just another disinterested nobody on his way someplace warmer.

The trench coats weren't amateurs. Their heads were on swivels as they continually scanned the area around them for any sign of a threat. Transitioning into a vehicle could often be one of the most dangerous parts of an assignment, and they appeared to know that. Fifty feet more, though, and this would all be over. At least, that was what they were thinking. But at twenty-five feet away, all hell broke loose.

Either because of his worn appearance, his age, or his stooped posture, Carlton hadn't registered as a threat. That was the first mistake the trench coats had made. The second was not having their weapons more easily accessible.

With his right hand, Carlton drew his suppressed 1911 from inside the paper clutched beneath his left arm, brought it up, and depressed the trigger.

The first shot went high and to the right.

"Gun!" yelled one of the trench coats as he let go of the arm of the homeless man he was muscling to the street and fished beneath his jacket for his weapon. The other two men spun and went for their weapons as well.

Carlton brought his weapon back under control and hit the man he'd been aiming at in the shoulder. He then turned his .45 on trench coat two and three.

Number two took a round right to the base of his throat. He fired at number three and missed, but as number three loosed his weapon, Carlton lined up his sights and succeeded in hitting him in the head, killing him instantly.

Running forward, he arrived at trench coat number one, who had lost all use of his right arm and was trying to draw his weapon with his left hand. Carlton aimed his weapon and shot him in the head as well.

The two homeless men were in shock. "Get the hell out of here," Carlton said, shoving them back toward the park. "Go! Run!"

The tourists waiting to board their buses had fled, screaming as they ran. Carlton looked up to see the Suburban, and its white-haired driver slumped over the wheel. Standing on the other side of the door in a puddle of broken glass was Tommy Banks. In one hand was his .357 revolver, the butt of which he'd used to smash the driver's side window. In the other hand was the dual-shot Taser X2 that Carlton had given him. Its twin wires were attached to two barbed probes that had been embedded in the white-haired man's chest.

"Get everything else out of our car and throw it in the back of this one," Carlton said as he took the Taser from Banks, depressed its trigger, and let the white-haired man "ride the bull" again, as it was known.

Carlton figured they had less than a minute. Yanking the driver out of the Suburban, he Flex-Cuffed the man's wrists behind his back and dragged him to the rear of the SUV. Opening the hatch, he half lifted, half pushed the man into the cargo area, where he Flex-Cuffed his ankles and then bound them to his wrists, leaving him facedown.

When Tommy had finished transferring their gear, he had the older man sit in the backseat with the Taser to keep an eye on their prisoner. Carlton hopped in the front seat, put the Suburban in gear, and took off toward the Tidal Basin and Independence Avenue, praying to God they'd make it out of the city without being captured.

CHAPTER 58

As they drove past the bright brick house in the Capitol Hill neighborhood, it appeared that Chuck Bremmer had kept his word. There was no sign of the surveillance team that he had following Kurt Schroeder. At the end of the next block they found his vehicle parked exactly where the Colonel had told them it would be.

Harvath checked his watch. "Ten minutes," he said to Rhodes and Casey as he looped around the block, getting a feel for the neighborhood before settling on a place to park. Both of the ladies wanted to go in with him, but he needed someone to stay with the truck, especially if Schroeder tried to run. Harvath decided to take Rhodes and have Casey stand by outside.

Bremmer had given them everything he could remember about Schroeder and where he was going to be this evening. Without having the file in front of him, there was only so much he could bring to mind. It would have to be good enough.

The row houses looked like neighbors had taken turns throwing darts at a paint wheel at Home Depot. There were red, blue, orange, aqua, white, and then their target—a bright yellow house with white mullioned windows. If someone told Harvath he'd just been transported to Old San Juan or somewhere else in the Caribbean, he might have believed it.

The homes all had fenced patios in back that abutted the fenced patios of the homes behind them. Had Harvath wanted to come in the back door, he would have had to start at the top of the block and jump numerous fences until he got to theirs, halfway down. The chances of being spotted or running across a dog were too great to risk it, and so he'd decided to go right in through the front door. If he was right, no one was going to notice.

Harvath knew that Casey didn't want to sit outside in the SUV. She wanted to be inside, where the action was. He couldn't blame her. The two were very much alike. Nevertheless, he had no idea how big Schroeder was or the size of the person he was meeting with inside. If it got rough, he had no doubt Casey could hold her own, but Rhodes was taller, with more upper body strength, and could handle a larger opponent if need be. To her credit, Casey didn't complain. But she didn't have to; Harvath could tell she was unhappy with him.

There was something odd about the way she was acting toward him that he couldn't put his finger on. He didn't know if it had to do with letting Bremmer live, whether she held him responsible for Riley's death, or what it was. Frankly, he didn't care. They had a high-value target inside that building, and all that mattered was getting him out alive.

After checking their weapons, Harvath took a deep breath. At his nod, they climbed out of the car.

"Remember—" he began to say, but Casey interrupted him.

"Signal if I see anything. Good suggestion. Thanks."

Shaking his head, he closed the door and began walking up the block with Rhodes.

There were lights on inside the row house on both the first and second floors, the plantation shutters inside closed. "You think it's going down yet?" she asked.

Harvath checked his watch again. "Probably. Let's just keep our fingers crossed."

A hedgerow ran in front of the house, bifurcated by a low iron gate. Three concrete steps led from the sidewalk to a narrow, pristine, landscaped walkway that stretched fifteen feet to the front door. "Classy," Rhodes remarked, and Harvath held a finger to her lips to silence her.

At the front door, he removed the lockpick set Casey had brought with her from North Carolina and told Rhodes to stand so that any neighbors who might be looking couldn't see what he was doing. Pressing his ear against the door, he listened for several seconds before going to work on the lock.

Used to working with a lockpick gun, he fumbled with the tiny pieces of metal. "Want some help?" Rhodes whispered, but Harvath shook his head.

A few seconds more and there was a click, followed by the bolt being drawn back. Harvath removed the picks, placed them back in their small leather case, and tucked it back into his pocket. Pressing his ear against the door again, he listened one last time.

When he was confident that they were good to go, he nodded at Rhodes, depressed the thumb latch on the handle, and slowly pushed the door inward.

It slid noiselessly back on its well-oiled hinges, and Harvath and Rhodes slipped inside. Drawing their weapons, they stood stock-still, taking in every sight, every sound, and even the smells of the home's interior.

It had wood floors and exposed brick walls. There were electric baseboard heaters and instead of a fireplace, only a faux mantelpiece. The furniture was tasteful but nothing special. A few pieces of art hung along the walls, but there were no personal photos anywhere. In fact, there were no personal touches at all, no books, nothing. It looked more like some sort of impersonal corporate rental than anything else.

Moving as quietly as they could, they crept through the tiny dining room, past a bathroom, and into the galley-style kitchen, where they located the rear door to the patio beyond. Rhodes pointed at two half-empty wineglasses next to the sink.

Harvath pointed at a men's belt on the opposite counter. Then, from the floor above, they could make out what sounded like an argument. A man attempted to speak but was instantly shouted down by a woman with a booming voice. Harvath gestured to Rhodes that they should go upstairs.

They passed back through the dining room and into the living room.

Harvath hated wooden stairs. No matter how quiet you tried to be, there was always that one squeaky board you didn't know was there until too late. Focusing his weight on the very outside of each stair, he signaled Rhodes to do the same and carefully climbed toward the second floor.

As they neared the landing, the argument became louder, but it was muffled, most likely behind a closed door. Whoever the woman was, she was giving the man absolute hell. Suddenly there was the sound of someone or something being struck, and Harvath stopped. Turning to look at Rhodes, he flashed her the thumbs-up and continued to climb.

At the top of the stairs, a narrow hallway gave way to a door for the bedroom over the living room, a bathroom, and the rear bedroom over the kitchen area where all the shouting was coming from.

Slowly, Harvath crept down the hallway, his weapon up and at the ready. He didn't need to look back to know that Rhodes was doing the exact same thing. Everything was going perfectly until, four feet away from the door, Harvath put his foot down on a warped floorboard that groaned beneath his weight.

Instantly, he froze. And just as quickly, the woman's voice from inside the rear bedroom fell silent. There were a couple of muffled words of protest from the man, wondering what was going on, but those were cut off so fast, you would have thought the woman had clapped her hand over the man's mouth.

Harvath didn't move a muscle, but his brain was screaming, *Damn it!* He had to make up his mind. Would the man convince the woman it had been nothing? Maybe, but he doubted it. They'd lost the element of surprise. It was time to hit the bedroom.

CHAPTER 59

Taking two steps forward, Harvath raised his foot and kicked in the bedroom door. What he discovered was much less dungeon-like than he had expected.

It looked like some sort of a cell, the kind which would have been appropriate for the SuperMax prison or for holding Hannibal Lecter. The walls and ceiling were lined with sheets of stainless steel and studded with attachment points—for what, one could only imagine. The floor was concrete and had a drain in the center. The window was also covered with stainless steel, leaving only the width of an arrow slit covered in opaque Lucite and lit from behind by a dim fluorescent bulb. Another fluorescent bulb hung inside a fixture attached to the ceiling. In the corner was a cage so small that the only way you could get a human being inside was if he folded himself into the tightest fetal position possible.

The only thing that could have taken the freaky factor any higher were the room's two occupants. Sitting on a rolling stool next to the stainless steel cot suspended from the opposite wall was a very tall woman in her late fifties. She was dressed in some sort of police or military uniform and next to her was a tray of bizarre and unmentionable items. Harvath had no desire to know what any of them were or what any of them did.

In her hands was a pair of medical shears, which she had used to cut through the clothing of the man shackled to the cot in front of her. She had just begun cutting off Kurt Schroeder's underwear when Harvath kicked open the door.

"What the hell is this?" the woman demanded as Harvath and Rhodes burst into the room with their weapons drawn. "Who the hell do you think you are?"

"Shut up," said Harvath as he snatched the shears from her and kicked her tray over.

"You'd better have a fucking warrant because my lawyer loves going after dumbshit cops."

"Elizabeth, do what the man says," Schroeder stated.

The woman was taken aback and, for a moment, didn't know how to reply. "What?"

"These aren't cops."

"How would you know?"

"Number one, they're carrying suppressed weapons, and number two, I know one of them. Or more accurately, I should say I know who he is."

"This is because of you, then?" the woman asked, her indignation growing. "People break into my place of business, kick in doors, and wave guns in my face and I'm supposed to go along with it? I don't think so. In fact, *I* think somebody better tell me what the fuck is going on here or I'm going to call the police myself."

Harvath looked at Rhodes. "Get her out of here."

"Like hell you will," the woman declared as Rhodes tucked her pistol away and approached.

"Easy way or the hard way," said Rhodes. "It's up to you."

The woman scoffed. "I'm not afraid of you."

"Wrong answer," Rhodes replied, knocking the woman off her stool with a lightning-fast jab to the face.

The blow was meant to stun more than injure, and before the dominatrix had even hit the floor, Rhodes was on top of her and had her Flex-Cuffed.

"Make sure she stays quiet," Harvath said as he kicked over a rubber ball-gag that had spilled from the tray.

Rhodes secured it around the woman's mouth, picked her up, and led her toward the door.

As they reached it, Harvath added, "Find out if she has a CCTV system in here. If so, I want to know where the DVR is."

Rhodes nodded as she exited. Harvath and Schroeder were now alone.

Walking to the overturned tray, Harvath set it upright and tucked his pistol into his waistband at the small of his back. He then began emptying out the contents of his coat pockets and methodically arranging them on the tray. The contents included a knife, a pair of pliers, two road flares, and a hickory-handled Ball Pein hammer. To these, he added the woman's medical shears.

The young man tried to appear calm. "Those won't be necessary."

Harvath ignored him.

"I said those won't be necessary."

Taking off his coat, Harvath tossed it into the corner and rolled up his sleeves.

The young man's calm was beginning to crack. "I'm serious, you don't need those."

Harvath checked the young man's restraints and then drew the stool and tray table alongside him and sat down.

"Can you not hear me?" Schroeder pleaded as Harvath gave his tools a final once-over. "You don't need those!"

"Really?" Harvath responded, still focused on his instruments. "Why wouldn't I?"

"Because I don't want to be tortured."

Glancing slowly around the room, Harvath looked back at him and said, "I thought you liked it."

The irony wasn't lost on Schroeder. "Something tells me you and I aren't going to have a safe word."

"No, we're not."

"Then I can do us both a favor. There's nothing in my head you need to torture me for. Whatever you want, I'll give it to you. Just please don't hurt me."

Harvath was so used to dealing with ideologically hardened jihadists that he'd almost forgotten what it was like to interrogate a man who was only out for himself. Could he trust him? That was yet to be seen.

"What's your name?"

"Kurt Schroeder," the young man replied.

"Do you know who I am?"

"Yes. Scot Harvath."

"Who do you work for?"

"I work for a company called Advance Technology Solutions."

"Who specifically?"

"The chief executive officer, Craig Middleton."

Harvath was studying his face, looking for any sign that he was being lied to. Thus far, everything indicated that the young man was telling the truth. Even so, Harvath wanted to make sure he remained incentivized. And with someone whose whole identity was defined via a keyboard, there was one very direct route for doing so.

Picking up the Ball Pein hammer, he spoke very slowly. "There are twenty-seven bones in the human hand. On the first lie, I'll break all of the bones of your right hand. On the second lie, I'll break all the bones in your left. If you lie to me again, I'll either cut off your fingers or I'll go for your eyes."

Schroeder was terrified and his voice shook with fear. "But I'm not lying. I'm telling you the truth."

"Tell me why the Carlton Group was targeted."

"Because of the attack you're planning."

"What attack?"

"I don't know," Schroeder insisted. "I wasn't given the details."

"You just took it on face value that we were behind a terrorist attack on the United States?"

"That's what I was told. I was only following orders."

Un-fucking-believable. It was the one rationalization that had been used to justify the murder of more people throughout human history than any other. "And what exactly is your role in all of it?" Harvath demanded.

"Nothing. I really didn't do—" he began, but his protestation was cut short as the Ball Pein hammer came crashing down on his right hand.

Schroeder screamed in excruciating pain and his body went rigid. He tried to pull his hand away, but the shackles held it in place.

"Keep lying to me," Harvath said into his ear, "and I'll keep swinging until every bone in that hand is broken, and then I'll move on to the other."

He waited for a full two minutes for Schroeder to stop crying. It took slapping him to get him to stop blubbering and focus.

Harvath asked him again, "What's your role?"

This time, Schroeder answered with the truth. "M-M-M-Middleton had me compile d-d-d-dossiers on all the targets," he sputtered.

"Which were given to the kill teams."

"Yes. B-b-but, I was only doing my job. We-we-we track people. We f-f-f-find people. It's wh-wh-wh-what we do."

Harvath wanted to crush the man's skull like an overripe melon. "What you *did,* you son of a bitch, was help kill a ton of innocent people; people with more character and integrity at the bottom of their coffee cups than you'll ever have in your pathetic body. How many Carlton Group personnel dossiers did you do?"

"A-a-all of them."

"You knew their backgrounds, their service histories, all of it; yet you believed every one of them was guilty of treason?"

"I-I-I—" he stammered.

Harvath interrupted him by raising the hammer. "If you tell me once more that you were only following orders, I'm going to fucking knock all of your teeth out. You killed people I care about. You *killed* them."

Schroeder drew his lips in and closed his mouth.

"Smart boy," said Harvath, dropping the hammer onto the tray. "Who's Caroline Romero?"

Schroeder was afraid to open his mouth, but he knew he had to answer the question. "She-she-she—" he began.

Harvath had no idea the man had a stammer. At this rate, the interrogation could take weeks. The last thing he wanted to do was show him any mercy whatsoever, but it couldn't hurt to pull him back a little bit from the edge. "Kurt, I want you to take a deep breath," he said, and waited for the man to do so. "Now take another."

When Schroeder did, Harvath continued. "You lied to me and that's why your hand is now broken. Are you going to lie to me again?"

Schroeder shook his head.

"Good. Take one more deep breath, relax, and tell me who Caroline Romero is."

"She used t-t-to work at ATS. She's dead."

"You mean she was killed."

"She ran into traffic and got hit by a-a-a car."

"While being chased by ATS goons."

Schroeder nodded.

"Do you know why she was being chased?"

"She stole data from ATS to help the Carlton Group with their attack."

This guy was an idiot. "There is no Carlton Group attack," said Harvath. "Caroline Romero stole that data to expose what ATS is up to. They're the ones planning the attack."

"ATS is planning the attack?"

"What do you know about a digital Pearl Harbor?"

Schroeder looked at him. "It's o-o-one of the worst kinds of attacks we c-c-could face. A large part of what we d-d-do is try to guard our clients against a d-d-digital Pearl Harbor. It would crash the Net and bring the country to its knees."

"So ATS is especially qualified to know not only how a successful attack like that would be carried out, but where the weaknesses in America's cyber infrastructure would be."

"Y-y-yes," Schroeder replied as what Craig Middleton was planning began to dawn on him. "But w-w-why? Why w-w-would they want to do that?"

"That's where Caroline Romero comes in, but first, where are the clothes you planned on wearing home?"

"In t-t-the coat closet. Why?"

"Because we're all going to take a little drive."

CHAPTER 60

The same tenant had rented the dilapidated barn and its run-down loft apartment for more than fifty years. In all that time, Tommy Banks had never told anyone about it, nor had he ever brought anyone here, until tonight.

The barn was an insurance policy; the kind that he had encouraged all of his students over the years to invest in. Some had listened to him, some had not. When transferred to permanent desk duty at Langley, or under the financial stress of raising a family, many had shut down their phantom bank accounts and had allowed their rental agreements at similar properties to expire. While Banks refused to judge anyone else's financial situation, having an unattributed redoubt was like owning a fire extinguisher or wearing a seat belt—you might not ever need it, but the day you do, you'll thank God you thought ahead. Tonight was that moment for Banks.

Once they had successfully made it out of D.C., they had disabled the vehicle's tracking systems, disassembled the white-haired man's cell phone, and made their way to the farm.

They hid the Suburban inside the barn, and after cutting away the restraints at the white-haired man's ankles, they pulled a hood over his head, yanked him out of the cargo area, and encouraged him to walk up the wooden steps to the apartment by threatening to use the Taser on him again if he didn't comply.

Once there, they secured his arms and legs to a sturdy dining chair, and Carlton used a pair of pliers to yank out the Taser's barbed probes.

Near an old TV set was an equally old VCR and rows of VHS tapes. Banks was a fan of Westerns and WWII films. Carlton only wanted background noise, but he didn't want anything that their prisoner might find heartening or inspirational, so he kept looking. He found a tape with Cyrillic writing and assumed correctly it had been from the Cold War days and was either research or material to keep Banks' Russian language skills sharp. Either way, it would do the trick. Carlton slipped it in, turned on the TV, and turned up the volume.

With the white-haired man unable to hear their conversation over the TV, Carlton stood in the bathroom with Banks and explained what he wanted to do.

The only question the older man had was, "Hood on or hood off?"

"Hood on," Carlton replied. "Sight deprivation increases the effect."

"He's a good-sized fellow. I'm afraid I can't be much help with the up-and-down."

"It'll work like a fulcrum. It won't be pretty, but it'll do the trick. Don't worry."

"This is your specialty, Peaches. I'm just here to help carry your briefcase."

With everything decided, the men walked back into the one-room apartment and their prisoner, whereupon Carlton cupped his right hand and struck the man through the hood against his left ear.

"First question," Carlton shouted so he could hear him above the ringing. "What's your name and who sent you?"

"Go fuck yourself," the white-haired man said from beneath the hood.

"You first," Carlton replied as he reached down, grabbed the man's testicles through his trousers, and gave them a vicious twist.

The prisoner's howl went from a low-throated roar to a high-pitched scream.

"You want to play cute with me, asshole?" Carlton demanded as he let go. "I can do this all day long and it only gets worse and worse and worse."

"Fuck you."

"You're not going to disappoint me, are you? I hate it when they give in right at the beginning." Looking at Banks, he said, "Heat up the iron."

"Fuck you! *Fuck* you," the prisoner spat from under his hood.

"You've never had your suit pressed while you're still in it?" Carlton asked. "It saves a shitload of time, but it's quite literally the equivalent of being burned alive. By the way, I hope you don't have any polyester on. It sticks worse than napalm."

"You're a dead man! I'm going to fucking kill you! Do you hear me?"

"You hear *me*, motherfucker. I've planted more people than you can begin to imagine, and I have zero reservations about killing you. But get one thing straight, you are going to talk to me. Your men are dead and no one knows where the hell you are. Whether you get out of this alive or your heart gives out before I'm done with you, it's your choice."

"Go fuck yourself!"

"Yeah, you said that already," Carlton replied. Turning to Banks again, he said, "Grab the bucket and those crates from under the sink and follow me."

Carlton then walked behind the prisoner's chair and, with an explosive show of strength, tilted it onto its rear legs and dragged it, along with its occupant, into the bathroom.

"You don't fucking scare me," the prisoner taunted from beneath his hood.

"Don't worry," Carlton replied, "I will."

Banks stood outside with the bucket and crates as Carlton stepped into the tub and retrieved a block of yellow soap on a thick brown rope that was hanging from the showerhead. He then stepped out of the tub, moved around to the front of the white-haired man, and began beating him brutally with it.

The man was one tough bastard and didn't even make a sound until the fifth or sixth strike. Carlton didn't give a rat's ass and let the blows rain down.

He wasn't out of control. On the contrary, he was in complete control and knew exactly how far he could push it. When he let up, the prisoner was in agonizing pain.

"What's your name?" Carlton demanded.

The prisoner didn't answer.

"What's your name?" he repeated.

The response came, same as before, but with considerably less vigor. "Fuck you."

"Fine by me," Carlton replied. "Next circle of hell it is. Buckle up." Nodding to Banks he said, "Bring in the crates."

Sliding the chair up against the tub, Carlton squatted down, grabbed hold of the rear legs, and counted to three. In another burst of power, he brought the chair up, balancing it on the edge of the tub so that the prisoner was now horizontal, facing the ceiling. Banks stacked the two crates and placed them beneath the legs, so that Carlton could let go.

Out of breath, his pulse racing, Carlton leaned against the sink for a moment. He was about to say he was too old for this kind of stuff anymore, but realized he probably wasn't going to get any sympathy from Banks and kept the remark to himself.

When he was ready, he snatched a towel from the nearest towel bar and traded with Tommy for the bucket. He didn't need to step Tommy through the next part. As he was fond of saying, this wasn't his first rodeo. He knew how waterboarding worked. And despite his age and reduced upper body strength, he could pin a restrained man's head in one spot and keep a towel over his mouth long enough to get what they needed.

Simultaneously, Banks placed the towel across the white-haired man's hooded face and Carlton turned on the tub's faucet to begin filling the bucket with cold water. No sooner had they begun than the prisoner began writhing violently. He knew what was coming.

"Hold him tight," Carlton said to Banks as the bucket filled. The chair was sturdy and well made. Along with the plastic zip-ties securing him to it, there was no way old Whitey was going to be able to break free and get away from them.

When the bucket was three-quarters full, Carlton turned off the faucet, leaned down near the prisoner's ear, and soothingly shushed him. Once the man stopped thrashing, Carlton waited a beat and then whistled the first few bars of "Singing in the Rain." Immediately, the man began thrashing again. It was very possible that he was already prepared to talk. Carlton, though, wasn't interested in "possibilities." He wanted to be certain.

Standing upright, he went from whistling the song to singing it as he slowly poured water onto the towel over the prisoner's nose and mouth.

The white-haired man's previous thrashing was nothing compared to what he was doing now. Banks had all his weight against the towel, and it was everything he could do to keep the prisoner from twisting his face away from the flow of water.

Finally, Carlton stopped pouring, and Banks was able to remove the wet towel and straighten up.

Immediately, the prisoner turned his head to the side and began coughing and gasping for air. As he did, Carlton turned the faucet back on and began refilling the bucket. This time, though, he waited until it was filled to the top and allowed it to run over. He knew the psychological effect the sound of water overflowing into the tub would have on the prisoner.

After a few moments, he turned off the tap and started whistling again. He nodded at Banks, who picked the wet towel back up and got ready to press it down over the man's nose and mouth. The prisoner, though, stopped coughing long enough to rasp, "Vignon. My name is Martin Vignon."

CHAPTER 61

The shootings at the World War II Memorial were all over the news. Craig Middleton didn't need to wait for identification to know to whom the bodies had belonged. He also didn't need to wait for the late Martin Vignon to turn up in a drainage ditch somewhere to know he was the man in the black Suburban that witnesses saw carjacked and driven away. Middleton had been able to pull up just enough footage via the local traffic cameras to put it all together.

That said, the coverage of the actual event was pretty lousy and by the time he tried to track the SUV, all of its GPS systems had been immobilized. He wasn't able to remotely activate Vignon's phone either. Reed Carlton and Thomas Banks, both of whom should have been playing shuffleboard somewhere down in Florida, had killed three of his security team, taken his security chief hostage, and had made a clean fucking getaway. He was beyond pissed off.

He held no illusions as to what they were probably doing to Powder at this very minute, the poor bastard. He had pretty big balls, but everyone broke eventually. Sooner, rather than later, Vignon was going to give him up, which was why he had to move fast.

He had already made up his mind. Too much sand was getting in the gears. He had no idea if Harvath had helped in the ambush or not, but at this point, it didn't matter. He needed to launch the attack. It was the only thing left that mattered.

Pulling out his cell phone, he dialed Schroeder again, but once more it went straight to voice mail. *Of all the nights to have sent him home.* God only knew where the man was or what he was doing, and Middleton shuddered at the thought. Schroeder's personal life was not only a wreck; it was disgusting.

After copying the files he needed onto his portable drive, he removed a stack of currency from his office safe and dropped it into his briefcase along with the drive and his encrypted laptop. Then he turned his attention back to his computer and thought about the repercussions of what he was about to do.

Once the attack was launched, every corner of the country would descend into utter chaos, including D.C. His board members knew this and had scheduled a team-building exercise for members and their families at the retreat so they could be there safe, sound, and well stocked when pandemonium broke loose. Many had children and grandchildren across the country they were bringing with them. It gave them perfect cover and plausible deniability for why their loved ones would survive. They could watch the country melt down from the safety and warmth of Walworth, all without raising a single eyebrow, as the event had been planned months in advance.

But now, Middleton was about to unilaterally move up the date. The board would be very upset and would have to scramble. Staring at his screen, he tried to figure out a way they could all mobilize their families yet avoid revealing that they had advance knowledge of the attack.

As his mind sorted through the options, an entirely different thought came to him. What if the board disagreed? What if they didn't want to launch immediately? What if they wanted to wait a week, or two? It would be a disaster and he couldn't allow that to happen.

He rolled it around the hallways of his mind a little more, and then it hit him. The best way for him to get what he wanted was simply to avoid blame. There was no reason the attack couldn't go early, as long as he had a scapegoat. Of course, that's exactly what he and the board had been positioning the Carlton Group to be, at least publicly. What he needed was a scapegoat *inside* ATS; someone to take the blame completely for the attack being launched prematurely. Not only did he have such a person, he had someone who would never contradict any of the narrative he was rapidly crafting in his head. That was the great thing about dead men, or more specifically, dead women—they told no tales.

All he had to do was make it look like Caroline Romero had not only discovered what they were up to but had attempted to thwart them by hiding her own program within their attack package. The board didn't have enough technological savvy to even begin to investigate such a charge on their own. If he told them that was what she had done, they would believe him.

He'd explain that she had inserted what she thought was a time bomb into their software, but in reality it turned out to be a fifty-gallon drum of accelerant and a pack of lit matches. In attempting to stop ATS, she had actually sped up the attack. And the way the program was written, once the horse was out of the barn, there was no getting it back.

It was brilliant, and a smile quickly spread across Middleton's face. Pouring himself a scotch, he sat back down at his desk, flexed his fingers, and pulled up Caroline Romero's workstation on his computer. All he had to do was backdate a small amount of digital evidence. Once the attack package began running, it destroyed itself, so even if someone wanted to challenge him by searching for Caroline's Trojan Horse, there'd be nothing to find. It would be like looking through the remains of a nitroglycerin factory for a match. Once it had been vaporized, you were never going to find it.

Within an hour, Middleton had sprinkled just the right amount of bread crumbs, most of them buried so deep they'd probably never be found. Not that it mattered. Once he gave the board the heads-up that the attack had been set in motion, all they would care about was getting themselves and their families to the safety of the estate in Virginia.

Pouring himself another scotch, he shot off a handful of e-mails and ran through the script he had prepared. Then, after inserting one of his Crypto Cards into the STE on his desk, he dialed the first board member.

"Allan, it's Craig," he said when the call went through. "We need to talk."

CHAPTER 62

Kurt Schroeder's loft was located in Columbia Heights, just north of the U.S. Capitol Building. It had rough-hewn beams, exposed brick and looked every bit the single, twenty-something, bachelor pad. There was a huge flat-screen television, multiple gaming systems, and a retro stand-up arcade unit, but no dining table.

The couch and other few pieces of furniture were straight out of an IKEA catalog, as were the unchanged sheets in his bedroom and the towels in the grungy master bath. The one thing Harvath didn't see, though, was any computer equipment; not until Schroeder unlocked a small second bedroom.

The door and its frame were of heavy, reinforced steel designed to look like a regular interior door. Beyond was a room that stood in sharp contrast to the rest of the pigsty. It was perfectly clean—there wasn't an empty cereal bowl, a half-eaten bag of Doritos, a stray article of clothing, or an empty beer bottle to be found. The room was pristine.

A wall of flat computer monitors hung from a series of polished nickel poles and gave the impression that they were floating above Schroeder's sleek glass desk. All around were racks and racks of equipment with lights blinking in a myriad of colors. It looked like a mini Mission Control.

"Sometimes I work from home," stated Schroeder as he pulled over an extra desk chair and offered it to Harvath.

As he sat, Rhodes entered with a plastic bread bag filled with ice. "This was all I could find," she said, tossing it to him.

Harvath caught the bag and handed it to Schroeder, who placed it upon his swollen right hand. Using his left, Schroeder navigated to the log-in page for ATS and went through the hoops required to access their servers remotely. As he did, Casey brought in bar stools from the kitchen for her and Rhodes.

Once he was logged on, a string of icons appeared. He clicked on the one second from the left, and the picture of a gaunt man, made up to look like an evil clown with sharpened teeth, appeared.

"What's that?" said Casey, turning up her nose.

"It's my avatar for Middleton. Fits him perfectly. Chuckles, the laughing boss."

Harvath rolled his index finger, signaling for Schroeder to get on with it.

"I'm going, I'm going," replied Schroeder as he typed in a few more passwords.

"How'd you ever get access to his computer anyway?" asked Rhodes. "I thought he was paranoid about security."

"He is, but the guy practically shits e-mails. I get hundreds from him a day. So, one time, I just included a little Trojan I had created in my response. I set it up so that he wouldn't find it and neither would any of the tech people who are constantly sweeping our systems for viruses and things like that. This rest is what I told you while we were in the car."

And what he had told them was that Middleton was a fetishist when it came to data, even his own. The man recorded and analyzed everything. If Harvath wanted to know where Middleton was going to be, when he'd be there, and whom he might be with, the best way was to look at his planner. It would tell him everything he wanted to know, everything.

"That's funny," Schroeder said suddenly.

Harvath leaned in closer to see what he was looking at. "What is it?"

"A couple of hours ago, Middleton wiped his planner."

"Wiped it?"

"Yeah. He totally nuked any future appointments. All of them."

"Why would he do that?"

Schroeder shrugged. "I have no idea."

"Could it be a mistake?"

"Mistakes aren't exactly Middleton's style. He's the kind of guy who makes backups of the backups of the backups."

"Then he had to have a reason. What was he doing before that?" asked Harvath.

Schroeder pecked away at the keys with his left hand, followed by three mouse clicks, and a log window opened up. He scrolled through its contents for several moments. "Hmmm . . . ," he remarked.

"What is it?"

"I don't know. It looks like he was over on the dark side of things, areas that even I don't have access to, but what's weird is that he did it via Caroline Romero's workstation."

"Really?"

Schroeder nodded. "And he backdated all of it to make it look like she did it before she was killed."

"He must be setting her up for something."

"Why else would you do something like that?"

Harvath nodded. "The question, though, is if he's setting her up, what for?"

The young man scrolled further down and then clicked on something. "That flash drive Caroline smuggled out of ATS. You said there was a code name on it for the digital Pearl Harbor that was being planned?"

"Blue Sand," replied Harvath. "Why?"

"Because he also buried that term in Caroline's internal search history."

"By *internal,* you mean a search of ATS servers?"

"Right. It wasn't a search out on the Web, it was strictly limited to inside."

"But she's dead," said Rhodes. "What difference would it make what she looked at?"

Harvath had the same question. But more to the point, Middleton was planting evidence to make it look like Caroline Romero not only knew about the attack, but that ATS did too. Why?

That was the hardest piece for Harvath to figure out. You plant evidence to implicate someone for a crime. What crime was Middleton trying to frame Caroline for? Of simply *knowing* about the attack? She was dead. What good would that do?

Was he trying to frame her for causing it? No, that couldn't be it. That was the Carlton Group's role. They were the ones who had been set up to publically take the fall. Besides, ATS wouldn't want to be associated in any way, shape, or form with the attack. Whatever Caroline Romero was being made to look like or to have done, it wasn't for outside purposes, it was for something inside.

So what would that be? Why would Middleton need an internal scapegoat for an attack he and the powers that be at ATS all wanted to see take place? What would you need to blame someone for, and why would someone who was dead and couldn't defend herself be the perfect patsy?

The simplest reason he could think of was if the attack failed. Was that it? Had Middleton had a change of heart, and was he now trying to sabotage the plan and blame it on Caroline? He doubted it. There had to be something else.

Harvath kept running possible scenarios through his mind, filtering all of them through what he knew about Caroline Romero from Nicholas. None of them explained why Middleton would want to set her up. Finally, he gave up and asked Schroeder, "Was that it, or is there more?"

The young man looked at the log and replied, "He was inactive for a while. Maybe he got a phone call or something, because then he was back, and he sent three e-mails and logged off."

"Can you pull them up?"

Schroeder nodded and pulled them up one at a time. "The first one has the subject line 'Walworth.' That's the name of the company's corporate retreat out in Virginia. It went to the security scheduler and told him to get a full contingent out to the estate ASAP. The second e-mail also had the 'Walworth' subject line and went to the estate manager. It says that an emergency board meeting has been called and that members would begin showing up shortly and they'd be bringing family members."

"And the third e-mail?"

Schroeder pulled it up. "The last one is for me. Subject line, 'Hey Shithead.' He's such an asshole. He says he's tried to call me, but my 'fucking' phone has been turned off. When I get this e-mail, I'm supposed to pack a bag and get my ass out to the estate as soon as possible. Then he adds, 'P.S. Keep it quiet. Don't tell anybody where you're going. Hurry up.'"

"Have you ever spent the night there before?"

"Me?" replied Schroeder with a shake of his head. "No. It's only for board members."

"And their families," Harvath clarified.

"They have the families out once a year in the summer, but never for board meetings. Those are always very private. They don't want kids and grandkids running around. They don't even allow spouses. That's what doesn't make any sense. Why would they be bringing family members to an emergency board meeting?"

"Because they're about to launch their attack," said Casey.

"But the next big family event at the estate was going to be in about three weeks," Schroeder replied.

Harvath looked at him. "I thought they only did one family event a year, over the summer."

"They do, but this year they added some sort of team-building seminar, and the board members were bringing in the families for that. They'd already begun stocking up the estate."

"Do you think that's when they were going to conduct the attack?" Casey asked.

Harvath nodded.

"So what changed? Why would they need to move up their timetable? What could have possibly spooked them that bad?"

Raising his index finger, Harvath brought it to his chest and said, "Me."

CHAPTER 63

Carlton kept Martin Vignon secured to the chair and interrogated him right there in the bathroom.

The pasty, white-haired man had taken so many blows to the face and head from the soap on a rope that the swelling made him look like the Elephant Man. When he spoke, it was difficult to understand him. His lips as well as one of his eyes were swollen. Several of his teeth were loose. Blood ran from his mouth, his nose, and one ear.

It had been an incredibly effective beating, but what had pushed him into acquiescence was the waterboarding. It was absolutely impossible to hold out against, and for a man who was afraid of very few things in life, it had created inside him a surge of raw, animal panic. In short, it was terrifying and something he never, ever wanted to experience again.

After winding two spirals of toilet paper and shoving them into the prisoner's nostrils, Carlton had begun his questions. Banks stood in the hallway, with the iron kept hot and nearby as requested.

Vignon didn't have a lot of answers. He was a thug and a drone. He did, though, have one key piece of information to share—the names of those whom he worked for. Both Carlton and Banks had heard of Craig Middleton and of ATS, but neither had ever met the man.

One of the many questions Vignon was unable to answer was who had killed Carlton's security team and tried to burn his house to the ground with him in it. Vignon swore up and down it wasn't him or his people and that he didn't know anything about it. Carlton believed him.

He also believed the white-haired man when he said he had no idea who had killed the Carlton Group's operators. Though he admitted to having a paramilitary background, his job was running corporate security for ATS.

Carlton asked dozens of questions more, but Vignon was of no further help. When it came down to the inner workings of the company or why Middleton would have wanted Carlton and his people dead, the white-haired man knew absolutely nothing.

Carlton decided it was best to stick with what the man did know and try to uncover something from that. Slowly, he had him unpack his side of the operation that had ended up with his capture.

Halfway through his account, Carlton made him stop, back up, and repeat something. "You were prepared to engage how many men?"

"Three," Vignon replied.

"But there weren't three of us. There were only two."

The white-haired man nodded. "Middleton thought you might be making contact with a third man."

"Who? What third man?"

Vignon paused for a moment, trying to remember the name and then it came to him. "Harvath. Scot Harvath. A former SEAL. Middleton said that if Harvath showed up, he wanted us to kill him."

Carlton couldn't believe what he was hearing. For the last week, he had grieved for Harvath. He thought he was dead. He didn't want the possible disappointment of allowing himself even a sliver of hope, only to have it dashed. All the same, it was the first good news he'd had since this entire thing started, and his heart leapt, even as he fought to keep his emotions under control. "Harvath is alive?"

The white-haired man nodded. "According to Middleton; alive and extremely dangerous. That's all I know."

"And Middleton believed he might show up at the meeting in D.C.?"

Vignon nodded.

Stepping out of the bathroom, Carlton walked into the kitchen and motioned for Banks to follow.

"That's a piece of good news," the older man said.

"I need to get to a computer," Carlton replied. "Right now. Do you have a laptop or something?"

Banks shook his head. "I don't have any of that here. Staying off the radar means using as little electricity as possible."

Carlton parted the curtains above the sink and looked out toward the farmhouse. "What about your landlord? It's pretty dark over there right now."

"That's because they're out of town."

"They've probably got a computer and an Internet connection, right?"

Banks shrugged. "Maybe. It's definitely worth a look."

Carlton didn't even bother to respond. He was halfway to the door when Banks yelled to get his attention. When Carlton turned, he tossed him his ring of keys. "One of those opens their back door. The missus has a home office under the stairs. If there's a computer, it'll probably be in there."

He should have known Tommy would have availed himself of a key to his landlord's house and would be familiar with its layout. He was still the best field agent Carlton had ever met.

Bounding down the stairs and out of the barn, he took off across the grass to the house.

It took four keys before he found the right one and was able to let himself inside. He was grateful for the tip to check under the stairs, because it was a place he would probably not have thought to search for a computer. Sure enough, there it was.

Pulling the chair out from the desk, he squeezed into the tiny space, sat down, and fired up the computer. It was an old Dell model on a dial-up connection. Once it was ready to go, Carlton opened its Web browser.

He chastised himself for having left the IronKey drive back at the barn. While not perfect, it did help hide one's IP address and location. It wasn't the only way, though, and Carlton took several minutes, using a variety of different methods to cloak himself and his trail before landing on the dating site he and Harvath had designated as a means of communication of last resort.

As he clicked on his ad, he held his breath. The damn page seemed to take forever to load, but finally it did, and there, among multiple responses, was Harvath's. Carlton exhaled, and out of joy, slapped the narrow desk so hard that the bulletin board behind it fell down.

He quickly hung it back up and clicked on the tab along the top of Harvath's response inviting him to "private chat." Once inside the private chat, he left Harvath a message coded in pickup terms that authenticated that it was really Carlton communicating and that he was doing so of his own free will, not with someone holding a gun to his head. He closed by giving Harvath the number for his last clean cell phone.

Leaving the dating site, he shut down the computer, pushed back in his chair, and closed the door to the little office beneath the stairs.

Walking back to the barn, he pulled the phone from his bag in back of the Suburban and turned it on. Now all he could do was wait.

CHAPTER 64

W hen Bremmer had dangled Kurt Schroeder as a means to get to Craig Middleton, a million things had gone through Harvath's mind—one of which was that Bremmer was a pretty devious son of a bitch. Another was that Harvath didn't fully speak the language of a man like Schroeder, but he did have someone on his team who could—Nicholas.

It was a risk, a big one, taking him from the Strieber's farm in Texas and bringing him to D.C., but no one knew technology and data the way Nicholas did. He not only wanted him to be part of debriefing Schroeder but also close by in the event ATS launched its digital Pearl Harbor.

When they had cut loose the stunned and visibly shaken Bremmer at his daughter's field hockey game, Harvath used one of Casey's clean cell phones to reach out to Strieber. Despite the fact that the man had landed back in Texas only a handful of hours before, he told Harvath not to worry and that he'd have Nicholas on the next Strieber Airlines flight to Manassas.

When he landed at the airport, he texted Harvath who dispatched Rhodes in the Suburban to pick everyone up and bring them back to the loft. Because they had left Schroeder's vehicle around the corner from the dominatrix's house, they were able to come and go via the building's underground parking structure and park in his full-size spot.

Elizabeth, the dominatrix, had been another problem. They had brought her from her town house at gunpoint and she now sat bound and gagged in Schroeder's master bedroom. Rhodes and Casey had taken turns supervising her bathroom breaks, but he was going to need them to help go after Middleton. It was a good thing he had called Strieber, and he was thankful that Strieber would be arriving with extra manpower.

When Rhodes, Strieber, Nicholas, Nina, and the dogs poured out of the elevator, it looked like the circus had come to town. But judging by the equipment cases they were lugging, this circus had brought a little slice of hell with them.

Harvath, who didn't want Schroeder left alone for a second, again Flex-Cuffed his hands behind his back, and when the crew arrived, dragged him out of his computer room. Schroeder didn't say anything to Nina, but the way he looked at her was enough to set Nicholas off. Literally going toe-to-toe with him and actually kicking the larger man's shoe to get his attention, Nicholas looked up at him with the ultimate don't-fuck-with-me expression and proclaimed, "Back off. She's mine."

Schroeder was so surprised he didn't know what to say. He simply nodded.

Not wanting to undermine his friend, Harvath swallowed his grin, handed over custody of Schroeder to Casey, and motioned for the little man to follow him into the computer room so they could debrief.

Harvath kept it as short and as simple as possible, bringing him up to speed on Bremmer, Schroeder, and Middleton. Nicholas chose not to sit down and instead listened as he examined all of the room's equipment.

When Harvath had finished filling him in, Nicholas's first question was about Caroline. "Was one of Bremmer's kill teams responsible for her death?"

"No. Schroeder says that on the day she died, ATS had its own people pursuing her. She ran into traffic and was struck by a car."

Nicholas didn't like the answer, but it seemed to satisfy him for the time being. "Does Schroeder know Nina is Caroline's sister?"

Harvath shook his head.

"Good. Let's keep it that way. What about the attack?"

"Bremmer knows nothing about it and Schroeder seems to have been kept out of the loop as well. Middleton and the people around him are playing this very tight."

"Maybe not tight enough."

Harvath looked at him. "Did you find something else on that drive?"

Nicholas nodded. "Something called the Community Comprehensive National Cyber-security Initiative Data Center."

"What the hell is that?"

"I think it's the answer to the 'why now' question we've been asking, the trigger for a digital Pearl Harbor."

"I don't understand."

Nicholas held up his index finger and explained. "The Community Comprehensive National Cyber-security Initiative Data Center is known by its acronym, CNCI, or better yet by its nickname, Spy Center. The cover story is that the NSA had amassed so much data and drew so much power to cull, analyze, and house that data, it outgrew its capacity at Fort Meade. Therefore, a new facility needed to be built."

"Wait a second," said Harvath. "A whole new facility needed to be built? What was the point of the server farms they've been building, like down in San Antonio?"

Nicholas winked at him. "You're a little too informed for your own good and should know better than to ask questions like that. The thing is, you're right. The NSA, or more importantly ATS *through* the NSA, succeeded in pitching the need for a totally brand-new facility. The NSA really is beyond capacity at Fort Meade. It's like a black hole; they can't get enough electricity there. But here's where things get interesting.

"They assembled a list of thirty-seven possible locations, giving each a code name. Camp Williams, in the high mountain desert outside Salt Lake City, was code-named Site Blue."

"Blue Sand!" Harvath said.

Nicholas nodded. "And guess which location ended up being selected?"

"Camp Williams. Also known as Site Blue."

"Precisely. There, the NSA began its two-billion-dollar construction

CHAPTER 65

*T*hat *was it*, Harvath thought to himself. It didn't matter *how* they planned to do it, all that mattered was *what* they were planning to do, and now all of it made sense to him.

When the Internet was collapsed, it was going to be deadly—airplanes and trains would collide, the power grid would shut down, banks and financial services would fail, utilities and emergency services would grind to a halt and so would the delivery of fuel, food, and medicine. Tens of thousands of people, if not hundreds of thousands or even millions, would die. And while society crumbled, Craig Middleton and the board of directors from ATS would sit on their secure, well-stocked 200-acre estate in Virginia and ride out the storm. Harvath, though, wasn't about to let that happen.

Even if he stopped the attack from happening, the political fallout would be off the charts. The board of directors at ATS read like a who's who of the most powerful in government. Politicking and diplomacy had never been his thing. That was an area in which the Old Man excelled. Which reminded him of something.

Turning to Nicholas, he pointed at the wall of screens and asked, "Can you open up a connection to the Net on one of those for me?"

The little man climbed into Schroeder's chair and got to work. A few moments later he said, "Got it."

project. Spy Center covers more than one million square feet of data storage, technical support, and administrative space—five times the size of the U.S. Capitol. It includes its own power stations, backup generators, and massive stores of fuel and water.

"But here's the most dramatic feature. According to Caroline's notes, the Comprehensive National Cyber-security Data Center isn't just about collecting and storing data. Its real purpose is to be the nucleus of the brand-new, government-controlled Internet. So, in answer to your question, *Why now?*, it's because ATS is ready. Finally, all the technology exists. The only thing they need to make the change—"

"Is a crisis," Harvath said, finishing his sentence for him, "explosive enough to justify it."

Harvath gave him the URL he wanted him to plug in. Nicholas paused and looked over his shoulder. "Seriously?"

"Long story. Just do it, please."

Nicholas turned back around and did as he was told. When he had navigated to the page, he pushed back from the desk and surrendered the system to Harvath.

Harvath rolled his chair over, grabbed the mouse, and began to click through the ads until he got to the Old Man's. There was a response! He couldn't believe it. The response invited him into a private chat section. Harvath decided to follow the link.

Based on the wording, he had zero doubt that it had been written by the Old Man. It was him and he was alive. There was also a phone number.

Harvath had to assume it was a burner, a chat-and-chuck that the Old Man could dump if and when he needed to. The question was, was ATS on to it? Would calling the Old Man lead their goons here to Schroeder's loft?

Harvath thought about going downstairs, getting in the Suburban, and driving somewhere to make the call, but if someone was listening and trying to track him, they'd probably use one of the many CCTV cameras in the city to pinpoint his vehicle and follow it when he drove back.

On the other hand, according to Schroeder, he was the only one Middleton had tasked with tracking down Harvath and the Old Man. There wasn't an army of analysts at ATS working on it around the clock.

It made sense. Middleton was all about compartmentalization. The less his staff knew, the better. Schroeder had proven capable enough. He had tracked Harvath to Paris, Spain, and Texas—not to mention all the other operators he had tracked. Roping more employees in, regardless of how little he told them, would only end up risking exposure for Middleton. Harvath decided it was worth it.

On the third ring, Reed Carlton picked up the phone. After a quick back-and-forth to establish their bona fides, the Old Man said, "I can't tell you how good it is to hear your voice."

"Yours too," Harvath replied. "We need to meet. There's a lot I need to fill you in on."

"Are you in town?"

"I am. How about you?"

"No. I needed some fresh air," said Carlton.

"That's probably a good idea. Why don't I come to you?"

The Old Man agreed and once their call was complete, he transmitted the specifics.

An hour and a half later, the two men were reunited in a tavern parking lot, not far from Tommy Banks' barn apartment. Carlton wrapped his arms around Harvath and gave him a huge hug. "I *thought* you were dead."

"I thought the same," Harvath said, hugging him back, happy beyond words that the Old Man was still alive. His mood, though, shifted when he let go of Carlton and shared, "It happened so fast. There was nothing I could've done for Riley."

The Old Man shook his head. "We're going to make those bastards pay. I just wish we had more help."

"We're not completely alone," he replied. Removing his flashlight, he cupped his hand partly over the lens and gave it two quick flashes.

Harvath had dropped off the two Athena Team members a half mile up the road and they had circled back. Casey appeared out of the darkness first, followed by Rhodes, who was carrying a long nylon case that contained a LaRue PredatAR rifle outfitted with a night vision scope that Strieber had brought along on his return trip "just in case."

The women had never met Carlton in person. After shaking hands, he suggested they continue their conversation back at the farm. Harvath agreed and they climbed into their two vehicles. Once the Old Man had pulled out onto the road, Harvath fell in a safe distance behind him.

Back at the farm, Banks kept watch over Martin Vignon above the barn, while Carlton made coffee for the team in the kitchen of the farmhouse. Tommy told him not to worry and assured him he would straighten everything out with his landlords when they returned from their trip.

Harvath filled Carlton in on everything that had happened, and then Carlton took his turn. He began by explaining why he had sent Riley to

Paris. A French banker had been helping several rogue nations circumvent financial sanctions and had also begun assisting in arms transactions. There was a fear that the CIA station in Paris might have been compromised, so Carlton had been asked to send in his own team. Before he could task Riley and Harvath with the assignment, though, the night of the long knives had come.

The Old Man walked him through everything else that had taken place. In his inimitable fashion, he revealed only those facts he thought Harvath needed to know and kept the rest to himself. Casey and Rhodes sat quietly and listened, taking in all the details.

After he had finished and they had fired questions back and forth about ATS, Carlton looked at Harvath and said, "You're right about the political fallout. An accusation alone, without some sort of corpus delicti, isn't going to be enough to bring them down."

"What about what's on the flash drive?"

"Even if I had read through all of the material, I don't think I'd want to bet all the marbles on it."

"What about testimony?" Harvath asked. "You've got Vignon. We've got Schroeder, and we can roll up Bremmer at any time."

"All three of whom were kidnapped by us at some point in this process and will refuse to testify on grounds of self-incrimination. They'll only talk with some sort of immunity deal. To get that, we'll have to go to either the President or the Attorney General and give them something substantial—something tangible and incriminating."

"That's all well and good, but we don't have that kind of time. This attack is about to happen, and you know what? I don't give a damn about political repercussions. I want to prevent this attack. We can worry about the fallout later."

Carlton took a sip of coffee, the gears turning inside his mind. "I agree. No matter what we gave to the President or the DOJ, because of the players involved, they're going to make damn sure they've investigated this up one side and down the other before they make a single move."

"In other words, paralysis."

"No, not paralysis. We're talking about political and career radiation from any misstep or mistake. I think exceedingly meticulous caution is what the watchwords will be. But you're right. It's going to move very slowly. They're going to do everything by the book, dot every *i* and cross every *t*."

"And that's fine. The bigger the case they can build, the better. All I care about, though, is disrupting the attack."

The Old Man took another sip of coffee. No one spoke. The only sound was the ticking of a Regulator grandfather clock out in the hallway.

Finally, Carlton looked and him and said, "What do you want to do?"

Harvath didn't need to formulate an answer. He knew exactly what he wanted to do. "I want to go in. Tonight. Now."

CHAPTER 66

Mike Strieber was a godsend. Flying people back at night, he had taken the initiative to bring along the new rifle Rhodes was using, as well as night vision equipment for Harvath. It was part of the multiple Storm cases' worth of gear Harvath, Casey, and Rhodes had loaded into the Suburban before leaving D.C. to meet up with Reed Carlton. Now, as Harvath made his way through the darkness of the wooded, northern edge of the ATS estate, he was very appreciative.

Schroeder had sketched out what he knew about the estate, but it was Vignon, the security chief, who really provided them with the best overall view. Of course, it was under extreme duress, but there was enough there to help in planning a halfway decent assault.

Most helpful were the anticipated personnel levels, what their backgrounds were, and how likely they were to engage an intruder they viewed as a threat. Vignon didn't mince words, especially when it came to the last issue. The estate security agents were highly skilled and were authorized to kill any hostile intruders. As Harvath wasn't pedaling up on a bike selling magazine subscriptions, he had no question which category he'd be placed in if they caught him. The key was not to get caught.

As he picked his way through the woods, Riley Turner popped into his mind. He couldn't allow himself to think about her, not now. He needed to focus. Placing her back inside the iron box he kept in that far, dusty corner of his mind, he slammed the lid shut and locked it. There'd be time to come to terms with Riley's death; now wasn't it. Shifting his attention to what lay ahead of him, he went back over everything he had been told about the ATS compound.

According to Vignon, they didn't use dogs on the estate. That was a big relief. But according to Schroeder, and this was seconded by Vignon, they did use multiple layers of highly sensitive intrusion detection systems. Luckily, Schroeder had helped install and centralize them. From his loft back in D.C., with Nicholas supervising his every move, Schroeder was able to create dead zones through which Harvath could slip and approach the main building. He also helped their radios pierce the signals blackout that normally blanketed the estate.

When Harvath came across the first guard patrol, right about the distance Vignon had assured him they would be, he quietly alerted Rhodes to their position. "Overwatch. This is Norseman. Do you copy? Over."

"This is Overwatch," she replied. "I copy you, Norseman. Over."

"I've got two guards on foot just east of my position. Can you see them? Over."

"Negative, Norseman. Stand by."

Seconds passed before Rhodes came back over Harvath's earpiece and said. "Norseman, this is Overwatch. I have them now. Over."

Mike Strieber had brought along one of his high-end M4-style rifles, which had been zeroed in with a powerful night vision scope. It wasn't lost on Harvath that he was launching an operation very similar to the one ATS had launched against him in Texas. Reflecting on this, he had warned Rhodes to be careful not to get ambushed.

While Rhodes covered Harvath's approach from the rear of the property, Casey was coming at the property from the front. Her job was to be there and create a diversion if necessary to draw attention away from any escape Harvath might need to make.

It was a good night for an assault; cold with thick cloud cover. The wind rattled the branches of the trees and sent patches of leaves skittering across the ground. It was the kind of night where senses got dulled standing a security post. The more the wind blew, the more apt you were to attribute things to it. A lot of second-guessing happened on nights like this, and Harvath was counting on that.

Staying in the trees, he moved southeast. The idea was to limit his time in open terrain as much as possible. The problem was that sweeping expanses of manicured lawns predominantly surrounded the main house. It was only by coming up on it at an angle, where the support buildings were, that an intruder had any chance of cover. ATS knew this too, though, and had focused heavily on defending this approach. For Harvath, it wasn't the technology being employed that was a problem, it was the amount of personnel.

One of the advantages he had on his side was surprise. Another was that none of the men standing guard tonight had expected to do so. Middleton's decision to rush them to the estate had been very last-minute. As a result, most of them were probably tired and more than a little bit punchy. That didn't mean, though, that they weren't a threat. Harvath could last longer than most without sleeping. And while he didn't like it, it didn't lessen how deadly he was. In fact, it might actually heighten it, as lack of sleep often put him in a bad mood.

What also put him in a bad mood were terrorists, and that was exactly how he saw Middleton and everyone else associated with ATS. Spouses and family members aside, there were no innocents on this property tonight. That thought was at the forefront of his mind as he came to the edge of the trees, one hundred yards from the beginning of the support buildings.

From where he crouched, he could see another patrol of two men. Hailing Rhodes again, he said, "Overwatch. This is Norseman. Do you copy? Over."

"Norseman, this is Overwatch. I copy. Over."

"I have another patrol. Two guards on my side of the long utility shed. Do you have eyes on? Over."

"Roger that, Norseman. Overwatch has eyes on. Two guards, north side of the utility shed. Over."

"Do you see anything else? Over."

"Negative, Norseman. There was movement near the stables, possibly another patrol, but it has moved on. You're good to go. Over."

"Roger that," replied Harvath. "Stand by."

He was carrying a suppressed, hyperaccurate short-barreled OBR rifle chambered in 5.56. Mounted to the top was an EOTech XPS3 holographic weapon sight and behind it a PVS-14 night vision monocular. With it, Harvath had been scanning the darkness for threats, and that was how he had picked up the first two patrols. Steadying his breathing, he peered through the optics once more, scanned the area, and then said over his radio, "Overwatch, this is Norseman. You are clear to fire at utility shed guards. Over."

"Roger that, Norseman. Overwatch is cleared hot. Engaging guards on north side of utility shed in three . . . two . . . one . . ."

Harvath watched as the first sentry was shot in the head, followed immediately by the second. Before either of the bodies had hit the ground, he had already taken off running.

It was one of the fastest one-hundred-yard dashes he had ever run. Skidding to a stop in the loose gravel and dirt behind the utility shed, he almost lost his balance.

After sweeping the area for threats, he dragged the first sentry and then the second closer to the shed where their bodies would be harder to spot in the shadow of the building.

He was now in an area where it would be difficult for Rhodes to cover him. There were too many buildings and miscellaneous pieces of equipment he would be using for cover that would impede her view. Only in the final sprint to the house would she be able to see him again. "Overwatch to Norseman. Good luck. Overwatch out."

Harvath took a deep breath, let it out, and then listened. The wind was really blowing and he thanked God again that they weren't using dogs. They would have smelled him coming from a mile away, especially now that he had begun sweating.

Keeping his back against the wall of the utility shed, he slid down to the far corner. Readying his weapon, he counted to three and poked around the corner ready to fire. There was no one there. Quietly, he made his way up the small hill, using the shed to hide him from view of the main house. So far, so good.

At the end of the shed, there was an open area about forty yards long before the next building. Parked two-thirds of the way between was one of the estate's utility vehicles. After using the night vision device to scan for threats, Harvath took off for it.

Coming to another abrupt stop, he crouched behind the engine block and listened. There was nothing he could discern, other than the wind.

Peeking around the front of the vehicle, he scanned for threats with his weapon site and, seeing nothing, stood up and took off running once more.

The next building was the stables. This was where Rhodes had said she had seen movement. Moving around the back of the structure, Harvath hugged the outer stable wall.

Halfway up, his foot caught on the edge of something and he almost tripped, but was able to recover his balance. No sooner had he done so than two armed men appeared. They were talking to each other and were obviously taken by surprise. Before they could get their weapons up and fully on target, Harvath depressed his trigger dropping the first man and then shifted to the second and did the same.

"Guards down," he whispered over his radio as he crept toward the riding arena. Beyond the arena was a long row of garages and after that, the final sprint to the house.

Harvath moved past the riding arena and made it behind the garages without any further incident. He now only had one last open area to cover, which they had code-named "the bridge," to get to the main house.

"Norseman to Overwatch. Do you copy? Over?"

"Roger that, Norseman. I copy. Over."

"Ready to cross the bridge. How does everything look? Over."

"A team just moved through. You should hit it before they come back. Over."

"Roger that," replied Harvath. "Stand by." He swept the area with his weapon, took three deep breaths, and then said, "Now!"

Springing from behind the garages, he ran for the back of the house. It was another hundred-yard dash, and then some. He ran with all the speed he could summon.

He was less than halfway there when he caught movement out of the corner of his left eye. There were two more sentries, and there was no way he'd be able to spin and engage them in time.

CHAPTER 67

Before Harvath could turn and engage the shooters, he heard Rhodes over the radio say, "Guard down," followed by another, "Guard down," as the bodies dropped at his nine o'clock.

Rhodes was amazing. She obviously had his back, so he kept moving as quickly as he could.

When he finally arrived at the house, his lungs were on fire. He pulled up alongside, crouched out of view, and drew large breaths until he'd oxygenated his blood and steadied his heart rate. Throughout the entire process, he never moved the muzzle of his weapon, which was trained on the back door.

As soon as his pulse and breathing were steady, he prepared himself to enter the house.

According to Vignon, the security staff came and went through the kitchen, so the door was left unlocked. Sliding over to it now, Harvath gave the knob a slow twist, and found that it was indeed unlocked. Over his radio, he whispered, "Norseman making entry in three, two, *one.*"

Pulling the door open, he came into the kitchen low. There were two guards at the kitchen table and a third doing something at the sink. He double-tapped each of them and cursed under his breath when the man at the sink dropped the coffee mug he was holding and it shattered in the sink.

Had anyone else heard it? It had sounded earsplitting to him, and not just because his finely tuned senses were on high alert and he was allergic to making noise. It had been loud. Too loud. *Damn it.* Time to move.

Stepping to the far side of the room, he pulled even with a set of stairs that led up to where the bedrooms were. Vignon had laid out who normally stayed in what rooms, all of which were named after characters from literature. But before Harvath went upstairs, he wanted to clear downstairs.

Moving through the kitchen, he checked a small breakfast atrium and then scanned an adjacent butler's pantry. Stepping into the formal dining room, he made a quick check before sweeping back into the kitchen and up the servants' hall to the front of the house. As he did, he heard a noise from somewhere behind him.

Pressing himself up against the wall near the entrance to the dining room, he strained to discern what it was. He picked up the sound of footsteps. They were slow and methodical, cautious even. Based on the fact that there had been three guards in the kitchen, Harvath was willing to bet he was listening to the approach of a fourth, who must have been somewhere sneaking a cigarette or in one of the home's bathrooms.

Allowing the weapon to hang from its sling, Harvath unsheathed a flat, skeletonized dagger and made ready.

When the figure appeared in the doorway, Harvath wrenched his pistol to the side and drove the dagger into his throat. He quickly thrust up toward the man's right ear and tore through and back toward his left.

Easing the large man to the floor, he withdrew the dagger, wiped it, and slid it back in its sheath.

He transitioned back to his OBR and swept through a card room, a rather substantial library, and then the living room. There was no sign of life. At least there hadn't been until he exited the opposite end of the living room where light spilled from an open doorway across the hall. Very carefully, Harvath made his way toward it.

Sweeping into a lavishly decorated study, with animal heads on the wall and a huge fireplace, Harvath found Craig Middleton. He was seated in a high-backed leather chair at an ornate partner's desk. A pair of reading glasses were balanced on his nose as he studied a series of maps laid out in front of him. His shirtsleeves were rolled up and his jacket and tie lay across a nearby chair. In his right hand he held a rocks glass with what looked like scotch.

"Don't move," said Harvath as he entered the room.

Middleton looked up from his papers. A smile slowly unzipped across his craggy face. "Look at this. The mountain has finally come to Mohammed."

"Don't move *includes* not moving your mouth."

Middleton rattled the ice in his glass, as if his right hand were trembling.

"Who else from the board is in the house?"

"How about a drink first?"

Harvath replied by firing two rounds into the top of the leather chair on either side of his head.

"Four," Middleton replied. "Though I heard a car about an hour ago, so there could be a fifth. I've been a little bit busy."

"I'll bet you have. Get up. You're coming with me."

Middleton smiled at him and leaned back in his chair. "I'd offer you a real nice position with us, but I know you wouldn't take it. It's a shame. We could use a man of your talents. The world is changing, quite rapidly, in fact. Guys like you are going to have to adapt or be crushed underfoot as our country progresses forward."

Harvath put two rounds through the desk, barely missing each of Middleton's knees. "I said get up."

Middleton scooted himself back from the desk and took a long draught of his drink. "I hope wherever we're going, there's plenty of this." Sitting the glass down on the desk, he smiled and added, "Are you a scotch fan, Mr. Harvath? I mean a fan of really, really good scotch. I've got a special bottle I have been saving for tomorrow."

Harvath was about to tell him to shut up and step from behind the desk, when there was a *pop* and two barbed probes embedded themselves between his shoulder blades.

When the electricity ripped through his body, his muscles seized and he fell forward like an oak tree that had just been chopped down. He hit the floor face-first and blood gushed from his nose.

They rolled him on his back and stripped away his pistol and rifle. When his brain came back online and he was able to process what was going on, he was stunned to see Chuck Bremmer standing right next to Middleton, the Taser gripped in his right hand.

"It took all night," he said with disdain, "but we knew you'd be here eventually." With that, Bremmer pressed the Taser's trigger again and held it down, giving Harvath an excruciatingly long shock.

When he stopped and Harvath had regained his faculties, Bremmer stepped forward and kicked him as hard as he could, right in the ribs. "That's for using a sniper to target my fucking wife." The kick was very painful but not as painful as the one that followed, which caught him under the chin and sent a searing lightning bolt right through his skull. "And that's for targeting my daughter. My daughter! You son of a bitch."

As Bremmer stepped back, Middleton looked down at Harvath. "You actually had old Chuck for a little bit. In the end, though, he figured it was worth one more try at getting rid of you. I'd say that was a pretty good gamble. Wouldn't you?"

Harvath spit a glob of blood onto the Persian carpet he was lying on and worked his jaw side to side.

"Since you had Vignon and Schroeder, we figured it was pointless to try to stop you from accessing the estate. In fact, it was Chuck's idea to let you walk on. If security caught you, perfect. If not, we figured this would work and it did. Now, to tie up all the loose ends."

Harvath watched as Middleton gestured for the rifle. Bremmer checked to make sure there was a round chambered and then handed it to him.

He hefted it up and down a couple of times and then seated the stock at his shoulder. Stepping away from Harvath, he raised the weapon and pointed it at several of the animal heads mounted on the wall. Bremmer gloated with a smile that stretched from ear to ear.

But the smile vanished when Middleton aimed the weapon at him and pressed the trigger.

A spray of pink mist hung in the air like some sort of obscene halo as the round took out half the man's head.

"Very nice," said Middleton as he walked over and picked up the Taser. "Very nice indeed. Now, about the rest of those loose ends. I'd like to know where you're keeping Kurt Schroeder as well as my security chief, Mr. Vignon."

Harvath looked up, smiled, and shook his head. He was already gritting his teeth, aware of what was coming next.

Squeezing the trigger on the Taser, Middleton gave Harvath another burst of electricity.

Harvath's body went as stiff as a board and then began to bend as his spine arched and his tensioned shoulders pushed him up off the floor.

When the effects of the Taser passed, Middleton repeated his question.

"Go fish," Harvath replied.

The Director of ATS was visibly upset with that answer and sent Harvath back into agony with the device.

He pulled the trigger two more times just to prove how far he was prepared to go.

When Harvath's eyes, which had rolled back into his head, came down and refocused, Middleton leaned over and pressed him one last time. "Listen to me, motherfucker. One last chance. After this, I'm going to the rifle and I'll start by putting holes in your fucking knees. Where are my people? More importantly, where the fuck are Banks and Carlton?"

"Right here, asshole," said a voice from the doorway.

Middleton spun as Reed Carlton pantomimed a kiss and two shots sped from his custom 1911.

EPILOGUE

Though Reed Carlton knew plenty of heavy hitters in Washington, it was Tommy Banks who was able to secretly get the heads of the FBI, CIA, NSA, and the DoD into one room on such short notice. Harvath had no desire to be at the meeting and had politely declined. Carlton understood why he wanted to remain in the background. He only asked that he and Nicholas, who had gone back to Texas to spend time with Nina, be accessible via secure communication in case there were any questions.

As it turned out, there were many questions, most of which were aimed at the Director of the NSA. All of the agency heads viewed ATS as a monster that the NSA had allowed to get out of control. They had long held suspicions about what the quasiprivate company had been up to, and now many of their worst fears were confirmed.

With no staff in the room, there was no one the NSA Director could divert to and ask questions of. Not that it would have mattered. If even half of what Carlton had said about ATS was true, and he had no reason to doubt it, they had a major clusterfuck on their hands—regardless of how much sway the NSA did or didn't have over ATS. In a town like D.C., perception was reality, and that was all that mattered.

The other problem NSA was staring down the barrel of was how physically intertwined they were with ATS, particularly when it came to the Utah Data Center. They were going to have to shut it down, immediately, at least until a thorough investigation could be conducted. They needed to know how ATS had specifically planned to carry out its attack and make sure that safeguards were put in place so that such a thing could never happen in the future.

After the participants tired of putting the boot to the NSA Director, they turned their sights to what the next several steps should be. All present agreed that there were two that needed to be taken care of right away. First, a cleanup team needed to be sent to the ATS estate to relieve Casey and Rhodes.

Per Reed Carlton's suggestion, the CIA would handle the cleanup, as well as develop a cover story that showed Chuck Bremmer had deep financial difficulties. In addition to a daughter leaving for an expensive Ivy League college next year, he was carrying on multiple extramarital affairs. He had decided to leave the Defense Department and transition into the private sector in order to make more money. To that end, he had lined up a job with ATS, but when it fell through, he went on a rampage, killing several ATS personnel at the company's rural Virginia retreat, including the company's managing director, Craig Middleton. The evidence at the scene would show that Middleton was able to get a shot off in the struggle before he died, killing Bremmer.

According to Casey and Rhodes, none of the board members had arrived at the estate yet. Having control of the scene worked to their advantage, but they would have to move fast.

The other step that needed to be taken was informing the President. The hardest part about setting up the meeting was limiting the amount of people in the room. The Director of Central Intelligence, though, was quite blunt and informed the President that the only people that would be allowed in the room were the Attorney General and the Treasury Secretary. The President's chief of staff and the rest of the opinion shapers he was wont to surround himself with were not allowed. This was a national emergency, but the circle of people chiming in needed to be very tight.

To his credit, the President respected the counsel of the DCI and did exactly as he asked. When Reed Carlton arrived at the White House along with the heads of the CIA, NSA, FBI, and DoD, the President met them in the situation room with only the Treasury Secretary and Attorney General in tow.

Carlton spoke for fifteen minutes, followed by the Directors of the NSA, FBI, and CIA, as well as the Secretary of Defense. The Attorney General and the Treasury Secretary were floored by what they had heard. The President, though appalled, retained his composure.

After everyone had been given a chance to speak and ask questions, the President raised the issue of damage control. The story would be so corrosive to the American psyche and would so undermine the people's trust in government, that he wanted it buried and cemented over. His intelligence chiefs cautioned there was a very fine line to be walked here. If they attempted a cover-up, it would suggest that ATS had been acting with the knowledge and support of the United States government, which wasn't true. If that caught hold in the American consciousness, it would be a nosedive from which there'd be absolutely no recovery.

The intelligence chiefs asked the President to order a thorough investigation first and have them report back what they felt were the best options. The President agreed.

In the meantime, the President wanted a stake driven through the heart of ATS. He wanted it completely broken up and all of its dirty deals unwound. If they had immediate access to all of the financial records at ATS, the Treasury Secretary said, they would make it their number one priority. The Attorney General said the Justice Department would back Treasury with whatever it needed. The question was, could the government, and the countless agencies and departments ATS provided technical solutions to, survive if the company was collapsed?

The NSA Director and the Secretary of Defense conferred for a moment off to the side. As they did, the President wrote on a notepad, outlining three legislative issues he wanted his staff to get moving in Congress right away:

1. A state of national emergency could last for only one year. Any period beyond that would need approval by a two-thirds vote of Congress.

2. All warrantless surveillance of American citizens was to be terminated immediately. Going forward, it would be a capital offense to surveil American citizens without proper judicial review and written authorization.

3. In order to curb insider trading, all members of Congress, as well as all federal employees who work in the defense, technology, and intelligence sectors of government, were to be prohibited from investing in the stock market.

The President was developing a fourth point about bringing better oversight to classified programs so that the nation's leaders couldn't be kept in the dark, when the NSA Director and the Secretary of Defense adjourned their sidebar and replied to the President's question.

It was their opinion that ATS could in fact be broken up and sold to a myriad of contracting firms who would be able to maintain the existing service agreements.

The conversation then turned to Craig Middleton and his coconspirators. The only two people currently in custody were Kurt Schroeder and Martin Vignon, neither of whom appeared to have had any knowledge of the proposed attack or the overall big picture plot. But both were guilty of a string of other violations, as were a significant portion of the rank-and-file at ATS. When they began discussing legal strategy, all eyes turned to the Attorney General.

He had already been playing various scenarios in his mind and didn't need time to collect his thoughts. All of the charges against ATS employees could be handled in federal court. That didn't worry him. His concern was the company's fifteen-member board of directors. Because of their prominence, openly trying them in public could be the equivalent of a public relations loose nuke. If it detonated, the fallout would be devastating. The knowledge that so many well-known and trusted figures had been conspiring against their own country might actually do more long-term damage than anyone could predict. Though it would demonstrate that the United States eventually discovered and stopped the plot, and might act as a deterrent, he didn't think the nation's psyche would survive it.

Citing the Patriot Act and the National Defense Authorization Act, the AG stated that an argument could be made for indefinite detention of any and all board members and possibly even military tribunals. There was another option available, but it would be up to the President. *The Black List.*

Upon mention of the list, the Treasury Secretary was asked to leave the situation room and wait outside. Discussion of the Black List was outside his purview.

It might have been argued that the only people who should have been allowed to stay in the room at all were the CIA Director and the Secretary of Defense, but the President asked Carlton, as well as the FBI and NSA directors, to remain. Going around the conference table, he asked the men one by one to weigh in on utilizing the Black List.

The FBI Director was adamantly opposed to it. He did not like the idea of the United States government being able to target and kill American citizens without due process. Immediately, the Attorney General jumped in to argue that there was a process, it just didn't take place in a courtroom.

The FBI Director finished his argument by saying that if you couldn't face your accusers and personally answer the charges against you, it was not due process, and it was not what the Founders intended.

Not only did the CIA Director disagree with his FBI colleague, so too did the NSA Director and the Secretary of Defense. They argued that ATS had intended to overthrow the United States. After failing to achieve their goal, the board members couldn't then come back and lobby for the full rights and protections that they had been actively working to subvert.

As the debate wore on, the FBI Director continued to remain steadfast in his position. No argument could change his mind. Eventually, the President thanked him and excused him from the room.

The final person the President queried about using the Black List was Reed Carlton. Very carefully, he laid out his argument.

As he saw it, the President had no choice. He agreed with the Attorney General that the spectacle of a public trial was out of the question. Indefinitely detaining the board members or trying them via a military tribunal would also be a huge spectacle. When word got out—and it would—that so many once-respected national political figures had been involved in a plot to subvert the nation, the effect would be irreversible. The Black List had to be used. Around the table, every head nodded in agreement.

The only weak point that the NSA Director could see was that even if the kills were handled covertly, someone at some point was going to connect the dots. You could only have so many "accidents" before suspicions were raised.

The CIA Director looked at Carlton, who then looked at the President and said, "There's actually a way to handle that."

FORTY-EIGHT HOURS LATER

The Gulfstream G550 business jet registered to Advance Technology Solutions reached its cruising altitude and leveled off over the ocean.

Each of the aircraft's fifteen passengers had received a phone call from Martin Vignon, a man they had all known for many years and trusted. Citing security concerns, he had kept the conversations brief.

With Reed Carlton listening in on each call, Vignon relayed two pieces of information. The first was that Middleton had been able to short-circuit the attack. As they'd all heard that it was imminent, yet it failed to materialize, Vignon's claim made sense. It also made the second piece of information even more believable.

According to Vignon, Middleton had established a contingency that required the board's immediate attention. Because the Virginia estate was an active crime scene and the ATS corporate headquarters were crawling with investigators, Vignon had arranged transportation for the board to the company's Grand Cayman property.

After the flight attendant had gone through and conducted the second cocktail service, the pilot summoned her to the cockpit. Stepping inside, Gretchen Casey closed and locked the door behind her.

As the CIA pilot began reducing the oxygen in the main cabin, Scot Harvath, uniformed to look like the copilot, handed Casey her equipment. One by one, they took turns getting suited up in the tight cockpit. When the pilot flashed them the signal, they donned their helmets and began the flow of oxygen into their face masks. Ten minutes later, they opened the cockpit door.

It was obvious from where they stood that hypoxia had kicked in. Quickly, Harvath and Casey moved through, certifying that each of the ATS board members was in fact dead.

Once complete, Harvath returned to the cockpit and flashed the pilot the thumbs-up. As the CIA operative finished tweaking the autopilot settings, Harvath and Casey gave each other's HAHO equipment a final inspection, then did the same for the pilot once he stepped into the main cabin and joined them.

Harvath looked at his wrist-top computer and gave the two-minute sign to the others. He then stepped forward and made ready to open the main cabin door.

At the one-minute mark, he signaled his team and opened the forward cabin door.

As alarms blared from the cockpit and the roar of the slipstream filled their ears, Harvath counted down the remaining seconds and then gave the team the signal to jump. The CIA pilot leapt first, followed by Casey and then, after one last look back into the cabin, Harvath.

The jet continued its flight out over the ocean toward its rendezvous with a deep, watery grave. Papers would carry the story about how the ATS board of directors, already reeling from the tragic loss of their managing director, had also discovered that he had embezzled significant funds from the company. They had been on their way to an emergency meeting with their bankers in Grand Cayman when their plane crashed. None of the bodies would ever be recovered.

Harvath navigated Casey and the CIA pilot to the drop zone out over the open ocean where a U.S. Navy vessel was waiting.

A flotilla of rubber Zodiacs rushed out to meet them, fish them out of the water, and return them to the ship.

From there, a Sikorsky SH-60F Seahawk helicopter ferried the team to Naval Air Station Key West, where the CIA pilot caught a flight back to D.C. Harvath and Casey, though, had other plans.

Cash, a change of clothes, and a vehicle from the motor pool were waiting for them when they arrived. Climbing in their car, they headed north on US-1 toward Little Torch Key. With the windows rolled down, the car was filled with the scent of the ocean. Though they were both quietly concerned about being late, they smiled when a Jimmy Buffett song came on the radio. Somehow, it felt like Riley Turner was sending them a message.

Undergoing the same training the Delta Force men did, the women of the Athena Project attended the U.S. Army's Special Forces Combat Diver Qualification Course in Key West. But unlike for the guys in Delta and SF, who enjoyed spending their R&R in a handful of bars in Key West, Little Torch Key had become the destination of the Athena women when they had downtime.

It was Riley Turner who had discovered the Little Palm Island Resort and Spa on Little Torch Key, and she had dubbed it her favorite destination in the entire world. It seemed a fitting place for Harvath and Casey to say good-bye.

They checked in and were shown to their waterfront bungalows with a few minutes to spare. Poking her head into Harvath's, Casey asked, "What do you think? Margaritas?"

Harvath shook his head, walked over to his coffee table, and grabbed the ice bucket, bottle of champagne, and two glasses he had ordered in advance. "We need to say good-bye in style."

Casey smiled. He still had a little bit to learn in the leadership department vis-à-vis second-guessing the people under him, but he did think of everything. That had pissed her off about him more than once. She also knew that she had unfairly held him responsible for what had happened in Paris. She had blamed him for allowing Riley to die, even though she knew he would go back and trade places with her in a second. She was ready to forgive him.

As he held the ice bucket and champagne up for her to see, she smiled and said, "Perfect."

They walked out onto the soft sand in front of the bungalows, and as the sun began its lazy drop into the ocean, Harvath released the cork and poured them each a glass.

When the sun touched the water, they toasted to Riley's memory and each took a long, slow sip of champagne. Sitting there on the beach with the thatched bungalows behind them and the waves gently lapping at the shore, they could see why she had so loved this spot. Harvath topped off their glasses.

They stayed there, neither speaking, and drank until the bottle was empty. It was only then that Harvath looked over his shoulder and realized that the staff had quietly been lighting torches illuminating the path to the tiny restaurant. "Hungry?" he asked.

Casey, her eyes closed and her hands behind her in the sand, smiled. "Is the champagne all gone?"

"All gone."

"Think there's any more in our minibars?"

"Probably," replied Harvath. "Do you want me to go check?"

Casey nodded, her eyes still closed.

"I'll be right back then," said Harvath as he stood and walked back barefoot to his bungalow.

Stepping inside, he left the door open as he crossed the room, opened the little refrigerator, and looked inside. He fished out a small bottle, and knew it wouldn't be enough. They were saying good-bye to somebody special. They needed another adult-size bottle.

Walking over to the nightstand, Harvath picked up the phone to contact room service. He had lifted the handset and was about to dial when he noticed someone appear at his bungalow door. A breeze from the ocean billowed the curtains into the room. It was Casey.

"I was just about to order us another bottle," he said.

"Forget it," she replied.

"You don't need another drink?"

Unbuttoning her shirt, she let it fall from her shoulders. "No. Right now, we both need something else."

AFTERWORD

The concepts of "Total Surveillance" and "Total Information Awareness" have fascinated me for years.

While writing this novel, not a day went by that new material didn't appear. Deciding what technology to include and what to leave out was particularly challenging. At times, it was like trying to drink from a fire hose.

I have assembled a list of my research material at BradThor.com.

ACKNOWLEDGMENTS

I remember living in Paris, attempting to write my first thriller, and reflecting on what a lonely profession being an author is. Little did I know then, that this was one of many white lies I would tell myself because I was afraid of failing. Only years later, after completing my very first novel, would I realize how wrong I was. Writing and publishing are team sports, and I am happy to be working with some of the best in the business.

First and foremost, my thanks always go to you, my **readers.** It is because of you that I am able to engage in a career I love. It is also because of you that I strive to improve my craft and get better with every book. Thank you for your support and for that most important ingredient of an author's success—all of the wonderful word-of-mouth.

My thanks go out to the magnificent, worldwide network of **booksellers** who stock, sell, and recommend my books. Without them, you wouldn't be holding this (in any form) in your hands right now.

My dear friend **Barrett Moore** continues to be an amazing fount of ideas, inspiration, and knowledge. His help on this novel, its concept, and so many of the details was invaluable. Thank you, Barrett, for everything.

Another dear friend, **James Ryan,** was there (as always) whenever I needed him during the writing process. Thank you for all you have done for me and for what you continue to do for our great nation.

Several more very good friends contributed to this novel and always picked up on the first ring. My thanks go out to **Sean Fischer; Scott F. Hill, PhD; Rodney Cox; Chuck Fretwell; Ronald Moore; Steve Tuttle; Jeff Chudwin;** and **Mitch Shore.** I very much appreciate all of your support.

I wish to also thank **Katarinna McBride** and **Clark Pollard** for the details they helped authenticate, as well as **Jerry Saperstein,** who graciously stood on deck ready to help with anything and everything computer related. Any errors in the novel are 100 percent mine.

There are several people who asked that their names not be mentioned in the acknowledgments. All I can say is thank you, and that I am deeply humbled not only by your friendship, but by your undying love and dedication to our country. Thank you for all you do for us.

Now, I get to thank my amazing publishing team. This is my first novel to be published under the new Atria/Simon & Schuster imprint of my stellar editor, **Emily Bestler.** Emily, I wish you huge success with Emily Bestler Books and look forward to publishing many, many more #1 bestsellers together.

My deepest thanks also go to my phenomenal publishers **Carolyn Reidy, Louise Burke**, and **Judith Curr.** Anyone who knows publishing knows how blessed I am to work with Carolyn, Louise, and Judith. Here's to many more years of success.

Great buzz helps build a great book and nobody builds greater buzz than my extraordinary publicist, **David Brown.** "Outstanding" doesn't even come close to describing him, nor does *thank you* come close to expressing how much I appreciate him.

I also want to thank the superlative **Atria/Pocket sales staff,** the **audio division**, and the **art and production departments.** They do amazing work and I am very grateful for everything.

While on the subject of amazing work, I additionally want to thank the superb **Michael Selleck, Gary Urda, Kate Cetrulo, Caroline Porter, Sarah Branham, Irene Lipsky, Ariele Fredman,** and **Lisa Keim.** I hope each of them knows how fortunate I feel to be working with them.

The day I met my sensational literary agent **Heide Lange,** of Sanford J. Greenburger Associates, Inc., was one of the best days of my life. Every day since then has only gotten better and for that I owe Heide a huge thank you. I hope you know how much you mean to me and how much I appreciate you.

In addition to Heide, I also want to thank the rest of the incredibly talented team at SJGA, particularly the fabulous **Rachael Dillon Fried** and **Jennifer Linnan.**

Out on the West Coast, the world's best entertainment attorney, **Scott Schwimer** never ceases to amaze me with his business acumen, but also with the depth of his friendship. Thank you, Scottie.

As has become my custom, I always save the best thank-you for last. My two greatest accomplishments in life are as a father and as a husband. I try to be at the dinner table each night, but in the throes of writing, that isn't always possible. Through it all, I have the undying love and un-wavering support of my amazing family. I couldn't do what I do without them. To my beautiful wife, **Trish,** and my beautiful **children,** I extend my biggest thank-you of all. Now that the book is complete, it's time to have some fun!